THE BODY ON THE SIDEWALK

THE RELUCTANT MURDERER

TWO NOVELS BY BERNICE CAREY

INTRODUCTION BY CURTIS EVANS

Stark House Press • Eureka California

THE BODY ON THE SIDEWALK / THE RELUCTANT MURDERER

Published by Stark House Press
1315 H Street
Eureka, CA 95501, USA
griffinskye3@sbcglobal.net
www.starkhousepress.com

ISBN-13: 978-1-944520-94-6

Book design by Mark Shepard, shepgraphics.com
Proofreading by Bill Kelly

First Stark House Press Edition: May 2020

THE BODY ON THE SIDEWALK

A body is found outside the Grady home, a man whom they all know, shot in the back. There is no getting around the fact that someone in the family must have done it. Then the murder weapon is found, with several different family fingerprints on it. And what was once a fairly stable group quickly dissolves into suspicion and distrust. The police decide to arrest the son, Don, who seems to be the most likely suspect. His sister Pauline believes the crime was committed by friends of Don's, a couple she does not approve of. Peggy was the last to see the victim, and is wracked with guilt. The youngest sister, Maureen, just wants to be left alone. And their mother, Mamie, is torn between them all. But which one pulled the trigger? And who will pay the price?

THE RELUCTANT MURDERER

We know that Vivian Haines intends to commit murder this weekend. She tells us so. But who is her intended victim? Could it be her wealthy aunt, who is supposed to leave her half her fortune one day? Or her frivolous sister and her seemingly penniless boyfriend? Or perhaps her aunt's mousy companion, or her long-suffering chauffeur? Or Vivian's own fiancé, the fastidious Cuthbert? All we know is what Vivian tells us as her efforts to plan and execute the perfect murder are constantly thwarted. Now Vivian is beginning to panic. Could one of them suspect her? Could one of them be planning to kill *her* before she can murder them first?

Bernice Carey Bibliography
(1910-1990)

Novels:

The Reluctant Murderer (1949)

The Body on the Sidewalk (1950)

The Man Who Got Away With It (1950)

The Beautiful Stranger (1951)

The Three Widows (1952)

The Missing Heiress (1952)

Their Nearest and Dearest (1953;
abridged as The Frightened Widow, 1954)

The Fatal Picnic (1955)

Stories:

He Got What He Deserved (*The Lethal Sex*, 1959)

BERNICE CAREY: THE RELUCTANT MURDERER

BY CURTIS EVANS

In the years following World War Two, Bernice Carey was one of a cadre of clever women writers—mostly American, but some British as well—who wanted to do something different with the traditional detective novel. Like Raymond Chandler and his hard-boiled followers, these women wanted to separate mystery from the "body in the library" whodunit convention and portray crime and its dreadful consequences with greater realism and psychological acuity. Murder in their skillful hands was not merely a problem to be solved but an event to be experienced as real people experienced real crime—with intense feelings of terror, recrimination, agony, suspense and, in the end perhaps (or perhaps not), some measure of relief. Reflective of this change in crime fiction, *The Reluctant Murderer*, Bernice Carey's 1949 debut crime novel, is a deviously suspenseful tale where the question is not whodunit, but just who will get done in, while *The Body on the Sidewalk* (1950), Carey's second crime novel, is the first of her fine essays in criminal social realism, wherein the author removes murder from the Venetian vase, as Raymond Chandler famously urged, and drops it, if not in the alley, then at least at the side of a rather scrungy thoroughfare.

□ □ □

In *The Reluctant Murderer*, Carey's focal character is not some know-all eccentric series sleuth, like Philo Vance, Hercule Poirot or Ellery Queen, keenly intent on solving a baffling crime, but rather a hard-bit-ten, forty-year-old San Francisco career woman, Vivian Haines, who is scheming to commit one. Perhaps in her crimped heart she does not really want to murder anyone (hence the title), but the idea comes irresistibly to her mind while she is reading a letter from her sister Anne that invites her to a weekend house party at Anne's cabin in the Santa Cruz Mountains above Los Gatos (the area where Carey herself resided with her second husband and two sons). "I had never cared for detective stories, and for a moment I regretted it," reflects Vivian, the narrator of the tale, as she gets down to the mechanics of murder. "If I had read more of them I might now be familiar with different means of doing away with people. I am not one to leave things to the last minute, nor to be vague about my plans; but somehow I had put off really getting down to business on working this thing out. After all, one has a natural reluctance about taking human life...."

With her new flash of insight that "murder was the answer" now firmly lodged in her bitter mind, however, Vivian departs for Anne's house with her salesman fiancée, Culbert, an old friend of the family's. At Anne's country place Vivian and Culbert encounter the war widow's handsome new scapegrace boyfriend, Johnny Lloyd, for whom Vivian expresses decided disdain:

I got his number the first time I ever saw him, lounging around on [Anne's] fancy outdoor furniture in sloppy slacks and huaraches, and no shirt—so he could show off his muscles and his nice, evenly browned skin, and the black hair on his chest....He was, it seemed, going to be the next John Steinbeck, or maybe it was William Saroyan—I forget which. He had a shack two ravines over from Anne's house, and I judged that he was at that time living off his discharge pay from the Army and his unemployment insurance. She had known him for a year now and to my knowledge he hasn't done a day's work in all that time.

Also present for the weekend at the cabin—a shingled structure with multiple levels and decks—is Vivian and Anne's wealthy and eccentric spinster aunt, Maud Twilliger, and Aunt Maud's demonstratively doting companion, the seemingly self-abnegating Miss Pringle, and her chauffeur, Alphonse. Of Aunt Maude Vivian sourly observes (recalling crime novels like Dashiell Hammett's *The Dain Curse*): "Any northern Californian knows that the southern part of the state is populated almost exclusively by screwballs, and I do believe Aunt Maud is the epitome of southern California crackpots." Anne and Vivian are Aunt Maud's joint heirs, although Vivian fears the undue influence that Miss Pringle and Alphonse might have on her odd aunt. So we have all the ingredients for a "nice" domestic murder, set at a weekend house party of sorts located not at a between-the-wars English country house but a mid-century California country cabin—yet there is a difference.

Just who is it who will be murdered, that is the question. Like in Pat McGerr's celebrated crime novel *Pick Your Victim*, published three years earlier, the author maintains in *The Reluctant Murderer* considerable suspense over the matter of the identity of the "murderee." It only adds to the already mounting suspense when scheming Vivian begins to suspect that someone is trying to murder her! Will this be the case of a biter bit? Yet in addition to the impressive suspense element over the matter of who the victim (or victims) will be, the reader also is pulled into the story by the compellingly dark picture which Carey draws of Vivian Haines herself. As *New York Times* reviewer Elizabeth Bullock glowingly wrote of *The Reluctant Murder*, which she deemed a "grim but good" novel: "It is no small accomplishment that the author has been able to sustain the repulsive but fascinating character study to the end."

□ □ □

While *The Reluctant Murderer* is in some sense a classic country house mystery (with the emphasis shifted to more noirish suspense elements) and, like Golden Age country house mysteries, rather tony in milieu, *The Body on the Sidewalk* presages, with its purposefully drab San Francisco setting, the impressive social realism of Bernice Carey's third crime novel, *The Man Who Got Away with It* (1950), reprinted by Stark House in 2019, and other, later books. *Sidewalk* anatomizes an "everyday" family put under great pressure when the body of a murdered man is discovered on their front sidewalk. The murdered man turns out to be Hank Grueber, whom at least several people in the extended family of matriarch Mamie Grady might have had motive to kill.

Mamie is currently comfortably married to the slackly amiable if not overly intelligent Frank Grady, but also living at the house are her four variously disgruntled children: Pauline and Donald, by her first husband, Don Thomas, a vanished merchant seaman, and Peggy and Maureen, by her second husband, Ramón Garcia, a restaurant owner of Mexican heritage. (Additionally, there are as well Don's wife, Lola, and their two young children, Jo Anne and Donnie.) Pauline, a poised and attractive secretary, harbors personal social ambition, hoping to land an upwardly mobile male catch in the corporate world (one Ellery Hodges, recalling Ellery Queen perhaps). Conversely, Donald Thomas works in the warehouse of Enderby Liquor Supplies and is a committed union man and "radical" who believes passionately in equality for black people. Peggy has discarded her husband, Len Thomas, in Oakland and is living at her mother's home again, while Maureen, the youngest, is a moody and sardonic adolescent, not yet eighteen.

Don is known to have had spats at work with Hank Grueber, who was, in Don's disgusted view, a sneaking toady to the suits at Enderby Liquor Supplies, while Peggy, wanting to have some fun again, had been running around with Hank since she left Len. Also drawn into the affair, much to Don's mortification, are his and Lola's black friends, Ernie and Nell Simpkins, who were visiting the couple at Mamie's house on the night of the murder. Mamie's second husband, Ramón Garcia, the father of Peggy and Maureen, gets involved as well. Thus it is a wide field of suspicion which presents itself to the presumably ironically named Inspector Holmes of the San Francisco police.

One of the fascinating things about *The Body on the Sidewalk* is the way the author attacks and subverts the social biases of traditional mystery fiction, which often was profoundly reactionary, portraying leftwing politics as dangerously radical and placing minority groups in a negative and often cruelly mocking light. Don's politics unfairly make him a target of suspicion, while several characters, particularly the odiously self-centered Pauline, make bigoted comments about other racial and ethnic groups. As Maureen ironically comments, "Everybody seems more worried about having people find out a member of the family associates with Negroes than at being suspected of murder." Even the ingenuous Lola comments of black people and criminal investigations, "A person always feels the police won't be fair to them." When Ernie is visited by Inspector Holmes and his myrmidon, he instinctively fears "these living embodiments of white law." As his eyes move from one policeman to the other, he checks himself, "angrily aware of how the movement would look to these white men. Another 'darky,' 'rolling his eyes.' And of course this is precisely how scores and scores of vintage crime tales referred to this natural human reaction. *The Negro rolled his eyes in terror*, lines from these tales would read, followed by some egregiously exaggerated, putatively black dialect.

For his part, Ramón Garcia, we are told, at a young age had "correctly assessed the disadvantages involved in being Mexican in a white world"; and at one point in the novel, after having observed the bitter back-and-forth bickering within the Grady family, he comments pointedly: "And they say it's us Latins who are excitable" (another frequent demeaning observation in vintage mystery fiction, made not only of people of Spanish but of Italian descent). And when Ramon hires jaded Jewish defense attorney Joel Freeman—"People! They make me sick," the lawyer announces—Mamie finds herself confusedly sorting through her own gently bigoted thinking, which recalls that of the fictional television character Archie Bunker, who commands, when he gets into legal trouble, "Send me a Jew!":

[Freeman] was a Jew—that was to the good—Jews were shrewd and cun-

ning and smarter than other people. A ripple of uneasiness crossed her mind, an unspoken apology to Don. He was as queer about Jews as he was about colored people. You weren't supposed to think they were different. He jumped on the rest of them impatiently when they spoke of Jews being this or that—which everybody knew they were. Don said some of them were as dumb as anybody else, and some were as shy and unassuming as others were pushing and forward.

But nevertheless, Mamie thought stubbornly, it was a good thing Freeman was a Jew.

The political and social views of Bernice Carey—a progressive thinker who during the Thirties with her first husband, Walter Fitch, a mechanical engineer and foreman in California oil fields, subscribed to the Communist Party USA's newspaper, the *Daily Worker*, and declined to state her political affiliation—obviously were very different from those of her naively complacent character Mamie Grady; yet perhaps Mamie's chaotic fictional family situation somewhat reflected her own real one.[1] Bernice married Walter Fitch at the age of eighteen in 1928 and during World War Two, after over a dozen years of marriage, abruptly left him and her two young sons for a couple of years, when she went to live in San Francisco. After her return she and Fitch divorced and she married Gilroy, California high school history teacher Richard Martin, a man with whom she remained happily married until his death and to whom her sons were very much attached as well. "Who would have thought that the romantic girl who had adored Don Thomas and been excitedly in love with the dashing Ramón Garcia," reflects Mamie bemusedly about her third, companionate marriage, "would one day be satisfied to love a man simply because he was kind?" One of Bernice's sons recalled in a telephone conversation with me that in the traditionalist Fifties Bernice, preoccupied with her mystery writing career, "wasn't the greatest" example of housewifery and mothering, which is the case as well with the rather casual Mamie Grady, who guiltily reflects, "Her children….hadn't had a normal home….They had to explain odd names, different from hers. Other kids' mothers didn't have love affairs…."

Bernice Carey seems clearly to have been aware of personal missteps she may have made, but she still wanted more out of life than her character Lola Thomas, who in the homogenous American mid-century sim-

---

[1] A year before the publication of *The Reluctant Murderer*, amid the height of the Red Scare, Bernice Carey was named as a Communist in the California Legislature's Fourth Report of the Senate Fact-Finding Committee on Un-American Activities (Communist Front Organizations), based on her having published pieces in the *Daily Worker*.

ply desires nothing other than "the same things millions of other women like her wanted: a white house set by itself in a lawn, with a fishpond in the backyard with rocks and waterlilies in it, and painted garden furniture standing about, and underwear with lace on it, and parties with decorated cakes where you played cards or did fancywork in company with friendly women, and trips downtown on Saturday might to eat in a restaurant and go to the movies."

These reflections on the author's own life I hope lend interest to *The Body on the Sidewalk*, but what makes the novel most memorable, in my view, is its expansive social consciousness and its credible depictions of the dilemmas of regular people when they are forced to confront that gravest of personal crimes—murder.

—February 2020
Germantown, TN

Curtis Evans received a PhD in American history in 1998. He is the author of *Masters of the "Humdrum" Mystery: Cecil John Charles Street, Freeman Wills Crofts, Alfred Walter Stewart and British Detective Fiction, 1920-1961* (2012) and most recently the editor of the Edgar nominated *Murder in the Closet: Essays on Queer Clues in Crime Fiction Before Stonewall* (2017) and, with Douglas G. Greene, the Richard Webb and Hugh Wheeler short crime fiction collection, *The Cases of Lieutenant Timothy Trant* (2019). He blogs on vintage crime fiction at The Passing Tramp.

THE BODY ON THE SIDEWALK

BY BERNICE CAREY

Chapter One

The street was still asleep under the gray flannel blanket of fog stretched over the city.

The little man hurrying along, his rubber-soled shoes striking out a dull rhythm on the cracked sidewalk, his topcoat collar turned up under his hat brim, was walking downtown to make the early shift at the cafeteria where he worked as a dishwasher.

Still dopey with sleep, he noticed little of the external world. But the body lay just inside the low, wrought-iron gate between the sidewalk and the high stairs. For a moment his sluggish mind and his unlimbered-up muscles barely paused over the sight. Another drunk, passed out before he could make it up the steep steps, that was the little man's immediate, impersonal impression.

But still the sight was unusual enough to slow him for a second glance; and then he noticed the brown stain on the squares of rough gray cement, the sprawled, dead position of the figure.

The little man halted and stared, and came fully awake. He glanced up and down the empty street, seeking aid or advice, but in the face of the deserted scene he had to fall back on himself for a decision.

One block over, on Ellis, and three blocks down, there was a police station. He thought of the time, realizing that the detour would make him late; but this was an excuse which would impress even Mr. Timpkins, the manager. With the police to back up his story he would create a sensation at work.

He took another look at the fallen man. Young he seemed—no more than in his thirties anyhow, dressed up, too, in a dark blue suit and a tan topcoat. You could see the hole in its back and the dried blood stiffening the material down the side.

The little man hurried away then, crossing the street diagonally, hoping no other pedestrians would come along to spoil the moment of drama when he returned in a police car. In less than ten minutes a dark blue automobile with the first letters of the San Francisco Police Department in gold on the door pulled up before the tall gray house, and the little man revealed his find to two officers in dark blue who looked the scene over impartially and assured themselves that it was indeed a dead body.

One of the policemen stepped back to the car and instructed his colleague at the wheel to "call headquarters." His eyes rested dispassionately on the little man. "Take him back to the station and get his statement. Riley and I'll keep an eye on things here."

Rather reluctantly the little man climbed back into the car. He would have liked to stick around for the excitement. A passing automobile had already stopped in the street, and a head protruded curiously from the window. A man with a lunch pail was coming down the block, his pace quickened by the sight of the little congregation on the sidewalk.

Riley took a stolid stance in front of the iron gate, and Sergeant Ferris stepped around the dead man and climbed the wooden stairs. The little man looked over his shoulder as the car pulled away.

It took several minutes for the sergeant to get a response to the doorbell, but finally the net curtain, held tightly over the glass in the upper half of the door by narrow rods at the top and bottom, was pulled to one side and a face crumpled with sleep peered out.

Sight of the uniform snapped Mrs. Grady's eyes awake, and she opened the door quickly, pulling a pink chenille robe closer about her voluptuous bust.

The sergeant looked down at a yellow-blond head encased in a coarse pink hairnet which bound down innumerable pin curls impaled on gold bobby pins. Sergeant Ferris could not know it, but he was one of the few males outside those walls ever to see Mrs. Grady's face in its natural state. What he saw were plucked eyebrows, light eyelashes, a too-soft skin minutely flecked with blue veins, and a small, pale-pink mouth.

Although curiosity and apprehension predominated in her expression, Mamie Grady also looked annoyed at being caught thus cosmetically undressed.

"What is it?" she demanded in a sleep-thickened voice.

The officer stood aside and pointed impassively. "Know this man?"

Mrs. Grady stepped out on the doormat and gazed down at the six feet of sidewalk between the steps and the gate. She refused to wear glasses except for reading, so all that her weak blue eyes took in was a brownish mass on the walk. But she glanced up at the officer fearfully.

"Is he—sick?"

"Dead."

"Oh-h-h!" It was a strangled screech.

"Live here?" Ferris inquired.

"I —I— No, I don't think so. Who is it?"

"Thought you might know."

She looked up at the calm red face, and, gathering up the long skirt of her robe, ran down the steps in white kid slippers that had wispy fur to warm her ankles.

She pressed the hand which was not holding the robe across her mouth. "Hank! My God, it's Hank."

The sergeant had descended a few steps. "Some of your folks?"

Mrs. Grady shook her head blindly. "No. Oh, my God, what happened?"

"Looks like somebody shot him. In the back." Sergeant Ferris looked at the figure and at the steps. He did not say so, but he had made the first deduction in the case, one which the detectives on the homicide squad would later confirm, that, from the way the man lay, he had probably been shot from above by someone standing on the steps.

"Better come back inside now," Ferris said equably. He followed her into the long, narrow hall at one side of which a stairway ascended.

"Anybody else here?"

"My family."

"Better call 'em. There'll be some men here from headquarters in a few minutes. They'll want to talk to you."

He glanced at wide double doors to the right. "That the front room?"

"Yes."

He opened one of the doors to look into the dim room crammed with over-stuffed furniture. "Tell 'em to come in here."

He followed her as she started dazedly down the hall. "Don't do no talking to anybody."

Mrs. Grady looked over her shoulder uncertainly, rather antagonistically. Then she knocked on the first door after the parlor doors.

"Girls! Peggy, Maureen!"

A muffled groan answered.

"Girls, get up!"

"Whassa matter?" came a sleepy response.

"Get up. Something's happened. There's a policeman here!"

"Wha-at!" It was a shrill squawk in the same voice.

"Put something on and go in the front room."

As Ferris proceeded down the hall behind his hostess, the door behind him opened and he glanced back to catch a glimpse of tousled brown hair, startled dark eyes, and bare shoulders. Peggy gasped and closed the door quickly. Then he heard indistinguishable voices in the room.

Sergeant Ferris wended his way along behind Mrs. Grady through a dining room with cream-colored wainscoting which opened off the last door to the right in the hall and on into a large, old-fashioned kitchen in which the white-enameled gas stove and refrigerator looked out of place. One would rather have expected the high-ceilinged, dark room to harbor a wood range and the "kitchen cabinet" of the nineties.

Mrs. Grady turned left in the kitchen and pounded on a paneled door leading to the first of two bedrooms which elled off at the back of the house.

She received an immediate answer to her "Pauline!"

"Yes?" The voice was sharp but polite.

"Put something on and go in the front room."

"What is it? Is something wrong?"

"There's been an—accident."

It was unnecessary to knock on the second door against the west wall.

It had been left ajar when Mrs. Grady went out, and now her husband appeared in the opening, his thick shoulders bare in a sleeveless undershirt and suspenders which held up brown-and-green-plaid slacks above run-over leather slippers. Thick gray hair sprang disheveled above a florid face covered by a pepper-and-salt stubble along the cheeks and chin.

"What's up?" he grunted, suspicious eyes on the cop.

"Hank—he's killed. Out on the street."

Frank Grady stared at his wife incredulously. "The hell you say."

The sergeant motioned toward the front of the house. "Want you all in the front room."

Grady looked at him with but slightly concealed resentment and picked up a pale blue dress shirt from a chair near the door. Struggling into it, he came out of the room as his wife darted inside.

"I'll only be a minute," she said determinedly, and closed the door.

Ferris surveyed the door skeptically, but was diverted when the one next to it opened and a young woman stepped out in a severely cut flannel robe with a side opening at the high neck. In the navy blue folds which hung to the floor, scarlet braid binding the cuffs and the neckline, Pauline was a regal figure even without make-up, with her light-brown hair hanging to her shoulders, hair which lay so smoothly that it was obvious she had already run a comb through it.

She raised her eyebrows coldly. "Did I hear Mother say something about an accident?"

"That's right. Go on in the living room and you'll find out all about it."

Ferris glanced at Mamie's door and back to the others who were proceeding through the dining room. He decided to follow them. The narrow hallway was congested as they moved along it, for the two girls were coming out of the front bedroom.

As the group massed itself wonderingly in the center of the nearly dark living room, Ferris went to the bulging windows across the front and pulled up the shades. It was not yet six o'clock, but the windows faced south, and the room became a lighter gray.

Pauline clicked on an indirect-lighting floor lamp, and the people were unflatteringly revealed to one another's gaze.

Peggy was a small, dark-haired girl of twenty with anxious brown eyes and a little mouth like her mother's. Over her nightgown she had put on a red rayon house coat, a garment somewhat fussily gathered and adorned with ecru lace. Ferris noted that she wore a wedding ring on her heavily nail-polished hand.

Maureen was the youngest. She had an intent yet composed expression, like a person watching a reasonably engrossing play. Between her two sisters in height, she had a somewhat boyish appearance in her knee-length flannel robe, seersucker pajama legs showing below it. Her brown hair was done in regulation high-school style, parted low on one side, smooth across the top, held back by a wide tin barrette, fluffing out at the ends.

None of the three sisters looked alike, yet they were bound together by an elusive family resemblance. There were fewer flaws in Pauline's features, yet she was the least striking of the three. Peggy, though her nose was shorter and flatter, her mouth too narrow-lipped and small for the broad cheekbones above, was obviously the "cute" member of the family. Maureen was in-between, her mouth larger than Peggy's, her face narrower, her eyes an indeterminate hazel. It was her air which gave Maureen distinction, a sort of careless composure, interesting at her age, which was between sixteen and eighteen, Ferris estimated.

He jerked his head toward the stairs in the hall. "Who lives upstairs?"

"My wife's son," Grady replied.

Ferris glanced around the group with an expression which in a less contained countenance would have been inquiring.

"Mr. Grady is our stepfather." Pauline answered his unspoken question with dignity.

At this moment Mamie sailed into the room. If it had not been for the same pink robe and white slippers, Ferris might not have recognized her. She had worked fast and expertly. A flowered silk scarf covered her hair turban fashion. A brown eyebrow pencil and mascara had done their work, and powder, raspberry lipstick, and a pink rouge had completed the metamorphosis.

"You might as well all sit down," she ordered. She turned to Peggy. "Did they tell you? It's Hank. He's killed out on the front walk."

Peggy stared at her mother. "What?" she said scratchily. "What did you say?"

"It's Hank. I saw him. The officers found him, I guess."

Peggy looked around at the other faces with her mouth open. Then she put out her hand blindly. It fell on Maureen's sleeve, and the other girl obligingly moved closer, her eyes interestedly on her sister whose fingers were digging into her arm.

"I—don't—believe—it," Peggy whispered hoarsely.

"Well, it's so. I saw him. And I simply can't understand it."

Pauline's voice cut the air coolly. "We'd better just sit down and keep quiet."

Ferris was eying the stairs doubtfully. But he decided to let the second floor wait till his superior officers arrived.

They had not long to wait. The high old houses, most of them—unlike the Gradys'—in dire need of paint, and converted into rooming houses, soon looked down upon an ambulance and two more official cars which discharged a photographer, detectives, and a medical examiner. Early as it was, a small, curious crowd had collected when Detective Jeffries of the homicide department was admitted to the front hall by Sergeant Ferris.

At the same moment Donald Thomas came running down the inside stairway in a bathrobe and pajamas, his reddish-brown hair standing up in tufts.

"What's up?" he called, his alarmed eyes upon the policemen.

"A little trouble," Detective Jeffries replied urbanely. He glanced at the group in the parlor. "This everybody in the house?" he asked Ferris.

"Everybody on this floor. I figured I'd better stay with 'em till you came and round up the upstairs then." Ferris looked up at Donald, who had paused to listen with both hands on the banister. "Anybody else upstairs?"

"My wife and kids. What's the trouble?" He could see the family in the parlor, and he was frowning in bewilderment.

"Little matter of a murder," Ferris replied cheerfully.

Jeffries spoke to Donald. "Will you come in here with the others?" He turned his head to Ferris. "I'll just check with you on what you've found here, and then you can go up and tell this man's wife to come down."

Donald walked around the three officers in the hall, eying them warily, and joined his relatives.

"For Christ's sake," he said in a low tone. "What gives?"

"It's Hank," his mother informed him, not lowering her voice. "Somebody killed him, shot, it looks like to me. And right on our doorstep."

"Hank *Grueber?*"

Peggy nodded mutely. She sat in a heavy overstuffed chair, looking terrified.

"Smooth your hair down, Don," his mother said parenthetically; "it looks awful. And to think Peggy went out—"

"Mother"—Pauline's voice was low and curt—"don't tell them anything."

"Don't be ridiculous, Pauline." Mamie looked around at her children authoritatively. "Just everybody tell the exact truth and we've got nothing to worry about."

Pauline turned away impatiently toward the window. "Oh, God."

Frank had settled morosely into an armchair. He glared at his wife. "I was ag'in her stayin' here in the first place. Now you see what happens."

Mamie was turning toward him with a placating expression; but at that moment, having concluded a low-toned conference in the hall, Jeffries and his assistant walked into the room. He looked them over measuringly and sat down in an occasional chair. Officer Flannery pulled a straight chair up to a long table standing behind the davenport and poised an Eversharp pencil over a writing pad.

Everyone watched the officers uneasily. Detective Jeffries's eyes settled on Frank.

"You're the head of the house?"

"I am."

"Your name?"

"Franklin L. Grady."

He turned to Mamie. "Mrs. Grady?"

"Yes."

"I believe you recognized the deceased."

"Yes, he's Hank—Henry, that is—Grueber."

"A relative?"

"No, just a friend of the family."

"Live here?"

"Oh no."

"When did you see him last?"

"Last night when he called to go out with Peggy."

Jeffries looked from one to the other of the three girls; and Mamie nodded at Peggy. "This is my daughter Peggy—Mrs. Johnson."

"Mr. Grueber—he was *your* friend then?"

"We all—knew him," Peggy said faintly.

Jeffries glanced about blandly. "Perhaps I'd better find out who everybody is."

Mamie leaned forward efficiently. "These are my daughters," she nodded. "Pauline—Miss Thomas; and Maureen—Miss Garcia; and my son Donald—Mr. Thomas."

Jeffries's eyelashes batted together once, but he remained suave. "From the names, I gather you have been married before, Mrs. Grady."

"Yes. Twice. Pauline and Donald by my first husband, Peggy and Maureen by my second," she enumerated glibly.

"I see. And, Mrs. Johnson—your husband, is he here?"

"I—I'm separated."

"Ah—yes. Mr. Johnson, he lives in the city?"

"No, in Oakland."

"His address, please."

Peggy leaned forward desperately. "Oh, you mustn't think—"

Jeffries's eyebrows went up inquiringly.

Pauline spoke sharply. "It's merely routine, Peggy."

When Pauline had given him the street and number in distinct tones, Jeffries addressed Peggy once more, "You went out with Mr. Grueber last night?"

"Yes," she whispered.

"Just give me an account of the evening up till you last saw Mr. Grueber."

Peggy glanced nervously at the members of her family. Mamie had opened and closed her mouth, as if she would like to relieve her daughter of this chore. Frank stared heavily at the throw rug before the double doors, scowling. Pauline's lips pulled into a tighter line, and Maureen's eyes went from Peggy's face to the officer's and back again. She listened intently. Donald looked as if he were preoccupied with disturbing thoughts which had just come to him.

"He came to the house about eight-thirty last night," Peggy began in a thin voice, "and we sat in here for a while, and then we went out in the dining room where Mother and Frank were sitting and talked a while and had a bottle of beer, and then we went out—"

"At what time?"

"Between nine-thirty and ten, I think. We walked over to Geary and down toward town and stopped in a bar, Tommy Harris's. We had a few drinks and left about midnight. On our way back we stopped in a Chinese restaurant near Larkin and had chow mein, and then we walked on home here—and—that's all."

"What time was it when you got back here?"

"A little after one, probably. I never noticed."

"Did Mr. Grueber come in with you?"

"No. We stood on the porch by the door a few minutes talking before I came in."

"Did you see him go down the steps?"

Peggy frowned and thought. "No. I unlocked the door and went inside. I said good night, standing in the opening of the door, and when I closed it he was just turning to go down the steps."

"Did you see anyone, or did anyone come in or go out while you were standing there?"

Although her head did not turn, Peggy's eyes shifted uneasily toward Maureen.

The younger girl answered in a clear, flat voice. "I came in while they were—talking—on the steps. I had been to the movies with a couple of girl friends. We went to the late show at the Fox and stopped at Compton's to eat afterward. It was pretty late."

"I see. What time, exactly, did you come in?"

"Must have been one-fifteen or one-twenty. I noticed the clock in the cafeteria as we dashed out to catch the streetcar, and it was just one then."

"Your sister did not come on into the house with you?"

"No. I spoke to them and went in."

"Did you speak to anyone else after you came inside?"

"No, the house was dark, on this floor, anyway."

"There were other lights?"

She glanced at Don calmly. "The hall light was on upstairs. It's a dim light. Sometimes it burns all night."

"Did you see your sister again when she came in?"

"Yes."

"How long after you came in?"

"Oh, fifteen minutes."

"But, Maureen," Peggy interrupted, "you're giving the wrong impression. I came in just a few minutes after you, no more than five minutes."

"He asked when I *saw* you," Maureen explained patiently.

"Oh yes, you were in the bathroom."

"You share a bedroom?"

"Yes."

"And your sister was not in that room when you entered, Mrs. Johnson?"

"No."

"Was the light on?"

Peggy looked surprised. She glanced at Maureen quickly. She answered promptly, but her voice was hesitant. "Just the little lamp on the bed table."

Maureen spoke calmly. "We leave that on when we go out at night. I didn't go in the bedroom first. I went straight to the bathroom. I was in there for ten or fifteen minutes. When I came back to the bedroom Peggy was there undressing."

Jeffries looked thoughtful. He rose. "You stay here, Flannery. I want to look over the layout of the house before we go on." He went out into the hall where he met Ferris and a young woman coming down the stairs.

"Mrs. Thomas, I presume," he said pleasantly. The woman in a long cotton house coat zipped up the front, nodded, her eyes worried.

"Just wait in here with the others. Ferris, will you come with me a moment?"

The officers went down the hall. Jeffries glanced into the girls' room where the bedside lamp shed a golden glow over tumbled beds in the dark room, the shades of its long windows still down. Opposite the dining-room door, at the end of the hall, a door led into a bathroom. Jeffries opened it and glanced about. A second door on his right opened into Pauline's room.

The officers proceeded around through the back of the house. A long screened porch opened off the kitchen, and steps ran down into a small back yard with grass and a willow tree. From these steps Jeffries saw that a narrow cement path ran around the corner of the house between the two back bedrooms and a high board fence. He remembered the front of the house. The ell at the side left a narrow yard traversed by a cement walk which connected with the walk where the body had lain. In the side plot running back to the jutting rear wall, whose two high windows must be the bathroom ones, there had been a strip of grass and several unhealthy rosebushes. The cement path turned in front of the rear ell of the house and squeezed between the house wall and the fence.

When Jeffries and Ferris returned to the front hall, they paused for a low-voiced conference with two men who had entered from the front. Hank Grueber's remains had already been removed in the ambulance.

As Jeffries turned back to the parlor the two officers tramped toward the rear of the house.

Mamie sat forward with an anxious frown. "What are those men up to?"

"We have to search the house," Jeffries replied mildly.

"Got a warrant?" Frank snapped.

"The occupants of this house are under suspicion of murder. I assume those who are not guilty would be happy to co-operate by assisting the investigation in every possible way."

There was silence. Lola Thomas, Don's wife, said faintly, "Just this floor, I suppose."

Jeffries's eyes fell on her measuringly. "No. We should like to examine your flat as well."

Lola's and Don's eyes met and dropped. Pauline glared at them. Mamie said, "Oh dear." Frank looked sour, and Maureen let her gaze rove interestedly over all of them. Peggy seemed too encased in her own dreary reflections to respond to what was going on.

Chapter Two

When Jeffries had elicited the information that Mamie and Frank had gone to bed after listening to the news on the radio at ten, and to sleep uninterrupted until Ferris rang the bell, and that Pauline had come in at eleven after visiting two girl friends who shared an apartment on Gough Street, and had also slept soundly until Ferris's ring, he turned to Don and Lola.

"Well," Don began, "we stayed up late, talking and reading. It was twelve-thirty by my alarm clock when I turned out the light. Both my wife and I stayed home all evening, never came downstairs from the time I got home from work."

Although the policeman's eyes were on Don, he was intently aware of the alertness with which everyone else in the room watched and listened as Don spoke. The atmosphere was nervous, as it had not been before.

"You were alone all evening, you and your wife?"

Don's eyes moved to his listening relatives before he said "Yes."

At that moment one of the officers appeared in the double doorway and motioned with his head to Jeffries to come out. The detective rose and went to him. The man had stepped back out of sight of those in the parlor. Silently he held out his right hand, which had been concealed behind him. On a heavy piece of string tied in a loop around the barrel hung a Colt .45

revolver.

Jeffries raised his eyebrows questioningly.

"Looks as if this was it," the officer said in a low tone. The gun was an old-fashioned six-shooter. He pointed to the exposed cylinder. "One gone."

"Where did you find it?"

"In that top drawer of the buffet in the dining room, back behind a lot of crap—playing cards, poker chips, writing paper, and stuff."

"Come on in here."

The officer followed Jeffries into the room, holding up the heavy gun like a trophy.

"Who does this belong to?" Jeffries demanded.

They were all staring at the weapon.

"It wasn't *that!*" Mamie gasped.

Frank, who had previously participated in the proceedings with an air of sulky detachment, pushed his head and shoulders forward, his eyes on the gun. He pressed his hands against the crocheted tidies on the chair arm and came to his feet, taking a step nearer.

"It's mine," he said incredulously. "Did somebody use it?"

"Do you have a permit?"

"No. But I've had it for years. I won it in a poker game at a logging camp up in Humboldt County, must have been twenty-five years ago."

"You kept it loaded?"

"Yes. For protection. In case of burglars—or—or anything. I take it along on vacations if we go to the mountains or any place like that."

"If you kept it for protection, how come it was in the dining room? Most people keep their gun close to their bed at night if they're afraid of robbery."

"I wouldn't let him." Mamie spoke up. "Guns make me nervous."

Jeffries glanced about. "You all knew Mr. Grady owned this gun."

They nodded, all except Lola, who looked at the revolver with loathing. "*I* didn't."

"All right," Jeffries said to the policeman, "take care of it. Have the boys go over the upstairs as soon as they've finished down here."

Lola said timidly, "Could I go up with them? The children are asleep, and I'm afraid they'd be frightened at seeing strangers."

"O.K." As the officers came through the hall, Jeffries nodded at Lola. "You can go now." He turned to the others with a businesslike manner.

"Now this Mr. Grueber. Where did he live?"

Mamie answered. "In a hotel downtown, on Eddy Street."

"Family?"

"Not now. He had a wife, but they're divorced, and she lives in L.A. now."

"What did he do for a living?"

"He was a salesman."

"For what firm?"

"Enderby Liquor Supplies," Mamie said firmly, and added defensively, "But that has nothing to do with Don."

Jeffries moved impassive eyes toward Don. "That's where you work?"

"Yes."

"Did you meet Grueber there?"

"Yes. He worked in the warehouse when I went to work for the company."

"How long ago was that?"

"Almost three years ago—just after I got out of the service. Hank got into the selling angle about a year ago, worked himself up—one way and another."

Jeffries turned abruptly to Peggy. "How long have you been married?"

She blinked. "Not quite two years."

"Did you go out with Grueber before you married?"

"A few times, yes."

"How long have you been separated from your husband?"

"About—about a month."

"Been seeing Grueber regularly during that time?"

"No. I—I just ran into him at a night club about a week ago. I've seen him twice since then."

Don was surveying his sister gloomily. Everyone else looked uncomfortable.

When the two officers who had gone upstairs descended, Jeffries rose.

"That will be all for now. But you'd all better stick around today. We may need you for further questioning."

"What about work?" Frank asked.

"Not today. We'll want to talk to all of you again later. We'd like to get this thing straightened out as soon as possible."

They were quiet as the officers closed the front door and trooped down the steps. Pauline went to the window and watched them pile into the official car.

"They're gone," she said flatly.

As if they had been waiting for a signal, everybody began to talk; the voices were either angry, petulant, or accusing, sometimes all three.

Frank was scowling at Peggy. "Well, you see. If you'd stayed home with Len, like I told you, we wouldn't be in this mess."

"Now, Frank." That was Mamie, trying to be soothing.

Peggy began to bawl. Maureen said, "Oh, for cripes sake, Frank."

Don said, "What in the hell happened? How did he come to get bumped off?"

"Yes, Peggy," Mamie prompted. "You must know something."

"I do-on't," she wailed.

"Don't heckle her, Mom," Pauline snapped. "It's Don who probably knows something, him and his—friends."

Don stood up and regarded the others sternly. "Listen, we're going to keep Ernie and Nell out of this. Nobody knows they were here but us; and I don't want to be responsible for getting Ernie in trouble. Him working at Enderby's, too, they'd probably put him on the pan, too, if they knew he was here last night."

"And what about the rest of us?" Pauline spat at him. "Living in the same house with you. It's bound to come out. The police manage to find out everything. It'll probably even be in the papers. What kind of people will people think we are? We'll all be disgraced." She turned to her mother furiously. "It's your house. You're renting to him. I told you to put your foot down."

"Don't talk to your mother like that," Frank roared. "I didn't like it, neither, but who'd-a thought anybody was going to go and get murdered on the front steps?"

"We'll just have to make the best of it," Mamie declared.

"I'm ruined, that's what I am," Pauline barked angrily. "And I was practically sure to be Mr. Forbes' secretary when Anne gets married next summer. And who wants somebody suspected of being a nigger lover or even a murderer for a private secretary?"

Maureen laughed; and it was shocking. "Everybody seems more worried about having people find out a member of the family associates with Negroes than at being suspected of murder."

"Your flippancy is out of place," Pauline said coldly.

"What we need is breakfast," Mamie said, getting to her feet decisively. "Peggy, stop blubbering. We know you couldn't help it. Maureen, come along and help me. And Frank," her tone softened, "don't let yourself get all excited. Remember your blood pressure." She paused in the doorway and declared brightly, "Someday we'll look back on this and laugh."

"Oh, God," Pauline groaned.

Maureen laughed right then.

Don repeated anxiously, "Remember what I said. You didn't see anybody go upstairs last night."

"All right, all right," Frank retorted testily, "We ain't anxious to let the police know we have darkies comin' to our house."

When Don went upstairs he followed the narrow hall back to the kitchen. Lola was settling the baby in his highchair. As she tied his bib she looked across the round, soft-haired head with worried eyes.

"They're gone?"

"Yeah, but not for good."

"Don, I'm scared."

"You and me both, baby." He crossed to the stove and took the percolating pot off a burner and poured coffee into one of the cups on the sink.

"Where's Jo Anne?"

"In the bathroom." She nodded at a bowl of cereal and a glass of milk on the table. "Her breakfast is ready." She sat down and began to spoon Pablum into Donnie's wet pink mouth. "The four coffee cups from last night are still in the sink. They noticed 'em, too, don't worry."

An archway led to the long living room which extended over the area occupied by the parlor and the hall bedroom downstairs. Don carried his cup to the arch and stood looking at the tumbled room, unemptied ash trays, the card table still standing with the pinochle cards scattered on it.

"They noticed everything," Lola continued in answer to his silent question.

Don leaned against the casing moodily sipping coffee. "I suppose it was a fool thing to do, lying about their being here. But the whole thing hit me so sudden. And the minute I remembered Ernie, all I could think of was keeping him out of it. And, partly, it was to protect the folks. I thought of the publicity and how burned up Pauline would be, her and her social aspirations."

"I know," Lola said comfortingly. She pulled the back of the baby spoon slowly over the edge of the bowl, ridding it of excess cereal. "I felt sort of guilty—toward the Simpkinses. We—encouraged them to be friends. You could tell when we first invited them up they were kind of leery of it. So you hate to have it turn out that you've involved them in a murder case. A person always feels the police won't be—fair with them."

Don moved to the sink and set his cup down, growling, "That rat even has to play the phony by dying in such a way and at such a time as to make it look bad for me."

"What worries me," Lola said slowly, "is if they find out you lied about us being alone, they'll think you're lying about everything." She kept her eyes on the baby to conceal the fear in them. "Don, who do you think did it, and why?"

He looked off across her head, his eyes narrowed. "Somehow we've got to find out."

"We?"

"Well, me, anyhow. No use beating around the bush. I know you're thinking the same thing I am. They'll try to pin it on me."

Her hands fell to the highchair tray, and the baby squealed and reached toward the cereal bowl. Four-year-old Jo Anne had come in and climbed into her chair.

"But Don," she said weakly, "they have to have evidence, motive."

"How long do you think it will take them to find out that Hank and I were like this?" He drew his finger across his throat. "That just before he was promoted out of the union we fought each other on the floor at every meeting. Some of Hank's pals in the front office would fire me in a minute if they could find a pretext that would get by the union. They'll be very helpful at building up a motive. Some of 'em will probably 'remember' Hank said I had threatened him—or some damn thing. No, the only way I can get out of danger is to get proof of who did do it."

"But how, Don?"

"Damned if I know." He looked down at her pale, anxious face and grinned. "I haven't got time to take one of those correspondence courses on how to be a detective that're advertised in the magazines Frank reads."

She did not smile, but wiped the baby's face with a piece of Kleenex. "It just can't be one of the folks."

"It almost has to be, it looks like, doesn't it?" he said gravely. "Unless Len—"

"Oh, Don, I don't like this, having to suspect your own people—almost hoping it is one of them, to save yourself."

She picked up the baby and carried him to the play pen set in the curve of the south windows, and Don followed her. He stood by the table which held the extension phone, and drummed on the top with his fingertips. "The police will probably check up on Len today, but someway I feel as if I'd like to see him myself. I think I could tell something from the way he acts. He doesn't go to work till nine. I have a notion to ring him up and tell him what's happened, get him over here if I can."

"Would he come?"

"Well, if you put it that his wife's in danger, mixed up in a murder, he might feel it's his duty to stand by. If he takes a belligerent attitude—well, that in itself would indicate something, though I don't know just what. But, damn it, Lola, the thing fits, jealous husband, a rival, a flighty young wife."

"Ye-es," she said slowly. She sat on the uneven cushions of the davenport which was covered by a dust-colored slip cover. "I just happened to think of Ramón. She's his daughter."

"What could he have to do with it?"

"Nothing, I suppose. But he's been coming into my mind. If the police don't get too engrossed in framing you, Peggy's the logical suspect. Ramón might feel that in an emergency like this he ought to be notified."

"Peggy's never been close to Ramón. I doubt if she's seen him half-a-dozen times since he and Mom split up."

"No, but he *is* her father. Of course Maureen's been the one who leans his way."

"Maureen! Why, she hardly knows him. She was only five when they were divorced."

"Maybe so; but she sees him regularly. Goes out to La Paloma all the time."

"What!"

"I never said anything, because she asked me not to, said it would just annoy your mother. You know how bitter she is toward Ramón. But when Aunt Betty was visiting me last summer, you remember, I took her to La Paloma for lunch one day, wanted to give her some real Mexican cooking. It was a Saturday afternoon; and who should we see coming down the stairs from the mezzanine floor where Ramón has his office but him and Maureen? He had his arm over her shoulders and they were laughing. So I asked her about it one day, and she was kind of defiant. Said he was her father, and so what, if she wanted to visit him."

"Whew, I'll bet Mom doesn't know that."

"So anyway it came to my mind—Peggy's his daughter; she's in trouble; and—and—well, I don't know."

Don stared at the window with troubled eyes. "He *might* know something that would help. Maybe I'll run over to North Beach when I get dressed and talk to him. But right now I'm going to give Len a ring."

Downstairs Mamie and Frank and Peggy were left at the untidy breakfast table, the women still in their house coats and slippers. Pauline had withdrawn to her bedroom, presumably to brood over her ill fortune; Maureen also had departed unobtrusively.

Frank picked his teeth and regarded his stepdaughter moodily. "The smart thing to do," he had just informed her, "is call up Len and get him over here and make up. Won't look so bad for you then."

"I've told you and told you," Peggy moaned, "I don't love him."

"You don't love him; you don't love him. That's all we get out of you. What kind of talk is that?"

"Well, it's reason enough." Peggy sulked.

With the air of one who has been over all this before, Mamie urged, "But why, honey? He's making good money, and he's not a chaser. And he don't drink—no more than most, anyhow. What do you *want*, for heaven's sake?"

"That's all you think about. If a man keeps you fed and clothed and doesn't beat you up regular and go on three-day binges every month and doesn't step out too flagrantly, you don't look any further. Far as you're concerned, he's God's gift to women."

"You're damn right he is," Frank declared.

"Well, not for me. Sure, Mom can love anybody, just so he's something in pants to show the world she's got a man. But not me!" Peggy scraped her chair back. "I wish I'd never come back here."

"Just one more crack like that to your mother," Frank warned, leaning forward, "and you'll be out of here so fast you'll wonder what hit you."

"Now, Frank," Mamie soothed. "She's all upset. Hank and everything."

"I'll upset her."

Crying again, Peggy went down the hall to her bedroom. Maureen, dressed in a sweater and skirt, was combing her hair. She glanced at her sister in the mirror.

"Now what?"

Peggy threw herself on her unmade bed with her face on her crossed arms.

"For two cents," her voice came muffled, "I *would* go back to Len. Life is such a mess."

Maureen's eyes were faintly scornful yet compassionate as they rested on the top of Peggy's head reflected in the glass.

"You won't be going anywhere till they find out who killed Hank."

Peggy raised her head and looked at her sister in the mirror. "Who did, do you suppose?"

Maureen shrugged. "Whose gun was it?"

"Oh no, Maureen, he couldn't have. He had nothing against Hank."

"O.K. So he didn't. But somebody did. Do you want the cops to think it was you?"

She took a short boxy coat out of the closet and began to put it on. Peggy raised herself on her elbows. "Where are you going?"

"Out."

"But we aren't supposed to, are we?"

"Nobody told me not to."

She walked past the bed and out the door. As the front door closed, Mamie came into the hall and appeared in the bedroom doorway.

"Where did Maureen go?"

"Don't ask me."

"That kid. I've got no more control over her than as if she wasn't even mine."

"Well, she'll be eighteen next month. And she always has been independent. No use to worry about her; she'll be back."

As Mamie turned away with a disturbed murmur, Peggy began to straighten up her bed. Maureen had not bothered to pull up the shades, and Peggy looked across to the dark green blinds bordered by lemon-colored light. She walked over and pulled them up impatiently, lifting a little the gloom within the room. From habit she pulled the tie of her robe loose, preparatory to dressing, but her fingers paused listlessly on the silk, and she stood staring at the lace-curtained windows of the dining room next door.

"Do you want the cops to think it was you?" Maureen had said.

She swallowed panic with a convulsive movement in her throat.

To be happy, that's all she had wanted; and the trail had led her to this, a man murdered, herself in danger of her life, and her whole family battered by trouble whose effects not one would ever escape.

Where had the trail gone wrong? Frank would say by leaving Len. Maureen would say by taking up with Hank while she was still married. Pauline would say by getting married in the first place before she had made something of herself on her own. Mom—well, Mom would blame it on other people—Len for being too dopey to hold the love of her cute little Peggy, Hank for letting himself get mixed up with a married woman. In both her previous marriages Mom had laid all the blame on the men and gone right ahead with her life, her conscience clear.

But Mom's mistakes, her pursuit of happiness, had never brought herself or her family to this: notoriety, bloodshed, danger.

To be happy, that was all Mom had wanted too; and she had attained it—except for *this* which had come upon her through no action of her own.

Drearily Peggy thought, "But when have I ever been happy? Only in little spurts."

Once, so far back that it was dim, she remembered a Christmas morning when Ramón was still their papa. She had sat on his lap holding a baby doll with painted hair. Papa had been in his pajamas and an old maroon-colored bathrobe; and she remembered, as if it were a color snapshot, how his eyes had been bright, and the stubble of black beard, and herself looking into his face as she lifted her head after showing him how the doll's clothes were complete even to a diaper with little gold safety pins.

But, between, there were the yelling voices, his and Mom's, with words about "bills" and "your check" and "over the bar" and "your crummy friends."

And then the alternately gay and moody young papa had been gone, and Mom had been snappy and often red-eyed, and Pauline and Don had been sullen, spending most of their time at their friends' houses, and Mom had gone to work as a waitress and she was tired all the time, and you would wake up at night to go to the bathroom and there would only be Pauline doing her homework over the dining-room table because Mom was out on a date.

And at first, when Papa left, Maureen had made life hideous. She kept asking questions. "Where is Papa? When is he coming back?" And Mom snapping at her to keep still, and Maureen having temper tantrums or being sulky and stubborn.

It had been better as soon as Mom married Frank. Then Mom was there when you came home from school, and she was cheerful and interested in you again.

It was about then that happiness became associated in Peggy's mind with being in love and having a husband. Frank had roused no emotional response in her—he was just another grownup around the place—but stability had come back to the family with his presence.

And happiness, a measure of satisfaction at any rate, had come into her life at the same time in the attention she got from boys. Yes, that had been good, happiness even, kidding around on the front steps with high-school boys. She always dated the older ones, in classes a year or two ahead of hers.

She had met Len before she graduated. He had a car and lots of money to spend; he took her to the beach and to El Patio to dance, and skating at Sutro's. And it was the most fun of anything she had experienced yet, necking with him. All those pleasures she had wanted to hang onto, so she married him.

Peggy turned from the window and threw herself on Maureen's bed, clutching the corners of the pillow with tense fingers.

And now it was all wrong, wrong, wrong! She had found no happiness, only misery and fear and guilt. A man had died because of her, and she would never be gay or even peaceful again. There was nothing left.

And it wasn't as if she had cared about Hank, or even got a lot out of going out with him. He was simply something to do, someone to take her places she couldn't go alone. It hadn't been worth it, having this avalanche of trouble as a result.

Chapter Three

Maureen walked to Van Ness and Geary, took an H car going north, transferred to the E car at Vallejo, and rode over the hill to the North Beach business district where every other building housed an Italian restaurant or a bar. Her eyes all the way had been wary, cataloguing the occupants of each car she boarded, examining the traffic outside the windows, looking back at pedestrians behind her as they were reflected in windows along the sidewalk.

She walked along Broadway, past a restaurant whose windows bore in fancy script the name La Paloma and in more conservative lettering the information that here was to be obtained real Mexican cooking: tortillas, enchiladas, tamales.

She turned into an alley just beyond the restaurant and entered by the kitchen door. La Paloma opened at noon for business, but it was now after nine, and two men were working over the big black stove and a long wooden table in the center of the electric-lighted, smoke-stained room.

"Hello, Tony," she said to the plump man in a round flat white cap who was cutting garlic into a large iron pot on the stove.

"Hi. Early visitor today."

"Papa here?"

"Sure; go right on in."

"Morning, Joe," she greeted the younger cook who was shoving a pan of tostados into the oven.

She pushed open the swinging door into the dining room. It was like night in the long room with booths along the walls, square tables crowned with upturned chairs down the center. Up front the Venetian blinds were closed over the windows and door, but lights were on behind the bar where a man stood counting money into the cash register.

He glanced up and peered into the dimness of the dining room as Maureen approached.

"It's me," she announced.

Ramón Garcia stood with his hands on either side of the cash drawer and showed white teeth beneath a neat black mustache.

"Come down to help the old man open up for the day?" he asked in a musical, affectionate voice.

Ramón was dressed in a gray business suit with a pale blue shirt and a gay necktie hand-painted with swaying palm trees. His graying black hair was combed to show to advantage a deep wave on one side. When Mamie Thomas had married him, twenty-two years before, he had been four years younger than she and completely devastating in a romantic, Latin way. Now he was twenty pounds heavier, his skin was coarser, and his movements were slower. But women patrons of La Paloma still found his urbane manner irresistible as he moved among the tables, inquiring solicitously as to the quality of the flavoring in the chili sauce.

Ramón's parents were Mexican, his father a section hand for the Southern Pacific Railroad; but Ramón had been born in Los Angeles and had achieved an American education through high school. The Spanish tongue had left no accent in his speech, only an engaging softness of the vowel sounds.

He had been a bright child, and had not been very old before he correctly assessed the disadvantages involved in being Mexican in a white world. He had purposely set out to eliminate as many traces as possible of his foreign origin, going so far as to refuse to speak Spanish even at home. In school he had passionately absorbed every crumb of American culture, and after high school had separated himself even further from his disadvantageous background by hitch-hiking to San Francisco and starting life afresh there.

Ramón's drive toward assimilation into the mainstream of Anglo-Saxon influences had been for the most part an unconscious one, and it had not occurred to him to reflect that the success which had placed him at last in the secure social category of Prosperous American Businessman was based, ironically, on exploitation of one of the cultural accretions brought from Mexico by his emotionally rejected family—their taste in food.

Ramón had been a busboy, Mamie a counter girl in a big cafeteria on Market Street when they met. Her susceptible heart was bruised and sore from the cavalier treatment it had received from the irresponsible father of Don and Pauline, and Mamie had become hopelessly infatuated with the young Spanish boy who was so openly smitten with her china-doll blondness. He was always "Spanish" to Mamie, never "Mexican."

Peggy and Maureen, their daughters, were too young when the divorce came to know the reasons leading up to it. As they grew older that crisis faded in importance in their mother's mind so that she seldom spoke of it. When she did allude to her second "mistake," it was with definite, though unspecific, censoriousness of Ramón Garcia. Peggy had deduced and firmly believed that her father had made her mother miserable by running after other women.

When she was fourteen Maureen had secretly looked her father up and introduced herself. Legally he had a right to see the girls, and regularly each month, till Peggy was eighteen, a fifty-dollar check arrived in the mail, after which the check became twenty-five, to continue till Maureen reached the same age. Mamie had skillfully avoided letting Ramón exercise the privilege of visiting his daughters, under the argument that it was "bad" for them to be torn back and forth, and he had shown little desire to circumvent her attitude.

At first he had been amused and flattered at Maureen's independently seeking him out. It had amused him, too, to keep their "friendship" secret, as she desired. And they had with time become truly friends.

"I can't stay but a few minutes. Something's happened at home."

He closed the cash drawer and came forward inside the bar. "Trouble?"

"Double trouble. Murder."

Ramón halted, and his black eyes became steady on her face. Then he moved quickly and opened the little gate at the end of the bar.

"Come on up to the office."

As they went up the stairs she talked in a low voice, succinctly summing up the morning's events.

She sat on the edge of a cluttered flat-topped desk, and Ramón thoughtfully selected a cigar from the humidor on it.

"I came over to warn you to keep away from us till this blows over."

"Keep away? I think I've been in your house once in the last ten years."

"I know. But I'm not going to come over or phone again while the cops are hanging around. I—well, I thought you might get worried when you heard about it, especially if you didn't hear from me, and offer to help or something, and there's no need for you to get mixed up in it. It may be a mess—Peggy in court and all that."

He sat down heavily in the swivel chair. "You don't think she did it?"

"No. She hasn't the guts."

"Frank's gun, huh?"

"Yes."

He smoked, and said after a moment, "You were right to come to me. If they arrest her, I'll get the best lawyer we can. Tell her not to worry; I can afford it."

"But that wasn't why I came," Maureen said impatiently. "It was to protect you, not Peggy. She's innocent. She'll be all right."

"You're pretty sure about her being innocent."

"Of course. But while they're investigating there's no need for you to be embarrassed. It would be just like Mamie"—she usually used her mother's first name when they talked—"to try to throw suspicion on you if things should start to get hot for her precious Frank. Peggy being your daughter, Mamie might hint you were protecting her honor or some such silly thing. And Frank is always harping at her to go back to Len. He was sore about her going out with Hank in the first place. Not that I don't agree with him—for once. If Peggy keeps on like she is, she'll wind up just like Mother did—three husbands before she's forty. A girl like her, soft and dumb like that, should settle down and stay that way."

"Look, baby," Ramón interrupted the flow of seemingly disconnected ideas, "I've never said anything about it one way or the other. I've been glad you liked me and we got to know each other. But I don't like this bitterness against your mother. I don't want any part of turning you against her, especially now when she's in trouble along with the rest of you. It wasn't any more her fault than mine that we broke up. I guess she had plenty to complain about."

"Sure, I know. You got to neglecting her, running around with a bunch she didn't like. But who wouldn't get bored with her fussing over 'em day and night? And then you being young and full of life and having Don and Pauline underfoot and then Peggy and me before you knew what had happened. And being poor to boot and all living in four rooms. It must have been enough to drive a person crazy."

Ramón smiled for the first time since he had greeted her downstairs. "O.K., O.K. I was a saint. But don't forget, all those things weren't much fun for Mamie either. Now don't you think you'd better get back before the police start looking for you?"

She jumped off the desk and jammed her hands in her pockets. "You will stay clear though, won't you? You've got no idea what a mess we are over there. Everybody fighting, and there's Don, you know, him and his friendship with the Simpkinses. They were at the house last night. That'll probably all come out. And Pauline, especially, is simply burnt up. It's bad enough to have a murder on your doorstep, and, for her, having people know your brother associates with colored people is the final straw."

Ramón' raised his heavy brows. "That's right." He uttered a short "Ha" of wry amusement. Then he came and laid his arm about her shoulders. "Poor little kid. No wonder you came running to your papa. I wish I could take you away from all this trouble."

Maureen smiled. "I can take care of myself. I'm used to them."

"Now, listen." His swarthy features became stern. "The minute it looks like Peggy might be taken in, you let me know, and I'll get the best lawyer in town on the job." He paused and pursed his lips. "I think I'll call up your mother and tell her that myself, so she can get in touch with me if it's necessary."

"No!" Maureen stamped her foot. "I came on purpose so you *wouldn't* do that. Those dumb cops won't be able to find out who did do it. They'll just make things unpleasant for a while trying. And I don't want you in on the bad publicity. It might even hurt your business."

"That's enough of that," he said sharply. "I'm your father and you'll do as I say."

Maureen looked angrily into his unsmiling face and turned away sulkily. "Good-by," she said, and walked out, pulling the door shut smartly.

Ramón frowned at the door, his expression worried, paternal. He shook his head uneasily and turned to pick up the phone. Then he laid it down slowly. "No," he said under his breath. "I don't want to let them know she comes here. Better wait till I see it in the papers."

Ramón was starting to leave the room when the telephone rang.

"Hello," he said absently, his mind still on Maureen.

"Ramón?"

"Yes."

"This is Don Thomas. I'm calling from a booth down on Columbus. I wonder if I could come up and see you for a few minutes."

Ramón's voice did not reveal the surprise his face showed. "Sure. Come on up. I'll let you in the front door."

He waited only a few minutes, looking through the slats of the blinds, before Don's figure appeared outside and Ramón unlocked the door.

Upstairs in the office again Don seemed ill at ease but watchful. He sat in a straight chair with a cushioned seat, across the desk from Ramón. It had been hard to think up a plausible reason to conceal the real intent of his visit, which was to see whether Ramón's manner would reveal any knowledge or suspicions about the murder.

"I guess you'll think it's funny, my coming to see you about this, but Peggy being your daughter, I thought you ought to know ahead of time in case—well, in case things go wrong for her."

"Is she in trouble?"

"Well, she may be. You see, she went out with a guy last night. Hank Grueber. I don't suppose you know him."

Ramón shook his head.

"You see, Peggy left her husband and came home about a month ago. You see, she's kind of—temperamental."

Ramón's dark eyes held a gleam of humor as he interrupted, "I suppose that's blamed on the Latin blood."

Don grinned. "Well, maybe it has been mentioned. Anyhow, somebody shot Hank after he left her last night and he died on our front walk."

Don's eyes were intent on the older man, and he was nonplused at the composure which met this announcement.

"Tough," Ramón said commiseratingly. "Is Peggy suspected?"

"We don't know. She may be, of course."

"And you want me to help—financially, perhaps, if she is accused of murder?"

"That wasn't why I came; but now that you mention it, it might help a lot. My idea was just that—well, she's really your kid, and I thought somebody ought to tell you the spot she's in instead of just letting you read it in the papers. Mom—well, I knew she wouldn't think of it. She—" He smiled deprecatingly. "Well, she tries to make us feel that Frank is our father, but, well, there's such a thing as blood, and I thought the only decent thing was to let you know."

Ramón's black eyes became inscrutable. His mind was busy behind a skepticism of this sudden concern over his paternal rights. He picked up a small box of matches from the desk and scratched one of them and held it to the dead cigar.

When he had a glow on the cigar, he removed it from his mouth and said quietly, "I got to know you pretty well as a kid, Don, while I was your stepfather. I always tried to treat you fair, like my own son as much as I could. I got nothing against you now. So let's be honest; put your cards on the table. This about Peggy; it's only half the story. You had a reason for wanting to see me. What is it? I promise you I'll do what I can."

Don hesitated. He did need help. *Had* there been another motive in his following Lola's hunch to come to Ramón? Had he been unconsciously looking for help from someone who was outside yet bound to the family? For nine years, from the time he was five until he was fourteen, Ramón had been the only father he knew, one who treated him with kindly indifference; but still the man in the family whom a boy looked to for advice on building model planes and repairing scooters. Frank had entered the family when Don was nearly eighteen, already out on his own. And now Don was troubled; self-reliant as he was, he had perhaps instinctively looked for a father's hand.

And Ramón had money. He was the only "successful" connection the family had. During the war, when people were throwing money around San Francisco like confetti, Ramón had expanded from a little hole in the wall where he dispensed chili beans to the present twenty-table establishment which he had financed on a shoestring.

Parenthetically, Don thought wryly that it just went to show the psychological hold financial success had on the American people. Ramón had been smart enough to make good; so you automatically placed your confidence in him. He must be better, stronger than the rest of them who hadn't been smart enough to get rich. Even he, who intellectually scorned rugged individualism and based his hopes on united action of the working people, when he got in a tight spot, instinctively he looked for help to the one businessman he had ties with.

For why should he trust Ramón, why seek him as a confidant? Why did he have this naïve hope that Ramón's brain could penetrate to the solution of this catastrophe? If Ramón saw his own daughters threatened, would he not keep silent at Don's expense, even if his more objective vision did discern the truth in the situation?

It seemed rather foolish to Don now, his having sought out Ramón. But even as doubt restrained his tongue, impulse broke through.

"Well, you're right," he said with a frown, his eyes on the edge of the desk. "I'm afraid I'm in a spot myself. There's nothing you can do; but maybe one reason I came to you was to have a chance to talk it over with another man, one I could trust." He glanced up, and his lips twisted wryly. "Not that I'm sure I can trust you. After all, I guess your main interest will be to protect the girls. But disregarding that, you know the ins and outs of the family. You might have some ideas or hunches I could go on. You see, I found out this morning from my wife that Maureen sees you all the time. Lola hasn't told anybody else."

"Look here, Don, are you mixed up with this Hank? Are you worried about your own neck?"

"Frankly—yes."

"You—did it?"

"Good God, no!"

"Good. Well then, what's the story?"

"Well, to begin with, this Hank Grueber was working at Enderby's when I got on there three years ago. Him and I were in the stockroom together, and you know how it is, you get friendly with a guy you're working with every day. He came to the house once in a while. We asked him to a party once downstairs—Peggy's birthday—and he got to know the family. But after a while I got leery of him. He was one of those guys that'll stop at nothing to get ahead. He played up to the foremen, practically laid himself out on his face when one of the big shots from the front office came into the warehouse. Then there was another guy in our gang. A Negro. He and I got to be pretty good friends, and this guy, Ernie, he was always Hank's particular target, always trying to get him in bad with the union and the bosses both. So I dropped Hank cold, avoided any social contact with him. Well, you aren't interested in the details; but first thing we knew Hank was a foreman, and then he began to ride me and this other guy.

Nothing we did was right. One day he called Ernie a 'nigger,' and I called him on it, and we—Hank and me—almost had a fist fight there on the floor. A whole bunch of the guys heard it. That was a little over a year ago.

"Well, to make a long story short, first thing anybody knew Hank was transferred to the sales department. He used pretty good English and looked good dressed up, and there's no getting around it, he was pretty smart. Everybody was glad to see him out of the warehouse and out of the union. He came out cold turkey as an anti-union man after he rose to the front office. We all figured he'd been stooling to the bosses all along, and that was one reason why they advanced him—his reward.

"So there you are. The police probably know by now, if they talked to the manager at Enderby's, that there'd been bad blood between Hank and me. He was going out with my sister who's a married woman; and they can assume I didn't like it. I was home at the time he was killed. I knew Frank had a gun, and I had access to it. Add it all up, and it looks to me like they got a case against me. So I figure I've *got* to find out who killed him and get proof. Because I don't expect the cops to look any further. I'm too good game myself."

Ramón laid the cold butt of his cigar on the edge of a copper ash tray. His face, accented by the black brows and mustache, was grave. He kept his eyes on the cigar butt.

"If you should prove to your own satisfaction then that it was, say, one of the girls, or your mother, would you expose them to save yourself?"

"What else could I do?" Don cried desperately. "I wouldn't, unless it was necessary to save myself—and my own family, Lola and the kids. Should I be a martyr, pay for somebody else's crime?"

"I'm just asking: would you?"

Don was mutinously silent for a moment, then he broke out impatiently, "Hell, this is an abstract question. I *know* neither Mom nor one of the girls did it."

Ramón did not remind Don of his previous words: "You know the ins and outs of the family," nor that Mamie and Don's sisters were the only ones of the family he did know.

Instead, in a more businesslike tone, he went on, "Being the kind of guy he was there must have been other men where you worked that had it in for him. This Ernie you spoke of in the warehouse. Could he have held a grudge, maybe got in somehow and got the gun and waited outside?"

Don frowningly shook his head even before Ramón finished. Even if Ernie had known of the gun, Don would have rejected the possibility of his guilt. Ernie was his friend.

"That gun," Don said slowly, "is what stumps me. It makes it look as if it has to be some of us."

"What about Peggy's husband?"

"He's probably seen the gun. Frank likes to show off with it. He's the kind of guy that *would* keep a gun. Likes to pretend he's a hard character, always telling about the rough life he saw in the woods when he was young."

"Let's see, he's a machinist, isn't he?"

"Yeah, works for the Watson lines. No connection at all with Hank, as far as his job is concerned."

"I've never seen Len. All I know is what Maureen's told me about him."

"He's all right. Not much imagination, narrow. Never thinks about anything but his meals and the movies and getting a new car. I think Peggy just got bored with him. She thinks life should be like one long movie, all emotion and excitement. The whole family, to tell you the truth, is fed up with her sitting around exposing her love life and brooding about, 'Do I or don't I *really* love him?' One day she does and one day she doesn't."

"Is he jealous?"

"You got me. But I suppose anybody is if they've got reason to be." Don glanced at the watch in a leather strap on his wrist. "I called him up this morning, caught him just as he was leaving for work. I told him to hightail it over here, that Peggy was in a bad jam. I figure he'll be questioned anyhow, and it would look better if he came over of his own accord. I wanted to be there when he came. Thought I might be able to tell something by the way he took it. I thought I'd have time to whip up here and back first, but I guess I've been too long-winded. Him and probably an army of cops will be there by the time I get back."

Ramón rose and walked to the window which looked out across descending slopes of gray rooftops and on to the vertical planes of white walls ascending the side of Telegraph Hill. The sun was now bright on the distant windowpanes to the north. He shoved his hands in his pockets and stared expressionlessly at the blue behind the cluttered skyline.

"I'll run you over in my car," he said abruptly. "I'd like to help you if I can. Coming in more or less like an outsider, I may pick up something you wouldn't notice. Anyway"—he turned, and a gleam came into his dark eyes, his full lips curved in a whimsical smile —"a father ought to show up when his kids are in trouble."

Don looked up at him uneasily. "That wasn't my idea, to get you to come over. It may not be—agreeable—for you, that is."

"I have a legal right to see my children"—he quoted—"'at any and all reasonable times.' This seems like a reasonable time. And"—he shrugged—"if my being there stirs things up, who knows, it may stir up clues."

As they got settled in Ramón's long blue sedan Don said ruefully, "I feel like a damned heel, deliberately watching the rest of my family, looking for signs of guilt. My only excuse is I've got a wife and kids of my own, and

I have a strange attachment to my own neck; and I guess self-preservation is the first law of life."

Ramón's eyes slid toward him and then back to the traffic. His voice, when he spoke, was soft, with a distinctly Spanish lilt to its inflections in contrast to his ordinary American accent. "You're thinking of Frank. You hope it will be him. That would make everything easier, I think."

Don looked quickly at the imperturbable profile beside him, the slightly flat nose, the well-defined lips, the solid chin. Again he had the sense of Ramón's words having brought to the surface motives and inclinations that had been there all the time but which had needed an outside voice to reveal them to himself.

"I've got nothing against Frank. He's a good guy, treats Mom decent, and she thinks the sun rises and sets in him." He laughed dryly. "Sometimes I feel embarrassed at her. Seems kind of silly, a woman her age acting romantic about a man, actually making eyes at him sometimes."

Ramón smiled but kept his eyes on the traffic signal ahead. "You are all, you kids, I think, jealous of your mother's husbands. If it was your own blood father, yes, it would seem natural. You wouldn't notice. But she seems—unfaithful—to you, loving somebody outside the blood. Me, you felt it even then; not so much, but it was there. But now I am closer some way than Frank. Because I was first, and I was there when you were little."

"You're pretty shrewd, Ramón. You figure things out about people. I think that's why I wanted you. Somebody's got to figure out why one of us wanted to kill Hank. I'm not so good on people that way. I kind of take things at their face value."

Chapter Four

When they reached the house on O'Farrell Street Len's Chevrolet coupe was parked in front of it. There were no police cars in evidence, as Don had half expected, but a patrolman sauntered idly along the sidewalk, his eyes unobtrusively observant.

It had not been a "good" neighborhood when the Gradys moved in ten years before. Sandwiched between the business houses and hotels which advanced from Market and the frankly tenement district creeping down from Fillmore, now the Negro section of San Francisco, that block on O'-Farrell had steadily run down even further under pressure of crowded wartime housing and the shortage afterward.

Pauline threatened regularly to take an apartment with a girl friend if Mamie wouldn't trade or sell and get a house in the Richmond or Sunset districts out toward the beach; but the house was clear of debt, and the upstairs flat brought an income, and Mamie, abetted by Frank, professed to be quite satisfied, even in the face of a four-family house on the corner occupied by Negroes and a rooming house across the street also tenanted by Negroes, mostly single men.

Besides, Mamie and Frank had it all worked out that when all the girls were married they would convert the parlor into a bedroom and rent it and the hall bedroom as well as the flat upstairs. Even Maureen felt resentfully that Frank was waiting impatiently for them all to be married and gone so that he could quit work and live a life of ease as a landlord, that this was one of the reasons he found Peggy's return to the nest so annoying.

Two things kept Pauline there at home. The first was money. It was cheaper, boarding with the folks, and she was saving methodically for the day when she quit working.

The second was that soon now she thought it would be time to get married, and then, of course, she would move into an apartment. For several years afterward, especially if she got the secretaryship with Mr. Forbes, she intended to go on working until she and her husband had enough for a substantial down payment on a home down the Peninsula, probably in San Mateo or San Carlos. By that time the husband should have advanced to a salary big enough to keep them both in comfort.

Pauline had adroitly maintained friendship with several eligible men. One was an employee of the insurance company where she worked; but he was a claims man and traveled a great deal, which was a disadvantage. She kept him as a reserve.

Her main prospect was Ellery Hodges, who was already an executive in the accounting department for Pacific Oil in the big building facing Market Street.

He was in love with her. She was sure of that. And he shared her ideals. The program she had laid out, of post-marital work and saving, would suit him to a T. Ellery had hopes of "going far" with the company. He lived, worked, and breathed oil, with little thought of personal interests not identified with the company's.

And he had recognized Pauline as a patrician type who would be good for a man's prestige socially and perhaps in business. At least the company would be able to find no drawbacks in his domestic life with so steady, fashionable, and intelligent a wife.

Pauline, in her quietly decorated, "modern" bedroom, pressed her fingertips over her eyes and shuddered.

And was it all to be shattered because a cheap sort of person she wouldn't have admitted socially to the planned-for, six-room, ranch-house-type home down the Peninsula had the impudence to be shot on their steps?

She paced back and forth, back and forth, on the eggshell string rug between her bed and the striped flounce on her dressing table. Frustration tightened her jaws, drew ugly lines on her face.

She hated them all; yes, even Mom. Perhaps especially Mom. Dragging them through the social scum of waitresses, mechanics, truck drivers, all their lives, marrying from passion again, and yet again, never learning that it didn't pay. Never learning to plan, to lay out a course toward better things and stick to it till you arrived, as you would arrive, if you planned and had ideals.

And Peggy!

"God!" Pauline uttered through clenched teeth.

Wouldn't listen. Wouldn't accept Pauline's offer of a loan till she finished business college. No, she had to have a man to sleep with every night. And wouldn't try to make that work, till at least she might have been a respectable housewife in the East Bay somewhere, even if her husband was only a bricklayer. No, she had to be dissatisfied, expect life to be a glittering bubble of what she considered happiness. Looking for it with vulgar people like Grueber.

And Don!

Pauline paused by the window from which all she could see was the straight-up-and-down boards of the service porch on the next house, and pushed her palm upward across her forehead.

Don was her own brother, the same inheritance as her own. She had hoped for something from Don. They barely remembered their real father. He had vanished like a stranger passed in a crowd after he deserted her mother when Pauline was only two. All she knew was that he had been a merchant seaman. Objectively, she realized that that didn't sound like much; but out of the romance of the sea and his coming vaguely from "New England" she had built up a conception of a "black sheep," a romantic adventurer, originally of a "good family."

So she and Don had "better blood." They would be true to it. But Don had never co-operated. Never!

Of course she realized much had been against him. There was no question of going on with his education after high school. It wasn't right for Frank to have fully to support all of his wife's offspring by other men. And just as Don might have begun to get ahead in his job at the candy factory the war had yanked him out and he had married Lola while on leave, and Jo Anne had come, and then Donnie, the baby.

But what had really finished Don, from the start, was his reliance on labor unions as his economic answer, not on his own individual fighting ability.

And now—now it looked as if it was the end, not only for him, but for her. She had never let Ellery know about Don and his activity in the union. Even that smear of radicalism on Pauline's own skirts might have queered her with Ellery. Ellery hated labor unions enough to satisfy even the officers of the company.

Quite rightly he believed that only weaklings had to band together for protection, that a real man got ahead by his own ability and hard work and pleasing his employers. And Pauline believed that someday Ellery would be a living proof of his theories.

She had tried to talk to Don, sensibly and reasonably, had expounded this philosophy of playing your cards right and working up.

"There's too many slips possible," he had replied with a shrug. "Maybe you make it; maybe you don't. Meanwhile, what about the millions who don't? We can't *all* be big executives."

"You have to look out for yourself first. It's a law of life—"

Don had looked at her oddly. "Yes, it can be done. You'll probably do it, get financial security, that is. But I think it costs too much."

"What do you mean?" She frowned.

"It takes too much out of you, changes you. I don't think I want to change—that way."

"But it's worth it, worth working hard and playing all the angles so you can rise to a respectable place in society," she cried, still puzzled.

"Is it?" He smiled. "Not for me, thanks. Personally, I think it's already taken too much out of you."

"Such as?" she demanded angrily.

His eyes had been unfriendly upon her. "Kindness, sympathy, understanding. Humanity, I guess you could say."

That had ended the talk, and nothing had ever been the same between them since.

Unexpectedly Pauline found tears running down her cheeks. Oh, Don, Don! You were my real brother. Why did you have to go queer?

She turned abruptly and wiped her face. This was no time for tears and regrets or even fear. Something had to be done. It was bad enough, the risks this raised at the office and with Ellery, but there was a more immediate problem. One of them might be arrested for murder. That, above everything, must not happen. The murder *must* be solved.

When Pauline emerged from her room, trimly dressed in gray slacks and a pink shirt, her hair brushed away from her forehead and caught in a coil on one side of the back of her head, she had evolved a theory.

The others had dispiritedly congregated in the dining room, the actual "living" room of the house. Frank sat in the armchair by the radio, trying to pick something out of the air besides serials. Peggy, crumpled on the cushions at one end of the studio couch, had put on a flowered peasant skirt and a white blouse with a low round neck accentuated by a wide lace-edged ruffle.

Pauline noted to herself that Peggy oughtn't to wear that type of costume. With her naturally curly hair and brown eyes it made her look really Mexican.

Mamie had changed to a long, starched house coat and combed her hair, which clustered in a crown of blond ringlets around her head. She was drinking coffee and cheering the others up by a steady patter of platitudes whose refrain assured herself and them that "everything was bound to come out all right."

"I've been doing some thinking," Pauline said judiciously, taking a cigarette from a package on the table and lighting it. She prowled about the room restlessly as she talked, looking out the side windows which provided a fine view of the peeling paint on the blank wall of the house to the east, touching objects on the buffet, straightening a plate on the rack which traversed the walls at shoulder height.

They raised their heads and listened to footsteps on the stairs and the front door closing.

"That's Don," Mamie remarked. "I wonder where he's going. That's him and Maureen both out, and I don't think the police would like it. I think they meant for us to stay right here till they came back."

"That's just dandy," Pauline said petulantly. "Them both out getting us into more trouble. But I'll tell you what I've figured out. We know it can't be any of us that—did it. So it's got to be somebody else that was in the house last night and took Frank's gun—"

Mamie listened respectfully, ready to accept the result of her eldest daughter's speculations. She considered Pauline the brainy one of her children. Pauline was the one of whom she was the most proud, with her nice office job, her knowledge of etiquette, her flair for style. To her mother's eyes Pauline always looked like the models in fashion magazines.

"Well, so who was in the house?" Pauline paused meaningly. "Don's friends, that's who."

Mamie moved her coffee cup uneasily on the saucer. If Pauline was her pride, if Peggy the one of her children with whom she felt the most at ease, and Maureen her baby who worried her the most and toward whom she felt most protective, Don was her beloved. Guiltily she knew he was her favorite. There was something about your first, the first baby you held in your arms and knew you had created, and on top of that your only son. You never seemed to get as close to your son as to your girls, but there was a special feeling a mother had toward her male child. Every time his name had come up in connection with the murder, it was as if a giant hypodermic needle injected a shot of fear into her veins.

"Now," Pauline continued, "we all know those niggers that live on the corner were upstairs last night—"

"Oh, Pauline," Mamie interrupted uneasily, "Don would have a fit if he heard you use that word."

"To hell with Don!" she flared sharply. "He got us into this disgraceful situation, and I've no more patience with him. And if you don't put your foot down at last—after this—"

"Pauline! To talk that way about your own brother—your full brother too!"

"She's right," Frank grunted. "We been too lenient with that kid."

"Kid! He's twenty-seven years old!"

"That's neither here nor there," Pauline interrupted impatiently. "The thing is I saw them—those Negroes"—she elaborated with a sarcastic glance at her mother—"go upstairs last night about eight o'clock."

There were two bells outside the front door, and when Don's rang he could open the door by pressing a buzzer. All his guests were so admitted.

"I was in the front room getting a book I left on the table. So this is how I've got it doped out. Everybody knows how colored people steal. Well, I figure that when they came downstairs from Don's late last night they saw the house was dark, so they took a notion to see what they could pick up. The man found Frank's gun in the drawer, and figured it would come in handy if he ever wanted to do any burgling in a big way."

She glanced about and noted with satisfaction that her audience was fascinated.

"He didn't find anything else, any money or anything, and as they were slipping out down the hall they heard Peggy and Hank outside and ducked into the parlor to wait. When the girls were both inside they slipped out the front door. Probably Hank had stopped for a minute, to light a cigarette or something, or maybe he had started away and heard them come out, and came back. He probably said something, asked the darky what he was doing, and the fellow got scared. They're all kind of mean anyway, and he probably couldn't resist having the whip hand over a white man, with a gun and all, so he just shot him."

They regarded her admiringly, more in tribute to her inventiveness than in conviction. Peggy moved her head slightly, a sort of rejecting movement, and put her little fingernail in her mouth, biting down on it worriedly.

With a circular movement Frank rubbed his mouth and chin with the palm of his hand.

"One thing I can't figure out," he said slowly. "A course Lola and Don, even if they were still awake, must have been in the back of the house, in the kitchen or bedroom, and you and me, Mamie, was asleep in our bedroom, and Pauline's room is in the rear too; but Peggy and Maureen were awake when it happened. Must have been right after Peggy came in. Why didn't somebody hear the shot?"

"Would it be—very loud?" Mamie asked faintly.

"Well—not so much as a shotgun or a rifle, but loud enough. Like a car backfiring anyway."

Peggy straightened from the waist up. "Maybe it didn't happen here. Maybe somebody brought him back and dumped him on our walk."

Frank looked at Mamie. "You said there was blood dried on the sidewalk?"

She nodded.

"Then he must have fell right there."

Pauline, slightly irritated at the conversation's turn away from her theory, broke in impatiently, "Good heavens, this is a city. There's always noise on the streets at night. We're used to sleeping through anything. Think of this location, one block past the Geary carlines, the Twenty goes past right in front of the house going out and comes in on Ellis just another block over, and the Van Ness cars two blocks away, running all night. And automobiles at all hours of the night."

"Not many streetcars running after one o'clock and not much other traffic either."

"But they do run. Many's the night I've heard them after going to bed late. Who's going to notice one bang more or less mixed into the sound of streetcars clanging uphill the way they do for two or three blocks both ways along here?"

Peggy was frowning with frightened eyes. "I never thought of it," she said in a scared voice. "I was so upset, and there was so much to think about this morning when the policemen were here; but I remember now."

"Remember what?" Pauline snapped imperatively.

"The shot." She gulped. "That's what it must have been. Your talking about streetcars—it kind of made like a flashback come into my mind. It must have been about five minutes after I came in. I had my shoes off and had taken my dress off and put on my robe, ready to go to the bathroom and wash as soon as Maureen got through in there. I never even thought about it, but I guess it registered somewhere back in my mind. You know how the Twenty car crashes and grinds when it has to stop to let someone off on Franklin and then has to make a cold start up the hill. Well, there was one doing that, and I could hear another car climbing the hill on the other side of us on Geary, and at the same time I heard a kind of louder noise, like an explosion. I didn't even think about it. If I had, I'd have thought it was an automobile starting and backfiring like Frank said."

"Well." Pauline threw out her hands in an expressive gesture. "Doesn't that just confirm the way I reconstructed the crime?"

"But the gun was back in the drawer," Mamie reminded her doubtfully.

"I figured that out too. I just hadn't got that far. When he sneaked out, see, he left the door open a crack, probably to make it look the next day as if some of us had been careless about closing it. Well, after he shot Hank, he certainly didn't want the gun on his hands, so he sneaked back in after the girls were asleep and put it back. It served a double purpose, protected himself and threw suspicion on us."

"Sounds reasonable," Frank agreed sagely.

"If it's true," Mamie meditated, "it lets all of us out."

"Of course it does. And I'm going to tell the police."

"Oh, Pauline, Don asked us not to tell. It'll put him in the position of concealing evidence."

"Serves him right then. He's willing to let us be suspected of murder to protect his precious friends. How much loyalty does that show?"

"But this poor man—this Negro—suppose he *didn't* do all that?" Mamie demurred.

Frank had been pondering deeply, his face working with the effort. "It won't hold up," he said regretfully. "That's a good heavy door. It had to be closed, else the shot would have waked up everybody in the house. And the nigger didn't have no key to get back in after he fired."

"He could have stolen a key from Don's sometime," Pauline snapped.

Frank shook his head ponderously. "Won't hold up."

The doorbell ringing long and hard suppressed Pauline's irritated rebuttal, and she jerked toward the door, startled. "The police again. I'll go."

Mamie half rose from her chair and dropped back. "We probably ought to receive them in the front room—more dignified. But I guess Pauline will usher them in there, and we can come in, as if we'd just been about our business as usual. Yes, that's better."

But the excited voice they heard was not an official one. Peggy raised her head, surprised. "Sounds like Len."

Pauline came in first, looking not too pleased, and behind her, with the effect of charging a football line, came Peggy's husband. He was large and sandy blond, with a pug nose and short hair parted in the middle and combed back loosely.

"Peggy, you poor kid," he breathed hoarsely, and lunged toward the couch. She shrank back, but made no resistance as he hugged her protectively and looked about at the startled spectators with solemn eyes.

"Don called me up, thought I ought to know, so I rushed right over. At a time like this, irregardless, a man's place is at his wife's side."

His large hand patted Peggy's shoulder, and he gazed down at her tenderly. "Don't you worry, honey, I'll see you through. I've gotta admit I ain't felt too friendly, you bustin' off home to Mamma when, far as I can see, I ain't done a thing to you; but when Don told me on the phone about you bein' persecuted by the cops, I says to myself, 'Let bygones be bygones; maybe I ain't been thoughtful an' considerate enough, her bein' a high-strung, sensitive little thing like she is. Maybe the little woman had a legitimate beef after all. Anyways, my place is right beside her at a time like this.'"

Magnanimity suffused Len's face at this chance for once to play a hero role, and the unsteady state of Peggy's nerves and a general mental confusion, complicated by fear, left her too weak to keep from being overwhelmed by his fervor. Her face had been working as Len talked, and she began to cry, allowing herself to be held in the curve of his arm, her face buried on the shoulder of his gabardine windbreaker.

Frank and Mamie interpreted it as evidence that, there now, she did love Len all the time, and they regarded the tender scene with satisfaction.

While they told Len the details of the morning's events Peggy recovered her composure and unobtrusively drew away, pushing at her hair with her fingers and straightening her blouse.

Her eyes scraped her husband's face coldly as she asked bluntly, "What were you doing last night?"

"Don't you worry about me," Len reassured all of them blandly. "Lucky for me I got an airtight alibi. I was at Trader Vic's till closing time with—uh—some friends; and I gave a couple of 'em a lift home; so I was with people till past one-thirty."

"How nice," Pauline commented. "We had so hoped we could pin it on you."

"Now, Pauline," Mamie reproved.

Just then they heard the front door open and close, and Pauline went to the hall to see who it was.

"Maureen," she informed them, and came back and sat down on the couch.

As her youngest daughter appeared in the door and surveyed the group coolly, Mamie addressed her in an aggrieved tone, "Where have you been? Don't you know this is no time to be wandering around without telling us? Suppose the police had asked us where you were?"

Maureen ignored the questions and regarded her brother-in-law skeptically; but she said kindly, "Hello, Len. Where did you drop from?"

"Don phoned me. Thought I ought to know."

"And he's out traipsing around, too, goodness knows where," Mamie added accusingly, "instead of being here with his family like he ought to."

"What are we supposed to gain by all sitting around looking at each other?" Maureen inquired reasonably.

"Well, Pauline just figured out what probably happened, and one thing we could do is get together on a story," Frank volunteered.

"Oh, sure, Don would agree to my story," Pauline said sarcastically.

Maureen pulled out a straight chair and sat with her arms on the table. "What did you figure out?"

"Yeah, you think you know what happened?" Len prompted.

Pauline was halfway through a repetition of her theory when Don and Ramón opened the front door.

The confreres in the dining room paused and listened curiously to the quiet voices and the steady footsteps coming down the hall.

"I guess everybody's in the dining room," they heard Don say.

As the two men appeared in the doorway, both Mamie and Maureen came to their feet. In neither was the movement a welcoming one.

"What's the idea?" Maureen demanded.

"Well—Ramón! Of all people," Mamie exclaimed in the tone of one who has had the wind knocked out of her.

Ramón smiled amiably, and Don explained awkwardly, "I dropped in on Ramón this morning, and when he heard about Hank he offered to help if he could—Peggy being involved," he finished lamely.

"Didn't know as anybody needed help," Frank observed ungraciously.

"I thought I'd like to see the girls anyway," Ramón added easily.

"Hello," Peggy said, as if greeting him were an afterthought, and hesitated on the next word, "Papa." She glanced at Len and back at Ramón. "This is my—husband."

Looking bewildered, Len stood up and Ramón advanced, holding out his hand. Len put his in it with an air of succumbing to the invitation from surprise rather than from cordiality.

With growing disapproval Mamie eyed the scene.

Adding eight human beings to the space already eaten into by dining-room furniture, a couch, an easy chair, and a radio, had given the room an uncomfortably cramped atmosphere.

Don said with a futile attempt at joviality, "What say we all adjourn to the front room?"

There was no apparent enthusiasm for the proposal, but everyone seemed mesmerized by the dramatic potentialities of the situation and unwilling to miss whatever might come out of it, so they tramped unsociably down the hall.

Maureen crowded next to Don, muttering, "What do you think you're doing, little Mr. Fixit?"

As they stiffly took chairs Don, feeling a sense of responsibility for the occasion, observed sociably, "Looks like the whole family's here except Lola."

"By all means somebody call Lola," Pauline said acidly. "Nothing like a nice family reunion, I always say."

"That'll be enough of that," Mamie rebuked her sharply. Her eyes had been hovering worriedly on Frank, but she had evidently decided to make the best of an awkward situation. "It's only natural," she went on primly, "I suppose, for Ramón—Mr. Garcia—to be concerned when his daughters get mixed up in a murder." Her eyes flicked nervously at the sullen Frank.

"I don't mean to intrude," Ramón said diplomatically. "I've always felt the girls were well provided with a father's protection in Mr. Grady."

Frank raised his eyes suspiciously.

"But I felt it was my duty to put myself at your service in any way that I could be useful to the girls. This is a very serious matter. A person never knows what the police will do, you know."

"You said it," Len seconded him. "Why, they soaked me fifty bucks one time for goin' through a red light. Said it was reckless driving, and I'd only had a couple of beers a good hour before it happened." He surveyed the company with virtuous indignation.

Peggy turned her head away from Len where he had plumped himself down beside her on the davenport, and found herself looking into her father's considering eyes. For an instant complete understanding passed from one to the other. Peggy's lips tightened and she looked away with an annoyed contraction of her brow. She had trained herself to dislike of this man, and it displeased her to experience this rapprochement with him.

Maureen's eyes had moved back and forth between her father and her sister. She had not yet taken a seat, and now she went abruptly to a footstool near the mantel, pushed it with her leg closer to Ramón's chair, and sat down beside him.

"We can dispense with the fine sentiments and the heroics," Pauline declared coldly. "Just before people started arriving in such hordes I told the folks what I'm sure happened, and I intend to tell the police. Our mystery will soon evaporate then." She turned to Don. "Maybe you'd rather see your own mother and sisters being given the third degree than tell the truth, which would clear this thing up in a hurry; but I'm not going to let you get away with it. That Negro—*friend*—of yours did it, and I intend to—"

"Pauline! You don't know what you're saying!" Don's face was white.

Maureen had leaned forward on her stool. Her eyes were unusually bright. "How do you know?"

"Deduction, that's how. I used my brain. Nice exercise," she added sarcastically. "Some of the rest of you ought to try it some time."

Don had jumped to his feet, and red was now suffusing his skin. He made an inarticulate sound of rage.

"Just a minute, Don," Ramón put in quietly, and to Pauline, "Tell the rest of us, will you, how you decided this Negro did it."

Don remained standing, eying his sister incredulously as she tersely sketched her reconstruction of the crime. "Good God," he groaned as she concluded her story.

Len looked around, his eyes wide. "Sounds reasonable."

Maureen had listened fascinated, her face inscrutable. Now she said in a low voice, more to herself than to the others, "It's a lousy trick."

Ramón glanced down at her.

"Have you any better ideas?" Pauline inquired scathingly of her youngest sister.

Peggy started to cry softly. "I wish I was dead."

Don began to swear softly but brutally at Pauline, and she shrank back a little. Mamie got to her feet and rushed to her son, crying ineffectually, "Don, Don, you mustn't! Now, you kids, behave."

Len put his arms clumsily around Peggy. "Aw now, kid. There's no use in you feelin' bad. How could you know he was gonna get bumped off? A course," he stated virtuously, "you had no business runnin' around with other men, but you never—"

Peggy pushed his arms away and raised her head angrily, the tears streaking her cheeks, and backed into the corner of the davenport near which Ramón's chair stood.

"For Christ's sake, leave me alone," she squealed. "You—you big *dope!*"

Mamie wheeled. "Now, Peggy, that's no way to act when Len's being so good and—and broadminded and everything."

Pauline was screaming back at Don, "Don't you dare talk like that to me!"

Lola, halfway down the stairs, leaned over the banister and cried, "What's happening? My God, amongst you you're making enough noise to wake the dead."

Jo Anne, following her mother one step at a time, stared through the railing, and, seeing her father angry and everybody talking at once, got scared and began to whimper. "Mamma, what's the matter?"

Frank, who had been sitting with his hands on the chair arms, opening and closing his mouth impotently, now leaped to his feet and roared, "Shut up! All of you! God damn it, I won't have it! Not in my house, I won't!"

In the startled silence which his more powerful voice wrung from the others the doorbell pealed peremptorily. The silence became painfully distinct.

"Oh, God," Mamie sobbed. "It's probably the police, and they heard us carrying on like—like hoodlums."

Maureen had been sitting tensely, her bright eyes jumping from one person to another. Now she glanced up at Ramón, who had sat impassively watching.

As Mamie commanded huskily, "Everybody settle down. Try to look— well, try to look—calm. I'll answer it," Ramón smiled down at his daughter.

She smiled faintly and relaxed. He said softly, so only she heard, "And they say it's us Latins who are excitable."

Chapter Five

Inspector Holmes looked like a middle-aged businessman, except that he had kept his figure and most of his hair. He removed a soft felt hat and soberly introduced himself to Mamie. Another detective, a Mr. Avery, stood at his side and a step behind. Although there was no physiognomical resemblance between the two men, so alike in type were they that a casual observer might have been unable to tell which was which after one glimpse of either in a crowd.

Embarrassed, Mamie ushered them into the parlor whose occupants had subsided unhappily. Lola took Jo Anne by the hand and let her out the front door with the admonition, "Now stay inside the fence. You're *not* to go outside the gate. Understand?"

The baby had been put down for his nap upstairs, so Lola sidled into the parlor and stood beside Don.

The Inspector glanced thoughtfully about the room. With himself and his cohort there were now eleven people present, and it was not a large room.

"We've come to make some inquiries into the death which occurred this morning." He looked around again, apparently unable to fit Ramón and Len into the report he had received from Detective Jeffries before the latter went off duty. "Perhaps first if I could get a line on who you all are—"

"Of course," Mamie replied, assuming the air of a hostess and seeming to get a lift from the opportunity to put everything on a social basis by making formal introductions. "This is Inspector Holmes, folks, and Mr.— Avery, was it? They're going to help us get this awful business all straightened out. Now, this—"

And she went around the room efficiently, giving names and indicating their owners' relationship to herself and to each other. At Ramón she hesitated momentarily, and then explained in a dignified manner, "Miss Garcia's and Mrs. Johnson's father. He felt it his duty to be near his daughters in these trying hours. So difficult for all of us, you know, Mr. Grueber being a family friend, and," she finished with solemn elegance, "meeting such an untimely demise."

Maureen glowered at the rug and Peggy looked embarrassed.

Pauline was the last to be introduced, and she spoke up in a clear, composed voice, "I wish to make a statement, Inspector."

"That's fine," he said impassively. "I believe, however, it would be better if I spoke to each of you separately. We seem to be quite a crowd. Is there some other room where you could wait?"

"We could go back to the dining room, I guess," Mamie said.

"If you will, and I'll call you as I need you. Miss Thomas, then, we'll hear your—er—statement first."

With Lola at his elbow Don went out first. He did not look at Pauline. All the spirit seemed gone out of him. As they trooped down the narrow hall once more Frank muttered, "Seems like I've done nothing but run up and down this damned hall all morning."

Nobody had anything to say as they gathered in the dining room. It was as if they felt the time for accomplishing anything by talk was over.

Frank went on to his bedroom to get a pipe. Don sat at the table with his hands clasped in front of him, gazing at them with two furrows between his brows. Lola sat around the corner of the table and watched him yearningly. Ramón took a straight chair against the wall and sat with his feet parallel, his hands folded in his lap, his eyes interestedly bright. Maureen crouched on the footstool in front of the radio, arms around her knees, withdrawn once more into the detachment of a spectator at a drama. Peggy huddled, squelched by misery, in her former corner of the couch; and Len sat at the other end, obviously unhappy at the unsociable air of the others. He made several conversational sallies, but since no one parried them, he, too, subsided moodily.

Mamie observed with a glance at the oblong clock on the buffet, "Now I suppose they'll throw lunch all off, just like they did breakfast." She looked about solicitously, "Is anybody hungry?"

But no one replied.

After a moment Don looked up heavily. "She'll implicate Ernest. I can't stop her."

Lola put her hand on his arm.

"Well, of course, Don," Mamie said soothingly, "it's just her word. None of the rest of us saw anybody go upstairs last night. So how can we swear to who it was?"

Frank had returned, and Mamie looked about at all of them defensively, her manner demanding their acquiescence. Since nobody answered, she assumed she had it.

"Don't blame yourself, Don," Lola said softly. "You tried to protect Ernest. You couldn't help Pauline's knowing." Suddenly she leaned forward and whispered, "It's like Mamie says: it's just her word against ours. One against two."

Don shook his head bitterly. "It's no use."

Under her breath Lola enjoined him urgently, "You stick to your story. You can't let them know you lied."

Sunk in his own reflections, he hardly seemed to hear.

After a moment she got up casually. "I'm going to see if Jo Anne's all right. Guess I'll go around through the back so I won't have to pass the living room."

Lola had been gone only a moment when Pauline entered the room. She looked serious, but there was no longer antagonism, nor even gloating, in her manner.

"They want to see you now, Don," she said in a low voice, not looking at him.

As he went out she came to the table and sat down and buried her head in her arms. It was as if reaction had set in after her opposition to her brother, and now her basic affection for him reasserted itself. She raised her head and pulled a Kleenex from her pants pocket, pressing it to her eyes.

"Oh, why did Don have to get mixed up with those awful people?" she sobbed. "I don't *want* to get him in trouble."

"There, now," Mamie murmured, stroking her hair. "I suppose you thought you were doing the right thing." She paused, and then said vaguely, "After all, honesty is the best policy." She frowned slightly, as if examining the maxim critically for the first time.

Don walked into the parlor steadily, and Inspector Holmes nodded toward a straight-backed chair with a padded seat.

"I suppose you know it's against the law to withhold information in a murder investigation."

"I'd never thought about it one way or another."

"Well, you know it now. Who else was in your apartment last night?"

"Nobody." He continued dispiritedly, "I know I should have mentioned the Simpkinses, but I was sure they didn't know anything about what happened, and I figure Negro people have enough troubles of their own without having other people's dumped in their lap too."

"I'm not interested in your social theories. All I'm interested in is finding out who killed Henry Grueber. In order to do that we need complete and exact information. I might say that you have not placed yourself in a very favorable light, Mr. Thomas, by trying to prevent our getting that information. Now, what time did these Simpkins arrive here last night?"

"About eight, a little after maybe."

"What time did they leave?"

"Some time around eleven. I can't say to the minute."

"Have you seen them or talked to them since then?"

"No."

"You went out this morning. Where did you go?"

"Over to North Beach to see Mr. Garcia."

"Why?"

"Well, he was my stepfather when I was little. I thought he ought to know what had happened. Just wanted to talk to him, I guess. He's still sort of like a father to me."

"Don't you get on well with Grady?"

"Why, sure."

"I see. Was Simpkins acquainted with Grueber?"

"Yes."

"Did Grueber's name enter the conversation upstairs last evening?"

"Of course not."

"Why did these people come to your house? A meeting?"

"No. We're friends."

"How do you happen to know them?"

"We're neighbors."

"Where does Simpkins work?"

It flashed through Don's mind that he might as well give the answer, since, even if Pauline hadn't told it, it was easily ascertainable.

"Enderby Liquor Supplies."

"If there was anyone else present last night, you'd better say so now."

"But that was all. I told you."

Holmes decided the man might be telling the truth. The state of the card table and the four dirty coffee cups on the sink upstairs that morning re-enforced the assertion. He spoke to Avery, "There's a phone in the hall. Call up the office and tell them to bring Simpkins in for questioning."

While that call was going through, another telephone on the corner was in use. Lola had broken into a run when she reached the back steps, dashed across the yard and up the alley. Panting for breath, she climbed the back stairs of the frame house where the Simpkinses lived on the sec-ond floor. She knocked on the kitchen door and pushed it open without waiting.

Nell Simpkins was moving around the ironing board where she had been working, and she halted in surprise as Lola, breathing heavily, burst into the kitchen.

"Nell, don't say anything. Just listen. I can't waste a second. I have to get back before they know I'm gone. And no one must know I've been here."

Nell put her doubled fist on the board, and her dark eyes were appre-hensive on Lola's face. She nodded, and listened.

"Hank Grueber was murdered in front of our house last night—"

Nell nodded once more, signifying that she knew already. The whole neighborhood had talked of nothing else all morning, and the woman in the flat across the hall had spent an hour over coffee in Nell's kitchen, re-peating the rumors which were already rife up and down the street.

"The police have found out you folks were there—"

Nell did not move, except for the muscles of her throat as she swallowed.

"We told the cops this morning nobody was there, but Pauline spilled it just now to the detective. She saw you come in. But it's her word against the four of us. Now, listen! Phone Ernie at the warehouse on some legit-imate errand—anything you can think of that will sound on the level.

Don't try to tell him what's up. Someone might be listening on the switchboard. But get across to him somehow, casually, that you were not at our house last night. He'll understand. We don't want to drag you in."

The words had poured out in a cascade, and now Lola paused anxiously. "Got it?"

Nell nodded. "I'll phone right away," she said softly.

As Lola darted back out of the door and down the steps Nell's face drew into a weary frown; but then she put her hand up to her cheek and tried to think—an innocent but fairly important reason for the unusual procedure of calling Ernie in the stockroom? The telephone was outside the flat, in the hall, to be used by both families living upstairs. She started for it, still thinking hard. A message that would hold water?

Even while she was being connected with the stockroom her mind was still organizing what she would say.

Ernie's voice was tensely questioning. "Nell? What's the matter? Is something wrong?"

"No. I know I shouldn't bother you at work, but I'm coming downtown shopping this afternoon, and I just thought; I'll meet you at the corner of Fourth and Market, in front of Benatar's Drugstore, and let's have dinner downtown and go to a show."

"But I won't be dressed to go out," he responded irritably.

She made her voice girlishly pouting. "Now, honey, we haven't gone anywhere for ages. We sat home all last night. You can at least take me out tonight."

There was a small puzzled pause, and the man said, "I don't get it. You know we—"

She broke in. "I'm sick of staying home, like we did last night. I'll be waiting at the corner."

Abruptly she hung up, knowing he was left puzzled. But now when the police came he would surely catch on.

She leaned her head against the wall a moment. The police. A murder. "Oh, God," she prayed silently, "dear God, don't let them ..."

She walked slowly back into her flat. It had worried her, taking up with a white couple. But they had been nice, and fun to visit and play cards with. But it had made her nervous. The neighbors had talked. And for colored people, it was better to be inconspicuous. And now, here they were, smack in the middle of a white folks' mess.

Wonderingly Ernest went back to work. Fifteen minutes later, as he wheeled a hand truck laden with cartons across the floor, he saw Rogers, the foreman, pointing him out to a man in a dark suit and a felt hat. Uneasiness trembled to life inside him.

The man came directly to him. "Ernest Simpkins?"

"Yes."

The officer opened his hand to reveal a badge. "I've come to take you down to police headquarters. We want to ask you some questions."

Ernest's hands tightened on the bar of the truck handle. "Am I under arrest?"

"No. We want information you may be able to give us in an investigation we're making. We can talk better in the office than here. Come along."

For a moment the question of legal rights, of the desirability of refusal to go along, flashed through Ernest's mind. But he was a peaceable man, avoiding scenes or arguments whenever possible. And the officer's manner was matter-of-fact. Probably better to co-operate.

Ernest had not yet heard of the murder around the corner from his own home. There had been the usual hurry and scurry to get out of his flat on time that morning, a run to catch the B car laboring up the hill on Geary Street, the usual unsociably silent mass of working people crowded on the rear platform of the car; and at work, by request of the police, the news of Hank's death had not yet leaked out from the office into the stockroom with whose crew the slain man had once worked. The officers had been busy so far with questioning of the managers, getting a line on Hank's career, before they invaded the warehouse itself.

As they drove back across the business district toward Kearny Street, Ernest, in the back seat of the sedan with the man who had come for him, considered Nell's strange phone call. He wondered what the connection was. Vividly every word came back, and he resolved to hold her message tight in his mind.

At police headquarters Ernest was deposited in a sparsely furnished room and told to wait. Through the open door he could see men in shirtsleeves and men in plain clothes and men in uniform going cheerfully about their business. He looked at a calendar on the wall, at the water cooler in the corner, at the bare oblong table, at the other straight chairs, and he smoked cigarettes and waited.

Toward the end of Ernest's sojourn Inspector Holmes arrived in his office from O'Farrell Street.

Before seeing Ernest he conferred on the telephone with Jeffries, who asked, "You turn up anything new?"

"One thing. There were at least two other people upstairs last night. Got it from the oldest girl. Colored couple went up a little after eight. She saw them; and Thomas admitted it, said he was just trying to save the guy embarrassment."

Jeffries whistled.

"After we left Grady's just now we went up and saw the woman. She denied being there. Couldn't get any more out of her. Said she never heard of Grueber."

"Think it's them?"

"Could be. I'm going to talk to the man now."

So an officer finally came for him, and Ernest followed him down the corridor, obeying the man's gesture and walking into the room under the curious eyes of Holmes and Avery.

Holmes was seated at his desk, Avery at the side of the room at a small table.

Holmes nodded at a chair. "Sit down."

"I'd like to know what this is all about," Ernest said quietly, trying to control a rising fear. "If I'm being accused of something, haven't I got a right to get a lawyer?"

"Nobody's accusing you of anything. We just want information," Holmes said smoothly. "There was some trouble in your neighborhood last night, and you may be able to throw some light on it for us."

"What kind of—trouble?"

"I'll ask the questions if you don't mind. First, where were you from eight o'clock last evening until one-thirty this morning?"

Now Ernest understood Nell's message. The cops must have talked to her, and in an effort to keep out of whatever the trouble was she had lied. Her phone call had been to tell him that. The uneasiness he had felt before was nothing to the fright which now emerged full-grown. It was dangerous to lie. The truth had a way of oozing out around the edges of falsehoods. He wished to God he knew what it was all about. If it was something serious, to be caught in a lie might incriminate them beyond repair.

His eyes moved from one to the other of the watchful white men.

"Well?" Holmes prompted brusquely.

Ernest could feel the sweat on his forehead. He raised his hand and brushed his fingers across his brow. His eyes moved again from one man to the other, and he became angrily aware of how the movement would look to these men. Another "darky," "rolling his eyes." Consciously he held his eyes still on the gray-eyed man's face.

The Thomases. It must be something to do with them. Maybe Nell had lied—not for him and her—but for them.

He ought to trust Nell's message. But he knew Nell. Fearful, overcautious. Her very efforts to keep them out of trouble might get them into worse.

And he was a religious man, a trustee in his church. He tried to live by the Bible, and a Christian didn't lie.

Besides, the truth was easier. You could stick to it, not get confused, just because it was the truth. He was afraid of these living embodiments of white law. He had no confidence in his ability to outwit them under questioning. He felt, resignedly, that they would catch him if he tried to deceive them.

So he told them quietly. The going to Don's, the pinochle till nearly eleven, the getting home and to bed "at five after twelve." He remembered the time on account of looking at the alarm clock as he pulled the button to set it.

When he had finished, the detective asked, "Did you see anyone about the house either when you entered or left?"

"No."

"Anyone see you come into your own house?"

Ernest frowned, hoping to remember that someone had. "Nobody I know of. There may have been people walking on the street that saw us, but I don't remember anybody."

"How long did you talk to Hank Grueber?"

Ernest lifted his chin and his eyes widened as he stared at the detective. "Grueber?" he repeated stupidly.

"Yes."

"Henry Grueber?"

"Yes, you must have met him as you left Thomas's."

"No, I didn't even know he was there."

"You know him though?"

"He used to work in our stockroom."

Holmes paused thoughtfully. So far they had nothing on this man except that the Thomases had sought to conceal his presence at their flat the night before. Pauline's theory appealed to Holmes as a neat disposal of the case, but there was nothing yet to back it up.

The detective had sensed at once when he talked to Nell Simpkins that someone had got to her during the morning. It was not unusual for Negroes to clam up before the police, their faces and even their eyes becoming maddeningly blank and impervious in self-protective noncomprehension; but now that the man admitted his presence in the Thomas house, Holmes was certain the woman would not have denied it if she hadn't been sure of confirmative testimony to support her statement. It was the wife, Lola Thomas, of course, who had primed the Negro woman in an effort to protect her own husband. Thomas himself had been smart enough to see that his lie had caught up with him, but the wife was slower to figure things out, and Don hadn't had time to coach her after he decided to come clean on the Negroes.

Holmes turned a pencil over in his fingers and looked out of the window. Don Thomas. He was the one to work on. What the detectives had learned from the people at Enderby's established motives that would hold up. They were still questioning people in the block who might have seen or heard something significant. He'd keep working on the family. One of them was bound to slip up sooner or later on their stories. Those girls and the fifteen minutes after Peggy Johnson came inside, and the other one was supposed to be in the bathroom. They could be hiding something there.

His eyes came back to Ernest. The Negro hadn't lied about his being in the house. Thomas had. And when you started catching them trying to cover up little things, it was often a symptom. Their minds seemed to catch on the notion that if they could just conceal the minor point, then the major would also remain hidden. Yes, Don Thomas was the man to concentrate on. Might as well get the Negro's fingerprints and let him go.

Chapter Six

When the detectives had gone Don asked Ramón to come upstairs with him and Lola for lunch. Maureen invited herself along, and as they sat around the table in the kitchen eating, they considered the situation.

Lola's face around the eyes was crumpled from weeping. When they had retired to privacy upstairs, she and Don had learned of their conflicting testimony before the officer, and he had been aghast to learn of her secret call on Nell.

"Now we *are* in the soup," he had ejaculated despairingly. "You've fixed it so the Simpkinses'll be caught perjuring themselves—" He broke off defeatedly. "That ties it."

"But I *told* you not to change your story," she cried. "I was only trying to help."

By the time they sat down to eat, a discouraged truce had been established.

"Well, I tell you," Ramón said, breaking a piece of French bread in two. "I don't think you've got anything to worry about. Don explained why you were trying to shield the Simpkinses. And they can't arrest any of you without some definite evidence; and that they haven't got yet. Or unless they find a witness, somebody who saw or heard something. That's possible, of course."

"I'd feel better," Don said ruefully, "If the guilty party was safely behind bars."

"Papa's right," Maureen spoke up. "They've got nothing definite on anybody. As long as they can't pin it on any of us, why worry about who did it? Hank was no good to anybody anyway."

"You didn't always feel that way." Lola smiled, her spirits beginning to revive a little under the influence of Ramón's prosaic, reassuring attitude.

Ramón's eyes turned toward Lola searchingly and went on to his daughter. "What's this?"

The girl frowned. "Search me."

"Why, Maureen," Lola accused teasingly, "you remember when Hank used to come here, before he and Don got on the outs so bad, you had quite a crush on him." She smiled at Ramón. "She was just a kid—fifteen, you were, I guess, but she used to hang around Hank at our parties, and anybody could see how flattered she was because he kidded around with her. I think you were really jealous, Maureen, when he went out with Peggy before she was married."

"It was just a silly childish crush," Maureen said shortly.

"Do the police know about this—crush?" Ramón asked sharply.

"Why, no." Lola glanced about uncertainly. "It didn't mean anything. I was only teasing Maureen just now."

"Well, don't do it again," Ram6n admonished. "Have you had anything to do with him recently?" he demanded of the girl.

"Naturally not."

"You're right, Ramón," Don added soberly. "We've got to be careful about remarks that might be misinterpreted."

"But I never meant anything," Lola protested, distressed.

When the meal was finished the men went into the living room and Maureen stayed to help Lola with the dishes. Hearing the baby wakening from his nap, Don went back to the bedroom, and Ramón was left alone.

While, ready to go, he waited for Don's return, Peggy came up the stairs. All during the depressing luncheon downstairs she had been disturbingly aware of her father's presence in the flat above.

"I wanted to tell you," she said, ill at ease, "I—I appreciate your coming over and offering to help."

"You don't need to thank me." He smiled. "I haven't done much for you in the past."

She came and sat on the arm of a chair, and in her full skirt and low-necked blouse, her dark hair thick and curly above long-lashed brown eyes, she looked like his daughter, heavier and darker though the man's features were.

"We ought to be better friends. Why don't you come over to my place sometime and I'll treat you to the best dinner we've got."

"I'll do that." She looked down at a fold of skirt that her fingers were pleating. Practically they were strangers, but it seemed quite natural to say, as any daughter might to her father, "What do you think of my—husband?"

"It's not what I or anybody else thinks. What do you think of him?"

She raised her eyes and met his, kindly, waiting. "Everybody around here thinks I'm crazy. There's nothing *really* wrong with Len."

"How did you happen to marry him?"

"I loved him, I guess—then. At least I wanted to marry him. He was cute, and crazy about me, and fun to go out with."

"And now?"

She raised her face, and a little smile moved her lips. "I keep thinking of a little rhyme:

> *'I do not love thee, Dr. Fell.*
> *The reason why I cannot tell;*
> *But this I know, and know full well:*
> *I do not love thee, Dr. Fell.'"*

Ramón nodded thoughtfully, and then his white teeth showed in a smile. "I'm not much of a reader, but there's a quotation I've heard somewhere myself, and it stuck with me: 'To thine own self be true ... thou canst not then be false to any man.'"

She was serious, studying him. "Then you don't think I'm just—temperamental?"

"You're young. Twenty, is it? Sometimes a person doesn't know his 'own self' yet when he's in his teens."

She sighed. "I knew you knew how it was—about Len. I could feel it downstairs this morning."

"I'd say, after this, take it easy. Don't go too fast. And, above all, don't let other people think for you."

Maureen appeared in the doorway to the kitchen. "Well? What's this? A heart-to-heart talk?"

"Maybe." Ramón smiled at her teasingly. "Jealous?"

"Could be. I don't know that I like another daughter moving in on my father."

"Maureen, don't be a brat," Peggy said.

Ramón had risen, and he looked from one to the other, his eyes inscrutable.

Maureen smiled crookedly and came and put her hand through his arm. "I was only kidding. Anyhow, I know I'm the favorite," she finished with a mischievous upward glance.

"I play no favorites," he said lightly. "But I have to go now. I've been away too long as it is."

Lola came in with Jo Anne, and Don entered from the hall, carrying the baby. After they had said good-by to Ramón, the two girls walked down the stairs with him. Peggy went back to join the others in the dining room, and Maureen followed Ramón into the outdoor vestibule from which the steps led down.

A feminine figure in a shapeless sweater, a drooping pleated skirt, and saddle oxfords, was coming through the gate with an armload of books clasped to her stomach.

Maureen looked down ungraciously. "Oh—hello, Toni."

Toni hesitated for a second at sight of the strange man, but curiosity was too strong. She gave her tangled tawny hair a toss and kept coming.

"This is my father, Toni."

Toni's green eyes scrutinized Ramón with candid interest and then turned avidly on her girl friend.

"I heard about it at school. It was in the paper." She turned and looked at the walk where, despite hosing with water, a faint stain still showed. "Criminy, isn't it terrible!" Her wide eyes examined Maureen with respectful awe and she shifted the books on her arm. "It said, 'Henry Grueber.' Wasn't that the guy I seen you down in Chinatown with one night last month? Remember Betty and I met you coming out of that chop suey joint, and I don't think you wanted to interduce us, but you had to 'cause we were busting with curiosity and we stopped to say hello and you had to—"

Maureen stood motionless with anger, only her eyes burning at her friend, who finally paused uncertainly. Ramón, too, had become still, his eyes moving from one face to the other.

He spoke softly. "Did you and Betty tell any of the other girls about seeing Maureen with him?"

"No, I had even forgot his name. It just came back to me as I was coming over here now to find out all about it from Maureen. We never paid much attention to his name, and when we asked Maurie about it next day she just said he was an old friend of the family, and I never thought no more about it, and now, jeepers! he goes and gets murdered! Won't Betty just die when she finds out it was the same guy we seen you with?"

Ramón had put on the smile and the manner which female patrons found so charming as he sauntered among the tables at La Paloma.

"Would you enter a little conspiracy with us, Toni?"

The girl looked at him wide-eyed, her lips parted slightly. She was obviously thrilled.

"You see, the police are asking us all kinds of questions, and Maureen just kept quiet about ever having gone out with Mr. Grueber. It doesn't mean anything in connection with his death, but if they knew she had been that friendly with him they'd embarrass her with all kinds of questions." Ramón's eyes were judging the effect of his words; and he decided on a touch of melodrama. "They might"—he lowered his voice significantly—"even give her the third degree."

Toni looked admiringly and a little fearfully at the sullen Maureen.

"So will you enter the secret with us, and we just all never say a word again about Maureen being out with him?"

"Sure," Toni said breathlessly. "Wild horses couldn't drag it out of me." She turned to the girl and finished conspiratorially, "Don't you worry, kid, I'll stick by you."

"Thanks, pal," Maureen said dryly. She had again retreated into the detached air of a spectator.

Ramón turned his hat by the brim and regarded his daughter. "Ride over with me, Maureen, for company, and I'll send you home in a taxi."

"Sorry, Papa," she said coolly, "Mother wants me to help with the dinner this afternoon. You can't come in either, Toni. We're all at sixes and sevens today, and I've got a lot to do."

"Sure, kid, I understand. And remember, you can count on me."

Ramón surveyed his daughter gravely, and as she said defiantly, her hand on the doorknob, "Good-by now," he decided not to insist on talking to her.

As he drove across the city he responded mechanically to traffic and signals, his mind troubled, his expression withdrawn and somber.

There was a scattered luncheon crowd at La Paloma, but Ramón passed through the dining room without pausing or speaking. Upstairs in his office he closed the door, locked it, and tossed his hat onto the rack in the corner. Absently he chose a cigar from his desk, lighted it, frowning, and walked to the windows, where he gazed off toward the tower on Telegraph Hill, his eyes blank.

Finally he turned and sat in the chair before his desk, one hand closed over the edge of the top. Sorting out times, the layout of the Grady house, the activities of its occupants on the night before, weighing personalities, motives, the interplay of relationships housed within those walls. The longer he sat, the grimmer, the more impassive his face became. Once he glanced at the telephone. The hand holding the cigar reached for the instrument and dropped back; his head gave a rough little shake. The name of a well-known criminal lawyer was in his mind, but he rejected the impulse to reach him. It might be a finger pointing for the police if Ramón Garcia engaged the man to represent the family on O'Farrell Street.

Finally Ramón shook himself away from his thoughts and took up his own business affairs. He could only wait and see. With an effort he kept himself from phoning to learn if there had been any new developments. He read the afternoon papers anxiously, but there was nothing in them he did not know.

The early-afternoon rush was over. Only two tables remained occupied, one with a luncheon party of six women in fur coats and overornamented hats, another with a group of four men talking business over cigars and coffee. Ramón stood outside the bar at the end toward the dining room, smoking his own cigar and talking to the bartender who leaned on his elbow and cast his eyes professionally now and then toward a young couple, tourists obviously, also obviously honeymooners, having Tom Collinses on stools down near the door.

At the buzz of the telephone on a long cord among the fancy wine bottles on the counter against the wall the bartender reached over and held the instrument to his ear.

"La Paloma," he droned in a bored voice, and then held the phone out to Ramón. "For you."

"Garcia speaking," Ramón murmured perfunctorily.

"Papa? Papa, is that you?"

Concern tautened the man's face, but he spoke quietly. "Maureen? Yes. Yes, it's me."

The voice on the other end was high, ragged. "Oh, Papa. It's terrible. I didn't—I never thought they'd— Oh, Papa—" It came like a cry over the wire. "They've arrested Don. That policeman—the one who was here this morning. He came in a car with officers and they've—they've—" Her voice became shrill to the breaking point. "They've taken Don!"

The tip of Ramón's tongue ran over his lip under the neat mustache, but his voice was quiet, soothing. "What did they say? Are they going to charge him?"

"What?"

"Did they say they were arresting him for—murder?"

Absently Ramón saw the bartender's eyes swerve toward him and then return conscientiously to the manhattan glass he was assiduously polishing with a white cloth.

"They said—they said"—Maureen was still having difficulty marshaling words and getting her voice to pronounce them—"they said they were holding him for questioning—something about 'material witness.' We were all in the hall when they—when they—left. But Frank—Frank says—that does it." She ended on a sob.

"Is your mother there?" Ramón asked in a deliberately undisturbed tone.

"Yes. Yes, she's here. But she doesn't know I called you. She's just running up and down wringing her hands and saying, 'What'll we do?' and Frank saying, 'We'd better get a lawyer.' They've got the phone book in the dining room, trying to look up lawyers in the classified."

Ramón's lips pulled in and his brows drew together. The girl was babbling on hysterically, "I had to call you. I couldn't stand it. Papa, can't you do something?"

"Now, now, baby," he said soothingly, "keep hold of yourself. Of course we'll do something. They always take people down for questioning. Don'll probably be home for dinner. Listen, call your mother to the phone. I want to speak to her."

"O.K. But—but Frank won't like it—"

"That's all right. Tell Mamie I want to speak to her."

He waited, staring at the smooth mahogany bar top, his hand with the dead cigar resting on the rounded raised edge of the counter, until Mamie's distraught voice came to his ear.

"Maureen just told me what's happened," he said briskly. "Ordinarily I wouldn't butt in, but this is serious. Don's going to need a lawyer and a good one. You've heard of Joel Freeman? Well, if anybody can help Don, he can. There isn't a better criminal lawyer in the state. But it takes dough to get him. Now, this is what I thought. He'll know who I am, and that I'm good for his fee. So I want you to let me get hold of him and hire him to represent Don—"

Her voice was trembling, distraught. "But, Ramón, we're not—broke. We have our house—we can get a loan. And Frank—well, he—well, you know how it is—"

"I know, I know," Ramón said curtly. "Say it's a loan. Say Don can pay me back—on time when he gets back to work. But I want to get Freeman on the job, and I want to do it fast. Tell Frank I— Oh, hell, tell him Freeman's a pal of mine, that I can get him to take the case where he might turn down strangers. After all, he's a big man. He's busy. He might send you to somebody else if you called him."

Her voice, low, uncertain, yet with a spark of rebellion in it, Mamie said, "I don't know why you're so—concerned."

"Never mind why." The expression on his face was dark, irritated, and suddenly he spoke roughly. "This is Don's life involved. Are you going to quibble around about your pride or some damned thing?"

"No.... No." There was a momentary pause, and he could hear her breathing over the wire. "Do what you can. And—and let us know right away."

"O.K. I'll call you back."

Before she hung up she said faintly but defiantly, "And we'll pay you back."

Ramón motioned with the phone to Mike, who came forward and set it back on the cradle, which was out of Ramón's reach. Then he turned without speaking and hurried up the stairs, moving the cold cigar between his teeth. In his office he picked up the telephone again, impatiently turning the pages of the thick directory with his other hand, looking for Freeman's office number.

During the height of the evening business, about eight-thirty, a waiter summoned Ramón from the back of the restaurant where he was suavely chatting with a party of regular patrons.

"Gentleman to see you, Mr. Garcia."

Ramón's eyes darted toward the bar.

"The little fat one there at the end," the waiter explained.

"O.K."

As Ramón moved forward he eyed the stranger curiously. With an equally speculative air the rotund visitor was eying Ramón as he approached.

"My name's Freeman," the stranger said quietly.

Ramón's eyes became quicker under the dark brows. He led the way upstairs, and Freeman laid a limp gray felt hat on the desk and sat down without being invited to. His round face and little dark eyes were stern and displeased under curling grizzled hair which looked as if its owner seldom found time to use a comb.

"I gather from young Thomas that you're a man of some common sense. And I'd like to know why the hell you didn't call my office as soon as the boy came up here this morning."

Freeman irascibly drew a crumpled package of cigarettes from his coat pocket and lighted one.

Ramón had let out his breath quietly. "I did," he said, "think of calling you earlier, but—well, it wasn't exactly my place to take over."

"Why Thomas didn't have brains enough himself to call somebody the minute that rat turned up dead on his steps is more than I'll ever know. Now, of course, they've all shot off their mouths to the police till God knows what the D.A.'ll be able to make out of it."

Freeman rose and stalked across the room. "People! They make me sick."

He turned his head on his short neck and suddenly smiled over his shoulder, and his face was startlingly cherubic with the swift change of mood which made him nervously exhausting to witnesses on the stand.

"Basically, of course, that's not so. Only thing that makes me able to put up with the human race at all is that, by God, in spite of everything, I *like* 'em."

He came back and sat down, all at once relaxed and affable. "Don sent me to you. He seems to have it set in his mind that you can help us. Insisted I talk to you."

Ramón was not taken in by the change of manner. He knew that behind the pleasant shine of Freeman's dark eyes a quick, hard mind was on the alert.

Ramón put his hand up over his eyes. After a second he shook his head wearily. "It looks bad." His hand fell to the desk again. "I didn't think they'd dare take him in—not enough evidence."

"Evidence, hell! They'll *make* evidence. And they've got plenty to tell a jury. Damn' detectives have been snooping around Enderby's all day. Wasn't hard to get proof Don and Grueber hated each other's guts. Then throw in a sister who's been 'wronged' or maybe about to be, knowledge of the weapon, opportunity, no alibi except his wife's word—what more do they want? They may not get a conviction, but they can stir up a hell of a good stink trying."

"But I thought they'd have to have something more definite than all that."

"They've got something definite all right. His fingerprints were on the gun."

"What!"

"The testimony at the inquest will give us more information. But Thomas tells me that during the questioning this afternoon they confronted him with that fact. Came at a bad time, too, damn it! They had him so pooped and fuzzy-brained before I got to see him that when the inspector asked him what he was doing with the gun the last time he had it in his hands, Thomas said he'd never had the damn' thing *in* his hands. So then they had him. Asked how he explained the fact that there was a couple of nice clear prints of his on it. By that time, when it was too late, he remembered. Last week he and Grady were going to play cribbage after dinner. The radio was on and he was listening to the news while he went to get the cards out of the drawer. His mind wasn't on what he was doing; and the cribbage board wasn't in sight in the drawer, so he pushed a tablet and stuff out of the way and picked up the gun and pushed it aside, trying to locate the board, and finally found it in the back under some envelopes."

"There must have been other prints on it."

Freeman shrugged. "They don't tell their little secrets to me till they have to." He shut his mouth in a straight line for an instant before he snapped, "There *have* to be other prints on it."

"What if there aren't?"

"We'll point out the killer could have used gloves and still not have happened to touch the spot Don had touched."

The two men were silent a moment, each looking at something besides each other.

At last Ramón said heavily, "Do you think you can get him off?"

"I'll try. That's all I can promise. The only sure way is to find out who *did* do it. That's where you come in. You know these people. Thomas seems to figure you as some kind of a clairvoyant, thinks you might have some idea of which one *would* commit murder, and why."

Ramón's face stirred in a sardonic smile. "I don't want to see Don framed, but it seems to me it's asking quite a lot of me to go around pointing suspicion at other people, solely on the basis of what I think about their character."

"This is for me to use, see, in proving Don's innocence. The more 'reasonable doubt'—in other words, confusion—there is, the better for him."

"I'd do anything I could to help Don," Ramón said slowly.

"O.K.," Freeman interrupted sharply. "Then tell me how you've got the thing sized up. Damn it, somebody shot him."

Ramón moved his hands in a surrendering gesture. "By this time you must have as good an idea as I have of what went on there last night and who's involved."

"But I don't *know* these people. Your opinions are just your opinions, I know that. They aren't evidence. But they might give us something to go on. Unless"—his voice took on a matter-of-fact tone—"you're trying to protect some of them—one of your daughters, for instance, and are willing to see Thomas take the rap for somebody else."

Ramón remained calm. "No. No, under any circumstances I wouldn't want to see an injustice done. But there isn't anything more I can tell you than you already know."

"I see."

Abruptly Freeman stood up. His expression was cold as he picked up his hat.

"I guess that's that then. I thought Don was overoptimistic in his conviction that you could throw some light on the case."

Ramón stood up heavily. "I wish to God there was something I could do. Tell Don, if there's any question of money, not to worry. Everything I've got is at his disposal. I'll keep in touch with the family. If I learn anything you can be sure I'll let you know."

Freeman regarded him shrewdly for a second before he said dispassionately, "You'd better trust me, Mr. Garcia. Remember, it's the D.A., not me, who's out to get a conviction. And I want to repeat: the more I know the better I'll be able to handle things."

For a while after the attorney had gone Ramón sat inactive behind his desk. Then, with a glance at the little electric desk clock which read ten minutes after nine, he picked up the telephone and dialed.

A woman's voice answered promptly, and he said, "Hello, Francine.... I know, I intended to be there by now. But look, darling, I've got mixed up in something, and I can't make it tonight.... I'm sorry, too, but it's pretty bad business. Did you read in the papers today about that murder on O'-Farrell Street? ... Yes. Well, it's my daughters' family.... Yes.... They came to me for help, and I've been over there today, and now something else has come up, and I have to see the girls again.... I'll tell you all about it later.... Yes. I'll call you."

Francine Dubois set the ivory telephone carefully in its rack and looked slowly around the long, light room whose wall-length windows, concealed now by heavy silk curtains, looked out across Alcatraz to the Marin hills. The beautiful modern room might have been the prison itself, so bleak and empty were the woman's eyes.

So now Ramón had his children to think about, and she—she had "Francine's", the fashionable little dress shop off Union Square. She sat, looking stiff and formal in her pale green velvet lounging pajamas, on a lavender love seat, her intricately coiled auburn hair like an exotic flower above the other colors. She leaned forward and touched the copies of *Vogue* and *Harper's Bazaar* on the blond coffee table, cherry-colored nails bright at the end of long, soft fingers. She picked up one of the magazines and began to turn the pages.

Chapter Seven

Meanwhile Ramón slapped his hat on his head and went downstairs and out to his car.

Lights were still on in the house on O'Farrell Street when he rang the bell fifteen minutes later. Pauline answered the ring. She looked white and haggard and still wore the slacks and shirt she had put on in the morning.

"Oh. It's you." She waited for him to say something.

"I'd like to come in if the family is still up."

"We're back in the dining room," she informed him ungraciously, and preceded him down the hall.

Frank sat listlessly before the radio, not hearing the crime story which he had turned on from habit. From the kitchen came sounds which indicated the washing of dishes.

Frank looked up at Ramón with a momentary frown which faded into somber affability. "Hello, Garcia."

Frank had been doing some thinking since Don's arrest. Up to that time, after Ramón's departure early in the afternoon, he had loudly communicated his disapproval of "that man's" horning in where he wasn't wanted. But, faced with an actual arrest in the family and the resulting trial and lawyer's fees and God knew what other expense, his mood had tempered. If Garcia wanted to help out, well, there was no reason not to let him.

"Sit down," he instructed awkwardly.

"I guess you're surprised to see me again." Ramón paused to nod at Mamie who had come to the door. "But I thought I'd run over and see how things were."

Even Mamie's bright hair and lipstick were no disguise now. Like an old woman she pulled out a chair and sat with her arms on the table. Tears had long since washed the mascara from her light eyelashes, and for once she had not bothered to replace it. The only light in the room came from two bridge lamps, one beside Frank's chair, one across the room by the studio couch. The room itself was homey and quiet in the shaded light, but the crushed human figures robbed the scene of its warmth.

Pauline had sunk bonelessly onto the studio couch, and Peggy followed her mother into the room.

"Hello, Papa," she said drearily, and crouched on the edge of the couch beside her sister.

"Where is Len?" Ramón inquired casually.

"He went home."

"Peggy should've gone with him," Frank contributed disapprovingly, "but she said the cops would probably expect her to stay here."

"Oh, Frank, don't start that again," Peggy muttered. From under her lashes she looked at Ramón, and then she lifted her head and stated clearly, "I'm never going back to Len. I'm going to get a job when this is over and start all over again. For the looks of things I'll be civil to him until—until—we know."

"Her brother is in jail for murder, and she talks about her love life," Frank declaimed disgustedly.

"Frank, not now," Mamie protested miserably. "I can't stand any more."

"I don't see Maureen," Ramón observed vaguely.

"She shut herself up in her room after they took Don," Mamie answered, "and won't talk to anybody." Her voice broke, and she put her head down on her hands so that the darker streak showed in her parted hair. "Oh, my poor boy, what will they do to him?"

Ramón's eyes were compassionate as they rested on her head. He knew how Mamie had always felt about Don. Once it had even been a slight source of jealousy to him.

"It isn't hopeless, Mamie," he said gently. "He'll have a trial; and Freeman is a shrewd lawyer. Look at all the cases he's won when everybody knew even the courts were against him."

Pauline got up and stood by the window, fiddling with the curtain. With her brother actually in jail her resentment of his social attitudes and activities had been softened by concern over his safety.

"Why didn't they listen to me?" she broke out. "That Negro. It's the only answer there can be."

"Put on another record," Frank growled. "I'm getting sick of hearing that one. If you're so sure it was him, why don't you prove it?"

"I may do just that," she flared, turning her head angrily toward Frank. "You can depend on it that Jew lawyer he's got won't explore that angle. That's another thing. My God, why get *Freeman?* He's always defending people everybody *knows* are guilty. That in itself is a strike against Don already."

"I don't think so, Pauline," Ramón put in. "It's his only hope. At least Freeman will put up a real fight."

Pauline looked at him with an expression that read, "What right have you got to come around here with your opinions?" but she held her tongue.

"How is Lola?" Ramón asked sympathetically.

Mamie had raised her head and was wiping her eyes. "She's taking it very well. She had dinner down here with us, and has been upstairs since she took the kids up to bed."

"Them coons're up there with her," Frank grunted, and then he growled with more spirit, "I oughta go up and throw 'em out. Troublemakers."

"It's tough on her," Ramón murmured.

"Tough on all of us." Peggy spoke up hoarsely. "Oh, God, I feel so *responsible*. If only I'd never *seen* Hank Grueber."

"Well, I told you," Frank reminded heavily. "But no, you wouldn't listen to me. Running around with other men."

"Frank, you *stop!*" Peggy was on her feet. "You've just got to quit hounding me." Her eyes fell on Ramón, and she lifted her head to face Frank defiantly. "I don't have to stay here and take your nagging. I'll go home with my father!"

In the horrified silence which followed, Ramón moved in his chair, and then spoke in mollifying tones, "Frank's only trying to protect you, Peggy. You mustn't feel hard toward him. I would have urged you to be careful myself." He glanced about. "You know you're welcome to come to my apartment any time and stay as long as you want to, but right now, the way things are, I think you should all try to put up a friendly front to the world. If Don didn't do it, it's possible some of the rest of you did; and the police probably still have their eye on the way you act."

Pauline stamped her foot. "Damn it, you *know* it isn't any of us! Why keep saying things like that? If it isn't the Negroes, it's some of Don's union friends. And who's going to investigate them now? If you're so anxious to help why don't *you* try to get some dope on them?"

"I think the police will be only too glad to have an excuse to investigate Don's friends. If there is anything there, they'll turn it up, don't worry."

Ramón glanced about. "I'd like to see Maureen before I go. Is it all right if I stop in her room on my way out?"

"If she'll let you in," Mamie said wearily. "She locked the door on the rest of us. That child." She sighed. "I know she was always crazy about Don, being her only brother and older and all, but it's no way to act, going off alone to brood—or sulk, whatever it is. And the way she turned on Pauline, blaming her for implicating Don. As if Pauline could help it. She *had* to tell the truth."

"I'll see if I can't reason with her," Ramón said, rising. "And, well, if there's anything I can do—"

Peggy had subsided sulkily on the couch, and he paused and put his hand on her shoulder. "Don't worry, honey, it'll all come out all right. Come and see me whenever you can."

She nodded, unsmiling, and Ramón impulsively bent and kissed her cheek.

He went out into the hall alone and knocked on the bedroom door. "Maureen, it's me, your papa."

"What do you want?"

"Let me in. I want to talk to you a minute."

"Not now. I'm getting ready for bed."

"Maureen!" His voice remained low, but it was hard. "Open this door."

For a few seconds there was silence, and then a key turned in the lock and the door was pulled back about a foot, Maureen's body blocking the space.

"What do you want?" she asked sullenly.

Ramón pushed the door open and stepped in, brushing against the girl. He turned, relocked the door, and put the key in his pocket. Only the dim bedside lamp was on, and the man glanced about, then pressed the button by the door, turning on the ceiling light.

Mutinously the girl returned his measuring look. She was without make-up, her lips paler than usual, her eyes bright, her hair untidy. She showed no signs of having wept.

Ramón sat on one of the twin beds and laid his hat beside him. "What is it, baby? Why do you have to be alone like this?"

"Do you suppose I want to be with them?" Her hand angrily jerked toward the dining room. Forced to speak at last, she rushed on with a fevered note in her voice, "That sniveling Peggy. Why couldn't she have left Hank alone? Then none of this would have happened. And Pauline! A fine sister she is. Why did she have to harp on the Negro angle, making Don look suspicious because he tried to conceal something, *making* them concentrate on him? And Mamie, and Frank. My God, he's her *son!* Couldn't she have thought up some lie, some alibi? What are mothers *for* anyway?"

"You love Don, don't you?"

"Of course I do. He's a swell guy, the decentest member of this whole lousy family. He's always been swell to me, used to take me to the zoo and the beach when I was little, gave me money for shows and bubble gum when nobody else would—"

She let out her breath explosively and stalked over to the other bed, sitting on it and grasping the foot-post.

Ramón turned so that he was sitting sideways to see her. "You never dreamed Don would be accused, did you?"

Her head lifted with a jerk. "Of course not."

Ramón ran his tongue over his lips. "Do any of the rest of them know you've been out with Grueber?"

"No."

"Except for this—what's her name—Toni?—do you think many people do know?"

"No." Sulkily she added, "I've only been out with him three times, and it was before Peggy came home. I knew Frank would raise hell, think Hank was too old for me, so I sneaked out to meet him."

"Were you in love with him?"

Her eyes darted toward the man, then dropped to her fingers clenched on the spool post. "Not—really. Not lately anyhow. Maybe, once, I had a crush on him. But after he took up with Peggy—and he knew she was married—I hated him."

"You don't like irregularity about marriage, do you?"

"Would you, in my place? Look at us, separated from our own father, getting *Frank* as a substitute, your mother acting like a—like a chippy—over men ever since you can remember. Having dates, flirting on the telephone—till she hooked Frank, of course. Is there any dignity in a home life like that? Do you think I enjoyed seeing Peggy going the same way?"

Ramón's brows drew together and his lips parted and twisted as he looked down from his daughter's angry face.

"I'm sorry," he said. "Maybe I should have done more—to make it work—when you were kids."

"Do you think I blame *you!* How could you make it work with a lame brain like Mom? No, Frank's all she deserves."

Ramón shook his head, his eyes on the girl. "You're young. You'll learn not to expect so much of people when you get older."

There was a pause, then Ramón said quietly, conversationally, "Maureen, do you know who did it?"

Her head snapped up. They stared at each other silently for several seconds.

"How should I?" she retorted angrily.

"You were awake and moving around downstairs when the shot was fired."

Suddenly she uttered a strangled sound, and laughed. But tears began to run down her cheeks, and sobs fought the laughter in her voice.

Ramón came up from the bed and hurried around the foot toward her, gathering her up in his arms. "Maureen, oh, my poor baby—"

But the strangled, hysterical sounds went on.

Mamie's anxious voice was raised outside. "Ramón, Maureen! What's the matter?"

"It's all right," he called over his shoulder. "She's just finally let go and is crying. A little hysterical is all. Go away. I'll handle it. She'll get over it better if she's left alone. It's all *right*, Mamie," he cried as worried clucks and jiggling of the door handle sounded from the hall.

Abruptly he shook the girl and then slapped her. She gasped, and as she began to regain control of herself, Ramón called, "She'll be all right now. Just let us be quiet for a moment."

"Well, all right." Mamie's reluctant steps retreated down the hall.

"You've got to pull yourself together now, Maureen," he said quietly.

"Why," she gulped, fumbling for a handkerchief in the table drawer, "why did you say—those things to me?"

"Because I thought of them. You were acting very funny. There must have been a reason for it. You've got to realize there's other people in the world besides yourself. They notice things, and sooner or later they figure them out. You go acting queer and somebody'll get suspicious."

Under her lashes she looked at him. "You got suspicious?"

"Yes." His voice was flat, impersonal. "But I'm your father. I don't go around saying such things."

She shivered. "No. Don't."

"But we've got to help Don. Maureen, do you know anything, anything you haven't told the cops that would help Don, something you could tell Freeman? He'll probably be in to see you tomorrow. *Think*, is there anything you should let him know? He's safe. He won't tell anything that's against Don—or—or anybody else. But the more he knows, the better he'll be able to save Don."

"I've thought and thought," she said dispiritedly, and added ruefully, "What do you think I've been doing in here by myself?" Her voice became stronger. "I'd lie if it would help. I'd commit perjury. I'd do anything. But I can't think of a likely story."

"You'd—implicate somebody else?"

"If necessary—yes," she said defiantly. "Someone like Frank, or Len, or one of Don's friends. But I *won't* have Don killed."

Ramón shook his head. "Maureen—" He hesitated, and did not go on. Then he sat down on the opposite bed, facing her, and leaning forward took her hands.

"Listen, my baby." His voice had softened to its rare, faintly Spanish inflection, the vowels longer, the *ls* and *rs* more liquid. "I did not suggest that we make up lies to save Don. I only ask: do we know something, something which maybe we forget but which might point away from Don? You see, *querida?*"

Seemingly half-hypnotized by his pleading eyes and lulling voice, Maureen nodded.

"But, Papa," she said more softly than before, "I don't know anything, anything that's the truth that would help."

"The shot maybe. Where were you when you heard it? Things like that. Think of them."

She pulled her hands away nervously. "I didn't hear it. But I had water running in the bathroom. I flushed the toilet. It might have been then."

Ramón sighed and looked down at his empty hands. After a moment he stood up. When he spoke it was in normal tones. "Well, we can just hope—hope for the best, as they say. I'd better go now. And, remember, no more temperament, locking ourselves in rooms. And, Maureen, no stories! You hear me? Lies." He shook his head. "You don't know. You've never been in court. What those lawyers can do to a phony story. Questions, questions, till you wouldn't know what even the truth was when they got through.

They'd tie you up in knots."

"O.K.," she said limply.

He regarded her thoughtfully a moment. "I shouldn't have mentioned it, I guess, trying to think of some detail which would help Don. Your best bet is to stick to what you've already said. Go over it and over it so you'll remember, and don't change a syllable, no matter what."

"Yes, Papa."

He took her chin in his hand, studied her face gravely for a moment, and then kissed her. "Good night, baby."

As the door closed behind him, she stared at it, biting her lips, her forehead wrinkled like that of a child wanting to cry but not daring to.

Chapter Eight

Upstairs, three people sat huddled around the dead fireplace in Don's living room where the parchment-shaded lamps were too dim to dispel the shadows in the corners.

Lola had been crying, and though her swollen eyelids and the weary lines of her face showed it, she was calm now, listless even.

Nell and Ernest Simpkins had come over, a sympathy-combined-with-curiosity call. They had not known of Don's arrest until they arrived. The air was streaked with tendrils of smoke as Ernest puffed restlessly on cigarettes.

"What about—" Nell spoke hesitatingly. "How you fixed for money?"

"The family will take care of it. That is, Don's stepfather—not Frank, the other one," she fumbled. "Ramón, the Garcia girls' father, he's well off; he'll lend us all we need."

"They may," Ernest said thoughtfully, "drag us all in before they're through. Accessories."

Lola ran her cold hand up her face and pressed it against her cheek. "You don't know how bad I feel, involving you folks. We tried, we really tried, to keep you out of it. We wouldn't have exposed you to all this for—for anything."

Ernest uttered a dry chuckle. "The color of my skin has exposed me to so much for so long that a little more ain't going to make much difference one way or the other."

Nell looked at her fingernails and said nothing; but as they moved to the door, going home, she smiled at Lola and patted her shoulder.

"Chin up, honey. A lot can happen. They got nothin' on him, you know, nothin' *real*, that is. And any time you need to get away, just give me a ring and I'll take care of the kiddies."

Lola's eyes watered again. "Thanks," she muttered. "Thanks, Nell."

She watched them clumping as quietly as they could down the stairs, and waved as they turned with smiles and hands lifted in encouraging salute. Her chest felt hollow as the door shut them from sight and she was again so dreadfully alone.

She walked with her head down back into the big, empty room. They did not know how grateful she was for their coming and staying with her for an hour or so.

Most people, in time of trouble, would burrow for safety into the family group. But her mother and father were dead; she had no sisters and brothers, and she had no sense of "belonging" in Don's family. She couldn't talk naturally to Mamie. It always seemed as if Mamie's vague blue eyes were considering things Lola could not apprehend. And, unadmittedly even to herself, she hated Pauline. Partly it was jealousy, for she knew Don and Pauline loved each other with bonds which their differences could never really break. From childhood on they had known and understood too much together. They had had to cling to each other as they grew up because their mother's emotional energies were diverted from the children in concentration on the search for a man who would stay put in her life. Also, Pauline was aggravatingly everything that Lola was not, smart, shrewd, poised.

Maureen and Peggy she liked, but they had a way of looking at her when they thought she didn't know, as if they wondered what made her tick. They wondered, she knew, how she could so placidly accept such things as Don's practical application of his belief in social equality for Negroes, and what they considered his lack of personal ambition in being active in his union.

She pulled the chains on the lamps and went back to the bedroom. In the confusion and turmoil of the day the room had never been straightened up, and Don's outing-flannel pajamas still hung crumpled on the back of a chair. She saw them, and dropped sideways on the chair, clutching the soft cloth and burying her face in it.

She thought she had cried all she could, but again she was sobbing, weeping in desolation. It was like the feeling when Don was shipped overseas in the war. Not only the poignant sureness that he would not be home for many months, but the dreadful underlying fear of—maybe never.

Her mind floundered restlessly after she was in bed. It had exhausted the speculations, the whys, the how, of Hank's death, and moved jerkily among unrelated thoughts, of itself trying to trace the course that had led her to this miserable cowering alone in bed.

It was strange for a girl like her to be caught in tragedy. She was not cut out for drama. What she wanted in life were the same things millions of other women like her wanted: a white house set by itself in a lawn, with a fishpond in the back yard with rocks and waterlilies in it, and painted garden furniture standing about, and underwear with lace on it, and parties with decorated cakes where you played cards or did fancywork in company with friendly women, and trips downtown on Saturday night to eat in a restaurant and go to the movies.

And now there was probably no use even to hope and dream that someday, somehow, maybe she would get all that.

But she must not think so much of herself. It was Don who had the real trouble to bear. If only she could have gone with him, to share his cell so he would not be so alone.

When life went back to normal the next day for everyone but Don the normality seemed unreal. It could not be that the same jobs, the same routines were still continuing after the crash with which their lives had collided with Hank's dead body.

For Frank alone there were compensations. It was pleasant to walk into the yard at the shop and realize that every man in the place was thinking about his affairs. Not everybody got his house and his family in headlines.

Frank nodded gravely at the men he passed, wearing a suitably serious and somewhat preoccupied air, as one who has Things on his mind.

In the washroom his particular cronies crowded around respectfully.

"Tough luck, boy."

"Cops been giving you a bad time, I guess."

"Sure sorry to hear about it, Grady."

And the solemn expressions of sympathy burgeoning inevitably into open curiosity.

"D'you see the body?"

"Much blood?"

"How you figure it happened?"

"I saw your stepson's being held."

"Said in the paper he's prob'ly a Communist. That the straight dope?"

Frank paused portentously in zipping up his coveralls.

"Now look here, men. Let's get this straight. It's all a pack of lies, what they're sayin' about the boy, just because he's a good union man and has some screwy ideas about colored folks." He shook his head regretfully, and looked about with an air of pained paternity. "You know kids. Some of 'em a man can't talk no sense into 'em. Gotta just let 'em get it outa their system. I don't want no misunderstanding about it. All I got to say is," he concluded belligerently, "my boy never done it. It's a frame, pure and simple, a God damn frame-up."

"What makes you so sure? Wasn't you bumped the guy off yourself, was it?"

Frank turned angrily. "Who said that?"

"Aw, hell, Grady, can't you take a joke?"

"Not about this I can't." Frank put his dignity back on, and marched out through the men who fell back in deference to his notoriety.

Mamie at home had to quarrel with Maureen to get her to go back to school. It seemed silly to return to Portia's mercy speech and irregular Spanish verbs and hypotenuses which were the sum of angles, when her mind had matters of so much greater import to contend with.

"If I was sick," Maureen shouted at her mother, "you wouldn't insist on my going. And I'm worse than sick, I tell you! I'd *rather* be sick than the way I am."

Mamie had not slept until nearly morning, and as a result was temporarily deprived of ability to play the role of mother as she conceived it. She turned on her youngest savagely.

"That's enough out of you. Thinking of nobody but yourself as usual. How do you think *I* feel, or Lola—or Peggy?" she added as the latter came into the kitchen in her red house coat.

"I don't *care* how you feel," Maureen retorted passionately.

Mamie stared into the girl's defiant eyes, and her face sagged. The hatred she saw was not the childish flare-up of a moment, but a steady flame left briefly unguarded. She turned away, and her reddened eyes filled with tears yet once more. It was to herself, not the girl, that she moaned in an undertone, "What have I done to deserve this? Trouble, trouble, trouble."

"Everybody," Peggy was saying crossly to her sister, "has had enough of your brattishness. We've got important things to worry about, and I, for one, am sick of your tantrums and showing off, locking yourself up in your room, and running off by yourself to see Papa. You've been spoiled enough without him helping it along."

Maureen turned on Peggy with gleaming eyes. She surveyed the other for a moment, and laughed shortly. "You're jealous, that's all."

Pauline opened her door, dressed for work in a black frock of dull-finish material. Her eyes passed over the others and she said ironically, "That's what I like about family life, the warmth and affection and camaraderie."

"Oh, dry up," Maureen snapped.

"That's enough," Mamie quavered with an effort to sound authoritative.

Maureen stood frustrated and uncertain, and, with her angry defiance momentarily in abeyance, her eyes were those of a miserable, bewildered child.

"Oh, damn," she ejaculated pettishly, "I suppose I might as well be in school with everybody gawking at me as stay around here."

In the corridor at Girls' High she tramped along with her books on her arm, her head up, her expression coolly detached. Inwardly she shuddered as Toni and Betty swept forward, Toni trying to exchange secretly knowing, confidential looks with her, Betty hysterically curious.

"It's just like a movie," the latter squealed. "That's just what I said to

Toni, didn't I, Toni? I said, 'It's just like a movie, a mystery one.'"

Maureen shrugged off the exclamations and stares of all her classmates with a withdrawn manner which only heightened her fascination for them. But the teachers' bright cheeriness, which assured her that they intended to treat her "just as if nothing had happened," was the severest strain upon her air of sophisticated indifference.

For Pauline the day was no less a hell than it was for Maureen, with the difference that the older girl handled herself more skillfully. She had indeed spent most of the night charting her conduct for the day.

She entered the office restroom with an air of quiet dignity, and smiled with a trace of wistfulness at the eyes in which politeness barely concealed the avidity.

Her friend Gwen approached hesitantly. "Pauline, I'm—I'm sorry. I know how you must feel. They—the police—they called me up, and I told them about your being at my apartment that night."

In a low voice, but clearly enough so that the others could hear, Pauline said gently, "Please—I'd rather not talk about it." Her smile expressed patient, courageous martyrdom in the best soap-opera tradition; and the girls were disappointedly restrained from further references to her "trouble."

Before going to her place she humbly approached the manager's secretary at the desk outside his office. "I'd like to speak to Mr. Forbes."

"Why, of course. I'll tell him." Anne's smile was too hearty and casual.

She turned from the boss's door and smiled again professionally. "You may go in."

"Good morning," Forbes remarked noncommittally.

Pauline raised blue eyes which were utterly frank. "I know that you have heard of the—scandal"—her voice faltered—"which has touched me, and—and I felt the organization was entitled to some explanation as to my—position."

Mr. Forbes seemed not quite clear as to the meaning of the scene to which he was being treated. So one of his stenographers' brothers was being held for murder in connection with some vulgar brawl. What had that to do with him?

"I know," she continued courageously, "that the firm wouldn't want someone who was connected with the—the criminal classes in its employ—"

Mr. Forbes blinked but listened.

"And all I can say is that"—she had lowered her eyes, and now she lifted them piteously—"I am convinced of my brother's innocence. It's a case of"—her voice went lower—"bad companions, and his being made the victim."

"Uh—well, I'm sure it's all very regrettable."

"I don't know whether the company will wish to trust me now. I'm sure

I shouldn't blame you if—if you felt it unwise to keep me on, in view of what has come out about my brother. All I can say is, Mr. Forbes, that my loyalty to the firm is beyond question. I have been grieved more than I can tell you by my brother's—associations. I have tried to show him how wrong he is, but—"

She sighed wearily, the little gesture of her hands suggesting the whole tragic story of a brother gone wrong.

"Well. Well now, Miss Thomas, I'm sure no one has ever questioned your—uh—integrity; and as far as I personally am concerned, my confidence in you has not been shaken in the least by your—uh—your trouble."

"Oh, thank you, Mr. Forbes. You don't know how much that means to me."

"Now just don't you worry, my dear. Your standing with the company is A Number One."

As she went out Mr. Forbes looked at the closing door and thought sentimentally, "Brave little thing," and Pauline went to her work, breathing easier. That was one point she had taken care of. Next was Ellery. *That* would be the tough one.

She had telephoned him the evening before, to suggest that they lunch together today. He had not gone so far as to refuse, but he had hedged, and at the last she had been forced to insist. When she named a small restaurant well removed from the financial district, he had consented.

She had to take a taxi to save time, and when she entered the rather tearoomy place, she thought to herself cynically that Ellery looked as if he expected a man in a derby hat to be "shadowing" her.

"I'm sure sorry," he said when they were seated in a booth, "about all this mess you've got mixed up in."

"Oh, El," she said plaintively, "it's been horrible."

"Sure has."

"I had to see you this once," she burst out impulsively. "You've no idea how I've needed you."

"Well—uh—if there's anything I can do—"

"If I can just feel sure that you're thinking about me, that will be enough," she said softly. "It will be—something to cling to."

"Why—er—of course—"

"You see, I thought we'd better not see each other until—until this quiets down a little." A small flicker of anger flared up in her as she discerned the relief which relaxed him; but she went on with sweet renunciation, "I don't want you involved, no matter how remotely. In your position and all. And then I know how revolting all this would be to anyone of your sensitive nature."

He became expansive and a little reckless as he realized she was going to let him stay safe from any connection with the affair.

"Now, I don't want you to feel like that. You need support, moral support, that is, and I want you to feel you can rely on me."

"I knew you'd take it like that," she said tenderly. "And that's why I *had* to talk to you."

All through the split-pea soup and the cottage-cheese salad she nobly argued Ellery out of getting mixed up in the degrading contretemps until, by the pie à la mode, he was able to get down to business and question her eagerly about what the police had said and who she thought really did it, and had she seen the body and was there much blood.

Pauline was tired when she left him, but fairly well satisfied. He might drift away before the notoriety died down enough so that he felt his social position wasn't jeopardized by being known as her friend, but by voluntarily freeing him for the time being she had bound him as securely as was possible under the circumstances.

Getting solid with Forbes had been the main thing. Even if Ellery cooled off, if she continued to get ahead in the company, there would be other men. Though no one was so suitable as Ellery.

In the taxi, on the way back to work, Pauline's eyes were hard and disillusioned staring out at the windowed wall fronts along the street. She had believed she was in love with Ellery; but the way she felt now was not like love. Yet why should she be surprised that he had reacted as he had? She, too, would have recoiled fastidiously from a similar shoddily threatening situation involving him. So why was she unreasonably disappointed when he did not rise above his dependence on respectability and step forth in stalwart loyalty, defying public—and even his company's—opinion for her sake?

Her thoughts had kept coming back all morning to the scene with Mr. Forbes in his office, and each time a nebulous dissatisfaction took on more concrete form. In some subtle way there was shame mixed with the memory. She liked to think of herself as poised, aristocratic, commanding, head held proudly high, shoulders straight with dignity. But this morning she had crawled. Her whole attitude had been a deviation from her conception of Pauline Thomas.

And somehow it didn't help to remind herself that the act she had put on had been merely a necessary maneuver in attaining the status which would enable her successfully to maintain the character she inwardly saw herself to be: the cool, assured, impeccably correct woman who evoked universal respect and admiration.

It degraded her in her own estimation somehow, having had to lower herself in her own eyes to gain her objectives, both with the company and with Ellery.

That afternoon Peggy stayed with the children while Lola and Mamie went down to the jail to see Don.

They took the streetcar, and all the way they did not talk except for words like, "I'll get it; I have the right change," and "We get off at the next block."

Mamie was bereft of the pat phrases with which she usually smoothed out the course of life. None of the platitudes in which she thought seemed to have any bearing on what had happened, although such things happened every day on the radio serials she listened to from nine to one every morning. It would take time to identify herself with the role she had been thrust into and so to adopt proper reactions to the situation.

Lola felt closer to her mother-in-law in their silence than she had ever been able to feel when heretofore Mamie had advanced upon her with friendly intentioned prattle.

It was Don who was cheerful and "natural" when they met. He kissed them both and smiled and talked repeatedly of Freeman and "circumstantial evidence" and "things like this happening all the time."

They had brought him cigarettes and magazines and a box of the English toffee which he liked, not knowing for sure if the gifts were permissible. When they left him Mamie had already begun to cheer up and went down the street parroting the phrases Don had used: "No evidence," "Freeman was clever," "Something would turn up," "No jury could convict him."

Although she knew his optimistic talk had been delivered for the good of her and Mamie, even Lola felt more hopeful after seeing and touching her husband. There was always hope, and you *didn't* know what might happen.

Don himself, alone in his cell, sat on the hard cot and put his face in his hands. He did not realize what he was doing until he felt the wetness between his fingers, and then he straightened up and made a snuffling noise in his nose and harshly pulled the back of his hand across his eyes.

Ramón got around, that night, to go to see Francine. It was a restful thought with him all day. There was no one else anymore, and for three years he had felt with satisfaction that, as far as women were concerned, he had found the ideal situation. She was the best companion he had ever had; and their love was free, no financial entanglement of their affairs, each free to go and come as he chose, to make separate plans, to see each other or not as they felt moved.

She was interested, eager, sympathetic, as he told her the story; and he talked on and on, leaning back in the large buff-colored chair, smoking his cigar, while she sat before him on a hassock, her hands clasped about the knees of a black velvet hostess gown. It was pleasant to be the one who laid out his opinions, suspicions, fears, speculations, to be bringing them to sympathetic ears, rather than having others bringing their troubles to him.

Almost he delivered himself of the extent of his perplexity; but even to Francine he could not bring out in words the conflict which tore at the edges of his conscious thoughts.

Francine's eyes left his face and stared at the rug unseeingly. There was silence for a moment, and then she spoke thoughtfully. "It must be the stepfather, Frank. There must be a connection between him and Grueber which hasn't come out. It couldn't be any of the others."

"Why?" Ramón asked tensely.

"Why, no one else would let Don go to jail in his place. His wife—impossible. His mother, one of the sisters— Well—" She frowned. "Maybe one of the girls. Though I can't imagine anyone letting her own brother be hanged— Or no, it's the gas chamber here, isn't it?"

"Such things have happened," Ramón said heavily.

"Yes. Yes, I suppose so. Pauline—she sounds like a bitch. She's capable of it, I suppose."

"She wouldn't have done it in the first place. Expose herself to scandal—never!"

Francine shuddered. "It's horrible. This phase of it, I mean, someone sitting tight while Don takes the rap. People—one doesn't realize till you hit something like this how cruel and cowardly they can be."

"Don't be too harsh," Ramón broke out curtly. "The thing isn't over yet. Don may go scot-free, probably will. Why should someone be a martyr for nothing?"

Francine gave him a quick look, then she took his hand and pressed it to her cheek. "Poor darling, you mustn't worry yourself so. When something like this happens a person's mind goes wild, imagining all kinds of things."

She went on talking, asking questions of a practical nature: about police procedure, if there would be an inquest, how soon the trial would be, while Ramón answered abstractedly.

"I'm going to the trial," she said cheerfully, "just to get a look at all these people, if for no other reason."

"You've never met either of the girls, have you?" Ramón asked, as if the thought were surprising.

"No, but I feel as if I knew Maureen. You've talked about her so much."

"She wouldn't like you," he mused. "She's a jealous little devil. But Peggy"—he smiled—"Peggy would adore you. Peggy is—well, simpler—reminds me a little of a kitten, willing to purr for anyone who will be kind to her, a little like her mother that way."

He shook his head ruefully. "Poor Mamie. That was her trouble. She clung too much. Her love for a man got so it felt as heavy as—as a millstone," he finished inadequately. "When it was over between her and me

I figured that must have been what was wrong in her marriage with Thomas. Unless he was forced into it because it was the only job he could get, any man who went to sea in the first place in those days was a man who was fleeing from the responsibilities of a settled life. The constant moving from one port to another gave him an illusion of escape. I always figured Thomas must have come from poor people who had a hard life, tied to one spot by poverty. And Mamie and the way she makes you feel she *needs* you, that her own emotional life has to feed entirely on you, must have made him feel trapped."

He paused, and drew in his breath. "Well, I didn't mean to talk your head off, honey. But that's the effect you have on me."

She smiled, and rose and walked around behind his chair, leaning over to lay her cheek against his. Then she straightened, and her fingers strayed over his hair, settling into the wave and gently pressing it deeper into place.

As Ramón lay back in the chair, eased by her caressing presence, his eyes fell upon a square mirror above a table across the room. They became still on the reflection in it. Francine, looking down at her white fingers against the black of his hair, had forgotten the glass, and in it he saw the face of a sad and lonely woman. She never looked like this when she knew his eyes were upon her. He saw her lips fold in upon each other for an instant and her eyes close as her fingers pressed his hair. Then her face cleared and she pulled her hand back and with a light smile moved around the chair to stand beside him.

"I probably," she said teasingly, "save you a psychoanalyst's fees. You just come up here and unburden your mind instead."

He hardly heard what she said. He reached out and took her hand and pulled her down to the arm of the chair, studying her face.

"Francine," he said abruptly, "would you like to marry me?"

Her eyes went still, fastened upon his. After a second or two she smiled quizzically. "That is a request for information, not a proposal."

"Yes."

She stood up and moved away. "I want only what you want. If you wanted to marry me, I would say yes in a minute. If not"—she shrugged—"it makes no matter."

Her voice on the last words ironically took on the French manner that she used in the shop to impress patrons who expected it.

That night when Ramón made love to her it was with an extra, reckless frenzy, as if he were trying to make something up to her.

Across the nation, in the National Maritime Union hall in New York, an engineer shoved a newspaper over the table to a fellow seaman with the idle remark, "Here's a funny thing, guy in 'Frisco the same name as you being held for murder. Any relation?"

The man in a suede jacket, his hat shoved back on his nearly bald head, picked up the paper and looked at the article with a slight frown on his lined face. This Don Thomas was known in maritime circles as a seaman of the old school, no family ties, a hard-drinking, rough customer on shore, on shipboard a reliable fireman who shipped out regular and spent his time playing poker when not on watch.

"No. No relation," he said flatly when he had finished the article.

And then he sat looking sightlessly at the back of a vacant chair across the table.

So that was how it had turned out. It was his fault, marrying that little fluff ball in the first place and begetting kids she was incompetent to bring up.

His brows drew together as he looked back, trying to recall why he had been foolish enough to try marriage in the first place. He'd met her at a dance hall, "Roseland," he thought it was called, in 'Frisco, and she'd been cute as a basket of kittens, big blue eyes and soft yellow hair and what they called a cupid's-bow mouth in those days. She'd been crazy about him but he couldn't get her any way but by marrying her.

His lips twisted a little grimly. Well, he'd learned since then.

It was a fool thing to do. Coming in off a trip and being expected to sit around a house listening to kids bawl, and catching hell when you came home off a spree. And you didn't always want to ship out of the same port. Times you wanted to lay over even in a different country.

His eyes went back to the paper in front of him, and he frowned, stirred by a vague sympathy, the kind one might feel at hearing of disaster among people of a foreign nation. They were not quite real to him, the people who lived stolidly on land. Even the new kind of seamen they seemed to be getting the last ten or fifteen years since wages and conditions picked up, half of them married, saving up for houses and babies on shore, champing to get back to the home port every trip. It was all changed since he first ran away to sea.

Chapter Nine

At the inquest Ramón sat impassively listening to the proceedings. Don, in his good blue suit and a white shirt, looked tired already. The faces of the rest of the family were strained.

Lola was composed and deliberately cheerful of expression, Pauline frozen in aristocratic hauteur, Peggy miserable and guilty-looking, and Maureen immobile, her eyes dark, her lips set. She did not look like a bobbysoxer now, in the unaccustomed formality of a close-fitting felt hat and a navy-blue suit to match, the skirt reaching sedately below knees covered by nylon stockings in a dark shade.

Mamie's hat was fussy with veiling and artificial flowers, and her printed black dress flaunted a pictured variety of still more flowers, none of which matched those on her hat. She had talked a great deal at home about "keeping up a front," but the lines in her face had grown harder to conceal with liquid powder, and the whites of her eyes were faintly pink with strain.

Ramón hardly listened to the technical testimony beginning with the little man who had found the body, the medical examiner, the various officers, and the ballistics expert. Only once did he pay attention closely, and that was to the man who had tested the gun for fingerprints. One of the jurors fussily asked questions which elicited the fact that, besides Don's, distinguishable prints belonging to two other people had been found on the handle, and they belonged to Mamie and Maureen. Several of Frank's had been found on the barrel.

Ramón, sitting back of the rest of the family, observed the exchanged glances of consternation which greeted this testimony. From Mamie's profile he read bewilderment and then real fright as her eyes sought Don's thoughtful face. His eyes were on the table before which he sat. Ramón noted that during the rest of the proceedings Don did not look at his family.

Maureen did not turn her head, and Ramón could not see her face.

Joel Freeman occasionally cast shrewd glances at his client. There was no doubt that the bullet stopped against a rib in Henry Grueber's body had been fired from Frank's gun, and there seemed to be little question that one of the owners of the clear fingerprints on the handle was the person who had fired the fatal shot.

Nevertheless the unwilling witnesses of the Grady family were incredulous and stupefied when the coroner's jury brought in their verdict along those lines, with the conclusion that Donald Thomas was the "person" in question.

Afterward Freeman spoke briefly to Lola and Mamie and Frank in the corridor, informing them of what to expect: the formal indictment from the grand jury, the setting of a date for the trial, the days, possibly even weeks, of waiting for the case to come up on the calendar.

With their eyes fastened numbly on his face, as if it were the only stable object in a shaken world, they listened to his brisk voice. He smiled reassuringly, promising to confer with them later, and shifting his brief case in his hand, clapped his hat haphazardly on his head so that it sat a little askew, bestowed a last bright, all-in-the-day's-work look upon them, and bustled off down the hall.

The girls and Len stood in a dejected group a little to one side, uncomfortably aware of themselves in the sparse traffic of the passageway where clerks went in and out of doors with papers in their hands and pairs of public officials passed talking to one another, not noticing other people, and members of the lay public, sucked into the halls of justice for one reason or another, wandered by, worriedly scrutinizing the numbers on doors, lost in the intricacies of corridors.

It was late afternoon when they came out to find their cars parked on a side street. Mamie had prepared a large pot of spaghetti in the morning, and had insisted before they left the house that all of them come back there for dinner together. Everyone but Peggy had come downtown with Frank in the family sedan, but Peggy had perforce been driven by Len in his coupe.

In the sedan there was something fretful, jerky about the talk as they took the uphill streets through the snarl of traffic with its frustrating red and green lights; and in the coupe Peggy talked feverishly despite a weary desire to sink into lethargic silence. Anything, however, to keep Len from directing the conversation the way he would want it to go. Fortunately the unfamiliar surroundings of the afternoon had provided a tailor-made subject for distracting his attention, and it was not hard to keep Len engrossed in pleasurably morbid retrospection of the day's drama.

The others had arrived before them, and as soon as they were in the house Peggy ducked into her bedroom with the excuse of removing her hat. When she came out Lola was bringing the children down the stairs and Peggy waited to accompany them to the dining room where Frank and Len sat talking.

"You been lucky," Frank was reminding the younger man, "havin' steady work right along. I hear things ain't moving so fast in the building trades."

"A big outfit like E. J. Corbett and Sons, they keep their men workin' when these little two-bit contractors haven't got nothin'," Len returned smugly.

Peggy could tell that her husband would have gone on to boast about the big jobs his boss had under construction if she and Lola had not interrupted the tête à tête. Jo Anne ran to Frank and began to climb into his lap. He pulled her up absently.

"Don't bother Daddy Frank now," Lola said perfunctorily as she and Peggy trailed through toward the kitchen.

Peggy reflected that it seemed funny, hearing the men talk about usual things like work.

Mamie with a ruffled oiled-silk apron over her good dress was organizing food on the kitchen table; and as Pauline came out of her own room, her mother directed, "You can start setting the table in the dining room."

Pauline said, "Okay," listlessly.

"What can I do?" Lola asked. She turned to Peggy. "Do you want to look after the baby while I help your mother?"

"Sure." Peggy dragged the heavy ten-months-old infant into her own arms. "I'll take him in the front room out of the way."

"Well, if you want to then," Mamie said, "you can cut up tomatoes for a salad, Lola. Maureen has disappeared, as usual, just when a person could use her."

Peggy plodded through the dining room once more, carrying the twisting, ungainly baby. The men were still talking, but even Len's ebullience had been somewhat subdued by the dull laboriousness with which Frank held up his end of their conversation.

It was so much the same as usual, people all over the house, getting in one another's way, the kitchen full of women doing things, Jo Anne pulling blocks out of the lower compartment of the buffet where they were kept for her entertainment when she came downstairs, the baby making slobbery gooing noises; yet is was all so different, the atmosphere stiff, unreal—no lift, no lightness in anybody, everyone conscious of having on his good clothes, and of their all being together at this hour on a weekday, having come from the strangeness of a courtroom instead of from the familiarity of the places where they worked.

Peggy sighed and shifted the baby in her arms and went down the hall to the front room. In the archway she paused.

Maureen stood before the windows, her feet apart, her hands clasped behind her back, still wearing her suit jacket. The younger girl turned and looked at Peggy. Maureen was scowling slightly; and Peggy's arms tightened on Donny. It had seemed for a moment as if there was something downright unfriendly in her sister's look.

"I'm trying to entertain him," she faltered inanely.

Maureen's eyes lowered to the child's round, fuzzy head and remained there. Peggy glanced down; and then she looked up again at the other girl with suddenly frightened eyes.

"Oh, Lord, kid. What's going to happen"—she ducked her head at the baby—"to them—if—if Don—doesn't come back?"

Maureen's scowl deepened as her eyes rested darkly on Peggy.

Maureen, Peggy thought, had a way of looking at you hatefully sometimes—as if she—as if she—*blamed* you for things.

Peggy's face quivered as if she were going to cry. But it wasn't her fault. It wasn't. She couldn't help the way things had turned out.

Maureen swung about full face and took a step forward.

"Papa's paying a lawyer," she asserted curtly, "to see that he *does* come back."

She moved on toward the double doorway, but as she came abreast of Peggy she paused with a tightening of her expression, and as if she couldn't hold back the words, spat out, "*You* should get all misty-eyed and sentimental about Don now! If it wasn't for you, he wouldn't be where he is right now."

She plunged on into the hall then, not giving Peggy a chance to retort. With a pouting expression Peggy set the baby on the rug, and then she stiffened in a bending position and looked over her shoulder in the direction Maureen had gone, her mouth slightly open.

Slowly she straightened and stared toward the doorway.

What had Maureen meant?

A look of fright came into Peggy's eyes. "If it wasn't for you ..." Had Maureen been referring to the actual shooting? Or had she only meant it was Peggy who had brought Hank there?

For the first time Peggy comprehended that since none of them believed Don had done it, each of them must wonder, then, who else among them had.

And they knew she had been the last to admit seeing Hank. All of them knew that, not just Maureen. Was her whole family thinking of her in guarded horror?

Donny had crawled to one of the end tables and was about to pull himself up by its legs, endangering a nest of glass ash trays on the top; but Peggy was unaware of his movements.

With a clatter of the glass dishes the end table came over and the baby went down hard on his bottom, letting out a bellow of fright.

Peggy turned and went to him. The rug had saved the ash trays, and the baby stopped crying as she lifted him.

"Have an accident?" Len called from the hallway, and came into the room.

"No bones broken," she replied breathlessly.

Len poked a finger into Donny's double chins and clucked fatuously, "Did um hurt ums, huh?"

"You have to watch him every minute. I—I think I'll take him back to his mother."

"Here, I'll hold him." Len awkwardly hauled the baby away from her. "He won't be no bother. I been wantin' to see you alone anyhow. Come on, sit down."

The room was growing dim, and Peggy moved across to an armchair and switched on a bridge lamp. Len deposited himself on the sofa, setting Donny between his outspread knees and joggling him up and down with a hand on either side of the baby's fat waist. Reluctantly Peggy perched on the arm of the chair.

"How about it?" Len began earnestly. "Why don't you come on back home with me tonight? There's no percentage in us goin' on like this. And I'd like to get you outa this mess here." He regarded her aggrievedly. "I never could figure out what it was all about anyway. Sure, I know we just seemed to have one beef after another the last few months, but when you get right down to it, what were they *about* anyway? Nothin', that's what. I'll bet you can't remember what started any of our fights."

"What makes you think it'd be any different if I did go back? We'd probably just fight again."

Len looked pained. "After what's happened we both oughta have learned somethin'. What I mean is, comin' up against *real* trouble firsthand like this, well, a person gets more of a perspecative on things."

Peggy could not look at him. She stared down at the toe of her high-heeled pumps.

She was tempted—a little. Over in Oakland, away from the family and this house, she would feel safer.

If she stayed here she would hate it, having to look for work again and probably having to take a job she didn't like. She thought of Papa. He was the only one really who gave her the go-ahead signal, made her feel it was O.K. to leave Len if that was what she wanted. The trouble before was she hadn't been sure it was what she really wanted. But somehow—even after that first time when she accidentally met Papa's eyes that morning when Len was making such a fool of himself—she had begun to know what she wanted. And now she knew for sure that the decision had been made. She would never go back.

But Papa had also warned her to be careful. The family must keep up a friendly front before the police. But they were not watching her now. They were sticking to Don. What difference could it make if she broke finally and completely with Len?

Peggy frowned with the effort of her thoughts. She hated having to figure things out alone, make decisions.

If Don were acquitted, would the police start all over, looking for someone else? Would they fasten on her?

"Well, how about it?" Len was urging. "Won't do no harm to try again anyhow. You know how I feel about you, honey. Christ knows *I'm* willing to try an' do better. I already told you that."

"I know," she said with a sigh. "But I tell you how it is, Len. I'm too upset. I can't go off and leave the folks now with all this trouble. I can't think about my own concerns with my brother in jail and all. Just wait till this is over."

He looked sulky, and let the baby slide to the floor; and at that moment Lola fortuitously appeared in the doorway.

"Getting tired of being nursemaid?" she said with a wan smile.

"Oh, he's no trouble," Peggy said insincerely, stooping to drag Donny away from the base of the floor lamp which was in danger of toppling.

But, of course, the children *were* trouble for the rest of the dinner hour.

No one thought of helping Lola upstairs with them at eight o'clock. She did not, as a matter of fact, want anyone to come up with her. Although she dreaded being alone again, at the same time she longed to get away from the necessity of talking and listening to other people, with the long rags of silence falling damply over the conversation as one by one people's minds were captured by their own thoughts.

She sank into a chair in the living room with her legs spread out, her arms limp on the chair arms. There was nothing now to cope with until breakfast. Breakfast. Was there cereal enough? Had she even bought milk when she went to the store that morning? She wasn't sure. Would she have to run down to the store before breakfast? And did she have enough change on hand? Would she need to cash a check?

She frowned, thinking of money. Don had a pay check coming Saturday. But now, for the first time, it crossed her mind that after that there would be no more pay checks until Don was released.

A new kind of panic joined formidably with the others ranked in threatening masses about the outskirts of her mind.

Even if she could get a job, she couldn't work, with the kids. She wouldn't throw them on Mamie. Mamie had raised four of her own and held down a job herself most of the time she was doing it. She deserved some freedom and rest now—not the care of two grandchildren.

Not consciously did Lola contemplate the possibility that this condition of sole responsibility might extend indefinitely into the future; but she began to speculate and fear as if such were the case.

Rent would have to be paid. Just because it was Mamie's and Frank's house she could not let the rent go. Here again the older people were trying to build up their security for the future when Frank would have to retire. They needed regular rent from the flat.

She rubbed her hand over her forehead. It was too much. Don's family could not take on her and the kids. Already they were obligated to Ramón. Thank God he had come forward with help. What a lucky hunch it had been, Don's going to him right in the beginning.

In a way it was strange though, his stepping in as he had after so many years of ignoring them all, and when he had no real obligation to the family. She wondered why he had done it; and suddenly her eyes were focused unseeingly on the drab rug.

Why had he? Of course it could be sentiment. A warm-hearted impulse. Latin people were supposed to be emotional, given to impulsive gestures.

That was it, of course. It was good of him to accept the certainty of Don's innocence like this.

Slowly Lola let herself realize that someone under this roof was a murderer, and that that someone was letting Don run the risk of the gas chamber while he sat tight.

One by one her mind singled them out. Mamie, Frank, Pauline, Peggy, Maureen. The police must have checked Len's alibi, letting him out. If it were not airtight they would have paid more attention to him. The triangle business. And it was absurd, of course, Pauline's accusation of Ernie. But it was equally absurd that any of the others had killed Hank. Only Len and Don had motives.

Lola's face twisted painfully. It was impossible, but it had happened.

Chapter Ten

Mamie and Peggy were busy doing the housework the next morning when the doorbell rang. Upon opening the door, Mamie found Joel Freeman standing at the edge of the porch, his hat on the back of his head, his face tilted upward as he surveyed the second-story windows above and to his right. He brought his eyes back down and smiled.

When he was in the hall he glanced about inclusively and observed, "Thought I'd better look things over so I'd know what the prosecution's talking about when they begin throwing around references to the scene of the crime."

Mamie caught her lower lip with the edge of her small, well-made false teeth. "You know," she said anxiously, "the more I think about it, Mr. Freeman, the more I think Pauline may have been right." She regarded him seriously. "If I do say it as shouldn't, Pauline is awfully smart. Intelligent, you know. We all know it wasn't any of us; and who else was in the house that night? And I don't see how a burglar or a prowler could have got in. At least nobody like that would have come *back* in. He'd have just thrown the gun in the yard and ran."

"Wouldn't Mr. Simpkins have done the same thing?" the lawyer asked gently.

Mamie met his eyes worriedly.

"Mind if I just prowl around?" Freeman went on. "Where is this buffet now where the gun was kept?"

Peggy had come to the dining-room door, and she and Mamie followed the man, watching him with anxious, intent eyes as he surveyed the location of the buffet, stood in the hall and thoughtfully measured the distance with his eyes from the bathroom door to the bedroom, from the bedroom to the outside door, as he paced down the hall and peered into the living room with the bay windows admitting long parallelograms of sunlight. He walked to the windows and looked out.

"These shades kept raised all the time?"

"Mostly," Mamie replied.

"They up that night?"

"I never noticed."

"They were down in the morning," Peggy volunteered. "I remember the policeman pulling them up to let in more light when we came in here."

Freeman bent his head forward and looked into the street. "No street lights right in front here."

Mamie came to stand beside him, and gestured toward the garage of the house on their left which came out flush with the sidewalk.

"Ormsby's garage shuts out the light of the one just down the street there. It's rather nice. We don't have it glaring right into our front entrance."

"Mrs. Thomas home?" Freeman inquired. "I'd better look around upstairs."

"Yes, she's home. Just go up and knock on the living-room door."

Mamie and Peggy watched him mount the stairs with his hand on the railing. He was aware of the doglike manner in which they had followed his every movement and word. It was nothing new to him. They were always like that, trusting him, depending on him, like children waiting for an all-powerful parent to help them out of some mess they'd got into. But even after so many years it touched him somehow, made him more determined than ever to win. It was their families that got you. And even when the client was guilty as hell he got to feeling sorry for the poor devil. *Tout comprendre, tout pardonner.* Sentimental bastard, that's what he was. Because it was tough for the ones on the other side, too, the ones who were left after somebody got bumped off. But they didn't have this helpless, scared look that got under your skin. They were usually vindictive and mad, and that stiffened your spine, made it easier to fight them.

He was convinced that Garcia suspected one of them. He wished to hell the Mexican would tell him which one and save him the trouble of ferreting it out for himself. It helped in your defense if you yourself knew what had actually happened, gave you ideas for gumming up the prosecution's contentions.

When Freeman had talked to Lola for a little while and taken note of the arrangement of the apartment and admired the children, he came back down the stairs. Mamie and Peggy were waiting in chairs in the living room, apparently immobilized by his presence in the house.

"I'd like to talk to Mrs. Johnson alone for a while," he said to Mamie with a smile. "Her testimony is going to be the most important probably in the case; and I need to have her story quite clear in my mind."

Mamie rose uncertainly and glanced down at Peggy. She left the room with an air of unwillingness.

Freeman sat in an overstuffed chair facing the windows and crossed his legs. He lighted a cigarette and regarded the girl benignly.

"I've told everything I can," she said weakly.

"What you've told so far to the police and to the coroner's jury is evidence. Now you're talking to your brother's lawyer. When I go into court I mean to have a much clearer picture of events than the prosecution has. If you've held anything back for any reason, let's have it now. You can trust me to use it safely for all concerned, or not to use it if it would cause trouble."

"I didn't hold back one thing from the police."

The man smiled facetiously. "Maybe you should have. But now let's just go over it inch by inch. For instance"—his eyes strayed to the sliding doors into the hall which were standing out a foot or more into the opening—"those doors—when you came in, were they closed, wide open, or partially closed?"

Peggy looked at them, frowning. "I never noticed. It was dark though in the hall, and a person wouldn't notice unless you were looking at them."

"You didn't turn on the hall light?"

"No, the little light at the top of the stairs made it light enough to see where you were going."

"Don't you people usually turn on the hall light when you come in at night?"

"Only if the upstairs light is off."

"I should think Maureen would have switched it on when she came in."

"Well—sometimes a person does, sometimes they don't."

Freeman leaned back easily in his chair. "Close your eyes and try to visualize the way it was when you came in."

Peggy closed her eyes dutifully, and Freeman's voice went on soothingly, "Just relax now and try to imagine yourself back in the hall after you opened the door. It was dim, shadowy. Was there any light except that coming down the stairwell?"

Peggy's brows drew together above the half-moons of her eyelids with their fringe of dark lashes. She shook her head slowly, and opened her eyes. "I don't think so; I don't remember any."

"The door to your room; it was closed?"

"Yes."

"You went straight in?"

"Yes."

"The bed-table lamp was on?"

"Yes."

"I noticed," the man said thoughtfully, "the bedroom door slides back close over the carpet, so there wouldn't be any light under it. But the bathroom door has no threshold. There's a space between it and the linoleum. Didn't you notice a band of light there?"

Peggy shook her head uneasily. "You wouldn't be looking for things like that."

"When Maureen wasn't in the room, what made you think she was in the bathroom?"

Peggy's hands moved in an abortive gesture. "Why, it's natural. A person comes in; quite often they've been—uh—waiting, and they head for there first."

"How were you dressed when Maureen came into the bedroom?"

"Why, I—I had on my robe and slippers. I was just waiting to go wash up. We always wash our make-up off before we go to bed."

"Was Maureen in her robe?"

"No. No, of course not. Like I said, she was probably in a hurry and didn't stop to undress."

"What did she have on?"

"Her coat, and—and the rest of her clothes."

"From your bedroom can you hear water and so forth running in the bathroom?"

"You can hear the pipes kind of—sing sometimes; but you can't hear it *running*." Her eyes had fastened on him concentratedly.

"Did you hear the bathroom door open and close before she came into the bedroom?"

Peggy leaned forward, and for the first time Freeman witnessed a spark of flinty spirit in the soft brown eyes.

"What are you getting at? Are you insinuating I *wasn't* in the bedroom while Hank was shot, that I couldn't have heard Maureen running water and all that? Are you trying to pin it on *me*, to get Don off?"

"Don't get excited," Freeman said equably, "I'm representing Don; but I don't forget who engaged me nor who is paying me. It is not my object to get anybody convicted. However, you can see already how important your testimony will be. We must decide, with absolute exactness, what you remember before you take the stand. Innumerable questions will be fired at you along the lines of the few I have just asked. And you see what's happened already. It looks funny, you hear and see nothing until your sister shows up in the bedroom door—maybe ten minutes after you enter the house."

"A person doesn't listen for the rumble of water pipes and the closing of doors. You don't look for light under doors. You're thinking about other things. And God knows I've had plenty on my mind, breaking up with my husband and all."

"Whether you realize it at the time or not, you do hear and see. I only want to find out what things you observed without consciously registering them. One thing, if you closed the front door when you came in, it had to be opened again immediately afterward, and opened and closed again sometime during the night when the gun was returned. Did you close the bedroom door when you went in?"

"Yes. It's a habit. Mom always insists we keep it closed on account of it opening on the hall with people passing all the time. And as far as the front door goes, anybody that was careful could shut it without making any noise."

Freeman sighed. "Yes, I know that." He seemed to cogitate, and then said casually, "You all had keys?"

"Naturally."

"You carried yours in your purse?"

"Of course."

"Was your sister carrying her purse when she came from the bathroom?"

"Maureen doesn't 'carry' a purse," Peggy said impatiently. "She has big pockets in her new coat, and she has a leather envelope purse something like a big wallet, and it fits in one of the pockets."

"Incidentally, how were you dressed that night?"

Peggy had never relaxed completely after her spurt of anger a few minutes earlier. The man had put her on the defensive, unexpectedly stiffening her spirit, and now she retorted with unwonted impertinence, "I was wearing clothes, of course."

Freeman smiled tolerantly. "Now, now, there's no need to get on your high horse with me." He went on dryly, "I'm mild compared to what the prosecutor will be. I have to know all these unimportant details. You were dressed up, I suppose?"

"I had on a black dress with a peplum," she conceded stiffly, "and a black hat with tulle around the crown, and a plain black coat."

Freeman smiled. "In other words, you were dressed for an evening out?"

"Naturally."

"You wore gloves then, I suppose."

Peggy's eyes looked black, and they darted at his face resentfully. "Naturally."

Finally Freeman pulled a white-gold watch from his vest pocket and looked at it, announcing that he must get back to his office.

"I want to talk to your sister, Maureen," he added. "Could you have her call at my office this afternoon after school? I seldom get away until six, so if she could be there by four-thirty or five I can squeeze her in."

"I'll tell her."

Peggy ushered him out and leaned against the closed door with her back, feeling exhausted.

Mamie put her head around the dining-room door as if she had been waiting, and came out quickly when she saw Peggy alone.

At the sight of her mother the stimulating anger the attorney had aroused flickered out in Peggy, and her lips quivered, her eyes filled with tears.

"What did he say? He stayed long enough. What did he want to know?" Mamie chattered, hurrying down the hall.

Peggy came forward, reverting to a childish tone as her mother came nearer.

"He was awful. I don't like him." She began to cry, and Mamie put her arms around the girl. Peggy put her head on her mother's shoulder, and felt the woman's soft cheek against her own.

"He tried to make out *I* did it," she sniffled. "He kept *insinuating*."

Mamie patted and clucked and reassured and drew the girl in to sit beside her on the sofa. Despite her distress, there was something pleasurable to the woman in holding her child against her, comforting her, being wise and maternal, the one the girl came to in her agitation.

Peggy recounted as much of the talk as she could recall, snuffling intermittently with a self-pity that gradually became rather enjoyable. It was somehow not unpleasant feeling abused and having Mom stick up for her.

"Why, my goodness, he's only trying to help us," Mamie asserted rallyingly. "He wasn't sus*pect*ing you. Nobody does. And like he says, he's going to have to talk to all of us and see that our stories don't—well—uh— you know— Not that we should lie; but he has to figure out what we *might* say in court, and then tell us if we *should* or not."

Peggy drew away from the cushiony comfort of her mother's bosom and ran her fingers under her eyes. "Guess I better go wash up. I'm a mess."

Mamie remained sitting on the davenport when the girl had gone. She wore a white slipover sweater and dark blue flannel slacks, and her fingers picked at the crease in the trousers. She ran the tip of her tongue over the dried lipstick on her upper lip. Pauline was right. They should have all stuck together in laying it on those nig—Negroes—she corrected herself with conscious loyalty to her son. Because if it wasn't them, anyone could see it had to be someone in the house.

Her sweater felt cold under her arms where she had perspired.

Mamie had always been good at closing her mind to what she didn't want to see. She had had to be. With her marriages and her divorces, for instance, she had had to think in terms of black and white, so that she was ineluctably always in the right, the men sweepingly at fault. It had been the only way to keep going, to survive with her life intact.

So now she could not think in terms of guilt within her family. She must think only of Don's innocence, refuse to be led astray into other kinds of speculation. Her thoughts fastened on the dark-haired, fat little lawyer with his inscrutable, shiny brown eyes. He was a Jew—that was to the good—Jews were shrewd and cunning and smarter than other people. A ripple of uneasiness crossed her mind, an unspoken apology to Don. He was as queer about Jews as he was about colored people. You weren't supposed to think they were different. He jumped on the rest of them impatiently when they spoke of Jews being this or that—which everybody knew they were. Don said some of them were as dumb as anybody else, and some were as shy and unassuming as others were pushing and forward.

But nevertheless, Mamie thought stubbornly, it was a good thing Freeman was a Jew.

She was simply not going to worry. Ramón knew what he was doing, getting Joel Freeman. He would get Don off.

She licked her lips again and ran her fingers up and down the cords standing out in her neck, pinching the soft flesh which was beginning to sag between them.

The girls, Don, Frank, Lola, all whirled in a terrifying kaleidoscope in her thoughts. She dared not sort them out, hold them steady, and consider all the implications of the places in which they stood.

She must simply keep focused on the lawyer in trust and optimism. Things had a way of turning out right if you just hung on and kept a stiff upper lip.

But she rose to her feet shakily.

Pauline, meanwhile, had gone to work that morning with her own upper lip as stiff as she could make it.

Usually she looked forward to the relaxed yet bustling few minutes in the girls' restroom before they all trooped down to their desks, with the talk about last night's dates, the last-minute powdering of noses and straightening of curls and attention to fingernails. But now she rode up in the elevator reluctantly, tired ahead of time at the thought of resisting their secret opinions of her and of her family, which had suddenly emerged in the notoriety of newsprint, not as she had painted it by offhand allusions in past conversations, but as it really was.

When she opened the door into the long room with its windows ineffectually opening on a light well and its wicker furniture filled with girls having a last smoke before they filed out to go down to the office, she found a large group obstructing the passageway to the locker rooms. Almost all of the girls were clustered around Marcia Bird, squeaking, twittering, excited. Marcia glowed, and passed her left hand around magnanimously so that everyone could see the diamond in a yellow-gold setting which had appeared on her third finger during the night.

"Pauline!" Gwen greeted her, squealing. "What do you think? Marcia's engaged!"

Marcia obligingly held her hand out toward Pauline, crooking her fingers to show off the ring.

"It's beautiful," Pauline murmured.

"Of course we *expected* it," somebody cried gayly.

"When's the big event?"

"Next month," Marcia said smugly. "Bob's being transferred to L.A., so we're going to be married before he leaves."

Among questions and jokes and comments Marcia moved out into the hall surrounded by fellow workers.

When she was gone Virginia Breckenridge spoke up decisively, "We'll have to do something. A shower or something."

"How about sort of a farewell dinner for her, at Lucca's or Monaco's?" somebody else suggested.

"No, I think it should be more sort of intimate—at somebody's house," Virginia announced definitely. "And it ought to be a surprise."

Pauline started to move along toward the lockers, but Virginia turned to her managingly. "There isn't much time. And of course we'll have to ask everybody. We should form a committee. Pauline, how about you being on it? You're good at things like that. And I'll be sort of chairman. And"—she glanced about speculatively—"you, Phyllis, you be on it too. We could get together for lunch today." She turned to Pauline again. "That O.K. with you?"

"Sure. I'll be glad to help."

"Well, look then, we'll meet in the lobby and try to get a booth down at the B and B this noon."

As Pauline started to walk on Virginia said with the air of one having through oversight made a social *faux pas*, "How is everything going, Pauline—about your brother?"

"There's nothing—new," she said stiffly.

"Well, it's too bad—"

A girl who had just entered crossed Virginia's field of vision, and she accosted the newcomer, forgetting Pauline, "Have you heard, Linda? About Marcia—"

Pauline moved away, feeling somewhat dazed. She had always been on casually friendly terms with Virginia, but right now it was more significant somehow, going out to lunch with her, especially since Virginia had so offhandedly made it clear that she had not forgotten The Disgrace.

Virginia was the only girl in the office who was a college graduate—not business college, but Stanford, no less. Her father was a retired businessman, living in Palo Alto; and Virginia had belonged to a sorority at the university and was always mentioning her connections. The girls in the office tacitly, though secretly a little resentfully, acknowledged her position; and considerable rivalry simmered about her in connection with the omnipresent jockeying for advancement. For Virginia made no secret of the fact that, for her, business was a career. She intended to rise as far as possible in the company; and although the men did not know it yet, she meant someday to be elbowing them out of the way in the contest for executive positions.

Crossing the main office to her desk, Pauline saw Charlie Daniels coming toward her with his topcoat over his arm, his hat in his hand. Charlie was the claims man who paid her consistent attention when he was in town. She braced herself mentally, ready to parry the covert curiosity which would hover in his eyes, revealing his prurient interest in the revelations about her family which had appeared in the newspapers. He would smile and speak as if everything was just the same; but he would be watching her in that speculative way she had begun to expect from people.

The desks nearby were still vacant at the place where they met, and he approached her purposefully. To Pauline's surprise, he was not even smiling; his expression was serious.

"God, kid," he said, "I've been reading about the murder. It's sure rough on you. I would've given you a ring, but I knew there wasn't much anybody could do; and I was out in the sticks on this case where you'd have a small-town operator listening in on every word."

Pauline looked back at him blankly.

"I guess it hasn't been any picnic," he said sympathetically.

She smiled thinly. "No, it's no picnic."

"I suppose everything's pretty upset and you're all pretty busy, but I was wondering if you're free any night this week. I'm going to be in town a few days, and I thought maybe we could have dinner and dance somewhere. You need to get your mind off things, get out and relax a little."

"Why—why, I'd love to," she responded in a tone of warmth and gratification of which she hadn't known she was capable right now.

"How about tomorrow night?"

"Swell."

"O.K. I'll pick you up about eight at your house." He smiled and touched her arm, and continued on his way toward his boss's office.

Pauline took her seat at her own desk and put her hands on the edge of the movable section preparatory to turning up the typewriter, but she only sat there with her hands idle, her eyes fixed unseeingly in front of her.

She thought of Ellery, and the thought was without emotion. Somehow she didn't care anymore. It wasn't important—all her plans, her blueprints for the future drawn around him.

With Charlie's undisguised recognition and acceptance of her situation had come a sense of safety that she had not known even before the murder.

Virginia crossed the aisle between the desks, her voice raised toward someone who was seated two aisles over, and Pauline's eyes focused on her.

Then her shoulders squared, and she flipped the typewriter into place with a practiced movement.

In her tweed skirt and red cardigan sweater set Maureen sat in Freeman's office that afternoon, her hands clasped in her lap, her feet in bobby socks and shabby brown loafers placed side by side on the tan carpet.

A young man with oily black hair sat opposite her in an armchair looking at *Esquire*, and a bleached blond in her forties sat with crossed knees on a settee, turning the pages of *Liberty* which she scanned with hard, indifferent eyes.

By contrast Maureen looked fresh and sweet and wholesome even in her wrinkled school clothes.

The secretary in a tailored suit and crisp, short-bobbed hair finally came out of a door and indicated with a bright, professional smile that the girl was next.

For an instant in the doorway to the attorney's office Maureen paused and took in the small room whose center was a flat-topped desk inundated with papers. Along one wall glass-fronted cases held rows of heavy, tall books.

Maureen took one of the leather-seated chairs and waited with a guarded air.

Casually, cheerfully, Freeman spoke to her as he had to Peggy in the morning, with the same line of questioning regarding the movements of both girls after they entered the house.

Maureen's replies were brief, exact—somehow parrotlike, the man thought. Behind a genial manner he studied her thoughtfully. It was unusual, most unusual, a young girl—practically an adolescent—to be so poised, so unexcitable. She never wavered in her replies, knew exactly, down to the last detail, what she had seen and heard and done. An ideal witness. The kind who would look flatly at her interrogator under cross-examination and refuse to say anything she did not wish to say.

He knew damn well she was lying, but about what he couldn't tell. There was one consolation anyway: if *he* couldn't crack her composure, neither could the prosecution. And her story was negatively advantageous to the defense. If Don had been lurking about downstairs, opening doors and trotting up and down the hall returning guns, she would have been likely to have heard some sound indicating his presence, and she swore she had not.

It was irritating though, your own witnesses not cooperating with their complete candor. Whatever they were holding back might have been useful, even though they in their inexperience couldn't see it.

Freeman had been silent for several minutes, staring at a bust of Daniel Webster on the bookcase and thinking these thoughts.

The girl's voice suddenly interrupted him. She was leaning forward, her hands clenched on the chair arms, her manner alive as it had not been since she entered the room.

"There's no question, is there, that you'll get Don off?"

He regarded her interestedly. "There's always a question," he said quietly.

Her body inclined farther forward in the chair. Still holding herself in restraint, she was nevertheless close now to flying apart, once she had slackened in her pose of cool disinterest.

"But you *always* win!" she charged him shrilly.

He was maddeningly unresponsive. "Nobody always wins," he said quietly. "I've had my defeats the same as anybody else."

Her features settled in a mold of strained desperation and she eyed him antagonistically. "You're just saying that," she said harshly, "to scare me. You think I know something I won't tell you."

She stood up suddenly, looking rather ridiculous in the awkward lines of the long, narrow skirt which was the style, the loose-fitting sweater, the flat shoes.

"You think because I'm young that I'm dumb. But I'm not as dumb as you think. They haven't got a case against Don. Any good lawyer could tear it to shreds. I know this much about the law. They have to *prove* you're guilty. And they can't. They haven't any proof against Don."

Freeman fitted his fingertips together and scrutinized them thoughtfully. "They seem to think they have."

She stepped forward and leaned on her arms with her knuckles on the desk. "You're playing with me. I don't know why, but you are. And all I've got to say is you'd better save your cute tricks for the trial. All I've got to say is you'd *better* save Don."

She drew in her breath sharply, turned, and strode out of the room. She stalked through the reception room and down the hall where she punched the elevator button viciously.

In the elevator she stood at the side, her hand grasping the rail, and leaned her temple against the polished wood as the cage plunged sickeningly downward.

When she stepped out on the lobby floor Maureen's breathing was regular again, her face impassive. She oughtn't to have flown off the handle like that in front of him, but she hated smart alecks at any time, and this was no time for anybody to be coy, least of all Don's lawyer. But that's all it had been. Freeman had been showing off. There was quite a lot of the actor in him, anybody could see that. For some reason it had pleased his fancy to pretend the case was going to be a tough one. But it wasn't going to be. It would be duck soup for a man like Joel Freeman.

The phrase struck her mind with a felicitous sound. Duck soup. It kept repeating itself in her mind off and on as she was jostled in the evening trolley crowds. It was like a silly talisman, steadying her thoughts when their fingers touched it.

Freeman sat at his desk, pinching his chin in his fingers with a stroking motion. He knew the signs of inner conflict when he saw them, and the foregoing scene had been more than a sign: it had been a demonstration. He was a little worried. The girl could crack up, and if so, it might redound to the advantage of the prosecution. He couldn't know whether it would or not, not knowing the source of her trouble other than that it was connected with knowledge of the murder.

On the other hand, the kid had guts. She might stick it through, go through the trial with that subtly contemptuous self-control intact. It was true she had flared out here; but here in his office she knew it was safe to let go. In the dangerous atmosphere of the courtroom it would be different. She impressed him as one of those people who react to a crisis by preternatural self-control.

Well— He dropped his hand and pressed the buzzer for his secretary. He had pretty much stirred the girls up. Between now and the trial he'd have to get on the good side of them again. He wished plaintively, though, that when he was working for people they'd *tell* him things.

Chapter Eleven

Until the trial began Ramón stayed away from the house on O'Farrell Street. He could do no more, he told himself, than he already had done by putting its occupants and their salvation into Joel Freeman's hands. When the case of the People versus Donald Thomas reached the courts, however, he was there unobtrusively among the spectators.

It took two days to select the jury, and when direct testimony began Ramón listened intently, observing the jury, following the objections and bickering of the attorneys. He did not hope to learn anything new. All the testimony given so far corresponded to what he had already heard. What he sought to learn was how it was going, what impression the facts made on the jury. Would Freeman's claims that there was no proof, that there was only circumstantial evidence against his client, hold up?

Ramón had expected Freeman to ignore as far as possible the fingerprint evidence. To him the finding of any prints at all seemed so damaging that Ramón had figured the smart thing for the defense would have been to play it down. Consequently he was surprised at the length of time Freeman spent in cross-examination of the expert who had identified the prints.

Frank's testimony had revealed that he had inspected the gun some ten days before the murder, having wiped it off tenderly with a handkerchief before laying it back in the drawer, handling it by the barrel as he did so, thus satisfactorily accounting for the marks of his own fingertips on that part of the gun.

Ramón had assumed that the other prints had all been marked neatly around the butt of the gun where it would be clasped in firing. But Freeman's questions brought to light that the two prints identified as those of Don's right thumb and forefinger were on either side of the handle close to the cartridge chamber, a fact which the attorney used to fortify Don's statement of having merely moved the gun out of his way in searching for another article in the drawer. It was logical that one might grasp the weapon so in moving it.

When it came to the prints the expert credited to Maureen, it seemed that again there were only two, the right thumb and little finger, one above the other on the inside of the handle; and Mamie was represented by one print, again the thumb, on the under part at the extreme edge of the gun butt.

"Is it not true," Freeman inquired offhandedly, "that for decisive identification all five prints on a hand are necessary?"

"Usually—yes."

"But you have definitely assigned these prints to the persons named in your statement?"

"They correspond," the expert replied curtly.

"Besides the decipherable prints you found, were there others, too smudged for identification?"

"Yes."

"Would you say that some other person besides these whose prints you identified *could* also have handled the weapon?"

"Possible, but unlikely."

"Could someone wearing gloves and handling the weapon deliberately, carefully, so as not to remove previous prints, have used the gun without erasing the prints you found?"

"I doubt it."

"But it's not impossible?"

The witness shrugged. "I suppose anything's possible. But it wouldn't happen once in a thousand times."

"Was it not unlikely in the first place, finding four reasonably clear prints on as small an object as this, which, according to your testimony, must have been touched by at least three people after Mr. Grady's polishing operations with his handkerchief?"

"Well—it doesn't happen very often."

Freeman's smile roved cherubically from the witness to the judge and the jury as he observed blandly, "A lot of unlikely things seem to have happened in this case." He nodded kindly at the witness. "That's all."

Ramón looked speculatively at the jury, all of whom had listened conscientiously to the preceding dialogue. They all looked thoughtfully blank. Ramón remembered what Freeman had said about "reasonable doubt—

in other words—confusion," and he was sure that now the jury in its deliberations would be inclined to pass quickly over the question of the fingerprints on the gun.

Eventually everyone who lived in the house had been questioned, their stories remaining what they had been on the morning of the murder. Ramón could see that the district attorney was using their testimony to show that Don had opportunity to commit the murder, that not one of the family could swear to who had or had not been in the downstairs hall or on the stairs after Peggy came into the house and closed the bedroom door. He made much of Don's original lie about Ernest and Nell's presence, using it to cast doubt on the defendant's veracity all down the line, while Freeman countered by emphasizing the positive meaning of Don's and Lola's unfortunate effort to protect their friends, building up the loyalty and generosity it had shown to be strong in Don's character.

Maureen was cool and detached on the stand, Peggy nervous and apprehensive.

It was when the past and present employees of Enderby's rose one by one to testify to the feeling existing between Hank and the defendant that Ramón felt the odds increasing against Don. Now the jury would believe that he had hated Hank Grueber, and this fact would color the preceding testimony.

As they moved despondently out of the courtroom that day, Ramón fell into step beside Mamie and Frank, ignoring the curious eyes of the crowd, and spoke deferentially, inviting the whole group to come with him to La Paloma for dinner.

"We can eat in the private dining room upstairs," he said. "It will save you folks having to bother at home. I know you must be tired."

Mamie looked doubtfully at Frank, who shrugged ungraciously. They had paused in the corridor, the girls silent on the periphery of the little group.

Lola spoke wearily, "Why don't you all go? Get away from the house for a while. I'll have to go home and relieve the sitter from watching the kids, but the rest of you go on."

After uncertain conferring murmurs inertia let them drift into acceptance. All were too weary to care whether or where they ate.

Ramón had a steak dinner served in the dining room opposite his office on the mezzanine floor, and Len, at least, became jovial with the warmth of red meat and red wine.

"I'm betting on little Joe," he declared heartily as the apple pie and cheese appeared, referring thus familiarly to Joel Freeman. "Believe me, he ain't missing any tricks."

"They got no *proof*," Frank said judiciously.

"But do they need it?" Pauline interposed cynically. "That jury doesn't look very bright to me."

Maureen directed a level look at her father. "How do you think it's going?"

He placed his fingers on either side of the glass and looked soberly into the burgundy wine. "Today they got motive. They already had opportunity. Lola's his only alibi, and a wife's don't carry much weight. And"—he paused intentionally—"the fingerprints on the gun."

"But Don explained that, and Frank remembers—about the cribbage board. And mine and Maureen's were on it too," Mamie said defensively.

All their eyes were on Ramón, and they were, in varying degrees, suspicious, questioning, uneasy.

"Of course Mom's and mine were on it. Every time you lose something in that drawer you move the gun, looking for it." Maureen spoke in a splintery voice. "There's got to be some way that gun was fired without erasing our prints."

"It could have been wrapped in a handkerchief or held in the folds of a person's clothes," Pauline said aloud but to herself, "and handled gently. It could have been done without damaging the other prints."

"But the jury isn't going to consider that possibility very seriously," Ramón pointed out.

"It was the fingerprints," Mamie said heavily. She poked at the fluted edge of the piecrust with her fork. "They eliminated me and Maureen because we didn't have a motive, and that left Don."

Maureen's hazel eyes were black under the artificial lighting as she spoke up bitterly. "I'll hate cops the rest of my life."

"They were only doing their duty," Pauline rebuked her.

"You think Don did it then?" Maureen shot at her, turning to look straight at her sister.

Pauline stared into the other girl's eyes, her lips parted. Her words, when they came, were a startled whisper seemingly forced out against her will, "I don't know."

Then she glanced wildly about the table as if shocked by her own words, and lifting her napkin, she covered her face with it, bowing her head. Strangled sobs were audible through the white cloth.

Maureen sat motionless, her body still half-turned, her eyes fixed on the feather ornament of Pauline's hat.

She seemed not to hear Mamie's ejaculation, "Pauline! Of course you know he didn't. Your own brother!"

Maureen's eyes slowly swept over the faces around the table. Len dropped his eyes, embarrassed. Peggy put her hand to her cheek and met Maureen's eyes with tears in her own. Frank was watching Pauline disapprovingly. Mamie's eyes were darting from one person to another worriedly. Maureen did not bother to continue her survey as far as Ramón, who was watching her inscrutably.

"My God," she said in a low voice. "Even his own family." Then she looked at Ramón.

"The jury will never believe he did it," Mamie was asserting argumentatively. "Beyond reasonable doubt. That's what they always have to be sure of. I was on a jury once. I remember. The judge tells them. And Freeman. Freeman's smart. All those legal things. There's loopholes ..."

As she babbled on, reassuring herself as well as the others, slowly the dinner party wobbled back to equilibrium again. Only Maureen was silent.

Once Ramón said, "Even if he's acquitted, it's a bad thing. Some people will always believe he did it."

Later, getting ready for bed, Mamie carefully tied the coarse pink net over her pin curls and drew off her chenille robe. In bed, in the dark, she moved close to Frank, who was lying silent on his back. He pulled up his arm and pushed it under her soft, bare shoulders, and she pressed her forehead against him.

She wanted to say something, but she had said it all so often that she knew he was tired of hearing her sighs and hopes and half-hearted self-encouragement. Not to irritate him, she held back the soporific words whose utterance helped.

Ramón now, he had never seemed to mind how much she talked, and he always had something to say in return, catching up and elaborating her observations. She had always known he was smart, that he'd get ahead someday. He had such style and a way with people. Too much, that was the trouble, she reminded herself virtuously. A natural-born chaser. She bet right now he was keeping some woman, maybe two.

Surprisingly, because she never thought of him at all any more, Don Thomas came to her mind. The heel! Deserting her with two little kids. And she had loved him so, enough to put up with his being away for months at a time, drinking up his wages when he did come in. She supposed it was always like that. You never loved again with the abandon of the first time.

Frank was falling asleep, and he turned over heavily. With a sense of relief her mind came back to him. Steady, reliable Frank. Maybe the kids did look down on him, thought he was common, and—well, dumb. But he was so good to her. And so well satisfied with her. Frank at least would never run away or flirt with other women.

She roughly suppressed the reflection which had tugged at the edge of her thoughts: who would have thought that the romantic girl who had adored Don Thomas and been excitedly in love with the dashing Ramón would one day be satisfied to love a man simply because he was kind?

But she must sleep. She must keep up her strength. Was it not a mother's duty to keep up the family's morale?

So she turned on her side with her butt touching Frank's, and conscientiously tightened her eyelids over her weary eyes.

Only sleep did not come. The day, its events, its words, tracked through her mind. It had been so queer at dinner over at Ramón's. Pauline's "I don't know." Her crying in her napkin. Maureen's "Even his own family!"

All at once she was tense with fear. The possibility that Don might not get off penetrated her determined optimism.

The self-assurances that were really only a thin veneer to keep up her spirits cracked and fell away. They wouldn't be lenient with Don. He was already in bad with the nice people, people like Pauline wanted to be in with, a person to be watched carefully because he advocated things like treating Negroes just the same as anybody else, and staying out on strike with your union till the bitter end—things that, despite his patient explanations, she didn't understand either. She was all right as she was now, and she didn't want to understand all that stuff that made people want to rearrange everything.

But they couldn't, they couldn't kill Don! Not her boy, who had been the sweetest, the cutest baby of all her children. He had meant even more to her after his father didn't come back to them. She had even leaned on his love then, little as he was, because she had needed so to feel that she was all-important to someone, even if his father didn't want her.

There was nothing, nothing she wouldn't do for Don. And here he was in danger, suffering, and she could do nothing. It was terrible to feel so helpless.

She lay very quiet. Her breathing hardly moved her chest.

Nothing? Nothing?

Her hand made a spasmodic gesture, as if pushing something away.

No, no, there were others she had to think of. She had her own life to consider.

But her fingerprint was there.

Her eyes were wide, staring at the fainter oblong below the pulled-up shade.

Thoughts she had never admitted to her mind came pushing out through the crevice this wild impulse had opened.

Her children—all except Don (*he* had never blamed *her* for his own troubles)—they felt she hadn't given them the right breaks. *They* hadn't had a normal home, with *two* parents and a father with a steady job. *They* had to explain odd names, different from hers. Other kids' mothers didn't have love affairs, like she did, first Ramón, then Frank. They had never (and now she knew she had always known it) been proud of her, the way they thought children had a right to be of their mother. They didn't even think she was very smart.

Pauline. Pauline was always correcting her grammar, criticizing her clothes, suggesting things to wear that Mamie didn't like.

Maureen. She closed her eyes against the memory of Maureen's look that morning after Don was arrested.

Peggy. Well, Peggy perhaps didn't hold anything against her. But Peggy was restless with life, never satisfied, looking for something that wasn't there. And I—maybe I am responsible, Mamie thought shrinkingly.

The decision did not put itself into so many words, but the meaning was there: if I am guilty, if I have failed them, perhaps now I can atone.

She lay still for a little, and then, as if propelled by some inner compulsion, Mamie quietly slid her legs out from under the covers. As she began to dress, she hurried, as if she must do it now and do it quickly before her courage failed.

Alone in his cell Don smoked one cigarette after another. At first it had been hard to face. Hardest of all, and most embittering, was the realization that one of them was letting him take the rap. Of course, he reasoned, trying to be fair, she was waiting, counting on acquittal. She could not actually mean to let him go to prison or to death in her place.

At first his mind had batted itself back and forth on the two possible "shes," and it was as if the whole world dropped away around him when "she" was Mom. All of a person's thinking denied the possibility that a mother would sacrifice a child to save herself. And in this case, paradoxically, the crime itself would have had to spring from maternal protectiveness—toward Peggy. To get rid of Hank so that Peggy would go back to Len.

But he could not see Mom taking Peggy's trouble that seriously. And even if she had, was it reasonable to suppose that she would murder to save one child's marriage and then turn around and let another of her children lose his life?

It was necessary to face the possibility of Mom's guilt; but, having faced it, Don had relaxed a little, knowing that he could reject it.

If it was not Mom, it left only Maureen. Lines deepened in his brow as again he turned the "why" over in his mind. None of the possible reasons seemed good enough. She was a funny kid, alternately withdrawn, knowing beyond her years, and stormily passionate, childishly spoiled. If it were she, what impulse, what sudden twisted emotion could have moved her at the decisive moment?

Whatever it was, he could understand her behavior now. Yes, he could understand. Self-preservation came first. There was fear, uncertainty, perhaps shame. But there had been love, he thought. Maureen had liked him. And was she devoid of fairness, a sense of justice?

Why, even Pauline and what she had become in her effort to escape from sordidness and insecurity, Pauline would never have let him go even this far in payment for a crime that was hers.

So heavy were his thoughts with dismay, with indignation, with pity finally, as he thought of his little sister and what she might have done and what the circumstances must now be doing to her that it was hard to decide on the course he himself ought to take.

If Freeman were to get hold of the girl and put pressure on her to confess, would she do it?

As he brooded over the problem, it was not the murder for which the girl stood condemned before his thoughts, but her silence while another took the consequences of her action. He did not know why she had shot the man; but he blamed the long twisting and distortion of emotional attitudes which had led up to the explosion in violence. He felt it was something that could have happened to anyone, and could feel no proper horror that his sister was a murderess.

It was a thing you could not easily do, to accuse your sister, the baby one at that, to turn her over to the penal institutions of the state. And he was not convicted yet. If he were acquitted it would be actually the two of them set free.

But afterward, what of Maureen? Would this experience have shocked and steadied her into better control of herself, or would it make her cynical, crafty, an underground enemy of all social laws? Would successfully accomplished violence make her permanently hard and unscrupulous?

Don sank on the cot and put his head in his hands. Somehow, if they escaped, he must try to help her.

But it might be that the fingerprints meant nothing. Freeman had attacked their evidence fairly successfully. Maureen looked for pencils, stamps, blotters in that drawer the same as the rest of them. She, too, could have simply grasped the gun to push it aside. It could be someone as yet unsuspected. Like Frank. He was more familiar with the gun than anyone else. He could have held it cunningly in two strong gloved fingers, deliberately trying to preserve any other prints that were on it—for purposes of confusing the police. Of them all, Frank was the most likely to let Don take the rap in his place.

But if he had done it—why?

Don moved his head back and forth in his hands. Why did he always come back in desperation to Frank? For it always made him feel that he was being unfair. Deep inside him he must, as Ramón had said, want it to be his mother's husband.

And he had no right—no reason—for this subterranean desire.

As a matter of fact, he knew Frank liked him, was proud of him in some ways. He had an irritating way of speaking of Don as "my boy" to his cronies. Although Frank was set in old-fashioned race prejudice, he was in other ways more understanding of Don's thinking than the women of the family were. Frank was the only one you could talk to about labor legislation and rounds of wage increases. He understood about union solidarity—not from any intellectual processes, but simply because he had worked for wages all his life and had learned the hard way about the need for sticking together with the men you worked with. Frank's idea of supporting his union was to put on a clean shirt and a good pair of pants and attend a meeting about once every three months, on those occasions taking the floor and bawling out irrelevant remarks—Don suspected—on each motion that came up. Frank alone thought it was a matter for pride, Don's being elected shop steward, and running for the executive board, even if he didn't win.

Restlessly Don chided himself for turning always to the thought of Frank when he had exhausted the guilt possibilities of the others.

But if not Frank, then who? Rather he than Maureen.

After Ramón had said good-by to his guests at the top of the stairs to the main dining room, he went into his office. He sat in his chair with his elbows on the desk, his head in his hands.

He had procrastinated long enough. Now he had to bring the truth out and look at it and make up his mind what he thought about it and what he ought to do about it.

Suspicions that his daughter was guilty had closed in like an octopus around his thoughts, and now that he fully admitted their pressure he realized that all along, with one part of him he had wanted the girl of her own accord to accept responsibility for her act, with another part of him he had co-operated to protect her, to wait for escape by means of an acquittal.

With his own words at the dinner: "Some people will always believe he did it," he had shown himself and probably the girl that their holding back was indefensible. They were still letting someone they both loved suffer in her place.

He felt sure that if Don were sentenced to death, or to life, she would confess to save him. There was comfort and relief in that conviction. It proved that, in Francine's words, his daughter was not entirely cowardly and cruel.

His heart ached with pity for his child. Even for a mature woman, toughened by the abrasives of experience, it would be a hard decision to make, to give oneself over to the vengeance of the law. There would be deathly fear in the girl's inexperienced mind. Probably the only outcome her thoughts envisioned as a consequence of confession was a sentence of death.

Ramón shook his head slightly, and reached for the telephone. He had had no right from the first to hold back. His silence had been a false protection.

He could not protect her. He could not save her. The damage had been done when she pulled the trigger. While he looked for a way out, through silence, through pretense between the two of them and refusal to admit the facts to himself, through waiting for a verdict from outside, the girl herself was being crushed by the things that had happened to her.

And meanwhile they had had no right to play fast and loose with Don's life.

Chapter Twelve

Twenty minutes later Ramón was ringing the doorbell of the old-fashioned house on Russian Hill where the attorney Freeman lived with his wife.

They entered the library at the left of the entrance hall where an open fire burned in the raised grate beneath an old-fashioned mantelpiece.

Ramón sank into the worn leather cushions of a Morris chair and accepted a scotch and soda. Freeman leaned back in a round-backed swivel chair and crossed his slippered feet on the edge of the desk top and peered quizzically at his guest.

"I figured you had the inside dope on this case right from the start," he observed placidly, "and so you've finally decided to speak up."

Ramón nodded gravely. "But it isn't easy—"

The doorbell rang as he spoke, and Freeman said whimsically, "I seem to be popular tonight."

When the lawyer appeared in the doorway again, Ramón came to his feet in amazement.

Mamie paused, taken aback, but then she lifted her chin and came into the room. When she was seated she spoke to Freeman nervously, "Probably I should have gone to the police, but it seemed better to come to you first."

"Whatever it is you have on your mind, I'd say yes to that," Freeman said dryly.

Mamie glanced uneasily at Ramón, and the attorney said, "Perhaps you'd rather speak to me alone."

"No. No, he might as well know. Everybody will pretty soon, I suppose." Her breast under its flowered rayon covering rose and fell once before she said steadily, "I did it."

Freeman put his hands on the desk top and peered at her. Ramón's lips parted, and then his face was still.

As neither man spoke, she glanced from one to the other, her eyebrows rising in annoyance. "Well? Didn't you understand me? I shot Hank Grueber. My fingerprints were on the gun. That should be evidence enough. And I can tell you why too."

Freeman let out his breath audibly. And then he and Ramón met one another's eyes.

Ramón rose, and going to Mamie, put his hand on her shoulder and bent and kissed her cheek. "God bless you," he said softly.

Her lips quivered and she turned her head and put her hand over her face.

Ramón remained on his feet and put his hands in his pants' pockets. He looked down at the woman thoughtfully.

"You have found out, too, who did do it?"

Her head jerked up, and she looked at him, puzzled, before she stammered, "Why, I—I did."

Ramón shook his head. "No. It's brave of you, Mamie, being willing to do this. But it isn't wise to protect her, and I don't think she'd let you go through with it, when it comes right down to it, any more than she would Don."

"She?" It was only a breath.

"It was Maureen, of course."

"No! Oh no." Mamie came to her feet. She looked frantically at the speculatively observing Freeman.

"It's possible," the lawyer said quietly. "She had a chance to get back and get the gun, wait in the parlor till her sister was in the bedroom, slip out and call Grueber back and let him have it, return the gun, and come back to the bedroom. Best chance of anyone, in fact. Any of the rest of you, you see, would have run quite a risk of being seen coming in or out of the front door, with both the girls still up when the shot was fired. With their bedroom off the hall that way, one of them could easily have come face to face with the murderer on her way to or from the bathroom."

Mamie sat down suddenly.

"Yes, that's the way I figured it," Ramón said reluctantly. "When I talked to Maureen the night Don was arrested I was sure she knew something. I told myself then that probably it was only that she knew who did it. For a while I thought she might be protecting Peggy. Sisters will stick together sometimes even at the expense of a brother. I even thought her fingerprints might have got on the gun, taking it away from Peggy and putting it away for her, Peggy going all to pieces maybe. It seemed more logical Peggy having some reason we didn't know about for—killing him."

He pulled the handkerchief from his breast pocket and wiped the palms of his hands, unconscious of the action.

"But it was hard for it to be Peggy. She would have had to go clear to the dining room for the gun and come back. And Grueber couldn't have gone far before he was called back. No more than a few steps outside the gate. It seemed more likely that someone was waiting in the front room until

Peggy got into her bedroom."

"The only trouble is," Freeman put in judiciously, "that there doesn't seem to be any reason for the younger girl to be led into killing the man, while, as you say, Peggy was involved with him, and the Lord only knows what issues may have arisen between them. These cases where sex enters into it, you never know what to expect. People do the damnedest things. It was natural, of course, for the police to fasten on Don's motive instead of getting tangled up in something sticky like a female's emotional processes. It's nice and clean and simple, two men hating each other and getting into a fight and one shooting the other. They figure any jury can *see* that."

Mamie had sat rigid, only her eyes moving, aghast, from one man to the other, as they cold-bloodedly analyzed her daughters' possible guilt.

"You can't—" she exclaimed in a bleating voice. "I won't let you talk like this about my girls. You—you're as bad as the police. Neither one of them had any reason to kill him."

Ramón looked down at her pityingly. "No good reason, no. But, like Mr. Freeman says, people sometimes do funny things when they get—uh—upset."

Matter-of-factly he continued, "Grueber had been making a play for Maureen himself, and he dropped her unceremoniously when Peggy came back. Maureen is young, only seventeen. It flattered her to have an older man rushing her, and it hurt just so much more when he gave her the go-by."

"But that—she wouldn't, she couldn't kill a man for that!" Mamie cried.

"I don't like to talk like this in front of you, Mamie, but there's more to it." He turned away, and when he spoke again it was to Freeman, as if he wanted to forget the woman's presence.

"It goes back. Her mother has been married three times. Maureen likes me better than Grady. Her childhood—it was unsettling, two fathers before she was eight years old, and a period between with none, and she doesn't care—isn't so congenial," he corrected himself, "with her mother, and she's fond of Peggy, her only full sister, you see. And she wanted Peggy's life to be—respectable, not like Mamie's. Then Maureen thinks in dramatic terms. Most kids her age do, I guess.

"What I think happened is she decides she'll run Hank off with a gun when she catches him necking with her married sister. It'll serve two purposes: relieve her feelings over his preferring Peggy to her, and save Peggy from making a fool of herself. And then something goes wrong. He either tells her to go to hell and keep her nose out of his affairs, or he laughs at her and tells her to go back to her mud pies, or laughs and says, 'Go ahead and shoot,' and starts off. Anyhow, she loses her temper, and the first thing she knows she *has* shot him."

Mamie turned her head toward Freeman, and then, in horror, back toward Ramón.

"You're not going to tell all that to the police! Ramón, you'd send your own child to prison? And how do you know it's true?"

"It has to be," he said resignedly. "You'll see, when we talk to her, she'll admit it. All that's held her back has been fear. She doesn't want to die."

"I'll talk to her," Freeman interrupted. "Her sentence shouldn't be too heavy. She's a minor; she had serious provocation—her sister's honor involved. We'll get some psychiatrists at her. There'll be more sympathy for her than for Don. Maybe, as you say, Garcia, she only meant to threaten him. The gun might have gone off accidentally. Or she didn't know it was loaded. We'll figure out something."

"I won't let you!" Mamie cried. "You heard me. I just confessed. I'll go to the district attorney. *He'll* believe me."

"I'm afraid not, Mrs. Grady. He'd see your motive for the confession all right. A mother protecting her young. But your motive for the murder—whatever you were going to cook up—probably won't hold water."

"Mamie," Ramón pleaded, "do you want the girl to go through life with this on her conscience? She's in a bad way already. I've watched her. She's under a terrible strain. That's one reason I haven't been able to get away from it, suspecting her. She wouldn't be so tense and wrought up if it was just the worry over her brother. In some ways she's—hard. She could take it if it was a simple case of Don wrongly accused. She wouldn't feel responsible the way she does now. I don't know how it will affect her in the long run, being branded as a murderess, but we can't let Don take her punishment. And if Don did get the death sentence, I believe she'd confess anyway; and her story would be convincing, because it's true. Believe me, I don't like this either. But there's no way out that I can see."

"But if—if Don is acquitted?"

"Did you," the attorney put in sardonically, "think he was going to be when you came over here tonight?"

Mamie put out a fumbling hand and sank into the chair again. The two men were too much for her. She had never been able to hold her own, opposing men.

When Ramón opened the door to his office back at La Paloma the light was on and Maureen sat with her knees drawn up in the armchair, her little dark hat on the desk. She did not speak. Only her feverishly bright eyes greeted him.

Ramón's lips trembled, and suddenly tears were in his eyes. He held out his arms, and Maureen, with the effect of one movement, unfolded from the chair and was clinging to him. He held her tightly.

At last she moaned, her fingers clutching at his flesh through the coat, "What am I going to do? What am I going to do?"

"It's all right," he muttered ineffectually, "I'm here. I'll take care of you."

Gently he guided her back into the chair, and taking the handkerchief from his breast pocket, he wiped her face, and then placed the folds of linen in her hand.

"You've known all the time," she said in a low voice.

"Yes, I've known." He turned away, pulling a rumpled handkerchief from his hip pocket. His head averted, he wiped his eyes and blew his nose.

Maureen sat in the chair, her knees and ankles together, her hands clasped in her lap.

"I'm glad," she said. "It was too much to take alone. I thought I could tough it out. But I can't."

"I shouldn't have let you." Ramón sat down in his own chair.

"What shall I do, Papa?"

"Tomorrow we will talk to Mr. Freeman. He'll represent you."

Her eyes were dark in a face gone suddenly white with fear. "Will I— Will they kill me?"

"Of course not," he said heartily. "Freeman will play up the—uh—the psychological angles; and you're a minor. I—" He hesitated uncertainly for a second, but went on with assurance for her benefit, "They don't give the death sentence to juveniles. But"—he became grave, sincere again—"there may be punishment, Maureen. Maybe some years of your life taken away. It—well, you have to learn, baby, you can't settle things, make anything in this world right, by going it alone, taking things in your own hands."

He ceased talking, feeling tired. Her eyes had been fastened on his face, earnest, intent, yet also somewhat blankly, as if she heard with only half her intelligence.

"You have no more to worry about now, baby," he said gently. "It's all out of your hands—into mine."

She let her breath out slowly. "You know—I'm glad. It was—too much." The last word was hardly audible.

The detachment, the thin hardness of her premature sophistication was gone, and only a tired little girl remained.

"I didn't mean to kill him—not really. I was just—acting smart, I guess, making like an actress in a movie. You know—hard-boiled, warning him to stay away—at the point of a gun. And then—it went wrong—changed. He—he made fun of me, told me little girls shouldn't play with guns. I was hating him already—on account of Peggy; and all at once I was mad clear through. I pulled back on the trigger. It—it surprised me—the noise, and his falling. I didn't think it was loaded. Nobody has ever used it that I know of since it's been there in the drawer.

"I was scared stiff. But after I was safe back inside and had the gun back where it belonged and nobody even knew what had happened, I calmed down. In the morning, though, I realized I had been stupid, putting the gun back in the drawer. I should have hidden it—even thrown it out in the street. Probably it couldn't have been traced to us. But after it went off and Hank went down—just like that"—she made a little dropping gesture with her hand, and shuddered—"my mind seemed to have been blown to pieces too. I didn't really know what I was doing. When I came into the bedroom and saw Peggy getting ready for bed, just as if nothing had happened, I bucked up a little. I knew I mustn't act as if anything was—wrong. When we were in bed I did think of it, that I should get rid of the gun, but I was afraid to get up. Peggy is a light sleeper, and she might hear me and ask what I was doing. So I just huddled there under the covers. I couldn't move.

"But when they didn't find him till morning, why then I felt safe somehow. It made me feel—well, superior, knowing all about it, when the cops came and didn't know anything. Knowing what *did* happen, I never dreamed they'd blame it on somebody else. I didn't think they *could*, because I didn't think they'd have evidence against anybody."

She lifted candid eyes. "It was a funny thing. That night—after I went to bed—I was afraid for myself, that the cops would be bound to catch me for it; but after they were there that morning, and I could see they didn't know anything from the way they had to look around and ask questions, like I said, I began to feel safe. It was as if I could look down on them, because I had done something and they were too dumb to catch me."

Within himself Ramón flinched. He had mingled with many people during the course of his own struggle for advancement, characters whom people like Pauline, for instance, would consider definitely not "nice" people, for whom anything was "fair" if it was to their benefit and if they could get away with it. Boys he had known in his precarious younger days who, when they couldn't find work, were cocky over picking up a few bucks with loaded dice, or of picking them up even more forthrightly by knocking out a grocer or a service-station operator and cleaning out the till. Men in his own line of business that he was friends with today who were smug about accomplishing complicated schemes for cheating on their income tax, who entered deals as a matter of course with known gangsters and murderers, because, with a cynical shrug, they admitted they "had to play ball."

So Ramón was familiar with that look, the superior assurance of one who "gets away with it" under the nose of the police. You took it as a matter of course—until you saw the expression on the face of a seventeen-year-old girl who was your daughter and who had gotten away with murder.

While he winced under these reflections, the girl was going on:

"And then—they took Don. It's been hell ever since."

She twisted her hands together, and lifted her eyes in agonized appeal. "But I didn't—I never intended for Don to be—killed—in my place. I wouldn't have done that, Papa. You believe me, don't you? I hoped Freeman could get him off, and then no one would ever need to know. But I know now it isn't—fair. Like you said, some people would still always think he did it—"

Ramón's voice was reassuring. "Of course, honey. Of course I knew you wouldn't keep still if Don was convicted." He leaned forward a little. "There's something I want you to know. While I was at Freeman's tonight, Mamie came there."

The girl watched him dully.

"She came to confess to the murder. She meant to save Don. It had never entered her head to suspect you. I had to tell her that it—wasn't Don. And then she still wanted her 'confession' to stand. She would have gone to prison, or to death, for you too."

Maureen's eyes were wondering, and then a shade of cynicism filmed them; but as her father's eyes remained steady on her own, the cynicism faded. Slowly her face puckered.

"Poor Mom, oh, poor Mom."

Ramón released his breath in a faint, relieved sigh. "You see," he said quietly, "she loves you."

Maureen leaned her elbow on the chair arm, her head on her hand. "I've made such a mess for everybody."

Ramón rose and came to stand beside her, soothingly stroking her sleek hair, his face drawn with responsibility, a certain bafflement in his eyes, but he spoke, for her, with an air of reassuring wisdom.

"Before, you blamed the rest of us because life wasn't the way you wanted it to be, but now you mustn't go to the other extreme and blame yourself too much. We are all, your mother and I, and even, I suppose, Don's father, partly to blame too. We might all, just as you might, have done things different...."

Defeated, wearily willing to accept whatever he had to say, she leaned her head against him and did not answer.

And Ramón, futilely stroking her hair, felt dissatisfied with his own words. If they helped the girl to resignation, to a calmer facing of her fate, it was all to the good; but the man realized that himself, he did not understand. It was all very well to bring out platitudes—something like Mamie, he thought wryly; but he felt that they really answered nothing. There must be more to it.

They were all simple, fundamentally innocent people, meaning no harm, only trying to find a way to live comfortably with themselves and with other people. So why had they all wound up beaten and bruised on that one moment when Maureen's feelings, which they had all helped to create, went out of control?

THE END

THE RELUCTANT MURDERER

BY BERNICE CAREY

Chapter One

It came to me while I was reading Anne's letter. That murder was the answer.

I slipped off my glasses—as if unconsciously I wished to blur the sight of concrete objects—and gazed dimly at the pattern in the wallpaper across the room.

Although I had worried and brooded for weeks, I had never considered killing before. At first there was the sense of triumph one has when the solution to a long-vexing problem reveals itself in one miraculous, penetrating flash. But there followed a moment of revulsion. I could never bring myself to do such a thing. Although it was a solution; I could see that. And I had almost worn my brain to ribbons trying to think of a way out.

Yet who would care—after it was done? And was I to let my life be ruined because of squeamishness—or fear? It could be handled somehow while we were all there together. I should have to use the means which came most conveniently to hand. There was a poison in the tool shed which Anne used in her rose spray, and her gun which she kept for "protection" when she stayed alone at the cabin, and knives, or—even—the swimming pool, where a drowning might be contrived. A judiciously engineered fall from the upper sun deck to the rocks of the stream on the south side of the house was also a possibility.

It could be done. It had to be. Other people could be ruthless. They could have an utter indifference as to whether you lived or died. They could see you faced with starvation, and turn away with cold eyes, as long as they were well fed and had a roof to go home to. No one knew all that better than I. So why should I have qualms about protecting myself at the expense of one miserable life?

No, I would do it.

The decision once made, I felt relieved, and calm as I had not been since I discovered the spot I was in.

I put my glasses back on and reread Anne's note.

DEAR SIS:

Guess who descended on me unannounced day before yesterday. Aunt Maud! She drove up in state in the old Lincoln, complete with chauffeur and companion. Touring the state. Getting gay in her old age, it seems.

So—enny-hoo-oo—I decided the only thing little Anne could do was organize a family reunion of sorts, in celebration of this very unacccustomed honor. So be sure to hie yourself down Friday evening on the commuter. No excuses, now, I know it'll be deadly—no liquor, and smoking only in our rooms; but after all, half a million is still half a million—especially with prices like they are!

Johnny will be here, though God knows how she'll take that, with me a widow only three years. And I'm writing to ask Culbert. I told her you had run across him, and since he's seemed to be giving you a rush lately, I thought it would be nice to have him—"old friend of the family" sort of thing.

So see you Friday night, darling.

Love,
ANNE

I was putting the letter back into the envelope when my phone rang in its built-in alcove in the entrance hall. I knew before I picked it up that it would be Culbert.

"Did you get a letter from Anne?" he asked without preliminaries.

"Yes."

"You going down?"

"Of course. You're going, I suppose?"

"But natch. Can I pick you up at the office?"

"If you expect to catch the train at five-fifteen, you'd better go there right from work," I said ungraciously. Culbert has so little sense.

"I'll wait for you at the gates, then."

"If you like."

I took my overnight bag with me to work Friday and wore my new beige straw hat with a wide brim and my tan gabardine suit which is suitable for country wear. Neither Mr. Harder nor Mr. Evans was in that afternoon, so I left the office at four-fifteen to be sure to make the train on time. Not that it would have mattered if they *had* been there. I have been secretary to Mr. Harder of the architectural firm of Evans and Harder for almost fifteen years, and am allowed certain liberties. I had some doubts as to whether, without me there, Mr. Evans' stenographer, a flighty young blonde who changes her hairdress every time the styles change, and Fred, the bookkeeper, and Irma, the receptionist and filing clerk, would remain until exactly five o'clock when we close the office; but I can't *always* see to everything.

Eric Nelson came out of the room where the draftsmen work as I was lingering for a moment in the reception office. He crossed his arms, hands on his shirt sleeves above where they were rolled to the elbows, and looked me up and down whimsically.

"All set for traveling?"

I had set down my bag and was drawing on my gloves. "I'm going to my sister's for the week end."

"Well, have fun, and give her my regards."

"Thank you; I'll do that."

As I went out Irma shook back her dark hair, which she wears much too long, and said, "Gee, Miss Haines, you look spiffy. Got a heavy date?"

I smiled somewhat dryly and said, "You might call it that." There was a macabre humor in the thought of how I could have replied that I *did* have a date—with murder.

As I waited I took a look at myself in the narrow mirror in the panel between the elevators. Those girls were always pouring on the soft soap, knowing my influence with Mr. Harder and Mr. Evans, and so trying to stay on the good side of me. Not that their fawning does any good. Efficiency, not personalities, is what counts with me as far as the business is concerned.

But I saw by the glass that Irma's comment was justified. I may be forty years old, but my figure hasn't an ounce of fat on it. Even though the styles now may lean toward unbecoming bumps and billows, I still have what in the twenties we called the boyish figure, and the standards of beauty we had then are still good enough for me.

There was a taxi parked near the corner, so I took it, just to be on the safe side. Where trains are concerned I like to allow myself plenty of time. Then, too, it was more comfortable than waiting on corners for streetcars and lugging an overnight bag up and down the steps in transferring at Fourth and Market. Also, a typical San Francisco wind was swooping around the corners of Sansome Street beneath a high, light fog, and I hadn't worn a topcoat, since they are such nuisances once one is out of the Bay Area.

I settled back luxuriously on the slippery leather upholstery of the cab. It always makes me feel like a plutocrat, riding in taxis. Because, I suppose, emotionally I have never forgotten the years when, on the trail of a job, I would walk from the Embarcadero to the heart of the industrial district south of Market, considering even streetcar fare a sybaritic self-indulgence.

Culbert was at the station when I arrived, waiting with a large brown suitcase beside him in front of the iron grille which separates the trains from the waiting rooms. Culbert is a salesman for a plumbing concern with offices in the industrial district, and from the office he has only a few blocks to walk to the station at Third and Townsend.

I thought to myself as I walked up, "He *would* bring practically a small trunk."

Culbert tends to be fussy, the way so many bachelors are, and I had no doubt that he had brought everything from swimming trunks to jeans, including extra tailored slacks and sport shirts for evenings.

He smiled possessively and said, "Ah, there you are, Vivian. Let me take your bag."

"Don't be absurd, Culbert. You'll have all you can handle with your own. Anyway, *mine* is very light," I said pointedly.

I have always made a habit of traveling light. Besides my pajamas and a thin robe, and a change of underwear and a clean blouse, there were only four other garments in my bag, all part of one ensemble, in blue-and-white striped seersucker: shorts and a halter which could serve both for swimming and sun-bathing, and a skirt and bolero which buttoned on outside and made the costume suitable for general wear.

Culbert chose not to notice my restrained manner and staggered along lopsidedly—on account of his suitcase. His round face, on either side of which he wears ridiculous sand-colored sideburns, was bland and smug, and he kept talking inconsequentially as we hurried down the aisle made by the waiting trains. I felt rather conspicuous walking beside Culbert. I have always admired really *tall* men; being five eight myself, and Culbert, even with his hat on, can't be more than five nine. I told myself grimly that I should be doubly glad he *did* have his hat on—a rather youthful affair with a small feather stuck in the bow on the side—since, considering that the top of his head has no hair at all, the sideburns look even sillier without a hat.

We were early enough to get a seat on the east side of the train, away from the sun, and when we were settled comfortably, Culbert folded his hands on his stomach and, with a sidelong look, remarked, "So Aunt Maud is making you girls a visit."

"It seems so," I returned noncommittally.

"It's been years since I saw the old girl," he went on ruminatingly. "Not since she came back to Sioux City for a visit when I was just a kid fifteen or so. As I remember it, she was doing very well then. Ver-ry well."

Culbert's family, the McCauleys, had lived on the same street in Sioux City, Iowa, that my grandparents did; so naturally his and my folks had known all about each other, although I, being born and brought up in Minneapolis, had not been a childhood playmate of Culbert's.

You wouldn't suspect it, seeing Culbert today, but his father had been a Methodist minister, and a very kindly, likable soul. I remembered him from the times I visited my grandparents during summer vacations.

Culbert, in his youth, had been rather wild. That is, he didn't settle down to learning a profession. He worked for a while in Chicago and in St. Louis, and once traveled through the East, selling something. Somewhere along the line he picked up a business education, by correspondence courses, I suspect. During the war he had found his way into San Francisco, and last year he looked me up, having discovered from someone who had known my grandparents in Sioux City that I lived in San Francisco. In that respect he was like most Middle Westerners in California, especially the Iowans, who, I believe, spend half their time running down perfect strangers whose sole claim to interest lies in their once having passed through the home town back East.

Culbert had the *Call-Bulletin* under his arm, and as the train pulled out he gave up trying to be sociable and opened the paper. A woman across the aisle had her head bent over a twenty-five-cent Pocket Book, and I saw the word "*Death*" in yellow letters on the cover. Her fingers covered the rest of the title, but there was a knife with great blobs of vermilion dripping off it, like balloons. It reminded me of my purpose for the week end.

I have never cared for detective stories, and for a moment I regretted it. If I had read more of them I might now be familiar with different means of doing away with people. I am not one to leave things to the last minute, nor to be vague about my plans; but somehow I had put off really getting down to business on working this thing out. After all, one has a natural reluctance about taking human life.

I looked out across the choppy greenish-gray water of the bay as we pulled out of the city and forced myself to concentrate. First of all, I must be sure not to get caught. Something that would pass for an accident; that was best.

But it might be hard to arrange. There was Anne's gun; but guns make noise, which would bring people running, perhaps before I could get away. My eyes wandered to the knife on the book cover. A butcher knife from the kitchen, and the thing done quietly during the night—the throat cut, perhaps. But here again was a difficulty. With so many of us there, people would be doubling up to sleep. Alibis would enter in, and I might be singled out as having none. You never knew who might be enjoying insomnia.

I hate loose ends, but it looked as if I were going to have to leave it to chance, watching and waiting for the right opportunity.

We were beginning to hit the stations down the Peninsula—Burlingame, San Mateo, Belmont—and Culbert folded his paper.

"Want to look at the news?" he inquired affably, offering me the paper.

"No, thank you. Anyhow, I don't care for sensational sheets like the *Call-Bulletin*. I read the *Chronicle*," I informed him.

He chuckled comfortably and observed, "Guess we'll have to take two papers after we're married," and glanced at me coyly.

"You going to start that again?" I said.

"Can't think of a better time. Come on, Viv, how about setting the date? We could break the news this week end while all the family's together."

I started to speak and then I pursed my lips a little and narrowed my eyes at the grove of live oaks we were passing. Maybe— After all, why not? It might help to throw off suspicion, if any came to rest on me. No one would think that a woman who had just become engaged to be married would have murder in her heart.

"We-ell, if you insist," I murmured. "I suppose we have to be definite about it sometime."

"Attagirl," he beamed, and patted my hand.

"Culbert!" I reproved sharply, withdrawing my arm. "Not in public."

"That's one of the things I like about you. Modest. A person doesn't run across a real lady like you every day."

"I guess I know how to behave," I retorted.

"How about next Saturday?" he prodded. "Now that you've finally decided to take the plunge, there's no real reason to wait any longer."

I suppose I could have pleased him by agreeing, but everyone knows I am not one to rush into things, and someone *might* think it was funny—after what would happen this week end—if they knew I had uncharacteristically promised to take only a week to prepare for marriage.

"Nobody," I said coldly, "could get ready for their wedding in a week. Since both of us have lived this long without being married, we can take a decent time about it. I have my vacation next month. We'll do it then."

"That's O.K. with me. Tell you what I'll do: I'll see if I can't get Bellows to trade vacation time with me and take his in August when mine comes up. Then we can have a real honeymoon, go to Yosemite maybe. Or— No!" He snapped his fingers, and his face lighted up. "We could run down to San Diego and visit Aunt Maud. It might please the old girl."

"We'll do nothing of the kind. Seeing her once a year is all I can stand. You needn't worry," I said tartly, "about keeping on the good side of her. Anne and I divide her money equally when she dies. We're her only living relatives, and she's told us point-blank that that's the way her will stands. And if you knew Aunt Maud better, you'd realize she's not the type who changes her mind. There's absolutely no use in making up to her in the hope that she'll give us a bigger share than Anne."

Culbert looked pained. "Vivian, how can you think I had any such idea? I only thought it would be an—uh—a *friendly* thing to do."

"Don't worry about Aunt Maud needing cheering up. She's happy as a clam with her carrot juice and her dried figs and her blue auras and her vibrations and her *very* peculiar conception of God."

"She's a strange person, isn't she?" Culbert said musingly.

Chapter Two

Any northern Californian knows that the southern part of the state is populated almost exclusively by screwballs, and I do believe Aunt Maud is the epitome of southern California crackpotism.

Not that she isn't shrewd. You don't start with ten thousand dollars left you by your parents when you're over forty years old and run it up, through investments in real estate, to around five hundred thousand, unless you know your way around. Aunt Maud, it seemed, had only to put a payment down on a stretch of empty sand dunes, and they turned out to be a fashionable beach resort, or buy a bare sidehill outside San Diego, and in five years it was choice residential property.

The part of Grandpa's "estate" which came to my parents was only four thousand dollars, for he left the bulk of his property to Maud, who had stayed at home all those years.

Papa died of a heart attack the following year, and by the time Mamma passed away three years later the money had simply been soaked up into old debts and hospital bills and the expense of educating two girls, so that Anne and I, after the funeral expenses, had only our fares to California and enough cash to live on for a few weeks until I should find work.

When the Depression hit in 1929, Aunt Maud didn't have her money in stocks. No indeed. Her assets were in cold cash in the Bank of America, and right through the terrible early thirties, when I myself was let out of one office after another until I finally got set with Evans and Harder, Aunt Maud was quietly buying apartment courts and duplexes which their desperate owners were disposing of for a song. Until now, as Anne had remarked, she was worth easily half a million.

Aunt Maud had never been what you would call "in business." She was something like the old-fashioned horse trader, operating independently and sporadically.

It had been during and since the war that Aunt Maud really cleaned up, unloading property at exorbitant prices, keeping only an apartment house and a couple of motor courts off whose rent she could live in more than comfort. She had, it seemed, grown tired of the dickering of buying and selling, and had "retired" to devote her thoughts to spiritual matters and to "enjoying" herself in ways like this trip to Anne's. During the winter, complete with limousine, chauffeur, and companion, she had spent a month at Palm Springs; and in a recent letter she had spoken of contemplated trips to Yellowstone Park and the Grand Canyon.

In the past Aunt Maud's various "deals" had made the services of a secretary necessary, and she had employed a succession of young women in that capacity. Usually they had lived at her house and had been a combination of stenographer, errand girl, and door mat. My guess was that the present "companion," Miss Pringle, carried on in at least the latter two functions. I had gathered from Aunt Maud's letters that she was an older, more settled person than the previous "secretaries," who had an annoying habit of getting married or just plain quitting.

Sometimes, thinking of Aunt Maud and the way she turned the Depression to account, I feel that life can be very unfair. For those lean years changed the whole course of my life. I was engaged in 1930, and Dwight and I would normally have been married that year or the next; but he lost his job and never did get another—not while I knew him, anyway—and people just don't marry in those circumstances. He had a roof over his head with his folks, but they couldn't take me in too, and so—well, the whole thing petered out and we drifted apart.

Never, until I die, shall I forget those years. After our folks died in the twenties, Anne and I had come West, young and full of hope and eager for adventure of a respectable kind.

Sensible girls, I suppose, would have retired to the protection of their rich aunt's wing when they saw how things were going. But we had pride, for one thing; and for another, we preferred starvation to giving up the control of our lives in payment for our keep. Aunt Maud is the type who, without giving it a thought, would manage you right out of your individuality if you let her, and when a person is supporting you, the tendency is to let them.

I had a good commercial education, and Anne was out of high school. For a while we lived together in a furnished room, and then Anne started to business college. Aunt Maud gave her the tuition outright; but as things tightened up more and more, Anne got a place with a well-to-do family on Jackson Street, working for her room and board till she finished school. Of course she couldn't get a job when she finished her course in 1931, so she stayed on with these people as a mere servant. It meant food, at least.

As for me, there were times when I just didn't eat—no more than one meal a day, anyway, and that of crackers and milk. Once when the landlady wouldn't wait any longer for her room rent, I wrote Aunt Maud and borrowed a hundred dollars. Every once in a while she would send Anne a five-dollar bill, which was all that enabled the kid to have clothes on her back. Aunt Maud was always rather partial to Anne—God knows why, for Anne is everything the old woman disapproves of. Maybe that's why she leans her way, because Anne represents all the things that Aunt Maud has repressed in her own nature.

One thing about the Depression made its mark on me. I could stand the being hungry, the mended underclothes and the last year's hat, and even the uncertainty about the roof over my head; but one thing I could not stand, and which I determined never to go through again, no matter what I had to do to escape it, was being the underdog. The insults—from landladies, personnel managers, from old employees who knew their jobs would last as long as the company did, and who treated the hungry typist, who would probably be let out next week, as if she were dirt under their feet, from the bosses who would as soon fire you as look at you, who often took it for granted that by giving you a few days' work they had also tacitly hired you to sleep with them if they felt so inclined.

No one would ever take advantage of me again if I could help it. Someday I was going to be on top of the heap. Independent. *I* would tell other people what to do—not they me. No more whips should be snapped over my back.

And sometime, I knew, Aunt Maud's money would put me there. Safe. Having to take orders from *nobody*.

After her rough start in the world, Anne had been lucky. When times picked up a little, she finally got a stenographer's job in an office downtown. One of the boss's sons was playing around in a minor position, learning the business; and he fell in love with Anne and married her, just like something in a book. Some people have always thought Anne was prettier than I, and of course she is five years younger; but I've always felt that where she has the edge on me is that she has so much *brass*, putting on a big smile and an "Aren't you wonderful!" air, and pushing right in whether people wanted her or not.

Anyhow, she and Tony were getting along fine, owned a fancy five-room apartment in a new building on Telegraph Hill, and him drawing down a big salary; and then the war came, and he went in—as a lieutenant, of course; and Anne just about went crazy, working: Women's Volunteer Services, Red Cross, bond drives, Stage Door Canteen, and I don't know what all. I told her she was doing too much, losing weight and looking pale; but, sentimental, the way she often is, she just grinned and said, "I have to, Sis. Everything I do here to help the war effort will help bring Tony home that much quicker."

But he never got home. He was killed in the final drive on Germany.

The Everetts, Tony's family, had a country home in the Santa Cruz Mountains above Los Gatos, and Anne went down to stay for a while with his parents, who were practically retired and spent most of their time in the country. Tony left her well fixed with insurance and some cash which they had put by, but I must say I was surprised when she phoned me from her apartment one day about a month after the news about Tony came and told me she was selling the apartment in town and buying a mountain cabin a few miles from the Everetts' place and intended to live there alone.

We lunched together downtown that day, and I will say she looked bad, no color and circles under her eyes.

She lifted her hands and let them drop to the cloth on either side of her plate and said wearily, "I'm so tired, Viv. You know how it's been ever since the war started. I've gone like a madwoman—committees for this, drives for that, going out to something or other every night. And always the worry about Tony. And now that he's not coming back, I feel as if I never wanted to see San Francisco again. You've no idea what it's like down there—so beautiful, so quiet, and, above all, so peaceful."

"But what will you do with yourself? You'll die of loneliness."

"No. Tony's folks are there a lot, and I've met people through them. The kind of people who'll do me good. They know how to live. They take time to enjoy their gardens, and their dogs, and just visiting around and sitting in the sun."

"Anybody'd think you were about eighty," I snapped. "You wait, you'll get good and sick of that lazy life."

Of course I should have known about Anne. She didn't get tired of it, and she didn't have a lazy life. After a few months, when she did get rested and take on a little weight and a good tan, she began to stir around. First of all she remodeled and redecorated the house she had bought, and changed the landscaping all around, doing most of the digging and planting herself; and before a year was out she had the place full of guests every week end.

One Sunday when I was there I asked her point-blank how long the money Tony had left her was going to hold out, and she grinned and said, "Not much longer, probably."

"Well, if you don't marry a rich man, or if Aunt Maud doesn't kill herself pretty soon with those crazy diets of raw peanuts and chopped olives, you'll have to do something. You can't live on scenery, or keep this place up on it either, for that matter."

At that time she had just put in a cement swimming pool. She laughed and held up her hands with the nails she kept neat and short but highly polished. "See these? They earned my living for me once, and they can do it again, if it becomes necessary."

I sniffed and told her right out, "You have no sense. You should have invested your money instead of living it up."

"Well, I'm having fun while it lasts," she said lightly. "Some people *never* have any fun, even with thousands wisely invested."

Even buried on a mountainside, she knew lots of men. Anne always did have men hanging around. So I had expected it would be only a matter of time till she snagged one with money. But instead of that she got mixed up with Johnny.

I got his number the first time I ever saw him, lounging around on her fancy outdoor furniture in sloppy slacks and huaraches, and no shirt—so he could show off his muscles and his nice, evenly browned skin, and the black hair on his chest. If she made it permanent with him, it was Anne who would provide the wherewithal for living.

He was, it seemed, going to be the next John Steinbeck, or maybe it was William Saroyan—I forget which. He had a shack two ravines over from Anne's house, and I judged that he was at that time living off his discharge pay from the Army and his unemployment insurance. She had known him for a year now, and to my knowledge he hadn't done a day's work in all that time. I figured he got by, by eating most of his meals at Anne's.

Of course any moment he was due for the big break. He spent all his time, Anne said—that is, when he wasn't helping her in the yard or repainting her guest rooms—writing novels and short stories. I asked her how many he'd sold and she admitted he hadn't actually *sold* any but that he'd had some things printed, and then she dragged out a little pile of magazines from the cupboard under the bookshelves. Personally, *I* had never heard of any of them, and I doubt if anybody else with any sense ever had either. And I told her bluntly, after I read two or three of Johnny's masterpieces, that if he expected to make a living with things like *that*, he might as well forget the whole thing right now. All the characters seemed to be mentally unbalanced, and I told her so; but she said no, they weren't really crazy, they just reflected the tensions and anxieties of our times.

Chapter Three

We were getting close to the station in Los Gatos, and I straightened my hat and pulled on my gloves. Culbert had fallen asleep with his mouth open, so I nudged him, and he started and blinked.

"Must have dozed off," he said stupidly, and I told him he'd slept soundly ever since we left Menlo Park.

Anne was standing alone on the platform, watching the train's doors as we pulled in; and for a minute I actually didn't recognize her.

I let her kiss me and then I stood back and just looked. "Anne Haines," I demanded (I can't get used to her being Anne Everett), "what happened to your hair?"

She giggled and touched it. "You don't like it?"

"*Like* it!"

"It's the last word. I read about it in a magazine. I had to go clear to San Jose to find a shop that would do it for me."

It was ghastly, that's all, ghastly. She'd been wearing her hair perfectly straight and pulled down over her ears and tied with a ribbon in the back so that a little tail hung down between her shoulder blades, which was hideous enough; but now it was gray, and I don't mean gray like decently natural gray hair, but a sort of bluish hue, like a light Maltese kitten. She had on a straight gray linen dress with no top except pink shoulder straps, and a pink leather belt, and pink sandals over bare feet; and it gave a person the weirdest feeling, the dress and her hair and her eyes almost exactly matching, and her mouth and her belt and shoes the same color.

"What," I inquired coldly, "did Aunt Maud say about your hair?"

"She didn't say. In fact, I doubt if she noticed. She started to commune with nature right off. She seemed to read some religious significance into the redwoods. They symbolized something—I don't remember what; but she and Miss Pringle—oh, wait till you see Miss Pringle!—all they did was stand on the sun deck and coo at the trees."

While I stood speechless at the sight of her hair, Anne had said hello to Culbert and squeezed his arm in welcome, and he had gibbered something complimentary, gazing at her fatuously. She linked her arms in ours, one on either side of her.

"You're being met in style, I want you to know," she announced with a bubbling sound in her voice. "My old coupé wouldn't do. Aunt Maud insisted that Alphonse—cross my heart, that's really his name—drive me down to get you in the Lincoln."

Looking down the line of cars, I had already recognized it. Aunt Maud's had the limousine for a good twenty years.

"It's a wonder," I said, "we didn't notice it as the train pulled in. It makes the other cars look like its litter."

Alphonse was a nondescript man of about fifty, wearing a chauffeur's uniform and cap, and he stood by the door to the tonneau of the heavy car, waiting to admit us.

"This is my sister, Miss Haines, and our friend, Mr. McCauley, Alphonse," Anne said brightly, and he bowed and touched his cap with dignity.

Inside the car Anne whispered to us, "I never know what to say to a chauffeur. Why, even Tony's folks don't have one."

"If I could afford it, I'd have one," Culbert chuckled. "I've always had a champagne appetite and a beer pocketbook."

"Aunt Maud," Anne volunteered, "asked you to excuse her for not coming down too; but the hour before dinner, it seems, is sacred to meditation. When we left, she and Miss Pringle were stretched out on chaise lounges on the upper sun deck, meditating like mad."

"Sounds restful," Culbert observed.

"I don't know. They seem to make such work out of all these—observances. She practically needs a timekeeper to keep track of the hours for rest and the hours for prayer and the hours for tomato juice. If she comes up with one more hour, I'll collapse."

From a clinical point of view, Aunt Maud's religious philosophy is an interesting study. She started out with sound fundamentalist views based strictly on the Bible, with a strong Calvinistic slant. She still, theoretically anyway, has the Puritan view that anything that gives physical pleasure is inherently sinful. However, as she went along, especially after emigrating to southern California, she proceeded to pick up whatever aspects appealed to her in the various cults she ran across, incorporating these points willy-nilly into the body of belief she already held, until now you are likely to run across dashes of Rosicrucianism, Christian Science, and even a soupçon of Aimee Semple McPherson in her over-all philosophy.

Apparently with no conflict at all, she has also an almost pagan obsession with bodily well-being, and has tried out every health fad she ever heard about, and a few that she figured out all by herself. Sometimes it is complicated calisthenics and going about in barefoot sandals; and once she even embraced nudism for a while, not as a social practice, but strictly in the solitude of her own roof top in San Diego. A sort of deistic attitude toward the sun accompanied this phase. As for diets, you never know whether she will be on a system that calls for nothing but raw meat or one that calls for all foods having the life cooked out of them and then being mashed up into a mess worse than baby food.

You can see why Anne and I didn't flock to our aunt when Papa died, but preferred going it on our own, even if it meant poverty.

Even with Alphonse's careful thirty-miles-an-hour speed, it didn't take long to get up to Anne's house which looked east over high slopes that couldn't seem to make up their minds whether they wanted to be redwood forests or open range. The old chariot mounted heavily along the narrow road made dim by the towering evergreen trees and turned into the graveled square made by the back wall of the living room and the garage which jutted out to the road.

Anne's house is, in my opinion, an architectural monstrosity. It was originally covered by redwood siding, but its flat-roofed descending squares made Anne think of a cliff dwelling, so she had it stuccoed in a dirty tan so that now it has a vaguely Aztec look more suitable to the desert than to a steep, wooded mountainside.

From the road where we pulled up one enters directly into the long, narrow living room to face a completely windowed wall, outside which lies the upper sun deck which is actually the roof of the first story of the house. To the left on this top floor are Anne's bedroom and bath, opening off the living room. A stair well descends from the northeast corner of the living room to a central hall below which leads into the kitchen on the left and to a dining room in the middle of the first floor, with a narrow corridor running off behind the dining room to connect with two small bedrooms on the south side of the house. The whole east side of this lower floor also opens onto another terrace, this one floored by flat stones, with a barbecue pit and a long picnic table at the end near the kitchen. An outside stairway in the center connects the two sun decks.

Below the house the ground falls away steeply in terraces held by rock retaining walls and planted with the brilliant cerise flowers known as ice plants. An earth path outlined by stones leads down in wide, shallow steps to the swimming pool, and at the bottom of the canyon a row of redwood trees shuts the property in like a serrated brownish-green wall. On windy days it is fascinating and rather soporific to sit on one of the sun decks looking off into the pointed tops of the trees swaying in a sort of stately dance.

To the north a tangle of madrones and maples and buckeye trees clothes the gentle slope against which the house seems to huddle, and to the south the grounds fall steeply from the walls to the bouldered stream overhung with giant sycamores. A steep wooden stairway with side rails descends from the lower sun deck to the bed of the stream through a clutter of Scotch broom and toyon bushes. Along the house, leading from the wooden stairway to the graveled parking lot by the road, an irregular dirt path is cut into the sidehill.

To one standing by the swimming pool, or down by the stream, looking up, the place has a rather dizzying effect, like gigantic steps climbing the hill. After a few days at Anne's you begin to feel like a mountain goat, always going up or down to get where you want to be.

It was no surprise when Johnny threw open the wide, heavy door into the living room and stepped out on the narrow stone-floored porch to welcome us, which he did as if he were already Anne's husband, a position I had no doubt he intended to occupy as soon as she could resign herself to accepting the loss of Tony.

He showed most of his teeth, which did look nice and white against his tan, and came toward me with his hands out. I knew what he was up to. He always did his best to worm his way further into a position of "member of the family," and kissing "Sis" when she arrived was one of the maneuvers; so I backed up and held out one hand at the length of my arm, and he was forced into merely shaking hands.

He slapped Culbert on the shoulder and pumped his arm, and ushered us all into the house, including Anne.

I started to turn back to the car for my bag, but Anne nudged me. "Alphonse will bring the luggage," she said *sotto voce* and winked. "Mustn't let on that we aren't used to service."

"Aunt Maud's out on the sun deck," Johnny informed us.

The middle windows across the room are hinged like doors, and they stood open to the now cool and shaded deck, where I could see Aunt Maud and a middle-aged person lying back in padded lounge chairs with white-painted steel frames.

As we trooped across the living room Aunt Maud modestly put her feet on the floor and smoothed out her dotted Swiss dress in which even the dots were white, and rose to meet us, looking distinguished and composed, with her white hair coiled on top of her head, the front puffed into the suggestion of a pompadour.

"Here they are," Johnny announced gaily, but Aunt Maud might neither have heard nor seen him for all the notice she took. She came straight at me, inspecting me keenly with her small gray eyes behind rimless glasses. After we had brushed our cheeks together in a polite gesture of kinfolkly kissing, she held her head very straight on her slight, square shoulders and, looking up at me, declared flatly, "You don't look well around the eyes. You look strained, not in harmony with the positive vibrations of the cosmos."

"I came straight from work," I retorted, trying however to sound affable. "I suppose I'm tired."

"The mind and body properly attuned to one another never feel tired," she stated positively, but with an air of quoting.

She turned her attention on Culbert next, and he smiled deferentially and extended his hand. "You probably don't remember me, Miss Twilliger; I'm Reverend McCauley's son, your old neighbor in Sioux City."

She shook his hand firmly. "I knew who you were. Anne told me you were coming." She inspected him frankly and informed Culbert, "You take after your mother—inclined to put on weight. Remind me to give you a copy of a diet I got from a friend in Los Angeles. It was particularly worked out for people of your glandular type."

Culbert smiled valiantly and muttered some kind of appreciative response. I didn't smile outright but my lips twisted a little. Culbert is sensitive about his tendency to pudginess, and one is expected to consider him merely muscular and athletic, not plump.

All in all, the visit was starting off well. I had already deduced that Aunt Maud has estimated Johnny and found him wanting, and while she seemed to be favorably inclined toward Culbert, it was obviously going to be amusing watching him squirm under her outspoken analyses of his character and physical attributes.

Miss Pringle had been standing modestly beside her chair, and now Aunt Maud turned and summoned her.

"Miss Pringle."

The companion stepped forward in a manner which made you feel she was backing away, even though you could *see* her moving toward you. She held her head a little to one side, with her chin down, and while I nodded and smiled as Aunt Maud introduced her, I was again inwardly amused; for my aunt's shadow was indeed almost a replica of her employer. Her graying ash-blond hair was also coiled on top of her head, and she too wore white, although Miss Pringle's dress was straight and skimpy and made of rayon, while Aunt Maud's dotted Swiss was full, blousing above a belt and sort of gathered below it. It was obvious that Aunt Maud had picked up a little gem in Miss Pringle, a yes-woman who would never think of entertaining the least little opinion until she had verified it by hearing it first from Aunt Maud's lips.

Anne excused herself to go downstairs and see to dinner. I offered to help, but Johnny jovially forestalled me.

"Now, Sis, you just stretch out in a comfortable chair and relax. I'm the

best little helper-outer you ever saw. We'll have things ready in no time."
And he cheerily followed Anne down the outside staircase.

I knew they would pause for a quick highball before they called the rest
of us, and I myself could have used the lift a drink would have given me.
But I sat down in a cushioned chair and smiled inanely at my aunt, taking off my hat and laying it on the wrought-iron table beside me.

"I'll have to go and wash up before dinner," I said, "but I'll rest a bit first.
I should have asked Anne where she intends to put me. I suppose your
chauffeur took our bags down the back stairs."

"I suppose," Aunt Maud said indifferently, "you and Anne will sleep in
one of those cubbyholes she calls bedrooms downstairs. Miss Pringle and
I are in her room up here. It was fortunate Anne had twin beds in her
room."

"Wasn't it?" I said drily. So it was just as I had thought. Everybody doubled up. Probably Culbert and the chauffeur would have to share the room
with bunk beds, and Anne and I would have the other downstairs, in which
there was about two feet of space to spare between the double bed and the
one dresser.

Aunt Maud was continuing to study me minutely from the position she
had resumed in the reclining chair, a cushion stuck into the small of her
back so that she sat upright with her feet, in neat, white-laced oxfords, out
in front of her. She always had this embarrassing way of looking people
over—as if she had a right to pronounce judgment on them.

"The older you get, Vivian," she said abruptly, and not approvingly, "the
more you look like your aunt Evelyn."

Culbert chuckled. "I noticed that myself. As a boy I knew your whole family, you know."

I gave him a dirty look, but he only gazed back at me blandly.

It had been a surprise having Aunt Maud pop out with her sister Evelyn's name. I had heard her mention Evelyn no more than half a dozen
times in my life. I wondered suddenly if time were softening Aunt Maud,
but the asperity of her next words dispelled that idea.

"Let us hope that you resemble her only in looks."

She squinted her eyes at me and went on thoughtfully, "There's someone else you remind me of. I notice it more as you get older. But I can't
place it. It's very annoying."

"Someone on her father's side of the family, maybe," Culbert observed
helpfully.

"No-o. No, it's an odd thing, but there isn't a Haines trait in Vivian. You
take Anne, now. The shape of her eyes. The lower lid straight, and the upper curved so her eyes look like half-moons, and her chin, very oval, almost pointed. Your father's was like that. Unbecoming in a man, I always
thought, showed something of a *feminine* streak."

"How do you like Anne's place?" I broke in as she paused, and I waved toward the slope which climbed to the sky in the east, the fringe of eucalyptus on the crest touched with rosy, golden light by the sun, which had already sunk behind the hills on the other side of the house.

"A truly inspiring spot," Aunt Maud said solemnly. "One *feels* the beneficent forces of nature here—"

While she went on to describe the effect the scenery was having upon her psyche, I let my mind wander, and it came back to the reference to Evelyn. *I* knew I looked a little like her, but Aunt Maud had never mentioned it before, and I was surprised that she was even willing to recognize a resemblance to her younger sister who had died during the influenza epidemic of 1918.

Evelyn had been the pretty, the popular one of the three Twilliger girls, of whom Aunt Maud and Myrtle, my mother, were the other two. Aunt Maud, according to the old family photographs, had been good-looking enough; but it seems she had never had the beaux, as they called them in those days, that the other two girls had. She was always a prim, exceedingly proper young woman, with, as I have said, strict religious attitudes. I suppose all this had a dampening effect on the ardor of young males, who probably weren't much different then, fundamentally, than they are today.

Aunt Maud was almost thirty when she had her first really serious love affair; that is, she began to keep company with a young man who had come to Sioux City from somewhere in Pennsylvania to work in a big farm machinery establishment downtown. No engagement had been announced, but everyone understood that there was an "understanding."

My mother was already married and living in Minneapolis, where my father was an accountant for a firm of grain distributors; and Evelyn was staying with my folks that winter, taking some courses at the University of Minnesota, a rather daring project for the young woman of 1907. When Evelyn came home for the summer she met Aunt Maud's beau, Henry Sanford, for the first time. I don't suppose either of them really meant to do it in the first place, but in a few weeks Henry and Evelyn were head over heels in love. It was an awkward situation, to say the least. Henry couldn't suddenly drop Aunt Maud like a hot potato. Apparently he decided to break it off gradually; but whatever else she is, Aunt Maud was never stupid, and by August she had tumbled to what was going on under her nose. It was, of course, not Henry, but Evelyn, whom she turned on. Evelyn apparently had more spunk than was good for her, because when Aunt Maud got abusive about people "stealing" other people's fiancés, Evelyn came right back at her and admitted she loved Henry and declared she was *glad* he also cared for her. Apparently the two girls raised so much hell at home that Grandpa decided they had better be separated, so Evelyn was shipped back to her sister Myrtle in Minneapolis.

Probably the lovers would have married in a few months, after everyone had had time to cool off; but early in September, Henry Sanford was killed by a runaway when he was out driving in a horse and buggy one Sunday afternoon with a young man friend.

When Evelyn came home to attend the funeral, Aunt Maud locked the door of her bedroom and refused to come out the whole time Evelyn was there. For Aunt Maud went simply wild when Henry was killed. Her feelings toward the pretty younger sister developed in one leap from outraged resentment to blind hatred. Evelyn became responsible, somehow, not only for Henry's emotional defection, but for his death. If it hadn't been for Evelyn, he wouldn't have been out driving with another man, but would have been sitting, that fatal Sunday afternoon, quietly and safely, on the Twilliger front porch with Aunt Maud.

So Evelyn returned to stay with her sister and brother-in-law in Minneapolis. My grandparents were sensible people, and they quietly kept the two sections of their family separated for that whole winter, at the end of which, incidentally, I was born. There was no visiting back and forth between the girls in Minneapolis and the parents and Aunt Maud in Sioux City.

Evelyn did come home early the next summer, for a week, but she went right back to Minneapolis at the end of it, finding the atmosphere in her old home too frigid for comfort; and soon she went to work as a private tutor for wealthy people whose children were too stupid to pass examinations without assistance outside the schoolroom.

Maud and Evelyn never spoke to one another again throughout the ten years that Evelyn lived after that.

You can see why it was not altogether pleasing to have Aunt Maud see a resemblance to Evelyn in me. I had no wish to become associated in her mind with the sister she hated. If she ever took it into her head that I was like Evelyn in more ways than appearance, it would be disastrous for me. For there is no law against people changing their wills, and little rhyme or reason sometimes in their doing so.

Chapter Four

When I finally found a suitable pause in Aunt Maud's monologue, I rose and excused myself to wash up for dinner. I used the inside stairs. There is a strip of carpeting on them, so my descent was noiseless, and when I came to the lower steps I could see into the kitchen, whose door to the hallway was open. Johnny and Anne were locked together kissing each other, motionlessly but apparently enthusiastically. My lips tightened, and I wondered to myself how Anne could be such a fool. Having married well once, one would have thought she'd have brains enough to do so again.

I turned and went down the hall without calling myself to their attention. Through the open double doors from the hall to the dining room I could see out through the also open French windows leading to the terrace, and I noted that Alphonse was sitting in a low chair stroking Rover's head.

Anne named her dog Rover in memory of Grandpa Twilliger's old pet, for he is the same type we had been familiar with in childhood, the kind of dog one still sees on farms in the Middle West, part shepherd, part collie, part—judging from his galumphing size and shaggy light-brown-and-white coat—Saint Bernard.

My bag was in the first bedroom, as I had expected. I took off my jacket and went into the narrow bathroom between the downstairs bedrooms, its one door opening into the hall, and washed my hands and ran my comb—gently, so they wouldn't have to be taken down—through the two pompadour rolls which rise away from my side parting.

After dusting my face with powder and brightening my lipstick I came out of the bedroom door and almost ran into Culbert, who was on his way to the end bedroom.

He halted and accosted me in a low voice. "How about us announcing our engagement after dinner tonight while we're all at the table?"

I wondered briefly why he was so anxious to make our betrothal public, but decided he thought the more definite it was made, the more likely I was not to back out.

I smiled, in amusement, although Culbert apparently took it to indicate softness; for he patted my arm and said, "Do you want to tell them, or shall I?"

"You'd better. I—well, I might feel embarrassed."

I smiled at him kindly and went on. It was, of course, best to tell them soon. Then I could seize the first opportunity to commit murder, with everybody thinking that such an act would be the furthest thing from the mind of a happily engaged girl.

Anne was alone in the kitchen, putting the last bits of radish into a combination salad. I offered to help, but she said everything was ready and that Johnny was finishing the table-setting out on the terrace. With daylight-saving time, it was still light enough to eat out of doors.

She lowered her voice to me. "I've been having Alphonse eat with the rest of us. I just couldn't feed the poor man alone, even if he is her servant. The first day I told Aunt Maud that was the way I was going to do it. She said he'd think it odd eating with the family, but I just told her I wasn't equipped for a servants' hall. *I* think she likes having people to order around, and she doesn't want anything to give them the idea they aren't her inferiors. But"—Anne opened her eyes wide at me—"what could *I* do? And Johnny thought it was all right—and, after all, with his background, if he thinks it's O.K.—"

"I suppose Johnny's background included whole platoons of servants?"

She put three fingers to the side of her mouth, like a little girl caught in a slip. "Oh dear," she said, flustered. "I shouldn't have said that. Forget it, will you, Sis?"

I looked at her sharply, wondering what kind of fantastic yarn that ne'er-do-well had been feeding her.

Aunt Maud said grace before we fell to on the dinner Anne had prepared. The companion and our aunt partook only of the salad—without dressing—the rye bread, and the fresh strawberries—without sugar and cream; but the rest of us also had corn fritters and deviled eggs, which Anne had thought might pass Aunt Maud's dietary censorship. Alphonse, stolidly, but with passable manners, ate everything that was passed to him and discreetly entered the conversation only when someone addressed him directly. The someone was usually Anne. I personally considered it unnecessary to annoy our potential benefactor by failing to observe her servant's "place." Fortunately he excused himself after the strawberries. I really didn't relish having the hired help participating in what one might call my "announcement party."

Culbert thoughtlessly started to pull out his package of cigarettes when we had finished eating, but I caught his eye and glared, and he got the idea, and looking scared at the thought of the lapse he had almost committed, he shoved the pack hastily back into his pocket. Aunt Maud considers the use of tobacco not only harmful to the body, which would be enough reason for her condemning it, but also immoral. Although the people who wrote the Bible did not explicitly prohibit smoking, she is sure they would have if they had thought of it.

As soon as Culbert found a convenient break in the flow of family reminiscences in which Anne had engaged Aunt Maud, he said with playful joviality, "Vivian and I would like to have your attention for a moment. This seemed like as good a time as any to take you into our confidence, now while we're all together like this."

He beamed at me patronizingly, and I lowered my eyes modestly, with a smile which I was irritatedly sure was turning out to look like a simper.

Everyone was regarding him blankly, as if unable to make themselves guess the obvious conclusion to these coy introductory remarks.

"I've finally persuaded Vivian to say 'yes,'" he informed them with an inclusive smile.

Anne spoke first, her voice low and breathless. "Vivian—really?"

I met her eyes, a faint smile on my lips. "Don't you think it's about time

I took the fatal step?"

"Yes, but—I— Well, I just never expected—"

"Well, say," Johnny chortled, "I think that's swell. Congratulations, old man." And, half standing, he reached across the table and shook hands with Culbert.

As a gesture of deference, Anne had set Aunt Maud at the head of the table. In the growing twilight I saw my aunt staring down at me with her eyes slightly narrowed, her face expressionless.

As usual, she spoke what was in her mind. "Are you in love with him, Vivian?"

I moistened my lips, angered and taken aback, although I had tried to be prepared for whatever attitude she might take, knowing her unpredictability.

"One doesn't usually become engaged if one isn't in love," I said gently.

"No, not usually," she said slowly. She turned her face toward Culbert and, after a thoughtful scrutiny, said, "Well, I suppose it's all right. Goodness knows, you're both old enough to know what you're doing."

Only then did Miss Pringle feel free to begin twittering little well-wishing sentiments.

Anne, still seeming a bit dazed, led the way in asking the usual questions about when the happy event was to take place and if we were going on a honeymoon. Finally I broke it up by offering to wash the dishes. The Pringle person insisted on helping me, so after the table was cleared Anne went out to sit with her guests on the terrace. Johnny built a fire in the barbecue pit, and they sat in the dusk, Aunt Maud with a shawl over her shoulders, looking off at the opposite mountains darkening against a mauve sky.

I had other things to think about than chitchat with my aunt's companion; but we couldn't just stand there picking up china and setting it down, so I observed conversationally, "It's rather confining, isn't it, working for my aunt?"

"In a way. That is"—she murmured a deprecating laugh—"my time is seldom my own. But it's very pleasant, being with Miss Twilliger."

"What of your own friends and family? You aren't able to have much contact with them, are you?"

"Well, you see, I haven't any family, aside, you might say"—her small laugh twittered again—"from Miss Twilliger's home. And she allows my friends to call at the house. And, occasionally, if we haven't anything in particular planned, I have a chance to run out and see friends."

It sounded deadly, and I thought to myself that one would have to be pretty desperate financially to enter voluntarily into this virtual slavery.

I glanced at the little woman speculatively. She wasn't decrepit yet. She could have held down a regular job, say in a store, and been able to have some private life. But then I realized that anything like that would be harder while one did work, and that there wasn't much physical exertion to being Aunt Maud's stooge, and she did get to go nice places, like up here and to Palm Springs. And probably Aunt Maud would leave her a little something in her will.

I glanced up sharply from the handful of silver I was washing, and Miss Pringle slightly raised her eyebrows, inquiringly.

The will. Could this Pringle be trying to muscle in on Anne's and my share? But no, that was ridiculous. A thousand or so at the most; that was all she could expect.

As I held the silver under the hot-water faucet to rinse it, I decided it was as well perhaps to be pleasant to this little woman. If she got it in for either Anne or me, she might try to influence Aunt Maud against us. She probably couldn't, but it was better to have her on our side.

So, as we finished our task, I said brightly, "There! Now that's done. It doesn't seem to take long when people work together, does it?"

When the dishes were put away, Miss Pringle went out to the terrace, but I quietly went upstairs to the living room, determined to have a few minutes to myself and to smoke a soothing cigarette while I had them. Rover was on the upper sun deck lying close to the low railing along the front. He thumped his tail and lifted his ears as I came out from the living room. I stood quietly by the stuccoed railing and looked over at the group below, tapping the ashes from my cigarette into one of the heavy cement *jardinières* set on the foot-wide railing which rose to a height of two and a half feet around the edge of the sun deck. There were half a dozen *jardinières* along the front of the house here, filled with dirt and planted with begonias. I wondered idly if ashes were good for begonias.

Below me, from the light of the log fire in the outdoor fireplace and from the light streaming out of the bedroom window at the other end of the terrace, which indicated that Alphonse had retired to one of the bunk beds and was probably reading Culbert's discarded *Call-Bulletin*, I could see the whole group, sitting in a semicircle.

Directly beneath me, in a low-backed, round wicker chair, no more than a foot out from the dining-room doors, sat the one I had to kill. My eyes came back to the big *jardinière*, and a shaking excitement took hold of me. I had been waiting for my chance. Here it was.

The dog had risen to his haunches and sat looking at me expectantly. There was even something to blame it on. I could say I had been inside and seen Rover walking back and forth, snapping at a moth, a rather silly habit he has, more feline than canine, and that he had jumped toward the railing, trying to catch the moth, and had knocked against the *jardinière*. The thing was heavy, but not so much so as to be immovable; yet the whole weight of earth and cement on top of a human head should do the job. Besides, even if the dog story were too weak, how could it be proved that I had deliberately pushed the jar?

Risky as it was, the opportunity was too good. I *had* to do it somehow. Life would be unbearable for me in the future if I didn't. I simply couldn't face it. No one knew how long Aunt Maud might live. The doctors said her heart was sound as a new dollar, and she was never sick.

Cautiously I looked over the edge again. They were all looking off to the east, and I was sure no one had seen me. I must not use my hands. There were fingerprints to be thought of. And I could not be too near the edge, in case someone should look up. I glanced about the sun deck anxiously. A pole of some kind, that was what I needed. The little wrought-iron table was empty. Its legs would do. I stepped back and picked up the table, holding its top against my stomach. Rover stood up and watched me with his head on one side.

I took a deep breath and closed my eyes. Now that the time was actually here, I felt held back. Suddenly I realized that with all my being I hated to do it. It was a dreadful thing, to take a human life.

But I was desperate. And there was hatred in me. That made it a little easier. It was only a few seconds that I stood there, gathering the moral strength to do it. Then I shoved with all my force, staggering a little as the *jardinière* gave under the pressure and toppled over the edge.

Even while I was hearing the crash below, I was setting the table back in place and darting toward the doors. I took a deep breath to steady myself and then took a few slow steps toward the railing, ending up with a little rush so that it would look, if anyone were gazing upward, as if I had hurried out from inside. I could hear the sputter of excited cries as I crossed the roof.

For a moment all I could take in was the wicker seat of the chair with a ragged hole through it. Stunned, I lifted my eyes and went over the group below, dimly but adequately illuminated by the light of the fire and that from the unshaded bedroom window.

They were all there!

I leaned over, pressing my palms flat on the rough stucco so hard that afterward I found a few broken places in my skin.

"What happened?" I croaked at last.

They were all talking at once, of course, and, as if they were on a jumbled sound track, I heard the shrill voices:

"The *jardinière*—must have been a slight earthquake shock ... Anne, those things are dangerous—I'll take them down tomorrow ... If I hadn't moved just when I did ... Sheer luck that you got up to turn on the lights ... If I'd been still sitting there—God, it's horrible to think of—"

I staggered back from the railing and ran my hand up one side of my forehead into my hair, not noticing that I had disarranged the roll.

Failed. By the merest chance. Seconds either way, and I would have succeeded. Those very seconds while I fought off my hesitancy to act had defeated me.

I must go down and join the excited comment, explain about seeing Rover playing around by the railing.

But it was bad, bad, bad. Now, when I did succeed, they would remember the *jardinière*, remember that I had been upstairs alone. Oh, I was a fool. It was not like me to be hasty, to act on impulse. And this was what happened when I did. It was just that I hated so to do it and yet was so anxious to get it over with.

Well, I must not be so stupid again. Next time I should have to figure out a foolproof way, and above all, *now*, a way that could not be traced to me.

Chapter Five

Rover followed me down the outside stairway, and they accepted my story of having seen him playing by the railing and knocking against the flowerpot. Soon the excitement died down, and we all chatted quietly until it was quite dark outside the radiance of the terrace light, which had been turned on. Aunt Maud was first to withdraw for bed, and the rest of us soon straggled after her.

I got my face creamed and a net over my hair, and was in bed first. Anne, in a brief nightshirt with short sleeves and a childish round collar, stood in terry-cloth mules wiping cream off her face before the mirror over the chest of drawers. She could see me in the mirror, and she regarded me curiously while she rubbed her forehead abstractedly with a piece of Kleenex.

"You could have knocked me down with a fender, as Jane Ace used to say on the radio," she declared, "when Culbert said you two were going to be married. You've never even hinted such a thing to me."

"You should know," I replied stiffly, "that it's a little lonely living alone, especially as one gets older. One wants—uh—companionship."

"Yes—yes, I know that. But you—well, somehow you've always seemed so—self-sufficient. You seemed happy the way you were."

I shifted my eyes from hers in the mirror and indulged in a moment's introspection. Happy? Yes, I suppose I had been. Irrelevantly, I thought of Dwight. I had heard a few years back, from a girl who had known us both, that he was married at last and living in Los Angeles. Things might have been very different for me—if either Dwight or I had had money or a steady job in 1932. I would hardly have been the same person that I am today; I'd be married and with a couple of kids, probably. But all that was past, done with. The Depression had lost my chance for me. And I had found a different way of living, on the whole a satisfactory one—if not happy in the sense Anne meant.

"Culbert's a dear, and I think he'll be very good to you," Anne was saying, "but—well, I didn't think you were *serious*. How about that new draftsman that went to work for the firm last winter? You had a few dates with him, didn't you? And I thought you liked him. I thought he was nice, the time I met him at your apartment."

"Oh—Eric. But a bird in the hand," I said flippantly, "is worth two in the bush. And he's never indicated that he thought of me in any way but as a—friend. And, after all, I'm not as young as I was. If I don't settle down now, I probably never will." I uttered a harsh laugh. "Why not be frank about it? At my age you take the sure thing, not the man who *might* propose someday. Besides, Eric's a widower, got two kids, a girl of twelve and a boy fourteen, to support. Why should I take on a half-grown family?"

"I suppose you're right," Anne said in a small voice, her face averted as she took a handkerchief from the drawer.

I knew she was not exactly disapproving of my attitude, but—well, disappointed in me.

Although I was right, of course. Eric Nelson had given me no reason to believe he had any tender sentiments for me. He had taken me to dinner once when we both worked late at the office, and driven me home in his old sedan before going on out to the flat in the Richmond district where he lives with his kids, their housework and cooking being handled by a woman who comes in three days a week.

He has rather a rough row to hoe, managing a house and family, and working too, though, goodness knows, it is no more than many a woman has to handle on her own, and does without squawking.

He took me to the movies once, and one Sunday I went on a picnic with him and the kids to Golden Gate Park; and I will say we had a very good time. Betty and Phil are likable children, as kids go. The time Anne met him he had dropped by my apartment on his way downtown to leave a book he had promised to lend me.

Eric is a nice person, very tall, with thin light brown hair growing to a point above his forehead because of the bald areas growing back from his temples. He has a twinkle in his eyes, and he even kids me about the way I keep things under control in the office. Out of the others' hearing, he calls me "the dictator"; but somehow he says it with such a—well, friendly quirk to his lips that I don't mind. I even grin a little self-consciously myself when he teasingly asks, "How about our having lunch together, Dictator?"

I suppose I do have a rather authoritative manner with the employees, but *somebody* has to keep the office force from getting slack.

It was probably no use to deny it. I could let myself become fond of Eric.

But, as I had told Anne, I have no reason to think he thinks of me—that way. He's never made a pass at me of any kind.

Anyhow, right now, with what I had on my hands, there was no point in stopping to build air castles.

Anne turned out the light and pushed open the casement window and climbed over me to the inside of the bed against the wall. I always take the outside, if I *must* sleep with somebody.

I didn't want any more cozy chatting about my affairs, so I said in a low voice that wouldn't carry out of our windows and in at the other bedroom's, six feet away down the wall, "Seems to me you're getting awfully thick with Johnny. *You're* not thinking of marrying again, are you?"

Johnny, incidentally, had taken her coupé to drive home in and was coming back for a day of swimming and sun-bathing in the morning. He doesn't even own a car, but walks a mile to the highway to take a bus when he has to go to town.

There was a brief pause, and then Anne murmured, "I'm not just *sure* yet. But I can't get away from it; he does appeal to me tremendously. He wants us to get married—soon. And—well"—she chuckled softly—"I'll probably give in. I guess I keep putting it off because I like to be coaxed. And"—she giggled suggestively—"Johnny coaxes so beautifully."

"And just what will you two lovebirds live on?" I demanded. "That is, until Aunt Maud passes away."

"Viv, don't be awful! I try not to think of our inheritance. It seems so—mercenary."

"O.K. But I still want to know what you mean to use for money. Two *can't* live as cheaply as one, you know, and I don't see any financial prospects in Johnny's future. I wouldn't gamble, even if I thought he had ability, on his writing success. The competition in that field is something awful."

Anne stirred a little. I could feel she had turned from her side to her back.

"Sis," she said solemnly, "if I tell you something in strict secrecy, will you promise, absolutely *swear*, that you'll never tell a soul?"

"Shoot," I said noncommittally. "You always have told me things."

"Well ..." She paused while she seemed to seek for words. "Johnny is really not what he seems."

"Humph," I said, letting her interpret the sound as she chose.

"He'd be furious if he knew I was telling you this, but for your own peace of mind about me—being your only sister, I know you're concerned about my welfare—I think it's only right to tell you."

She rolled onto her side and lay looking at me. I turned my head and could see the outline of her face in the darkness, which was becoming less obscure as my eyes adjusted to it.

"You know his name is John Lloyd?"

"Yes."

"Well, you've heard of *the* Lloyds?"

I had, of course. Anyone living in California has heard of Simon Lloyd, founder of one of the biggest gold-rush mining fortunes. The Lloyd mansion on Nob Hill, the palatial country estate in Atherton, now sold and ripped up into a subdivision for middle-class residences.

"Well, Johnny is one of *the* Lloyds."

I was speechless. I merely lay there staring at her face in the light of the stars outside.

"Not a direct descendant of old Simon, but a connection; and Johnny's immediate family—they're all dead now but him—came in for some of the boodle when old Simon died. They lost most of it, but Johnny has enough to get by on comfortably. The main thing is, though, that Priscilla Lloyd, the old-maid granddaughter of Simon Lloyd, is the only direct heir left; and when she dies Johnny will inherit a good chunk of the estate. Old Simon fixed it in his will so that a share of his fortune has to keep passing on to blood relatives as long as there are any left."

She paused, and my voice finally came back to me. "Do tell! Johnny—told you—all this? And why, may I ask, the secrecy about his—er—connections?"

Anne raised herself on one elbow. Still keeping her voice low, she continued eagerly, "*That's* a matter of Johnny's temperament. You know how it is with people connected with big names. Look at Priscilla Lloyd; she can't sneeze without the newspapers commenting on it. And Johnny hates publicity. But it's mostly on account of his art—"

"His what?"

"His work. His writing, you know. He feels that a writer must really know and understand people, and Johnny says that great wealth sets you apart from the people, creates psychological barriers that are fatal to really getting the *feel* of the common people's lives. So he prefers to be completely separated from the Lloyd reputation."

"I see," I said.

And I did see. Johnny Lloyd was smart enough to correctly estimate Anne's character and temperament. She was too trusting, too fundamentally innocent, even to think of investigating and verifying this cock-and-bull story, and he had thought the pledge of secrecy insured that the story would remain locked in her naïve little head out of loyalty to him. He had not counted on the fact, though, that a creature of loyalty usually has more than one loyalty, and that Anne felt a deep sense of it to me.

It was all very clear. His potential wealth would quiet any of her misgivings about taking on a financial risk for a husband, and when Priscilla Lloyd did come around to dying (she was in her late sixties now), all Johnny would have to do would be to concoct another plausible tale to account for his losing out on the inheritance. Meanwhile he would have a soft berth with Anne and Aunt Maud's money.

I wondered fleetingly if, after all, he might not succeed with his scribbling, in time. He seemed to think up stories glibly enough.

While Anne whispered on, extolling the grandeur and, at the same time, the beautiful simplicity of Johnny's character, I pondered whether to tell her then what I knew to be the facts about the Lloyd fortune.

For I knew. Just before the war Priscilla had sold the gloomy mansion on Nob Hill and built an elaborate apartment house on Russian Hill, where she now lived, when she wasn't traveling, in a luxurious penthouse on the roof. Evans and Harder had been the architects she had chosen for the job, and our whole office had been in a flurry for months over the deal. The fabulous Priscilla Lloyd aroused interest and notoriety by whatever she did, and troublesome as she made herself as a client, constantly thinking up new features for the building which couldn't possibly be incorporated in it without canceling out items that were equally absolutely necessary—to her mind, it had been a real feather in our cap to get the job, for other people would be instantly convinced that architects who were good enough for the immensely rich and particular Priscilla Lloyd must be good enough for anybody.

Naturally at that time we all became intensely Lloyd-conscious; and amongst us we read up on Simon Lloyd and were alert to every scrap of gossip about his granddaughter. Simon Lloyd had been an immigrant from Wales, an orphan. There was no record anywhere of any brothers and sisters, And when he died in 1904 his entire holdings went to his only son, who, in turn, after his death during the First World War, passed them on, still intact and with no strings attached, to his only daughter.

Once these facts had been widely known in California, but in the past thirty years people had had other things to think about than the course taken by once-great fortunes. They had had the booming twenties, unemployment, fascism, and another world war to engage their attention, and so it was no wonder that Anne was vague about the Lloyd background.

Something else I knew, or at least had on pretty good authority, and that was where Priscilla's property was likely to go at her death.

In the thirties she had joined the Catholic Church. Mr. Harder is a prominent Catholic in San Francisco, intimate with some of the Church's leading dignitaries, and they had all been pleased as punch at Miss Lloyd's conversion. After the contact I had had with her while she was building her apartment house, I took a rather dim view, however, of her religious convictions. I know the Catholic faith has ideals about goodness and human decency and brotherhood, but I knew these were not the things which drew Priscilla Lloyd. She was a thoroughly selfish, unscrupulous, coldhearted old woman, and, getting along in years, she had, in my opinion, simply decided it was high time to set about protecting her status in the next world if there was one, and so she embraced religion as a sort of insurance in the hereafter.

Mr. Harder, in an expansive mood one day while we were working on her building, told me in strict confidence that he had it on unimpeachable authority that she was leaving every cent to the Church when she died. It sounded likely. By that act, I estimated cynically, the old battle-ax probably figured she could cinch her harp and wings. The Lord would be very ungrateful if he didn't let her in after she gave all that money for His work.

I decided not to prick Anne's bubble right then. I would take care of the whole matter in other ways, ways that might spare her feelings. But I couldn't resist one malicious sally.

"I gathered," I said, "that Aunt Maud wasn't too favorably impressed by Johnny. She probably considers him too worldly. And then, too, not seeing any visible means of support, she may think he's trying to sponge on you. Don't you think it would be smart at least to let *her* in on his—uh—prospects, and relieve her mind in *that* regard. After all, it's to your advantage not to have her displeased with you. She might decide to cut the Pringle person—or even Alphonse—in on the bequests in her will. And, mercenary or no, we could both use her money. We don't want it split up a dozen different ways, and if she got down on one of us, she might do it."

"We-ell"—Anne had come down off her elbow and was curled up with her hand under her cheek—"if I thought she was really getting too down on Johnny, I might ask him if we shouldn't tell her."

"You do that," I said dryly.

I knew how friend Johnny would respond to *that* suggestion. For Aunt Maud would instantly look up the Lloyd family in minute detail.

Chapter Six

Anne was soon asleep, but I lay wide-eyed. My nerves and muscles must have been too tense to let my brain relax into unconsciousness. For a while I mulled over the new light Anne had thrown on Johnny. My opinion of him had not been high in the first place, but now he took on a rather sinister aspect. A four-flusher and a liar. Anyone who would concoct a fantasy like this to deceive a woman was certainly not to be trusted. God knew what Anne might get into if she were foolish enough to marry him.

I should certainly have to put a stop to Johnny. I would try to handle the whole thing without her knowing. She could be spared the humiliation of learning how she had been taken in.

My thoughts went on inexorably to my own problem.

How was I to do it? It might be more difficult than I had contemplated. The difficulty lay in not getting caught. But people did get away with it. So I, too, should be able to.

Having Anne in bed with me, I could not keep turning over, resting my muscles with new positions.

I do not smoke excessively, and never at night; but I found myself thinking longingly of a cigarette. It seemed as though, if I could just have a smoke, I should be all right; I could fall asleep.

The desire kept tearing at me until finally I eased myself out from under the covers and slipped my feet into my slippers. I stood up and pulled on my robe, and found my cigarettes in the darkness. Then I opened the door cautiously and stole down the hall and through the dining room onto the terrace.

I heard the sound of movement, and a thump, thump! on the stones; and my veins froze until I recognized the dark shape of Rover, stretched out on the floor next the stairway.

I went and sat on the second step from the bottom and lighted a cigarette. Rover got up and came over and lay down at the foot of the steps. Except for the incessant orchestration of the crickets and tree toads, it was very still. The shrill rising-and-falling chirping of the crickets seemed to set the silence apart, to give it an almost tangible quality, rather than dispel it. In the starlight I could distinguish the dark masses of the hills and the outlines of trees.

Ordinarily the still peacefulness of the night would have seeped restfully into my soul, but tonight's quiet was somehow not peaceful, only ominously empty, as if the world waited, breathless and black, beneath the glittering stars.

Now was a time for murder. I had a breathless, impatient urge to act, to get it over with. But that was insane, of course, with two people in every room. And Johnny not even there; for the more possible suspects there should be floating around, the better.

"Vivian?"

My name came out at me in a hoarse, questioning whisper; and with a gasp of fright, I shrank against the steps, my head jerking toward the dining-room doors from whence the sound had come.

A figure stepped out from the wall, and I saw that it was Culbert, vague in a light-colored robe.

"Oh—it's you," I sighed. "You scared me, materializing out of nowhere like that."

He came to the steps.

"I heard your door close, and then I thought I heard steps out here, and I saw the glow of your cigarette out of the window, so I thought I'd come and see if it was you."

I glanced at the bedroom windows and whispered, "Sh-h, we might wake Alphonse and Anne."

Stealthily I rose. "Let's go up on the sun deck. We can sit at the other end where we'll be far enough from these windows and from Aunt Maud's room so that she won't hear us either."

As he tiptoed up the stairs beside me, Culbert whispered loudly, "Have you got another cigarette?"

"Sh-h! Yes, I have. I'll give you one after we sit down."

One of the planks creaked as we tiptoed across the sun deck. I felt as if we sounded like a team of horses.

When we got to the end of the deck we sat side by side on the broad railing, and I offered him my package of Old Golds.

"I couldn't seem to get to sleep," Culbert confided, using his normal voice but holding it low. "Too much excitement today, I guess."

"Was Alphonse asleep?" I whispered.

"I guess so."

"Weren't you afraid of waking him up when you got up?"

"Oh, I was quiet. What was the matter with you? Couldn't you sleep either?"

I rose and turned to look south into the wooded hillside above the stream. The song of the crickets sounded shriller and louder than ever.

"No. Maybe I've had too much excitement today too." I went on ruminatingly, my voice low, "Have you noticed how when you're out awhile at night you get so you can see better. That big sycamore down by the stream. You can see the pale blotches in its trunk."

Culbert swiveled around on his hips and looked back and down. I put my hand on his shoulder as together we peered down over the wall and the steep bank.

The south windows of the room he shared with Alphonse were directly below us, and suddenly I heard the creak of springs through the open windows. I drew back a little, listening acutely. If he were awake, and if he heard any unusual sounds outdoors in this deathly stillness, he would probably get up and come out of his room. Alphonse somehow impressed me as the sort of person who investigates noises at night.

And then my conjectures about Alphonse were dissipated abruptly.

From the other end of the deck a voice demanded peevishly, "What's the matter? Who's there?"

We jerked our heads around and saw a roundish white object protruding from one of the bedroom windows. Aunt Maud's head.

"It's just us," Culbert answered softly. "Vivian and me."

I kicked his ankle sharply. "No use to tell her I'm here," I muttered.

We held our cigarettes behind us like guilty children as she demanded next, not troubling to subdue her voice, "What are you doing up at this hour of the night? Waking everybody up."

I came forward a little. "I couldn't sleep," I said huskily, "and I—I just came out for a breath of air."

"What? What did you say? I can't hear you when you mumble."

So I hurried down the floor until I was close enough for her to hear a low-pitched reply. *I*, at least, was not going to yell across the whole house at one o'clock in the morning. I explained my sleeplessness again and elaborated with an account of how Culbert had heard me and got up to see if anything was wrong.

"Since we were both so wide awake," I concluded conciliatingly, "we decided to come up here and talk for a few minutes."

"Well, you get right back to bed, both of you. You ought to know better, Vivian. How do you think it looks, you two gallivanting around alone in the middle of the night?"

I had to swallow a slightly hysterical laugh. What I had been doing with Culbert was hardly what Aunt Maud would call "gallivanting."

But I said meekly, "Yes, Aunt Maud."

And under her disapproving eyes we trailed down the stairs, the cigarette butts almost burning our fingers as we still held them out of sight, shielded by our bodies, unable to throw them down and step on them until she could no longer see us. If she had known we were smoking together, she *would* have thought we were having a regular orgy.

At my bedroom door Culbert detained me with a hand on my arm and with his other hand he pressed my head forward and kissed me determinedly. His lips were cool from the night air, but moist and soft. My nerves shrank from the touch, but reason told me to submit. A man you had promised to marry *expected* to be able to kiss you whenever he liked. His mouth moved greedily against mine, and I could feel his flesh growing warm from the contact. I tried to draw my face away, but he held my head more firmly. It was obvious he was sensuously enjoying the experience. But when his hand began fumbling for my breast, I pulled away roughly.

Inside the closed door, I drew the back of my hand across my mouth. I hoped he hadn't sensed my revulsion. I didn't want him getting sore and sulking at me so the others would notice tomorrow. I must keep up the appearance of a placidly engaged girl, fond of her man even if not wildly in love.

Back in bed beside Anne, still wide awake, I was sure of one thing. There was no use trying to accomplish anything at night in *this* house.

I woke reluctantly the next morning, for I had not fallen asleep immediately on returning to bed. My mind had instead gone clanking over the same ground again and again, forming the same phrases over and over until they became trite from repetition.

"I have to do it." "There's no other way out." "I must think of a way, a safe, sure way." "It isn't as if anyone would care very much, afterward."

I had read somewhere that one's brain will work almost automatically sometimes if you give it a chance. Just present it clearly and explicitly with a problem, go to sleep, and when one wakes up, presto, there is the answer.

But my mental machinery, I decided grimly as I lay looking up at the plastered ceiling after I woke, must be rusty. For it had not produced the slightest hint of a concrete plan.

Anne had evidently climbed over the end of the bed and slipped away without waking me. No sound of human activity reached my ears, but the lively birds outside, disjointedly shrilling forth comments on their busy, darting activities, would have told a sightless person that day had come.

Lethargically I pulled myself out of bed. My body felt heavy, my eyes dull, and my brain soggy. The night before, in my wakefulness, I had felt no fatigue; but now I was dead tired.

I drew back the monk's-cloth window curtains and, reaching over to the dresser, put on my glasses and surveyed the terrace and the stretches of cerise flowers below. It was all so bright under the morning sun that I closed my eyes against the light which seemed to bounce back off the silver frames of the chairs.

I put on my sun suit and was soon ready to meet whoever might be up and about. Anne was in the kitchen, squeezing orange juice.

"You the only one up?" I asked.

"Oh no, I saw Alphonse outside a few minutes ago, and"—she raised her eyes to indicate the bedroom upstairs—"they're up. They read the Bible and pray every morning before breakfast. Seems that puts them in the right frame of mind for contact with the wicked world."

I picked up a glass of orange juice and drank it, standing by the sink.

"She's sure thick with Miss Pringle," I said idly, "praying together, meditating, even sleeping in the same room."

"Oh, they have separate rooms in San Diego. But I was darned if I was going to sleep on the davenport in the living room, or in the glider on the sun deck, so Pringle could have the room we're in."

"This is the first time, though, that Aunt Maud's been so chummy with anybody. She's always been more or less a lone wolf. Her secretaries, for instance, they were just business employees."

"Well, it's nice she has someone to share her life more, now that she's getting old."

"I suppose so. Helps to keep her off our necks."

I wandered out to the terrace. Culbert must still be asleep after the late hour last night. I sauntered to the other end of the stone floor and looked off across the descending grounds. To eyes accustomed to the pervading gray of city streets and walls there was something pleasantly surprising in the varied greens which met one's gaze wherever it turned, the quiet brown-green of the redwoods below, the fresh, clean hue of the maples and oaks on the slope above, the paler tone of the broad sycamore leaves below. It was quieting somehow.

Down by the swimming pool I saw Alphonse standing with his hands in his pockets, gazing into the water which shone blue and sparkling, reflecting the sky below the gray walls of the cement tank. Rover sat beside him, looking up expectantly.

Curiosity stirred sluggishly in my mind. We were not the sort of people who were so used to servants that they became mere utilitarian objects scattered around for convenience. Alphonse, to me, was a human being, one who might possibly play a role, be a factor, in the pattern of my own existence.

I strolled down toward him and the dog, saying, "Good morning," as I approached. "Looks as if it's going to be a hot day," I observed pleasantly.

He was wearing a tan shirt open at the throat, and his dark hair threaded with gray was smoothed back damply from the domelike front of his head. His heavy, lined features smiled impassively.

"Always have a breeze up here, though," he replied, not relinquishing the respectful manner of a servant. I had a feeling, however, that the subtly servile manner was something he put on, that he didn't really feel like an underling.

I patted Rover's head. "You must have got up early."

"I always wake up around six-thirty." He was relaxing a little, and he nodded at the dog with a slight softening of the opaque expression in his eyes. "Me and Rover here've been walking around the place." He smiled then. "Tried to catch a fish down in the crick, didn't you, boy?"

As Rover wagged his tail happily, I noticed that his feet and legs were still damp and his paws muddy.

We heard voices then above, and I looked back. Aunt Maud was standing on the terrace in a long housecoat.

I said, "Guess we'll be having breakfast soon now," and started toward the house, Alphonse following.

As we neared the terrace Aunt Maud accosted me, "Well, I see you're up early, even though you did spend most of the night prowling around." Aside, and offhandedly, she acknowledged the man's presence with a "Good morning, Alphonse," going on again to me, "If you're troubled with insomnia, what you should do is work on your state of mind before you go to sleep. Utter relaxation, that's the secret. Let all your muscles go limp, and then think of something beautiful, let your mind be saturated with beauty, denying all thoughts of self."

I felt like asking her how she happened to be so wakeful that the faint sounds of our steps and voices had roused her.

Alphonse passed us and paused for a moment uncertainly as Aunt Maud rattled on about the need for being in harmony with the constructive vibrations of the universe in order to achieve complete relaxation and the psychic steadiness which accompanied it.

I felt a fleeting sympathy for the man. There seemed to be no *place* for him in the setup here at the cabin. He sort of rattled around amongst us, neither wholly in the effaced position of a servant nor yet with the assured standing of a guest. After his moment's indecision he mounted the stairs to the sun deck.

Aunt Maud kept talking, and I sat down in one of the chairs, putting in a "That's right" or an "Of course not" where the monologue seemed to require it. I could hear Culbert talking to Anne in the kitchen, and he came out with a stack of cups and saucers for the table, calling a cheery "Good morning."

Aunt Maud turned and appraised him skeptically, vouchsafing a grunt of greeting. When he had gone back inside, she turned and came over to sit in a chair on the other side of me, dragging it closer to mine. She leaned forward and spoke in a low voice.

"I've been meaning to speak to you, dear. I've had it on my mind since last night. Now that your own mother is gone, I feel that I ought to speak of these matters with you girls when the need arises, since there's no one else to do it. About last night, Vivian ..." She leaned back a little and regarded me gravely. "I know, of course, you had no thought of being indiscreet. But a girl must guard her reputation. And being up alone in a house in the middle of the night with a man you're engaged to—well, it just doesn't look right. And men—well ..." Her eyebrows went up and her lips pressed together in a straight line. "They misinterpret a girl's actions. And you're only flesh and blood, my dear, and, who knows, *you* might even find yourself tempted beyond your strength ..."

I swallowed and bit my lips, and I think Aunt Maud thought it was because of embarrassment, but it was actually to keep myself from laughing out loud in her face. Just wait till I told Anne about Aunt Maud giving me motherly advice, advising a woman forty years old to beware the pitfalls men would lay at her feet.

She went on reassuringly, "Of course I know *you* are a good girl, Vivian, but a woman can't be too careful. Her chastity is her most cherished possession." Her expression hardened coldly. "Some people, I know, take a light view of such things these days, but *I* do not. Right's right, and it doesn't change. There is never any excuse for—er—sexual laxity."

There in the hot sun I felt cold suddenly. I wished I had had a cup of hot coffee in the kitchen.

Vaguely I had been aware of an indistinguishable murmur of voices above us on the sun deck, and now I heard Miss Pringle's laugh ripple out, gentle, but gay and relaxed.

Aunt Maud lifted her head and frowned upward. "Who is with Miss Pringle?"

"Alphonse, I think. He went upstairs a few minutes ago."

"Oh." She brought her gaze down from the sun-deck railing, but there was still a slightly disgruntled cast to her face.

I realized with impatient amusement that Aunt Maud was actually jealous of the little companion. She didn't want Miss Pringle finding pleasure in any society but hers. It was appalling, yet rather pathetic; and I promised myself desperately that I would never get like Aunt Maud, so emotionally malnourished that I fed greedily on the affections of those upon whom I did have a claim.

Chapter Seven

We had hardly finished breakfast when Johnny stepped up on the south end of the terrace, having parked Anne's car above and come down the path around the south side of the house.

Aunt Maud never drank coffee, but fortunately Anne had refused to consider her sensibilities in that regard, and the rest of us were having our after-breakfast cup at the sunny outdoor table. She offered Johnny some coffee, and as he drank it he absently broke pieces off a hot buttered snail that was left over and continued to nibble on them until the whole cake was gone. It was obvious to me that snacks at Anne's expense helped to keep down his grocery bill.

He was helpful, though. I'll admit that. He insisted on washing the breakfast dishes while I wiped them and Anne did some necessary brushing up around the place.

He asked me a perfunctory question about my work and if the firm was busy, and deliberately I began to chatter about a new apartment building Mr. Harder was working on.

"Your name being Lloyd reminds me. We did a penthouse apartment building for Priscilla Lloyd a few years ago. You know, the gold-mining fortune."

He scrubbed at egg dried on a plate and did not look up. "Yes, I know."

I laughed lightly. "If I didn't know there wasn't a single other living connection of Simon Lloyd's, I'd ask if you mightn't be one of the famous California Lloyds."

He gave me a quick sidewise look out of his eyes that are so dark a brown that often one cannot distinguish the pupil in them.

I looked right back unwinkingly, and he turned his head as he pulled some cups into the dishpan.

"How do you know that?" he said, sounding careless.

"Oh, I know, all right. I became quite an authority on the Lloyd history while Miss Priscilla was our client. Woman's curiosity, you know. I even found out," I added calmly, "that she is willing every cent of her money to her church when she dies."

He stopped moving his hands in the sudsy water and regarded me directly. Again I met his eyes levelly, and although his square-jawed face did not change expression, I was sure he understood me.

We finished our common task in silence.

I went upstairs afterward, leaving him wiping off the top of the electric stove in the kitchen.

Aunt Maud, in her loose flowered seersucker housecoat, and Miss Pringle in "ditto," only with violets instead of pansies, were out on the sun deck solemnly lifting their arms up and down, and breathing.

Aunt Maud saw me and called, "Come on and join us, Vivian. We're doing our deep-breathing exercises."

I was wearing my shorts and the halter without the jacket, and I figured the sun would be good for me, so I went out and pumped my arms around and inhaled and exhaled with them for about ten minutes. Might as well humor the old girl.

When the exercises were over, Aunt Maud retired to the living room to write letters at Anne's desk, instructing poor Miss Pringle to take off her housecoat and lie on a mat in the sun for a while, the ultraviolet rays would be good for her anemia.

I myself was sweating from the arm-waving in the hot sun, and I felt a moment's pity for my aunt's little slave, who meekly slipped out of her robe, revealing a rayon slip and skinny, freckled shoulders, and stretched out on her face on the sun-bathing mattress.

I had a package of cigarettes and some matches in my shorts pocket, so I went down the steps to the terrace, crossed the stones, and started down the rustic stairway to the stream. It would be cool down there, and quiet except for the soothing murmur of the water. I could find a spot out of sight of the living room and the sun deck, and smoke a cigarette while I thought.

For I must think, devise some plan. The nights were out, of course. I should have to do it somehow in broad daylight.

There was arsenic in the tool shed under the garage, one of the ingredients of a spray for roses, the recipe for which Anne had read in a magazine. She had also tried it on gophers by wrapping the powder in lettuce and cabbage leaves and shoving them down the holes, which apparently didn't work, considering the number of gopher holes which still pockmarked the grounds around the house.

I chose a flat-topped boulder at the edge of the stream in the shade of a big sycamore and looked over my shoulder up at the house. A young oak at the top of the slope hid the living-room windows from sight, although I could be seen from the sun deck. Aunt Maud was inside, however, and likely to remain there. Rough steps gouged out of the earth zigzagged up the steep incline behind me to meet the path near the front of the house. They were bordered by rocks, at one time carried up from the stream bed, and this rude natural stairway wound in and out among the unkempt shrubbery.

I gazed at the pebbles under the clear water and, to the sound of incessant staccato bird cries, pondered my problem.

The arsenic was best, I concluded. It could be administered in a drink of some kind at some moment like the present when the whole household was scattered. Having so little experience with things of that sort, I didn't know whether the poison would act immediately or not. It would be better if it didn't. Then it would be harder to establish who had been with the victim. But if it did act immediately, I could simply wash up the vessel and get myself to some other part of the place before the body was found.

I flicked my cigarette into the stream and decided to slip into the tool shed as soon as possible and get some of the powder in an envelope. I reminded myself of fingerprints and felt mechanically in my pocket for my handkerchief. I would keep it over my hand whenever I touched anything, even the doorknob, in the shed.

There was a noise on the hillside behind me, and I turned my head languidly. There were always noises on the grounds at Anne's. Rabbits or squirrels in the bushes, or even, rarely, a covey of quail taking off with a sound like little motors running. But this was not an animal. What I had heard was one of the larger stones bordering the dirt steps, rolling down the embankment. It was at least a foot thick and was falling directly above the rock where I sat. I jerked back instinctively, not consciously knowing in which direction, and a guttural cry of fear rose in my throat. My start would have been too late to save me, for I didn't have time to get to my feet and off my boulder, which was directly under the bank. But one of the stones marking the path projected slightly, and the falling missile struck this other rock as it tumbled down the hillside. It was deflected just enough in its course and missed me by inches, landing with a great splash in the stream beside me.

For a moment I could not move. I felt as if every drop of blood in my body had suddenly drained away like water swooshing out of a basin when the plug is pulled. My eyes were riveted in horror on the big stone now peacefully lodged in the stream bed. But then fear swiveled my body around from the waist, and I looked fearfully back up the hillside. I could see no one, but I saw a toyon bush near the top of the slope move more violently than the breeze would have caused it to, and there was a flash of some drab color in the interstices of the leaves. My eyes are not strong enough to distinguish details at a distance, but I could see that something was moving swiftly there.

Someone had taken careful aim from the slope above, and not too far above, either, and dislodged that miniature boulder and sent it rolling down to hit me. If it had not struck my head and killed me outright, it would have at least knocked me off into the stream, probably throwing my head against one of the gray rocks protruding from the water, and there would have been a good chance that I would have drowned there in less than a foot of water, having been rendered unconscious by one or the other of the blows.

I scrambled to my feet, and my knees would hardly hold me up. I must get away, and quickly, from this defenseless position alone down here; but I felt as if I hadn't the strength to climb back to the house. My breath was coming in gasps, and I deliberately forced myself to breathe deeply.

Gradually, anger was mixing in with my fear; outrage at whoever had committed this cowardly assault on a helpless woman. I took the wooden steps as fast as I could, growing more determined, hanging onto the rail to help myself climb. I meant to reconnoiter quickly in the house and try to discover who had been alone and thus able to make the attack on me.

I was still too shaken to try to figure out reasons for the assault. When I came out on the terrace Culbert was just puffing up the steps from the direction of the pool, and he stepped onto the stone floor at the same time I did.

He could, of course, have run into the garage, down the stairs inside, which opened both into the downstairs hall and into the tool shed which had a door out to a narrow path running between the north hill and the wall of the house, have come out through the tool shed, and hurried around to come up on the terrace from outside. That would have accounted for his shortness of breath.

But there was no conceivable reason why Culbert should try to kill me— unless he had suddenly taken leave of his senses.

"Where," I demanded breathlessly, "have you been?"

He looked surprised. "Down at the bottom of the hill, below the swimming pool, looking around."

"Was anyone down there with you?"

"No."

Without another word, I ran through the dining-room doors and into the hallway, where I looked both ways, leaving Culbert gaping after me. I hurried to the open kitchen door, and Anne looked up from the drainboard where she was creaming shortening for a cake. She had been whistling softly to herself, and she stopped whistling and looked up inquiringly.

"How long have you been alone in here?"

"For goodness sakes, why?"

"Don't ask questions. Answer me."

"Why, I don't know. Fifteen minutes, maybe."

I wheeled and ran back into the hall and up the stairs. Aunt Maud was sitting at the desk in the northwest corner of the room, writing busily with a fountain pen. I gave her a quick glance and went to the sun-deck doors. Miss Pringle, wrapped in her seersucker housecoat once more, was sitting sedately in a covered swing with its back to the sun, reading the *Reader's Digest*.

"Have you been out here ever since I left?" I demanded.

She raised her eyebrows. "Why, yes."

"Anyone else been out here?"

She released a fluttering laugh. "Why, John—that is, Mr. Lloyd—came up the outdoor stairs while I was sun-bathing. I was so embarrassed—in my slip, you know. But he was awfully nice, smiled in the politest way and told me not to mind him, he'd had sisters and he knew how it was. He walked around, looking off at the hills for a few minutes, and went out through the living room. I don't think he spoke to Miss Twilliger. She concentrates so well when she's working, never notices people in the room ..."

I turned and went back inside while she was still babbling on, and, ignoring Aunt Maud's concentration, demanded, "Aunt Maud, did you see Johnny in here a little while ago?"

She glanced up, frowning through the gold-rimmed glasses that she wears for close work, and said coldly, "I may have. I don't allow myself to register nonessentials when I'm busy."

"Well, did you happen to register which way he went out of this room, and which direction he took?"

She took off her glasses with one hand and really looked at me. "Why?"

"Because I want to know," I said, for once not bothering with the buttering-up act.

Her eyes took me in shrewdly, and then she said in a businesslike way, "He went out the front door. I presume he went that way"—she pointed toward the stream side of the house—"since I didn't notice him pass these windows." She nodded toward the broad windows at her left. Then she looked at me intently again. "I couldn't swear he didn't go this way, though, because I *was* preoccupied with my writing. Why are you checking up on the young—man's—movements?"

I could have sworn she had an epithet other than "man" in mind, and even in my distraught state it tickled me a little.

"I'll tell you some other time," I muttered, and hurried down the stairs.

As I came to the bottom Johnny opened the bathroom door down the hall. He hesitated for a second as he saw me, and then, with a bland look, came forward. I turned sharply and went into the kitchen where Anne was. I didn't want to be alone with him. In a moment he appeared in the doorway.

"Need an assistant cook?" he inquired nonchalantly.

When he was clear of the door, without a word I made my exit through it and hurried down the hall. There was still Alphonse to check up on. I should have tried the garage upstairs, but at least I could investigate to see whether he was in his room or not. I knocked, and heard feet touching the floor, and Alphonse, in his shirt sleeves and a pair of khaki pants, opened the door and stood looking at me curiously.

"I—I—" I stammered, and then blurted out, "I just wanted to ask—are you—will you be able to drive us in to the train Monday morning?"

"Why, sure," he said courteously, but unable to conceal his surprise. "If you want me to."

I retired in confusion and went into the room I shared with Anne. There was no key to the door, but out of sheer nervousness, I propped the room's one straight chair under the doorknob and then sank weakly onto the bed.

It was incredible, but there it was. Someone had tried to kill me. Clumsily and hurriedly and rashly, as I had done last night, seizing circumstances which would make it seem like an accident. By a mere chance I had escaped, but I knew, being able to judge by my own intentions, that it was only a reprieve. Once you decided it was necessary to kill someone, you kept trying. Which meant another attempt would be made on my life. It was terrifying. Worse than being trapped. From one moment to the next, one didn't know if one would be alive, didn't know how or from where it would come. At least my victim was spared this agony of apprehension.

My eyes fell on the open window, and I sprang up and pulled it closed, fastening the metal catch tightly. At once the room seemed airless and oppressive.

For a moment I thought of packing quickly and asking Alphonse to drive me to San Jose to catch a train. But how could I be absolutely certain it wasn't *him?* Suppose he had homicidal tendencies and had taken an irrational dislike to me because of some fancied affront?

That was the trouble, I couldn't be positive. Anyone in the house—including even Aunt Maud—could have done it. Not one of them had been with another the whole time I was out of the way.

There was only one who had a reason I could think of, and that was Johnny. But I couldn't be *sure*, even, that it was him.

It must be, though. He guessed Anne had told me his "secret," and he had rightly interpreted my hinted threat across the dishpan. He knew I was cryptically telling him I would trade my silence for his laying off Anne. And naturally he wouldn't want to run the threat of exposure as a liar and a four-flusher. It would spoil all his plans for Easy Street at Anne's expense.

I pressed my hands to the sides of my head. Again I had been a fool. I should have waited about taking care of this until I had accomplished my own purpose for the week end.

But there was no use crying over spilt milk. All I could do was be careful, never allow myself to be alone or to be left alone with Johnny. But what would happen then to my own project?

I raised my head and stared unseeing at the opposite wall. If one murder, why not two? Perhaps I could kill two birds with—not one stone—but one dose. They said the best defense was a good offense. Johnny would probably wait for another time when the scene set itself for an "accident." Meantime I should lose no time in finding a way to get poison down both of them.

I straightened my shoulders with more courage. I would try to set him at ease right now, not let him know I suspected foul play about the baby boulder—so that he wouldn't feel that he dared waste no further time in getting rid of me, thinking I suspected him and might publicly announce my fears.

But I knew it would be useless to tell the others the whole story. They might believe he had lied about his family, but I realized with sickening dismay that no one would believe he had tried to kill me for fear of exposure. They were all so naïve. To them it would seem fantastic that hearty, hail-fellow-well-met Johnny had resorted to attempted murder. They would just put me down as a frustrated old maid with a persecution complex.

I stood up and wiped my face with a Kleenex, for under the emotions of the past half hour I had been perspiring. I smoothed the front rolls of my hair and the back one with my fingers. Then I took an envelope from the pocket of my overnight bag, where I always carried a few sheets of stationery, and folded it into my pocket.

Sternly resisting another upsurge of panic, I took the chair from under the doorknob and went out.

Chapter Eight

As I passed the dining-room doors I could see through to the terrace, and I noted that Anne, Johnny, and Culbert were seated out there, all with their backs to me. Quietly I tiptoed on past the stairway and carefully opened the door leading to the rough stairs that ascended to the garage, closing it noiselessly behind me. Then, with equal caution, and with my handkerchief in my hand, I opened the tool-shed door. It was dim and musty in there, with only the small window to the north. Rakes and hoes and a shovel and long-handled clippers hung on walls, and the floor was cluttered with discarded cardboard cartons, a pair of old rubbers, flower baskets, a keg which had once held nails. On a shelf at shoulder level were cans of ant powder, DDT, a fly-spray gun, old packages of seeds, and a squat can conspicuously marked "Poison." Hardly breathing, my hands trembling with haste, I brought the can down with my handkerchief around it. The cover was stuck tight, and I held the can against my leg, prying the lid up with a fingernail protected by my shorts. It finally came, and I laid the lid on an orange crate against the wall and poured at least two tablespoons of the powder into my envelope.

It seemed to take an unconscionable time. I felt a cold drop of sweat trickle down my skin from my underarm.

At last I got out of the shed. For a moment I listened beside the hall door and then opened it slowly. I closed my eyes and expelled my breath—which I felt as if I had been holding for hours—and leaned for an instant against my hand on the doorknob behind me.

The relief at having made the tool-shed trip unobserved was so great that also, briefly, my apprehension over Johnny's threat to my safety seemed to lighten and disappear, as if wafted away by the relaxation of this particular danger.

Almost jauntily I went through the dining room and out to the terrace.

"Where have you been all morning?" Culbert greeted me.

"Oh, here and there."

Johnny's expression, as he glanced at me, was a touch *too* indifferent, I thought.

"We were debating," Anne said, "whether to swim before lunch or wait till after. What's your vote?"

I sat in a chair with an awninged top, facing them, and stretched my bare legs out in the sun. "I'm lazy myself; I'd rather wait."

"Anyhow," Johnny put in, "it's twelve now. Soon be time to eat again."

I lay back, consciously relaxing, it seemed, for the first time in hours.

"Let's have old-fashioned lemonade for lunch," I suggested casually.

The proposal came apparently of its own impetus from my lips. I had not thought it out. But I knew as soon as I had spoken that here was my way. I would make the lemonade, use the set of tall glasses, each painted with a different California wild flower; and then I would serve the drinks, setting two in the right places.

Anne was saying doubtfully, "I don't know whether Aunt Maud drinks lemonade. Seems to me there's something about acid and starch combined—they do something dreadful to your liver—or maybe it's your kidneys."

"She needn't drink it, then," I retorted.

"Sounds good to me," Culbert seconded me comfortably.

I rested my head against the canvas chair back and silently considered another angle. The envelope. It must be burned. But how, without attracting notice? I opened my eyes, as if lazily, and glanced toward the barbecue pit. An empty egg carton from breakfast, some crumpled paper napkins, and a fold of old newspaper lay on the ashes. I would have to serve the drinks, then carry the tray over to the table by the fireplace, and then, casually, as if it had just occurred to me, set a match to that refuse, slipping my envelope into the heart of the blaze. I would turn away, observing carelessly, "Might as well get rid of that unsightly trash."

They were talking desultorily about whether to have liverwurst or tuna sandwiches, or both, for lunch.

I lifted my eyes to the railing of the sun deck. "I see you took the *jardinières* down," I said idly.

"I had Alphonse help me do that the first thing this morning," Anne answered. She threw back her head and looked over her shoulder. "They looked so pretty," she added ruefully, "but, you know, I always *did* think they were dangerous, not anchored down except by their own weight."

"I'm beginning to think," I said dryly, "your whole place is unsafe. I was innocently sitting down by the stream this morning"—I lowered my voice and glanced around the semicircle humorously—"having a quiet cigarette where Aunt Maud wouldn't see me. When the first thing I knew a big rock came rolling down the bank and splashed into the stream right beside me. Six inches closer and it would have brained me."

Johnny was eying me and listening both inscrutably and imperturbably. Culbert clucked in distress, and Anne frowned and pulled off her sunglasses to regard me with concern.

"Why, Sis, how awful!" She turned her eyes in the direction of the stream. "How could it? And where did it come from?"

"It was one of those rocks bordering the path. Probably loosened to begin with, sometime, and some jar, a truck going past or something, set it rolling."

Culbert pursed his lips and turned his body in his chair to gaze up at the sun-deck railing.

"No sir," he stated decisively. "It was earthquake shocks—last night and today, too, I'll bet. I know you saw Rover playing around, Viv, but it isn't likely he'd bump that jar hard enough to knock it over."

Johnny straightened himself in his low chair with his heels on the stones, stretching his arms lithely, his body on a slant from his feet to his short curly brown hair.

"Maybe," he said lightly, "it was Rover being playful again this morning. Dangerous critter, that."

I met his mocking eyes innocently. "No, I think Culbert's probably right.

We're not many miles from the San Andreas Fault here. You often get little tremors."

"Where is Rover, by the way?" Culbert inquired. "I haven't seen him this morning."

"Oh, he's around. This seems to be one of his hunting days. He was barking furiously at a gopher hole early this morning." Anne laughed. "The silly old thing sees a gopher stick its head up, and then he digs and digs at the hole while the gopher has retreated half a block away in his run. He'll probably come home smelling to high heaven of skunk."

She paused, seemingly struck by a thought. "I'll go look at the place that rock came from after a while. Rover could have been digging there and loosened the ground that supported it—"

"Vivian!"

I looked up, and the other heads also turned, startled. Aunt Maud, still in her pansy-scattered robe, stood at the top of the stairs leading to the sun deck.

"Come up here. I want to talk to you."

I stiffened, and there was probably an unpleasant glint in my eyes, if she could have seen it from that distance. I dislike being ordered around.

But I made myself relax and stood up obediently. Aunt Maud had already turned and retreated from sight.

"The master's voice," Anne said sympathetically, *sotto voce*.

"Oh well," I shrugged, "she's old—and spoiled."

When I reached the top of the stairs, Miss Pringle was still reading in the swing. She lifted her eyes from her magazine and smiled sweetly, and it occurred to me that her little ears had probably been pricked up to catch every word she could from below. And she was just the type, I told myself grimly, who would trot in later to tell Aunt Maud everything she had heard.

The latter was standing inside, waiting for me, and she motioned with her head toward the bedroom door. "We'll go in here where we won't be disturbed."

I felt a prickle of uneasiness. Was I being called on the carpet? And if so, for what?

She closed the door behind us and then deliberately pulled in the casement windows over the sun deck and fastened them.

"It's hard," she said calmly, "to get any privacy in a small house like this."

She sat down then in the slipper chair, and I perched on the edge of the nearest twin bed, noting as I did so that the Bible, a *Thought for the Day* book, and a volume called *Eating for Health* had succeeded Anne's ash tray and lending-library novel on the bedside table.

"Why," Aunt Maud said abruptly, "were you looking for Johnny a while ago?"

It is difficult to fool the old woman, and I thought for a desperate instant that she had caught me unawares, but I found myself answering fairly glibly, with a deprecatory laugh, "Well, to tell you the truth, Aunt Maud, Johnny has a way of getting me irritated over nothing. His temperament isn't congenial to me. And well, I had asked him to—uh—to help me move the bed in the room Anne and I are sleeping in—so we'd get more air; and then when I'm ready to do it"—I shrugged and spread my hands—"no Johnny. It seemed to me he was deliberately avoiding me this morning to escape helping in any way, and I got mad and decided, by golly, I'd find him."

Aunt Maud, with her hands folded in her lap, kept her eyes on me narrowly; but she seemed to accept this weak story, and suddenly she leaned forward a little.

"Is Anne going to marry that man?"

"I hope not," I said simply.

"I don't trust him."

We met one another's eyes for a moment, and I felt like saying, but didn't, "You and me both, sister."

"It's got to be stopped," Aunt Maud announced with finality, and went on virtuously, "It would be different if I thought there was Love there. I believe in the beneficent influence of Love. But the bond there is not a spiritual one." She tightened her lips. "It's entirely of the Flesh."

"But what can we do?" I said mildly.

"We must Expose him."

"How?"

"I thought," she said with a shrewd look, "you might have some ideas."

I shook my head regretfully. If I told the "secret" Anne had confided to me last night, and Anne learned of it, as she would, she would never forgive me; I would lose her, and with her the only close blood tie I had.

"Well, he didn't spring into existence here and now, out of nowhere. What do we know about him except that he was in the war? If we knew something of his past, we might find something, an unsavory episode with a woman or something."

Somehow I was sure that Anne would forgive and dismiss any scandals of that sort that we might dig up. But you couldn't tell Aunt Maud that people didn't consider sexual misbehavior so seriously any more. Her reading didn't run toward things like the Kinsey Report.

"I'll tell you one thing," Aunt Maud declared flatly, "if Anne marries that creature, he'll never get his hands on a cent of my money. I'd rather leave her share to Miss Pringle and Alphonse, if they stay with me and remain loyal. You've no idea what a comfort that little thing has been to me. She's a ver-ry Spiritual person, not a worldly bone in her body. And Alphonse has been very reliable, not always wanting to run off on his own affairs.

He's always there when I want him."

My hands clenched on the candlewick bedspread on either side of me. It was the first time I had heard it in Aunt Maud's hands, but there was no questioning the sound. The whip had been cracked. I felt cold and sick and ugly inside, but I smiled faintly and murmured, "For her own sake, her future happiness, you can be sure, Aunt Maud, that I hope and pray Anne won't lose her head and marry him. I—I'll do my best to—influence her."

"I couldn't, of course," Aunt Maud proceeded loftily, "*threaten* her by saying anything like what I've just said to you; but we can both let her *see* that I—that we"—she corrected herself—"disapprove the match. People, I must say, are a constant source of amazement to me. Now, why you should want to saddle yourself with a nonentity like Culbert McCauley is completely beyond me. Although I will give you credit. In your case I don't believe it's *lust* as it is with Anne."

I had to swallow before I could reply. My manner, I hope, concealed the blind fury her words had evoked. If I have a fault, it is probably my inability to take kindly to criticism.

"Culbert is a nice man," I said placatingly, forcing myself to remember her will and the—at least—two hundred and fifty thousand dollars I should realize from it.

"Oh yes. Understand me, I have no *objection* to Culbert. It just seems so strange, not quite in character."

"I'm fond of him," I said flatly.

Our discussion petered out, after that, into platitudes, and in a little while I told her I must help Anne with lunch.

She looked at her own small silver-cased clock on the chest of drawers and rose energetically.

"Goodness, yes. Our little visit threw me off schedule. Usually I've changed into an afternoon costume by this time and am already relaxing in preparation for the midday meal. Tell Miss Pringle to hurry right in and change clothes or she won't have time for our usual ten minutes of quiet."

As I came out of the bedroom I saw through the windows that Miss Pringle was no longer alone. Alphonse sat on the edge of a low chair facing the swing, bent forward with his elbows on his knees, his hands hanging loosely clasped between them. The bald front of his head glistened in the sun. They were talking intently in low tones, Miss Pringle also leaning forward a little, her magazine doubled in her hands, her fingers riffling the pages.

She saw me as I came to the doors, and she drew back a little, and instantly, in a higher tone, said, "Oh, I don't think Miss Twilliger will be going anywhere this afternoon. I'm sure she won't mind if you go for a little hike. But I'll ask her for you. I see she's free now."

Alphonse had slowly straightened himself as Miss Pringle spoke, and turned toward me; and now he rose and, after inclining his head deferentially in my direction, said politely to Miss Pringle, "Thank you, ma'am."

"My aunt," I informed the companion somewhat formally, "asked me to tell you it is time to dress for lunch."

She came to her feet in a swirl of lavender-and-violet seersucker, clasping the *Reader's Digest* to her bosom with one hand and pushing at the side of her hair with the other.

"It's been so *pleasant* out here," she fluttered, "I do declare I just *forgot* the passage of time. Miss Twilliger and I *always* change from our morning coats"—she brushed at the long skirts of her robe—"long before noon—"

Still twittering away, she glided past me with her head to one side.

I stood still, looking at the bedroom door, thinking about Aunt Maud's "companion." It was natural, of course, that a woman of seventy should feel safer with someone living in the same house with her. As one's years drew on toward the closed door of death, one probably felt a greater need for the reassurance of contact with other living creatures.

She had always had a man to drive her car and keep up the yard and do odd jobs around her square two-story stucco house on a corner lot in an old middle-class neighborhood in San Diego; but Fred, who had lived in a room behind the garage and done these things for years, had finally become too old to be a reliable driver and had had to retire to live in the overcrowded bungalow of his married daughter. Fred's retirement had come soon after Aunt Maud hired Miss Pringle, and shortly after that, Alphonse had turned up.

Now I began to wonder where she had found these two, what she knew about them. I knew now, after observing their manner toward one another when they thought they were unobserved, that their relationship had more in it than one would expect between a gentlewoman-companion and a chauffeur and handy man. The question was: had an intimacy developed after the two met in Aunt Maud's establishment, or had they deliberately planned beforehand to worm themselves into her life together?

In the light of Aunt Maud's remark about leaving Anne's share to them, the pair showed up in a new aspect.

Chapter Nine

I descended the inside stairs reflectively. Anne was coming out of the dining room in her extremely brief, tight shorts and strapless bra.

"We're going to eat inside here," she informed me, pausing in the double doorway. "It's too hot at the table outside during the middle of the day."

She hitched her bra up a little over one breast and added, "I was just going down to slip something over this outfit. I'm afraid Aunt Maud would consider me too naked for mealtime."

I followed her down the hall, my eyes resting on the indentation of her spine down the smooth brown flesh of her back, cut across by the blue band of her sun-suit top. There was enough fat on her bones so that her shoulder blades did not protrude, but she looked somehow thin and little—unprotected and vulnerable.

She chattered in a low voice as she walked. "I *hope* Aunt Maud will approve of the menu. I wouldn't mind seeing that she had her own special things if"—she glanced over her rounded shoulder as she opened the door, and continued as I followed her into our room—"she'd let the rest of us eat what we pleased. But every time she discovers a new 'scientific principle' about food, she expects everybody else to accept her word on it instantly and takes it as a personal affront if you don't fall right in and start practicing it."

I had forgotten to reopen the window when I left the room, and Anne broke off with a "Whew! It's hot in here. I wonder how this window came to be closed."

As she flung open both sides of the window, I said musingly, "I think Aunt Maud's getting more dictatorial as she gets older. She always did pour on the advice, but in the past she never waited to see whether you followed it or not. But now she's getting so she's more interested in seeing that everybody does what she wants."

"I suppose you have to expect it," Anne said resignedly, pulling a short, buttoned-up-the-front dress, which matched her sun suit, from behind the monk's-cloth curtain that hid a closet in the corner of the room.

As I drew on my own jacket and buttoned up my skirt, Anne went on with a little rueful chuckle, "It's a nuisance, having to use this bedroom. I tried to bring down everything I would need from upstairs, but I'm always wanting something that's in a drawer in my own room."

She lighted a cigarette and laid it on the edge of the ash tray on the dresser, and untied the ribbon around her blue-gray hair, which she began to comb out swiftly.

I sat on the edge of the bed and lighted a cigarette of my own.

"What do you know about this Pringle and Alphonse? Where did she get them?"

"She told me, but I didn't pay much attention ..." Anne frowned faintly, remembering. "Yes, she advertised for a companion. I couldn't think for a minute whether it was an employment agency or a newspaper ad. She tried both, she said. But it was the advertisement that got Pringle. I remember Aunt Maud saying how Pringle exactly answered the description in the ad: quiet, of refined tastes, serious-minded, unmarried, no dependents, desirous of a permanent home— It must have taken half a column."

"What about Alphonse? Was he an ad too?"

"No-o, now that you mention it, it was Miss Pringle who recommended Alphonse. I think he was working in a garage or a service station or something, and either he'd worked for people Miss Pringle had or they'd traded at the station where he did work. Anyhow, Aunt Maud said Miss Pringle knew *of* him and suggested Aunt Maud interview him after she decided to let Fred go. Anyhow, Aunt Maud's well satisfied with Alphonse, which reflects well on Pringle in her mind. Because he, too, is just what the doctor ordered—no family to distract his mind from his work, quiet and dependable, glad to have a permanent, steady job."

Anne straightened the bow on her hair and said, "There! Now I can go get the feed bags ready."

"Just a minute," I said. "We've got plenty of time." I moved my head up and back toward the bedroom upstairs. "They're still dressing, and they have to relax before they take on the serious work of digestion. I tell you, Anne, I'm getting suspicious of that pair. I don't think it was accident, Miss Pringle ringing Alphonse in on the deal. I saw them together a while ago when they thought no one was looking, and there's something between them. They may even be married—"

"Oh, *Vivian*, that's fantastic. Why would they keep it secret?"

"Aunt Maud's ad called for a single woman, and Pringle probably needed work. She's no spring chicken—past fifty, or I miss my guess—"

Anne regarded me skeptically through her cigarette smoke, leaning her buttocks against the dresser.

"Anyhow—they're in cahoots," I argued firmly. "Maybe they *aren't* married. Maybe they're just—going together; but one thing I *do* know, they're out to get Aunt Maud's money."

"Well," Anne said mildly, "faithful servants usually are remembered in their employers' wills."

I surveyed Anne measuringly for a moment and then I said, "I might as well tell you, Aunt Maud's talk with me was about you and your affairs."

Anne's lips curved upward at the corners. "So?"

"She doesn't like Johnny."

Anne tapped her ashes into the tray and sighed. "I had already gathered that. He's too—unconventional, to suit her."

"She as good as appointed me her agent to break you two up."

"Why, the old meddler!"

"That's what started me thinking about Pringle and Alphonse. She hinted that if you married Johnny she'd leave your share of the money to them."

Anne straightened. "Well, let her! Of all the nerve—trying to run my life."

"I thought you should know, though. So you could be a little discreet. There's no use in antagonizing her unnecessarily, not when those two leeches are hanging onto her. Don't do anything like suddenly announcing your engagement. Hold off awhile, and she may soften up or forget what she has against Johnny."

"It makes me feel," Anne said savagely, "like dragging Johnny over to the courthouse Monday for a license, just to show her what I think of anyone who'd use their money to interfere in your personal life."

"That would be just dandy," I said sarcastically. "Maybe *you* don't care about laying your hands on a quarter of a million dollars, but *I* do."

"What's your share got to do with it?"

"Just this. We're sisters. We're fairly close, as sisters go. I've been unofficially appointed to control you on this. You go defying Aunt Maud and it's ten to one, no matter what I say, she'll turn on me too, figure I'm on your side instead of hers. And change her will, giving everything to *those two*. And then"—I leaned forward and finished ominously—"there's no telling what they might do. They might even kill her for her money. They could do it easy enough, alone with her all the time as they are."

Anne stared at me, aghast. "Vivian! How can you say such things? What gives you such ideas?"

I settled back on my hips. "I'm a realist," I said coldly. Then I added, a pleading note in my voice, "I want that money, Anne. I'd do anything to keep on the good side of Aunt Maud. For my sake, please don't do anything rash. If you up and married Johnny right now, in order to insure myself with her I'd have to denounce you and break off relations with you, or else Aunt Maud would conclude I wasn't loyal to her. Don't put me in a spot like that. Give this thing time."

Anne was looking at me rather oddly. But she nodded her head slowly. "O.K., Sis. After all, as I told you last night, I haven't made up my mind fully whether I even want to remarry."

Anne left the room then to see to lunch, and I went to the bathroom. I needed a few minutes to organize my mind and get a grip on myself for what I had to do next. It was odd how my actions seemed to follow a course which was like a well-thought-out plan, even though I hadn't consciously worked out the details.

Now, by letting Anne know Aunt Maud hated Johnny, I had given her something to think about after Johnny turned up poisoned. It would be obvious that someone had done it, and it was well that motives be pointed out in other directions than mine. Also, by showing her that Pringle and Alphonse were conniving creatures, it threw them into a murky light. Before anyone could be accused of murder, evidence and proof were necessary. None should be found in this case, but I wanted Anne, especially, to be aware of sinister forces around her.

It had been a shrewd move, too, my warning her not to rush into anything. No one, remembering this conversation, would dream that I was all set to kill the man, that I knew she would never have a chance to marry him. I was almost surprised at my own cleverness.

Regardless of the personal safety angles, I didn't want Anne ever to have suspicions about me. A person needs someone close and friendly, and Anne had always been that. It would be hard to lose her. That was the reason, probably, I had held back on telling her the truth about Johnny. People are funny, and I know how they'll sometimes turn against the person who pricks their bubbles of illusion, even though that person is perfectly innocent. It had seemed better to try to eliminate Johnny—at first by direct pressure on him, now by killing him in self-defense.

I had my hand on the bathroom doorknob when another interpretation of this morning's near accident flashed across my mind. I froze with my fingers on the knob. Suppose it hadn't been Johnny who pushed the stone. Either Alphonse or Pringle would like to see both me and Anne dead! Then Aunt Maud's money would be a lead-pipe cinch. And Alphonse had looked surprised when he opened the bedroom door and saw me. Suppose I did poison Johnny to keep him from killing me, and, after all, Johnny wasn't the one who was trying to do it. I would still be in constant peril. My throat felt dry as I swallowed.

I passed my hand distractedly over my forehead. I felt as if I were in a nightmare where hopeless confusion holds one helpless and immobile.

For a moment I had a feeling of having entered into a new kind of existence, as if, from the time the solution of my troubles had come to me while I read Anne's letter, I had become somebody else, as if I had been out of character ever since. I said and did things without consciously intending to beforehand, having afterward to explain them to myself. Like telling Anne to lay off Johnny on account of Aunt Maud, only realizing afterward that Aunt Maud's attitude toward him really didn't matter, since he would soon be dead anyway, and then reasoning to myself afterward that I had done it to throw suspicion on the old lady and away from myself.

And then, with difficult clarity, I saw that even these explanations to myself were not the whole story. There may have been these devious, subconsciously calculated motives behind the things I had said to Anne. But it was also that, in talking to her in our usual sister-to-sister way, as if I were not hiding secret intentions which would terrify her, I had permitted myself the momentary respite of forgetting what I had to do. There had been a need to become confidential with someone—anyone—to feel the momentary intimacy of gossipy talk, and I had chosen things I *could* talk about, finding, in so doing, a little relief from the weight of the secret intentions I could never share. These thoughts that I must keep to myself drove me by their awful *loneliness* to a need for sharing at least *some* kind of secret in confidential, conspiratorial contact with another person.

It wasn't like me to have undergone this compulsion toward making contact with someone else—even, I was sure, unconsciously. I had always been self-contained, on good terms with myself, in control of my outgoing impulses, able to pick and choose as to when and with whom and about what I should give myself in confidence. But now I had done it without conscious control.

Standing there with one hand on the doorknob, the other pressed against my head, I had an eerie sense of disembodiment, as if I could not be sure it was I, this tall, slender woman in the familiar body.

The very vagueness and uncertainty as to the means of carrying out my decisions. That wasn't like me. I am a definite, efficient person. To decide *that* I want to do something has always been accompanied by knowing *how* to do it. I have always seen and judged people and events clearly—no fuzziness, no uncertainty. I am a person who always knows the score. I get people's number, and I am seldom wrong. This quality is what has made me indispensable in the office. It is why Mr. Harder relies on me so completely, why I hold the whip hand over the rest of the office force.

But my clarity, my certainty, my decisiveness, seemed, especially in the last few hours since the attack on my life, to have dissolved. People, including myself, and their motives and their conduct, seemed to have become as fluid, as changing, as the moving surface of the stream down the hill. I had no sooner pinned down a certainty than it shifted, flowed out from under my fingers, and left me terrifyingly with nothing to hang onto.

Chapter Ten

With a mental wrench I brought myself back to the immediate next step. I had planned it carefully; I would go through with it. If Pringle and Alphonse remained an imminent menace, I should have to deal with them next.

Going down the hall, I remembered that we were eating in the dining room. This was a nasty little shock in itself. It meant a more conspicuous act in disposing of my envelope. But perhaps I could slip out and burn the stuff before we sat down, without anyone noticing; and then, if it ever came up, no one could say for sure *who* had burned the trash in the fireplace.

Anne was setting a long tray of sandwiches, both brown and white bread, with lettuce sticking temptingly out at the edges, in the center of the table, and she called out gaily as I appeared in the doorway, "The boys got everything ready while we were getting prettied up. Aren't they darlings!"

"We aim to please," Johnny said with a grin, appearing in the kitchen door with a platter on which were arranged radishes, celery stalks, little fresh green onions, and slivers of raw carrot. As Anne took the plate from him he said, "This is Culbert's handiwork. Artistic, ain't it?"

"Beautiful," Anne laughed. "Remember this, Sis, after you're married. You can make Culbert do the fancy touches when you give intimate little dinners."

"How about setting a date now," Johnny suggested with a bold look, hooking his thumb in the tea towel he had tied around his waist, "and giving us an invite?"

"It's a deal," Anne said gaily. "We insist on being your first dinner guests."

My face wrinkled in a sickly smile, and I put out my hand to the door casing, mumbling something about consulting Culbert on the date. I had to stand still there for a moment, fighting back totally unexpected emotions. Like a fool, I felt like crying, weakly and pitifully, like a child.

This was all so nice, so light and jolly and washed with the sunshine now slanting in through the south corner of the screened windows to fall in a triangle across the north side of the room. Why couldn't it be real? Two sisters and their boy friends, kidding about the engagement of one pair, looking forward innocently to cozy little get-togethers in the future. It sounded so happy and normal. All I wanted was to be happy like other people. But instead I was destined to be a murderess. And two other people were marked for sudden death.

Rather stiffly because I was struggling for control of myself, I said, "Well, now I'll do my share. I'll make the lemonade."

Johnny raised his hand, palm outward, and announced, "It's all done, Sis. Not a thing to worry about. Efficient kitchen help like us forget nothing. Ain't that so, Culbert?"

He had turned sideways in the doorway to admit Culbert, who had on one of Anne's blue-and-white checked bib aprons.

"Couldn't be righter," Culbert burbled, beaming at me as he entered bearing a bowl of potato chips and another of corn chips, which he set on the table.

"Now all we need are the guests," Anne declared. "I can call Alphonse, but I suppose we'll have to await the queen's pleasure." She wrinkled her nose humorously toward the upper story.

Culbert cocked his head, and we all heard voices at the top of the stairs. "No, they're coming," he said.

I had moved to the table and clutched the back of one of the blond maple chairs. My eyes fastened frantically on the pitcher and the glasses on the big tray Johnny was bringing in from the kitchen. He set the tray on the sideboard next to the door and began to pour the lemonade into the tall glasses with flowers on them, the ice cubes in the pitcher clunking against its sides as he poured. The glasses looked perfectly empty and clean, and he was pouring everybody's drink from the same supply. But I watched his hands fixedly.

Aunt Maud and Miss Pringle entered behind me, but I did not turn my head. Johnny was standing sideways, and suddenly I heard him say jokingly, "What's the matter, Vivian? Afraid I'm going to poison somebody?"

I started, realizing that he had noticed my absorption in the movements of his hands.

"I—I was just thinking," I muttered.

And I had been thinking, despairingly. Why, oh why, had I succumbed to that impulse to tell Anne my suspicions about Aunt Maud's servants? Why had I wasted time letting her know Aunt Maud was set against Johnny? By that delay I had lost my chance.

Panic nearly suffocated me. Time was passing by. I couldn't, I simply couldn't, keep thinking up new ways to commit murder. I might not even have any more opportunities. And meantime Johnny would still be alive, a constant menace to my own life—if it was Johnny. And it must be. That remark about my being afraid he was going to poison somebody. He knew I suspected him. Which made him doubly dangerous.

As we took our places at the table, unobtrusively I changed glasses with Culbert, who was to sit beside me, explaining, with what I hope passed for light humor, "I like lupines better than poppies."

Glancing up, I met Johnny's eyes defiantly. He was not smiling; his eyes were level upon me, and two faint lines deepened between his brows as our eyes met. Through my lashes I saw that he looked thoughtful as he sat down.

I pressed my lips together as Aunt Maud said grace. Maybe he *had* somehow slipped poison into my glass. But if he had, Culbert would get it. I had to pretend to eat, but I could hardly swallow. I nibbled at an olive or two, chewed valiantly on a piece of celery, and got down half a sandwich.

Everyone else seemed in good spirits, and Aunt Maud launched into a lecture on the beneficial effects of sun-bathing, from the point of view that ultraviolet rays had a purifying effect on the mind as well as a stimulating one on the body. The skin on her own face was lightly tanned and surprisingly firm for her age, though marked with lines around the eyes and mouth. She was wearing a gray linen dress with elbow-length sleeves, and the skin on her forearms was an ugly, mottled tan.

"Of course," she declared, "you people are very unwise to stay out as long as you all seem to have done this morning. *After* the sun has reached the zenith and is *declining* is the proper time for sun-bathing."

My eyes rested on Miss Pringle's face across from me. Her fair skin was a light, brickish color and there were dried flakes of white skin on her neatly shaped nose.

It slipped out before I had time to think. I was so bottled up and throttled and disgruntled generally that I suppose I *had* to say something nasty to somebody or explode then and there.

"I noticed you ordered Miss Pringle out in the morning sun," I said curtly.

Anne, at the end of the table, shot me a quick, surprised, but slightly mischievous glance.

"Miss Pringle," Aunt Maud said majestically, "tends to be anemic. She needs a stronger dose than most people."

I glanced cynically at the companion, who was silently dipping a radish in salt, a fixed, meaningless little simper on her mouth.

In that moment I became entirely convinced that Miss Pringle—regardless of Alphonse—had designs on my aunt. Nobody would put up with things like this unless they hoped to profit largely by it. Being ordered out in the broiling sun when she obviously had a tender skin, having her physical condition discussed as if her body were an inanimate object belonging to Aunt Maud.

My gaze shifted calculatingly toward Alphonse, who was as usual eating steadily and quietly.

In a stilted little voice Miss Pringle spoke. "Mr. Quade, would you pass the olives, please?"

It was the first time I had heard Alphonse's last name, or, indeed, thought of his having one.

He handed the woman the glass dish full of olives, and she said, "Thank you," formally, and offered the dish, next, to Johnny on her left, while Alphonse responded politely, "You're welcome," and took a drink of his lemonade from the glass with Indian paintbrush on it.

Anne caught my eye as this exchange took place and meaningly shook her head in a slow, slight movement, pushing out her lips a little.

She meant that this punctiliousness showed there was nothing between those two. But I lifted my eyebrows at Anne in contradiction of her headshake. *She* might be too naïve to suspect, but *I* detected the unnaturalness of this stiff formality. They were overdoing it.

When the meal was finished, Alphonse rose first, as usual, excusing himself, and spoke to Anne respectfully. "I'll be glad to do these dishes, ma'am, if you want to just leave 'em here when you get through. I'll come back in and clear off."

"Why, thanks, Alphonse." She smiled at him in a friendly way. "That's very nice of you."

"There's no reason," Aunt Maud said firmly, "why he shouldn't make himself useful ..." She paused and nodded dismissingly to the man, who had hesitated when she began to speak. "You can go now, Alphonse." And again to Anne, "Goodness knows he has little enough to do here. Maybe you have some gardening or some repairs he could take care of."

Alphonse held the screen door so that it closed quietly behind him as he went out to the terrace. I heard a sharp little "Crack!" at the table and looked down to find that Miss Pringle had broken a celery stalk in two. Her eyes were downcast and her face dead-pan, however.

"Oh no, Aunt Maud," Anne was saying, somewhat embarrassed, "there's nothing that needs doing right now."

"Well, goodness knows, I pay him enough," Aunt Maud remarked complacently. "It wouldn't hurt him to do something to earn it."

I looked down at my plate, scattered with the bits of food I hadn't been able to eat, and wondered why Alphonse hadn't killed her before this. But, of course, they would wait until the heirs were disposed of and her will changed.

Anne's expression had become unconcerned once more as she made some bantering remark to Johnny, her bright eyes and her warmly brown skin looking even more lively in contrast with the dull gray hair. I felt physically cold. Vital, affectionate, carefree Anne, my little sister, brutally murdered so these vultures could get the money that was coming to her. And myself—cold and lifeless too. They would do it. I had no doubt of it. And probably this week end, while they had us together.

I was breathing fast and shallow, and I tried to stop, to draw my breath slowly and normally, so no one would notice my agitation.

I wanted to get up and run screaming down the mountain road where, here and there, other houses perched stolidly and reassuringly among the trees—away from this place which was becoming a house of horror.

I was afraid. Afraid!

But I mustn't go to pieces. Keep calm. Think of a way out. Get rid of that sinisterly hypocritical little woman, that silent, powerful man with the hard, workman's hands. I had noticed the thick, square-nailed fingers on the light-colored chair back as he stood after rising from the table.

Craftily, I began to think, growing calmer as I did so. Two I had already marked down, because I didn't dare take a chance about Johnny. Perhaps, somehow, I could get all four of them together. But how? Think! I must think! Distractedly my mind scurried about, getting nowhere, until I felt myself growing panicky again.

"What are you so preoccupied about, Vivian?" Johnny broke into my thoughts heartily.

"She's in love," Anne teased. "All girls act like that when they're first engaged."

I felt the blood rising to my face and heard Culbert laugh with Anne and Johnny, and somehow I managed to cackle a bit too.

"Well," Aunt Maud said briskly, "siesta time. Come on, Miss Pringle." She stood up, dropping her napkin so it stood in a pointed heap. "Now, don't the rest of you go rushing around, getting overheated right away after you eat. You ought to all lie down for an hour."

"We'll rest," Anne promised with a smile. "Don't worry about us. Later on we'll all go down to the pool for a dip."

"Miss Pringle and I will come down and watch," Aunt Maud volunteered generously, and they went off, single file, toward the stairs.

When they were out of earshot, Anne said meditatively, "Tomorrow being Sunday, we *will* be in for it. I might as well warn you, children, we shall all have to pile into the Lincoln and go to church in the morning—"

"Dibs on one of the jump seats," Johnny put in flippantly.

"She called up the Chamber of Commerce yesterday," Anne went on, "and got a list of the churches in Los Gatos. She picked the Presbyterian."

"Why?" Culbert inquired.

"I suppose it seemed sort of bland and neutral. Naturally no denomination is wholly correct. Only Aunt Maud has been able to discern the true and final meanings in the Scriptures."

We had lighted cigarettes after Aunt Maud left the room, and I smoked nervously, waiting to see what plans would be proposed for the hour before we could swim; but everyone sat lazily, the conversation drifting hither and thither. I hoped this mood would prolong itself until Anne and I could go off alone to dress. I didn't want to be alone in this place again.

But there are times when convention dictates privacy, and I was uncomfortably aware of one of those occasions coming on. Finally I couldn't stand it any longer, so I excused myself and hurried down the hall, locking the bathroom door behind me and closing and locking also the one high window of opaque glass.

When I came out and hastened back to the dining room it was empty except for Alphonse gathering up dishes. He glanced heavily at me, and I kept going till I reached the stairs. The quiet told me no one else was on the lower floor, and I didn't intend to stay there alone with *him*. And I hadn't the courage to walk past him to the terrace.

In the corner made by the two lowest steps of the stairway stood an umbrella stand, and my eye fell on Anne's walking stick, a sturdy piece cut from a limb of madrone, with carving cut out in the smooth, rust-colored wood. Instinctively I lifted it out of the stand and climbed the stairs. I didn't feel quite so helpless with the stick in my hand. It could serve as a defensive club if necessary.

There was no one in the living room, and as I reconnoitered the sun deck through the windows I saw that it, too, was vacant. Quietly I went out on the plank floor scattered with porch furniture. I chose a padded bamboo chair in the shade of the wall, from which I could see the top of the outdoor staircase and the doors from the living room. I stood the stick up against the chair arm and leaned back wearily.

Then I heard steps on the stairs from the terrace, and I straightened, alert in every nerve; but it was Culbert's round skull, inadequately trimmed with dust-colored hair, which rose into sight.

"Oh, there you are," he greeted me.

"Sh-h," I warned. "Aunt Maud and that woman are taking their nap in there." I nodded at the shallow windows standing open down the wall.

"That's right. I forgot."

He tiptoed over and took a chair in the shade near me.

I relaxed against the cushion and closed my eyes. I was glad Culbert had come up. If I was safe with anybody, it was with him.

"Where are Anne and Johnny?" I asked in a tired voice.

"I don't know where Anne is. She said something about walking down toward the stream to see where the rock came loose that almost hit you. Johnny's down by the pool, taking another sun bath. I was just down there, but I've had all the sun I want for one day."

He had kept his voice low, and since we were toward the opposite end of the deck, I was fairly sure we were not disturbing the siestas in the bedroom.

Reassured by the safety of Culbert's presence, my mind began to stiffen up out of its jellylike state of fear and to function again. Perhaps, if I went ahead with my original intention, in the resulting shock and confusion these others might be jarred or frightened out of immediate prosecution of their evil designs. There would be police about. Surely none of them would dare, under such conditions, to commit another murder. Everyone would be too busy trying to prove he hadn't done the first one to think of trying another—so soon. I might even be able to direct suspicion toward Johnny, eliminate him *that* way.

Why was not now as good a time as any? We were all scattered. Nobody could swear to where anyone else was. Aunt Maud and Miss Pringle were asleep in separate beds.

Culbert was rambling on, something about swimming, what an expert diver he'd been in his youth; but I scarcely heard him. I rose abruptly and walked to the railing. Down below, on the runway beside the pool, I could see Johnny lying with his face on his crossed arms, wearing only trunks. The terrace was bare, the shade now extending in a slanting wedge across nearly a quarter of it. I glanced around the grounds. Anne was nowhere in sight. Alphonse, judging from the sounds of china against silver, was still washing dishes.

As I came thoughtfully back to my chair, Culbert's voice cut through my abstraction. "What's the matter with you today, Vivian?" His voice, still held low, had an edge on it; and his eyes were sharp and disapproving, his lips pursed a little sulkily.

I forced myself to act natural.

"Matter? Why, I didn't know that anything was the matter with me."

"You've been acting damned funny. Kind of a wild look in your eye one minute; butter wouldn't melt in your mouth the next. What's eating you?"

"I didn't know. That is"—I halted, disturbed—"*have* I been acting—that is, do you think anybody else thinks I've been—well, not quite myself?"

"I don't know what anybody else thinks." He smiled sardonically, and, on him, the look was so out of place that it was almost frightening. "What's the matter? Is it so tough being engaged to me that it's making you act nutty?"

"Maybe I am a little—upset. Taking such an important step. Giving up my independence. They say every woman is nervous before her marriage."

I smiled ingratiatingly. I mustn't arouse his suspicions. But I must get rid of him quickly. I had to get it over with, now while I had a chance.

My hand closed over the walking stick's handle, carved so it fit the curve of the hand.

"What have you got that up here for?" Culbert asked curiously.

"Why, I—I had thought of taking a hike after I rested a little. Would you like to go along?"

"Not me." He stretched out his feet in brown canvas oxfords with rope soles. "I tramped around enough below the swimming pool this morning. It's too steep around here for walking."

"Well"—I rose, and my throat felt dry, as if I squawked when I talked—"I think I'll go walk around a little."

So intent had I become on my plans that I almost reeled back with shock when Anne's voice sang out softly from inside the living room, "You going for a hike, Viv? I see you have my stick. If you don't go too far, I'll go with you."

"I—I was, but—but I've changed my mind. It's—it's too hot—after all."

"I think so too."

Anne came and flopped on the swing, making it creak. "Soon be time for a good swim, anyway."

I sat down leadenly, the stick across my knees. Culbert was looking at me with his eyebrows pulled down, the sulky look more pronounced on his mouth.

Anne suddenly stopped pushing the swing with her foot. "Vivian," she demanded, "aren't you well?"

I rallied with all the faint strength I had left and smiled apologetically. "It's funny; Culbert was just now saying I didn't look well. I think probably it's the heat today. The sudden change after the cool weather in the city. Every once in a while I feel a little giddy."

"Maybe you'd better lie down instead of going swimming."

I thought of being alone in our room downstairs, which really would be hot and stuffy now, alone there with Alphonse prowling around in the house while all the others were down at the pool, and I shuddered away from the idea.

I laughed scornfully. "Heavens, I'm all right, Anne. Of course I'm going swimming."

I went on talking lightly then, but inside I was sick, sick, sick. It was bad enough to be in the spot I was in, and—from the way things had been going—never to succeed in escaping it by ridding myself of the person who had put me there, without being also surrounded by so many mortal enemies whose danger no one else could see. I could not even get help against Johnny, the main danger; for no one, not even Culbert, and, least of all, Anne, would believe he had tried to kill me once already.

That was the worst of it. I had no one to share my fears with. I had tried to reveal the Pringle-and-Alphonse setup to Anne and earned only a poorly concealed disapproval of my suspicions. And I couldn't explain why Johnny was after me without revealing that I had already partially betrayed my promise not to tell what she had told me. And if I told Anne's "secret" to anyone else, she would learn it sooner or later, and I would lose her good will, perhaps not only now, but forever.

I felt as if I were in a spiked cage with the walls drawing in all around me.

Chapter Eleven

When Anne and I went down to our room to get ready for swimming, I happened to catch a glimpse of myself in the mirror and I paused for a moment, surprised. It was no wonder she had asked if I felt well. I couldn't say just what gave my face its strained, haggard look. Perhaps it was the unnaturally bright, darting glint in my eyes; perhaps the lines standing out more than usual on my face, especially the ones marking off my cheeks between my nose and mouth.

I must get hold of myself. I couldn't go to pieces, not among the enemies besetting me on all sides.

All I had to do to prepare for the swim was take off my skirt and jacket, for the lined shorts and halter of my play suit also served as a bathing suit. Holding a towel and my rubber cap, I stood and waited for Anne to get into two pink jersey garments which were even less extensive than her sun suit.

As we walked down toward the pool, Rover came climbing up the terraced walk toward us, his tail drooping dispiritedly, his tongue hanging out, his legs and the underside of him wet and dirty.

"What did I tell you?" Anne said. "That dog has been out hunting rabbits, and anything else he could find, all day. Now I'll have to keep an eye on him that he doesn't get inside on the rug upstairs till he dries off. We probably ought to bathe him tonight."

Rover looked up at her wistfully, and his tail swung lethargically. Anne patted his head, and he turned and padded downhill beside her.

"And by the way," Anne added, "I found the place where the rock was dislodged, and sure enough, there was a gopher hole right beside it, and our friend here had been digging around it. Maybe not today, but anyhow, he had the earth undermined beside and under the stone."

I glanced down at the big dog sharply. His coat was a dull tan, with white feet and breast and a long diamond of white on his forehead. What I had seen moving in the bushes had been a drab color like his. Could it have been Rover, running through the brush after some little wild animal? Could this accident really have been set off by the dog? His feet sending a clod of dirt or a smaller stone rolling against the already precariously balanced rock, which at that moment jarred loose and fell toward me?

But no, it was stretching coincidence too far. The movement I had seen might as easily have been the khaki-clad legs of Alphonse. And both Johnny and Culbert had been wearing tan slacks. The blur of color might even have been the nondescript shade of Miss Pringle's housecoat. Or even—my mind tripped over the possibility as I walked with eyes cast down, seeing Anne's golden-brown legs flashing along beside me—even Anne's tanned limbs.

We were beside the pool where Culbert and Johnny were lying on their backs, toasting their chests. I crumpled on one of the stained canvas mats on the cement runway beside the pool.

Anne! She was going to great lengths to suggest that Rover was responsible.

Not Anne. Not my own sister. But how did one ever know what lay festering in the depths of another's mind? Who would have guessed, for instance, that *I* had come down from the city with murder in my heart? If I couldn't trust myself not to harbor such intentions, how could I trust anybody else!

And Anne, by her own admission, must be running short of money. She liked an easy life like this, sun-bathing, entertaining, spending money foolishly on her appearance—like that hair. And if I were gone, she would be Aunt Maud's sole heir. In ten—fifteen—years Aunt Maud would die, and Anne would have the means to continue this life of leisure forever.

It seemed fantastic, knowing Anne; but then anyone knowing me would have thought it equally fantastic that *I* should seek a way out of my difficulties via murder. She might have a long-range plan worked out. First me; then, in a year or so, Aunt Maud. And then she and Johnny could sit it out—as Anne thought—till Priscilla Lloyd kicked off. They might even be in this together.

I looked sickly at the pair of them: Anne had thrown herself down on her stomach beside Johnny and, propped up on her elbows, was tickling his nose with a geranium leaf she had picked off a bush above the pool.

I lifted my eyes and swept them wildly over the setting around us, the dark bank of redwoods below, the spreading green maples and the tall tanbark oaks with their long slim leaves, north of the pool.

Oh God! Oh no. The world couldn't be like this.

Trills of bird song ran out in little broken ribbons from the trees. Overgrown geraniums grew lush and deep pink along the bank above the pool. The sky was an unbroken brilliant blue canopy over the sunburned hills rising on all sides, the hollows in their sides padded with wooded growth. The leaves of the bushes all about trembled gently in the breeze.

It was all beautiful and peaceful and open and sunny.

I leaned on my arms braced behind me, palms out on the hot canvas, and closed my eyes.

But I knew what dark and cruel and violent purposes could lie in the depths of the human beings inhabiting these idyllic surroundings. I knew how little one could trust even those who pretended to care for you. Oh yes, I knew, by the surest of all criteria—that of personal experience.

Aunt Maud and Miss Pringle were coming down from the house, but I did not turn my head to look at them until they were with us. Aunt Maud ensconced herself on a folding canvas chair in the shade of the bank west of the pool, and Miss Pringle, in a modest black bathing suit with an overskirt, sat on the edge of the cement and dabbled her feet in the water, squealing in refined tones at its chilliness as she pulled a white rubber cap over her hair.

The others began to pile in, Johnny taking off from the diving board; but I answered their shouts to join them by saying I wanted to wait a bit.

Miss Pringle stayed in the shallow water, swimming a few strokes and then settling on her feet to watch the other three showing off, diving and ducking each other. I watched the play narrowly. I was afraid to get in. All that horsing around. On the pretext of playing, somebody could hold you under too long, or even break your neck, wrestling around as Johnny and Anne were doing at the moment, each trying to duck the other.

I rose and sauntered over to Aunt Maud, and sat down on the hardpacked ground beside her chair. We exchanged a few idle remarks, and Aunt Maud informed me that she always liked to be near water, probably because she was born in the zodiacal sign of Cancer. Since she was happily off on a subject that interested her, I didn't follow too closely.

I had been sitting there a few minutes when Alphonse emerged on the trail just below the pool. He was bareheaded, and as he came out on the level area he paused and, drawing a handkerchief from his hip pocket, wiped the sweat from his face. It is quite a climb up from the ravine, where there is another stream into which Anne's empties. He had obviously been for a walk, and he carried a stout stick he had picked up along the way to help him climb.

"Go get your suit on, Alphonse," Anne called hospitably, "and get cooled off."

"Yeah, come on in; the water's fine," Johnny seconded blithely.

The man's eyes slid toward me and Aunt Maud and then down to Miss Pringle.

"Well, if you don't mind," he said with a slow smile, "I think I will."

As he went past us he nodded, somewhat hesitantly, I thought, in our direction.

He was barely out of earshot, and perhaps he wasn't clear out, when Aunt Maud said primly, "I know Anne means well, but I wish she wouldn't be quite so familiar with Alphonse. After all, he is a servant, and I can't have him getting so he doesn't keep his place."

"You don't regard Miss Pringle in quite the same light?"

"Oh dear, no. Of course she's an *employee*, but more of a social equal."

"But *she* doesn't seem to consider Alphonse her social inferior," I said innocently.

Aunt Maud's head slewed around toward me. "What do you mean?"

"Why, nothing. Only they were chatting quite intimately on the sun deck this morning when I came out of your room, and I've noticed several times this week end their attitude toward each other when no one else is about is—well, sociable, to say the least. And anyhow, they were related to each other in some way before they went to work for you, weren't they?"

Aunt Maud was wearing sunglass lens over her regular glasses, and I could not see the expression in her eyes, but the rest of her face, looking down at me, was pulled into a thoughtful frown.

She turned her head toward the water, and I saw that Miss Pringle was standing against the end of the tank, her back to us, only a dozen feet away. She might have heard me, but I doubted it, with the cap over her ears and the others yelling and splashing a few feet away. My nerves fluttered a little, however, at the thought. It would be bad to put them on guard, to make them feel that I was an imminent menace to their standing with Aunt Maud.

The latter was saying impatiently, as if to reassure herself, "Miss Pringle had met him. She knew he was looking for a new position."

I kept my voice low as I said with a significant chuckle, "Maybe that's what she tells *you*. There's some sort of relationship there, though, or I miss my guess."

"Ridiculous," Aunt Maud sniffed.

But I knew I had planted doubt in her mind. Alone as she was, with only Anne and me in any way "belonging" to her, Aunt Maud was jealous of those close to her. She was really lonely, and hungry for attention. She didn't want the thoughts, and possible affections even, of the members of her household diverted from her own person. That was why she had been careful to pick a lone, unattached woman as a companion, why she had wanted a chauffeur who had no other demands upon him but hers. She wouldn't like those two thinking more about one another than about her.

Well, she couldn't say I hadn't warned her. And she might think twice now before she lightly disinherited her own blood in favor of deceitful strangers.

I knew, for the looks of things, I should have to take at least a little dip, and I decided to go in now, before Alphonse came back and I had still another one to watch out for in the water. I would stay at this end, away from the others. I was bigger and stronger than Miss Pringle anyway, and she wouldn't try any funny business directly under Aunt Maud's eyes.

So I pulled on my cap, pushing my hair well up into the top, and went over to the pool. As I lowered myself into the water, gasping from its first cold touch, Miss Pringle, with what can only be described as a dirty look, rather pointedly climbed out of the pool, pulling herself up on her stomach over the edge of the cement.

Standing waist-deep, my hands still on the side of the tank, I shivered with more than the chill of the water. She had heard me. Had I been a fool again? Indiscreet? Rushing blindly into worse danger?

"Well," I thought defiantly, "at least they know now they're not putting anything over on *me*."

And I struck out with a side stroke, almost welcoming the shock of the water against my hot flesh.

The others greeted me with loud cries, urging me down to the deep water. But I paddled around where I could put my feet on the bottom when I chose.

When Alphonse arrived and dived in from the side, Miss Pringle arose from where she had been sitting cross-legged beside Aunt Maud and, with her towel over her shoulders, climbed toward the house.

Now that Alphonse was in the water, the pool, which was only forty feet long, seemed, for me, too crowded for comfort, and I climbed out at the end near Aunt Maud. As I came toward her, she was looking full at me, and suddenly she reached up and unsnapped the sun lens off her regular glasses and stared fixedly at my face a few feet above her in the full glare of the sun. I met her gaze blankly for a moment and then turned my head to look for my towel and bent to pick it up. I passed the towel over my face and saw that Aunt Maud's eyes were still fastened upon me with something startled and incredulous in them.

"What's the matter?" I ejaculated, taken aback.

"Your head," she said in a strange, toneless voice, and went on, almost vacantly, "The lines—of a—face—they show so much more—plainly—in a bathing cap."

My own eyes must have grown fixed, widening in horror as my own mind appreciated what must have entered hers.

For seconds, perhaps, we remained so, each held in stunned fascination by the other, yet each of us hardly aware of the other as a person, so numbed were our minds by the knowledge to which each of us must adjust.

Then I jerked my gaze away and moved out farther into the sun, roughly pulling off my cap, shaking the softening hair loose around my temples.

Somehow I got my feet into my sandals and stumbled fast but blindly toward the house. I ran through the rooms and slammed the bedroom door closed behind me and wedged the chair under it.

Turning, I saw myself, wild-eyed and disheveled, in the mirror. Like a sleepwalker, I moved closer to the glass, put my hands up, pulling my hair back and off my face. Yes, it brought the structure of my skull out more plainly when the blurring hair was out of the way. And I had taken off my glasses for the swim.

I had never seen my real father, not even a picture; but he had probably not worn glasses, and a man's hair was always held back and close to the head, as the cap had held mine. My naked face, bare of all make-up, too, for once, had helped to expose the resemblance.

But would Aunt Maud figure it all out at once? Might she not conclude it was only a remarkable coincidence? If she did deduce the facts, she was not one to keep silent. She would confront me with her deductions.

My mouth hardened. Well, I had cold-bloodedly planned murder once. Not only once, but twice. I would kill before she had time to change her will.

I put my fingers to my temple with an air of bewilderment. (Looking into the glass, it was like watching another person uncover these thoughts.) Why had I not thought of it before? Aunt Maud. She had been the one to kill all the time. Her death would make all the others unnecessary—except possibly Johnny's. He would fear my exposing him even more then—with Anne's inheritance almost in his hands. But the others. I wouldn't need to worry about the others if Aunt Maud were dead.

I pressed both hands against my temples and sank onto the bed, unmindful of the damage my wet suit would do to the covers.

I had botched things up enough, made enough mistakes. I must think, really think, logically, clearly, this time. Why was it I had been so bungling all the way, my mind darting at this and at that idea, all of them confusing me until I didn't know which way to jump, making decisions only to have them canceled out by accidents; and not being able to take the failures philosophically, to proceed calmly to the next necessary steps?

I could not go on with this bungling. I had to be forceful, decisive, unemotional about the thing.

Chapter Twelve

There was a knock on the door, and it went like an electric current through my nerves. I stared at the ivory-painted door panels, barely breathing in my will to make no noise that would reveal my presence.

"Miss Haines!"

It was Miss Pringle's voice, determined, yet pleading. "Please, I want to speak to you."

My silence had brought a scared, entreating note to the voice.

"What do you want?" I asked harshly.

Anne's gun was upstairs in a drawer of the desk. This woman could be trying to get me to open the door so she could shoot me.

"I just want to talk to you. Please!"

She was almost tearful now, and I frowned uncertainly. Her tone implied that it was *I* who had her in *my* power.

I bit my lips, but then I rose and pulled the chair out and, standing back of the door, cautiously opened it. She sidled in, and my breath escaped in relief as I saw that she held no weapon.

Now that she was inside, she faced me with a sort of timid defiance.

"I heard what you were saying to Miss Twilliger down at the pool."

"Well?" I said coldly.

"I don't know how you found out. I couldn't overhear all you said, but it's obvious some way you learned of the—relationship between us."

"So—you *are* married!" I pronounced triumphantly.

Her face was almost comically blank, and before she had time to consider the ignorance my statement revealed, she exclaimed, "Oh no! Alphonse is my brother."

Then it was my turn to look blank.

Her lips tightened, and her sunburned little face grew even brighter pink over the cheekbones.

"I thought you knew," she said angrily. "From what I heard, you were talking as if you did."

"I knew something funny was going on, all right," I snapped.

"But there isn't anything—wrong," she protested pitifully. "We—lied, I know, to Miss Twilliger; and that wasn't right, of course. But—well, you know how she is. And I've worked for older people, wealthy people, before. I've learned to understand them. I soon found out—well, how she was— after I went to work for her. I don't mean any disrespect, but I knew she'd be—jealous, if there was someone else I cared for around all the time. So I—well, I just didn't tell her Al was my brother. He needed work, and this is such a pleasant job, and she pays well. We're able to save a little. And it's nice being near each other."

She paused, out of breath in her earnestness.

"Oh, please, Miss Haines, don't spoil it for us. I'm fifty-five now, and Al's past fifty, too; and, for people our age, you don't run across work as easy and pleasant as this every day. That's all we want, believe me, to feel safe in our jobs—"

She paused, as if a fresh idea had occurred to her, and her eyes fastened on me speculatively. Then she added with a softening in her tone, like one reassuring a child, "We aren't after her money, Miss Haines. Really we're not. Even if I could, I wouldn't do anything against your interests with her. So, please, don't try to turn her against us, will you? She would be angry if she knew we'd deceived her. She has such strict—principles. My lie would seem—immoral to her. And I don't see any reason she should be up-set by being told. And it means so much to us. That's why I—well, I low-ered my pride to come to you. I thought if I laid my cards on the table, you'd—forgive us, and try to reassure Miss Twilliger if she suspects us now. Someone has to look after her as she gets older, and I can promise you and Mrs. Everett," she finished earnestly, "that we'll take good care of her. I know you want that."

Somehow, despite all my reasons for distrusting her, there was some-thing convincing about this beseeching little woman. The sincerity of her voice and manner got through to me in spite of myself.

"I—I'll think about what you've said," I returned brusquely. "If you"—I swallowed uncomfortably—"if you're really being—honest with me, I guess it's not— Maybe I was mistaken," I finished abruptly.

She smiled hopefully. "Oh, I was sure it was just a misunderstanding. That's why I thought, if I just came and talked to you, frankly, everything would be straightened out."

We became aware then of Anne's and the men's voices on the terrace out-side, and Miss Pringle slipped away, murmuring, "Thank you, thank you so much, Miss Haines."

While Anne and I stumbled around each other in the aisle beside the bed and in front of the closet in the corner, trying to get dressed, I remembered the suspicions about Anne which had invaded my mind down by the pool, and I was silent and withdrawn.

Somehow I managed to jam myself into my suit skirt and my extra blouse with the frill down the front and lace edging on the cuffs.

Anne, too, dressed more elaborately for this Saturday evening dinner, in a square-necked pale blue linen dress with short sleeves and a flaring skirt, and high-heeled sandals.

As she put on coral earrings and a string of beads to match, she said, "Now, if it weren't for Aunt Maud, we could all stretch out on the sun deck with Tom Collinses for a while before dinner."

I grunted noncommittally, bent over drawing on my spectator pumps. Straightening, I saw Anne holding her head back slightly to observe the effect of her beads in the mirror. She *would* have looked sweet—if it hadn't been for her hair.

Irascibly I snapped, "I hope to God you'll get that stuff washed out of your hair the next time you have it done—if it'll *come* out. You look like hell."

Her face crinkled in a smile and she made a face at me in the glass; then she whirled, her skirt flaring like a ballerina's, and, putting a hand on each of my shoulders, she kissed the top of my head.

"It's a good thing I know your bark is worse than your bite, Sis, or my lil ol' feelings would be hurt."

She went out then, and I didn't even bother to put the chair under the door. I'd got to the point where I almost didn't care. I had an exhausted feeling of, "All right, let them all attack me in a body, and be damned to them."

Parenthetically I thought that it was funny, the way I seemed to be thinking in swearwords so often, which are something I never use, considering it vulgar.

After I had put on lipstick and a little more rouge than usual, I opened my purse, lying on the dresser, to make sure the envelope with the arsenic was still there where I had put it when I went down to the pool. I stood for a moment looking at it and then snapped the bag shut.

It would have to wait till tomorrow, about Aunt Maud. I simply didn't have the mental energy left tonight to work out plans for poisoning anybody.

Through the thin wall between our room and the bathroom I could hear someone running water. Probably Culbert, shaving before dinner. He would be good for another hour before making an appearance. It took Culbert longer than a woman to make his toilet.

I went down the hall and glanced into the kitchen. Anne was standing in front of the refrigerator, pulling out a tray of ice cubes.

"Starting dinner already?" I inquired.

She winked at me. "Nope; fixing a highball for Johnny and me. He's still down by the pool, and I thought I'd sneak down and we'd sit against the bank there where you and Aunt Maud were sitting this afternoon and have a quick one. Want to come along?"

I thought of being alone down there with those two, neither one of whom I trusted now, hidden by the bank from the others in the house, and I declined.

"Hasn't Johnny dressed yet?"

Anne giggled. "He probably has. He's very casual about those things. His 'dressing' consists of letting his trunks dry out and then putting his pants and shirt back on."

I wandered restlessly out onto the terrace, keeping well away from the edge of the sun deck above. From the north windows I could hear Aunt Maud's and Miss Pringle's voices indistinguishably. In a few minutes Anne came out, carrying a small tray with two tall glasses, and set off down toward the pool, first saying conspiratorially, "If you and Culbert want to sneak one in the kitchen when he comes out, hop to it."

I watched her go down and turn and disappear behind the miniature cliff topped with giant geraniums, which ended the yard area and began the swimming-pool level. Envy stirred in my heart as I pictured the two of them in canvas chairs, sipping their drinks and smoking and talking confidentially, cozily. Things never worked out that way for me.

I wondered what they said to one another when they were alone. Could it be that they were in cahoots to get me out of the way? It seemed fantastic. Not Anne. Irresponsible, impulsive little Anne. But how could one know, for sure, about anybody?

My eyes surveyed the yard speculatively. On the other side of the beds of violently hued ice plants Anne was trying to cultivate a border of roses along the north edge of her grounds. She had several varieties, Talisman, Cécile Brunner, an old-fashioned pink cabbage rose. At the end, an old vine of single-petaled white roses grew profusely over a trellis six feet high that had been there when she bought the place. It sat cater-cornered between the row of geraniums and the cabbage rose, and it was now a fan-shaped mass of shiny green leaves brightened by an occasional splash of white. Its main blooming season was over.

Idly, without any conscious intentions, I stepped off the terrace and wandered over to the rose bushes, touching a flower here and there, moving slowly down the yard. When I reached the trellis I glanced casually toward the house. It sat there still and placid, no one in sight on either level.

I could hear the murmur of Anne's and Johnny's voices below and, glancing up at the rose vine, touching the petals of a flower, as if I were lazily inspecting the shrub, I moved around behind the trellis on the dirt which Anne kept clear of weeds and grass. Back of the trellis, I was shut from sight, both of people in the house and of anyone at this upper side of the pool. Softly I moved along the wall of thorny vines and glistening leaves to where, although I couldn't see them, I could distinctly hear the two below.

Instinctively, then, I took a step backward. Eavesdropping was a cheap, underhanded thing to do. But I stiffened my mind and stood my ground. When one's life, perhaps, was at stake, one didn't quibble over ethics.

And my surmise had been right. They *were* talking about me.

"... I don't know what's got into Vivian this week end," Anne was saying. "She seems to be just a bundle of nerves. And snappy! Of course she always does have a rather abrupt manner and a curt way of speaking. But she's been simply on edge all day."

"There's something screwy about this engagement of hers and Culbert's," Johnny said thoughtfully. "He seems pleased enough about it, and he obviously tries to make up to her, but most of the time she hardly seems aware of his existence."

"Maybe that's what's upsetting her. She gave her consent in an unguarded moment, and now she regrets it. Because, honestly, I don't think she gives a damn about Culbert, though he's an awfully nice, agreeable little fellow. You could have knocked me down with a feather when I heard they were going to get married. It was just one of those things, you know, their going together. He was from back home, and he was somebody to take her out to dinner and to a show occasionally. She found it pleasant, naturally, to have a man to go out with now and then."

"I wonder why she's never married. When you get behind the prickly exterior manner, Viv's a decent enough sort. And she's not bad looking. Austere, but good bone structure, the type who will be handsome even in old age."

"Well, it's that very austerity. Her forbidding manner holds men off. And then I told you about the love affair she had. She changed somehow, slowly but definitely, after she and Dwight drifted apart. She cared for him—deeply; and as far as Viv was concerned, she'd have shared her furnished room with him and been willing for them to starve together, back there in 1931. But no, he had his pride. Sometimes she'd have work when he didn't, and he wasn't going to get married without a dime—and I mean that literally."

Johnny uttered a short, bitter laugh. "You don't need to tell me. I know."

"—and maybe have his wife have to share her pittance with him. And well—you know how things go. They just didn't stick together. He went to L.A. Somebody heard of somebody who knew somebody who *might* have a job for him there, but it didn't materialize; and by the time Viv got set with Evans and Harder, it was all over."

There was silence then, and I could visualize them sitting there musing on poor old Vivian's frustrated life. It made me boil, but at the same time I found my eyes were wet. I ran my finger furiously across my lashes under my glasses, disgusted with myself for this evidence of weak self-pity.

"I wonder," Johnny was saying meditatively, "if it's made her queer. Our late unlamented Depression was enough to screw up anybody's psyche for good. Sometimes I wonder I wasn't marked for life by the years I spent being a flunky for those rich bastards in Santa Barbara." He chuckled wryly. "Maybe I was and it'll show up yet. Waiting on their tables, carrying their bootleg liquor around on trays, polishing their shoes. I sure found out how the other half lives. Of course, with Vivian, there's another angle too, this being an unwilling virgin."

"I suppose she *is* a little frustrated," Anne agreed mildly. "She may have had an affair or two, although she's never admitted as much to me. But she's had boy friends off and on. Of course, not *many*."

My fingernails cut into my palms, and I had to relax my jaws. I had clenched my teeth so hard it hurt me.

"She was taking the damnedest tone with me this morning while we were doing the dishes," Johnny chuckled. "Something about my name being Lloyd, and dragging the Simon Lloyd fortune in by the heels. She positively *leered* at me, in an accusing sort of way. I wondered if she suspected me of being the heir to millions in disguise. I wish to God I were one of *the* Lloyds."

I leaned forward, hardly breathing.

"Oh dear. Oh, dear me." And then Anne gave a little gurgling, rueful laugh. "I suppose I'd better tell you. But you're going to think I'm an awful fool—"

"Darling, I *know* you are, but in such a nice way. That's why I love you, I guess, makes me feel masterful, as if I had to protect you from yourself."

"I'm quite able to take care of myself, thank you. This time, though, maybe I did let my imagination run away with me. I probably overstepped the mark."

"Out with it. What have you done now?"

"Well, I know how Viv is. She's prejudiced against you because you don't have a regular job. She thinks it's practically immoral not to be making money. Of course I understand and approve of your doing what you want to do till your savings run out, and then, if you must, get in and grub with the rest of them to keep alive. In effect, I'm doing the same thing myself. And, of course, it *is* impractical. I, for instance, should have invested Tony's insurance and saved our bonds, and kept myself busy building them *up* instead of living my money away. But anyhow, Vivian thinks it's indecent not to be concerned with making money, the way everybody else is.

"And she's right, of course. I don't blame *her*, especially. She's never forgotten or got over the humiliations of the Depression. She's terribly proud, always has been. It would be sheer horror for her to be dependent on other people again, have to beg for a job or humble herself in any way because she didn't have money enough to thumb her nose at other people.

"It's funny"—she broke off musingly—"the different effects poverty has on people. Now me, and you too, I guess, having known hard times, when we have any money we figure it's only good to have fun with. Eat, drink, and be merry, for tomorrow— But it's not like that with Vivian. Money means independence to her, independence of other people and their potential cruelties to her, the cruelties she met with during the Depression, for instance. She'd rather die than be in someone else's power. In fact, I believe—almost—she'd commit murder for what she considers security."

I heard Anne give a deep sigh.

"What's all this got to do with the way she's been acting, her sinisterly conspiratorial manner toward me?"

"Dear me, I did get off the subject, didn't I? Well, I want Vivian to feel kindly toward you. And she's very fond of me. And I know she worries about me. So I had one of my crazy impulses. I thought I'd just set her mind at rest, make her feel better about you and me—and, incidentally, quit picking at me about you—so I— You'll die at this! But I told her you *were* one of *the* Lloyds, that you would come into a fortune when Priscilla Lloyd dies!"

"My God!"

"Ain't I *awful*?" Anne giggled.

"How do you think of such things? By God, I'm missing a bet. I should set you to work drawing up plots for me. No wonder she was making mysterious allusions."

As they laughed together, I drew back. Shaking, I crept around the trellis and made my way among the rose bushes back to the house.

How could she? How could Anne lie to me like that? Talk about me behind my back? Humiliate me? Laugh at me with that man? *Pity* me, even!

Chapter Thirteen

Unseeingly I stumbled along between the patches of loose earth around the rose bushes, but when I had nearly reached the house my eyes focused on a figure standing rocklike on the path leading to the toolroom door.

Alphonse had his arms folded, and from the malignant look on his seamed face, the settled posture of his body, I knew he had watched me slip behind the trellis and come out. He had probably seen Anne go down to the pool and had correctly estimated my actions.

I started to cut across through the flower beds, to keep as far away from him as I could, but he spoke in a low, uncharacteristically imperious voice.

"Miss Haines. I want to speak to you."

I hesitated, then returned defiantly, "I'm sorry. I'm busy right now." And started on.

He took a deliberate step forward. "This won't take long."

I had an uneasy feeling that he would follow if I didn't accede to his demand. I glanced nervously at the house front. I didn't want others overhearing, no matter what he had to say.

So I came back to the bare ground by the roses, halting well out from the house. I was not going to get out of sight, alone with him around the corner of the house.

"Well?" I said impatiently.

He came a few steps closer, menacingly, it seemed to me.

"My sister's been talking to me. And I just want to say this. I don't know what you've got against us, why you're trying to do us dirt with Miss Twilliger; but I want it settled right now, so we'll know where we're at. If you're going to lose us our jobs with Miss Twilliger, let's have it straight. You either spill it now and get it over with or you shut up for good. We ain't gonna go along, feelin' somebody's workin' against us and we're liable to get kicked out any minute. I want to know now, so we can start looking around for somethin' else if we have to."

"It seems to me," I retorted irascibly, "you people are awfully anxious to stay with my aunt, and it looks funny to me—considering the way she treats *you* especially. And I don't intend to see my aunt get in the power of—of—adventurers!"

"We got no designs on the old lady, aside from holdin' down a couple of soft jobs."

"Soft!" I snorted.

"That's right," he snapped harshly. "Maybe I have to take a lot of crap from her. But I know what the score is, and my shoulders are broad enough to take it. She ain't always been rich, and so she don't always know how to treat her employees. She gets mixed up, still kind of surprised because she can afford to hire a chauffeur, and she thinks she has to show her authority now and then, just to show other people she's the boss. But, at bottom, she's a real good old lady. She treats us just like folks when we're alone, at home or out on a trip, the best accommodations, looks out for us to see that we get to see and do everything she does, worries about us if we're ailing, and even pays the doctor bills if we have to see one.

"But she'd feel we'd tricked her if she knew Alice lied to her about me. I told her it was foolish in the first place, but she said Miss Twilliger was so insistent the first time she interviewed her for the job about her not having any family that Alice just said she didn't, thinkin' it didn't really matter; and she was so anxious to get out of the place she was in, where she had to do the washing and all the housework, that she didn't want anything to stand in the way of this position.

"Now all I want to know is: Are you going to drop it or ain't you? If you're going to keep it hangin' over our heads, we want to start lookin' for somethin' else. My sister and me ain't as young as we were, and all we're interested in is somethin' permanent, where we can feel we're secure for a while, anyway."

His eyes held me coldly, and I realized that he hated me—no, despised me! I want to be respected—to be liked, even—as much as anybody does, and anger churned within me at this man's open contempt. I had allowed myself to be softened by Miss Pringle's cringing, but I could hardly restrain myself from bursting into a shrill tirade against this arrogant, defiant, antagonistic man. I wanted to rush at him, scratching and kicking. Standing up to me like this. Demanding a showdown. Daring to let his cold eyes and his stolid face reveal his contemptuous opinion of me.

My face must have been what they call livid, and my voice came out choked and unsteady with fury.

"How dare you stand there and deliver ultimatums to me? I'll do whatever I think best, and nobody's going to dictate my actions to me. You and your silly sister mean nothing to me. Nothing!" My voice ended in a sob of exasperation. "Nobody means anything to me. Nobody! You're *all* against me!"

I turned from his implacable figure and fled toward the terrace.

Culbert was standing at the other end of the stone floor in a clean pale green sport shirt, his hair combed down slick and wet around the sides of his head, his face frostily pink from a combination of sunburn, shaving, and talcum powder.

As I came up onto the terrace he said, "Come on and sit down here with me for a while, Vivian. I've hardly had a dozen words alone with you since we got here."

"Not now," I returned shortly. "I don't feel well."

"I knew there was something wrong," he declared, and moved closer to me solicitously. "You must be coming down with something. You've been acting funny all day. Maybe you'd better go to bed."

His fussy advice jerked me back to reality. After the "accident" which I was going to have to work out for Aunt Maud tomorrow, it was going to look fine if the whole bunch here popped up with remarks about how "funny" I had been acting, about something being "wrong" with me.

Tonight, if it killed me, I must act natural, play the part of the happily engaged girl.

So I laughed playfully—at least, I hope that's the way it sounded—and said, "Oh, Culbert, you're a regular old fussbudget. It's just that the sun has given me a little headache." I thrust my head forward slightly, conspiratorially. "What I need is a drink. Let's slip into the kitchen and have a quick one. Anne told me we should help ourselves."

He brightened. "O.K."

While we were mixing our highballs Anne and Johnny came in with their tray and jokingly "ordered" another one. I was proud of my acting ability in meeting those two face to face, after what I'd heard down by the pool. I was as gay as anybody.

"You stand where you can see into the hall," Anne instructed Johnny, "and give us the high sign if they start down the stairs."

He glanced at the electric clock on the stove. "Hell, they won't be down for another hour. It's only five-thirty. They're probably out on the sun deck meditating."

"Lord, I wish she'd read an article somewhere saying meat was indispensable to human chemistry," Anne sighed. "I'm just up against it to think of any more vegetable dishes. Poor Alphonse and Pringle. Think of putting up with boiled turnips and grated-carrot salads day in and day out. But thank God she can afford to keep them. Think of it, Sis, if we had to have her live with one of us all the time."

I shuddered laughingly.

Suddenly Johnny whispered hoarsely, "Jiggers, La Pringle!" And we all hastily hid our glasses behind canisters and coffeepots or whatever was handy.

Miss Pringle came to the door, her expression rather grim for her.

"Miss Twilliger asked me to tell you that she's not coming down for dinner this evening," she announced primly. "In about an hour she'd like to have me bring a tray to her in her room."

Anne came down off the stool she had perched on. "Isn't she feeling well?" she exclaimed in concern.

"She's not ill," Miss Pringle said coolly. "She didn't inform me of her reasons for not coming down."

Her eyes caught mine for a second as she turned to go back upstairs, and they were accusing.

Rather sardonically, I realized that Aunt Maud had not told Pringle what was the matter with her, and that the little companion thought her employer was upset over the suspicion I had aroused in Aunt Maud's mind about herself and Alphonse.

But I knew what was up. Aunt Maud had been thinking, going back into the past and piecing things together—and I had no doubt that she would put all the pieces together correctly and get the whole picture, and that she could easily verify her conclusions by referring to records in St. Paul or Minneapolis. That she was now digesting her conclusions was obvious, and that the process was such a shock to her nerves that she didn't want to see people for a while was also obvious to me.

To the accompaniment of puzzled comments and conjectures, the four of us set about preparing dinner. On the surface it would have been a jolly meal if it hadn't been for the stony presences of Pringle and Quade. I wondered idly which was their real name, or if perhaps they were half sister and brother and really had different names.

We ate before it was time to send Aunt Maud's tray up. The first course was homemade vegetable soup, and as I slowly spooned it up, untasting, it came to me what to do.

Chapter Fourteen

A sick, empty feeling followed the soup into my stomach. Oh God, I didn't want to do it! Actually I liked Aunt Maud. She was amusing, in a way, with her funny religious ideas and her sporadic, eccentric health fads. And she left us pretty well alone. She had been good to us, according to her lights. She had helped Anne through school, and she gave us each a fifty-dollar check at Christmas and on our birthdays. And she was fond of us. Even her opposition to Johnny was really a desire to protect Anne's happiness.

But, of course, I reminded myself sternly, it was all changed now as far as I was concerned. Already she would be upstairs there, brooding with hatred.

And with the coming of that hatred had come the crashing to earth of all my prospects. All I had to look forward to now was the piddling savings from my salary, and an old-age pension, and years of fear—fear of illness, fear of getting too old and, efficient as I was, losing my job to a younger woman. Nor could I hope, at my age, to find a man to support me. Even Culbert was depending on living off Aunt Maud's money in the future rather than on working to take care of *me*. And besides, I recoiled in every nerve at the thought of having to look to a *man* for livelihood, having him lord it over me because *he* earned the money.

No, there was no other way.

And this would be easy, really, and *sure*.

Everybody would be in and out while the tray was being prepared. It could never be pinned on anybody. It was an ideal setup actually. I wouldn't have wanted anyone else to be blamed. It might even pass for suicide.

While the boys were clearing the table, Anne started to prepare the tray in the kitchen. I went casually down to my room, slipped the envelope into the front of my blouse above my skirt belt, came back onto the terrace, and carried some cups and saucers into the kitchen. The soup was already steaming in a bowl on the tray. Miss Pringle was waiting in a chair outside in the shade, and Culbert followed Johnny out of the kitchen to get the last things off the table.

I had to act fast.

Anne had put a paper napkin on the tray, and I said, "Better get a cloth napkin from the buffet. She doesn't like paper ones."

"Oh gosh, I suppose I'd better."

As Anne went through the door to the dining room, I slipped the envelope out between the buttons of my blouse and swiftly shook at least a teaspoonful of the powder into the soup.

My back was to the terrace door, and I heard Johnny call to Culbert, "Better shake the tablecloth over the edge of the stones. Anne doesn't like mess on the floor."

I had the envelope back in my blouse before he came in the door with the teapot and sugar bowl.

I had been surprisingly cool and calm up till then, but as both he and Anne entered the kitchen by separate doors I felt suddenly so weak that I thought I was going to faint. I stood with my hips against the cupboard and put a hand out on either side of me on the tiled drainboard to hold myself up.

Anne laid a white napkin with forget-me-nots embroidered in the corner on the tray and said, "There! I hope she likes it." She slipped a rosebud out of a vase on the window sill and laid it on the napkin.

I wanted to laugh, to laugh and laugh. Roses with your poison! But I checked myself with all my will power. No hysteria. I must not get hysterical.

"Tell Miss Pringle the tray's ready," Anne instructed Johnny.

As he went out, I followed him and stood idly near the fireplace as Miss Pringle went into the kitchen. For one terrible moment, as I stared at the jeweled combs holding her hair up in the back above the slender neck and the sloping shoulders covered by figured voile, I wanted to cry out, "No! No, don't go. Don't take that tray up."

I leaned hard on my arm, the elbow stiff, my knuckles on the stones of the barbecue pit.

With my back to the kitchen, my body shielding the act, I pulled out the envelope and dropped it on the ashes where the egg carton and napkins still lay, dry from exposure to the sun.

There were matches in a little metal box next the stone chimney, and I scratched one and held it to the corner of the envelope.

Anne came to the kitchen door then, and I said carelessly, "Thought I'd burn this trash. It looks so messy."

"I usually save it to help start the next fire. But that's all right. It isn't neat, having the fire box full of junk; and I have lots of old papers."

I walked over to one of the long chairs and sat back limply, my legs sprawled on the cushion, eyes closed. I was tired, tired. I didn't think I had ever been so tired. And numb. Numb only on the surface, though. I realized that I must not let myself break through this strangely anesthetized state.

I didn't even offer to help with the dishes, although perhaps it would have been better to keep busy. But all my energies were taken up with waiting. I was such an amateur. Would it act instantaneously? Probably not. For surely she had eaten some of the soup by now. How long would it take? And had I used enough? But even a little of a deadly poison, I had heard, would kill a human being. On the other hand, maybe I had used too much. Didn't too much of a poison sometimes set up so violent a reaction in the stomach that it would be instantly thrown up?

I wondered if it would be quick and easy. Or would it be horrible and painful? My hands clenched on the tubular frame under the chair cushions. Oh God, not that! I never wanted anyone to suffer.

Why had I been so careless? I could have looked these things up in the library. Why had I failed to prepare myself—with information, at least? Could it be that part of me didn't want to do this, that with some part of me I had never really meant to, and so I had held back unconsciously, not going at it with my usual careful deliberation?

Well, it was too late now. I had done it. It was, in fact, only by accident that I hadn't committed murder last night.

Culbert came out of the kitchen and sank into the awninged chair I had occupied that morning.

"Anne suggested the four of us play some bridge after they finish the dishes," he observed lazily.

"It's O.K. with me. We'd better play in the living room upstairs, though. It cools off so after the sun goes down, and with the lights on out here or on the sun deck, the bugs bother you so. It's odd the way in summer hardly anybody ever uses the living room except as a passageway, while in the wintertime we're there all the time—"

I let my voice run on, barely hearing what it said. Anything to make it appear that I was at ease, that I was being "natural."

As I ran down, Culbert made some sort of comment.

Restless all at once, I swung my legs off the chair and walked to the edge of the terrace, my eyes grazing the irregular skyline to the east, following it northward as it descended in a jumble of unevenly cleared, rounded knolls. Birds were making a great to-do in the deciduous trees north of the house, discussing, I suppose, their plans for going to sleep. A hummingbird still darted at the golden blossoms of the little fremontia tree at the south corner of the terrace. Its swift, nervous movements fascinated me.

Culbert was saying, "I haven't seen any blue jays around close to the house. I wonder if there aren't so many this year."

I turned and came toward him with quick, jerky steps, answering abstractedly, "Anne and Johnny amused themselves by shooting at them with her gun this spring. If you have too many jays around, you don't get the other birds. Pretty ones, like tanagers and finches. Jays scare them off. They call them butcherbirds, you know."

Butcherbirds. Butchers— Killers of the avian world—

"Give me a cigarette," I commanded abruptly.

Culbert glanced up toward the second story, then pulled a package from his shirt pocket. "Guess it's safe," he said, lowering his voice. "She won't be down this evening."

"No, she won't be down."

I pulled a cigarette from the package and bent for a light as he held up a match in cupped hands.

Restlessly, I moved toward the kitchen door. I leaned against the casing and looked in at Johnny and Anne washing dishes.

As I stood there Miss Pringle came in at the door at the other end of the room, carrying the tray. Her eyes caught and tarried for a surprised instant on the cigarette in my fingers. I raised it and put it to my lips defiantly.

It made no difference now whether anybody did or did not do what Aunt Maud wanted him to.

She set the tray on the worktable between the stove and refrigerator, and Johnny turned half around, glancing back at it.

"I see she didn't eat her soup," he remarked.

"No, Miss Twilliger felt it was too warm for soup."

My hand became motionless on its course away from my mouth with the cigarette. And then, with a rough movement, I hurled the cigarette back of me onto the stones, not looking around to see where it fell.

It's a funny thing. I'm not religious anymore. That is, I believe in a Something, a Force, an Abstraction of some kind that you can call God, for lack of a better name.

But in that instant a silent cry reverberated within me. Thank God! Oh, thank God! And I had an almost overpowering impulse to fall on my knees, hands uplifted, still moaning, "Thank God." And it was the kindly, sad-eyed old gentleman with a beard and a long white gown who had been so real to me in my childhood that I would have been kneeling to.

Aunt Maud was not dead. I was not a murderer!

As if from a long way off, I heard Johnny's voice. "Shall I pour this soup back in the pot, Anne? No use to waste it."

"Yes, just dump it in."

As Johnny moved toward the table, I shot forward, crying hoarsely, "No. No! Leave it alone!"

With his mouth slightly open, he stared at me; and Anne turned her head in amazement.

I seized the bowl of soup, now with a film of cold grease across it, and dumped it into the sink beside Anne's white granite dishpan, watching it fiercely as it ran down through the holes of the chromium outlet. The bits of vegetable—carrot, onion, corn, tomato—were too large to run through, and I carefully scraped them up in my fingers, and with my toe on the lever of the garbage can under the sink, I lifted the lid and hurled them in on top of the coffee grounds and wilted lettuce leaves. Then I held the bowl under the hot-water tap and filled it again and again, each time sloshing the hot water around in the shiny white sink. At last then I washed my fingers hard in the stream of hot water which had filled Anne's soapy dishwater until the pan was running over.

I turned off the faucet hard and went around Anne to the towel rack at the end of the drainboard and dried my hands vigorously on the crash hand towel.

As I glanced up after hanging the cloth back, I found all of them still motionless, their eyes stupefied upon me.

Miss Pringle, in the background, was the first to stir. She looked frightened, and suddenly she squeaked, "Miss—Miss Twi-twi—" She swallowed and then managed to get the word out, "Miss Twilliger would like to see you, Miss Haines, in her room."

With that she pivoted and scurried away.

Nobody else said anything. I gazed at the doorway through which Miss Pringle had disappeared and then began to walk slowly toward it, ignoring Anne and Johnny, who, still silent, with blankly wondering faces, turned their heads and watched me go.

At the stairs I paused with one foot on the lowest step, my hand on the newel post. So great was my relief over the soup that I hardly cared what the coming interview would mean to me.

Standing there, seemingly suspended in time, I experienced a moment of exceptional clarity; and I was overwhelmed at the magnitude of what—by divine intervention, it almost seemed—I had escaped.

In these desperate attempts to escape the domination of others, to gain freedom and security, I had nearly surrendered myself to an even more terrible, more inescapable master—my own self. One might find respite, partial escape even, from the tyranny of others; but from what lay inside oneself, from what was integrally built into one's whole mentality and emotional make-up, one could never, never escape.

And I knew, now, that, reason as I would, recognize justification for my acts as I did, still something had been produced in me, something that was wound inextricably into my thoughts and feelings, that would never have let me forgive myself, that would have held a whip over me during every waking hour for the rest of my life—if I had succeeded in committing murder.

Call it what you would—conscience, ethics, moral sense—it was there. The childish God to whom I had mentally fallen on my knees, the social attitudes to which I had been bent in school, the ethical standards I had accepted all my life, they had done something to me which I could never safely oppose lest I be torn in two, a miserable slave, one side of myself forever at the mercy of the other.

Resignedly, too exhausted really to care anymore, I plodded up the stairs to face Aunt Maud.

Chapter Fifteen

I knocked on the door and Aunt Maud's voice said, "Come in."

She was alone in the room, standing by the open window. Apparently she had been gazing out at the view, but her head was turned toward me now.

Dully, I met her eyes. I didn't even care very much how she began, and I didn't bother to think of how I should answer. So naked and weak did I feel that I was incapable of anything but the unthinking responses of complete honesty. As far as she was concerned, all was lost; so it didn't matter anymore what attitude I took or how I answered.

"Sit down," she said, motioning toward the slipper chair.

I was dumbly surprised at the gentleness of her tone. As I moved stolidly to the chair she had indicated, I realized in a puzzled way that she had directed me to the best seat in the room.

She moved slowly past me and lowered herself to the bench before the vanity-dresser, her back stiffly erect, hands clasped in her lap. I raised my eyes, waiting; and I saw that she was watching me covertly.

She smiled at me brightly, uncertainly.

I frowned faintly. This was very queer. Aunt Maud—of all people—ill-at-ease. Again, swiftly, I looked at her obliquely. Her face had sobered, and there was an unfamiliar expression on it.

My gaze steadied upon her, for her expression had named itself to me. Compassion. There was no other word for the fleeting cast of countenance I had discerned.

Aunt Maud, who had ordinarily a Jovian disregard for the feelings of others, was feeling sorry for me!

I put up my hand and passed the fingertips hard across my forehead.

"You haven't been feeling well today?" she said solicitously, as if relieved at finding something to say.

"I feel like hell," I said bluntly, and met her eyes squarely. In a little last flare-up of spirit, I decided I would not be played with like a mouse under a cat's paw. "Is it any wonder?"

"Oh—" It came out little more than a breath. "Then—you know—about yourself?"

"Yes, I know. And what's more to the point, you guessed, too, this afternoon, didn't you?"

"Yes. Yes, it came to me—like that." She paused and said softly, "You poor child. I didn't ask you up here to talk about it, though. I only—well, I wanted to look at you again, was all. I wasn't sure you knew. And I didn't mean to tell you if you didn't."

I must have looked wooden, sitting there staring at her uncompre-hendingly.

"Have you always known?" she asked gently.

"Since I was seventeen. My mother—that is—Myrtle—Aunt Myrtle, I should say—told me. She—felt I should know. But she said no one else did, or needed to."

Aunt Maud shook her head commiseratingly. "What a terrible burden to bear all these years."

"It hasn't been a burden," I said flatly, "until recently."

"Myrtle oughtn't to have told you. There was no need for you to know that you weren't—legitimate." The tailored linen gown moved over her flat bosom as she drew a deep breath and then continued reflectively, "There was always a nagging familiarity about your face. And this afternoon, with the hair off your ears, the shape of the bones around your eyes and tem-ples not obscured by the glasses, I saw it was—Henry—you looked like. And your height. All of us Twilligers were fairly small people. And Fred Haines was a little man. But Henry"—she spoke softly—"Henry was so tall. I've always liked tall men," she said dreamily.

She recollected herself after a moment and added scornfully, "I've always known you had *her* nose and mouth. So, when I came up here by myself, I thought back, and it was all clear. The length of time. Henry's death—so soon. The way she never came home all winter. And it was the sort of thing Myrtle would do—to protect Evelyn's reputation. And they could have managed it. I remember they moved to another house, clear across town in Minneapolis, in May, after you were born in April. And Myrtle and Fred had only lived in the Twin Cities a short time. They didn't know peo-ple there."

I leaned forward, my eyes intent upon her, concentrating on her words. I had difficulty in following this.

I was long past pretense or diplomacy, so I blurted out, "You don't hate me, because I am *her* child."

Her face hardened briefly, and she moved one hand dismissingly. "Oh, *that*," she said. "A biological accident. Because, actually, you see, you are the child *I* should have had. And would have, if it hadn't been for *her*. Be-cause it was really me that Henry loved. Your very existence," she said bit-terly, "shows the—the *methods* she used to take him from me. She delib-erately *seduced* him. And," she added largely, with an air of one woman of the world to another, "we know what men are. Weak—in those respects. We can understand—women have always had to understand and for-give—those—weaknesses. And when another woman deliberately sets out to *lure* a man by exciting his—well, his Lust—what can you expect?"

She spread her hands resignedly.

I sat back silently, painfully trying to follow her logic. One thing was becoming clear to me. Through all these years she had clung to her love for Henry Sanford, my father, veiling his betrayal of her, which she still refused to accept, by throwing all the blame for it on Evelyn, my mother. Except for Evelyn's duplicity, Aunt Maud still believed that on the "spiritual" level, which was the only one she credited with significance, Henry had really loved her, not Evelyn.

And now she had identified me with Henry, not with the wicked Evelyn. Of paramount importance to her was the fact that I was *his* daughter. She had admitted me to the holy of holies where he was enshrined in her heart, the only man who had ever told her he loved her, even though he had later reneged on the declaration. But still, it was to him she owed the fact that she had been loved, that she didn't have to die knowing no man had wanted her.

Here and now I was being offered love that had been dammed up, deepening and intensifying for lack of an outlet, for forty years.

Neurotic and demanding and possessive as she might be in expressing that love, still I had become its main object. As long as she lived I would be the person my aunt valued above all others.

No matter from where it comes, there is nothing more reassuring, more bolstering to one's morale, than to feel oneself the object of another's devotion.

It seemed irrelevant, then, as it flashed through my mind, the realization that now I need have no more fear for my future financial security. It was more certain than ever now that I would surely get my half of Aunt Maud's money.

But, unimportant as the thought seemed to me at the moment, it brought with it an ineffable sense of peace. I didn't need to take thought, in the biblical phrase, for the morrow. I was certain now of my inheritance, and no one could kick around an heiress to two hundred and fifty thousand dollars.

When I came out of Aunt Maud's room I walked out onto the sun deck, scarcely aware of what I was doing.

Miss Pringle was sitting there alone, knitting. She drew her yarn closer to her stomach as she saw me, ceasing to work her needles. With an apprehensive look, she rose, obviously waiting for me to move out of the doorway so she could glide through it, away from me.

I felt a pang of guilt as I looked at her. She seemed to shrink as I approached her. But I put my hand on her arm anyway. There was an irresistible urgency in me—to make amends, as if by so doing I could wipe out the actions I had tried to commit.

"Don't worry, Miss Pringle, I'm not going to do anything to hurt you. I understand how you feel. It *is* a good job, working for my aunt. She's trying sometimes, and thoughtless; but I suppose you've had worse employers, and I can see how you and your brother wouldn't want to lose your jobs. So I won't tell her."

Miss Pringle still did not look entirely convinced of my good intentions, and after muttering her thanks she shied off and scuttled away through the living room.

I grinned wryly to myself. You couldn't blame the poor little thing for being afraid of me. I must have acted *damned* peculiar all this terrible day.

I walked to the railing and, with my knees against it, surveyed the horizon, a deep lavender in the east, turquoise rimmed faintly with the palest gold in the northwest. In the cloudily blue upper reaches of the sky a star gleamed dimly here and there. Everything was quiet, and still, and peaceful, the only sounds a few last feeble twitterings of the birds and an occasional fitful note from the tree toads, tuning up for the night's orchestration. The dark masses of the mountains on all sides seemed steady and solid and reassuring.

The texture of life itself had a different feel to me now in the cool, gentle twilight after the fevered day. Tentatively the fingers of my mind explored the changed fabric of life. With a sort of wondering relief, my thoughts kept returning to the central fact. I was safe. No one could hurt me anymore. It was certain now that I would have plenty of money the rest of my life. I could arrange my future to suit myself, go on working if I liked, quit when I chose. I could be nice to people, or ignore them, solely on the dictates of my own feeling for them. I didn't have to kowtow to anybody in order to protect myself against their taking advantage of me.

I was free. I was safe.

And now my fears of the day seemed grotesque. The malevolence I had seen wherever I looked faded into improbability.

I glanced down at the figures below on the terrace, Anne on the reclining chair with her arms behind her head. Johnny squinting at an open newspaper in the semidarkness. He oughtn't to try to read in that light.

It was strange how even people looked different to me now. Pringle and Alphonse, just a pair of scared little rabbits, hanging on to jobs where you didn't have to scrub floors or be driven to death on a factory assembly line.

And foolish little Anne. I smiled down at her tenderly. How could I have thought she was plotting against me? I remembered all of a sudden how once during the Depression she had the only pair of stockings without runs that either of us owned. And she insisted I wear them to an interview for a job, even though my feet were bigger than hers; and sure enough, I came home with both big toes out, and she only laughed.

And Johnny. He was still something of a fool. Probably never amount to anything. But he was just the kind Anne would drift in with. It was sheer luck that she had married someone like Tony Everett to begin with. I sighed. When they did get Aunt Maud's money, they'd never know how to build it up. They'd just gradually live it *down*. But there was nothing *I* could do about it.

If Anne was really determined to marry him, even against Aunt Maud's wishes and at the risk of her inheritance, I should have to do what I could with Aunt Maud, try to talk her around. She would listen to me now. If anyone could influence her, I could. It was sweet to realize that, through her love, I had this power. And I felt—rather fatuously, I suppose— virtuous and benevolent at the thought of using my new power over Aunt Maud to gain for Anne something she wanted.

Chapter Sixteen

As my eyes fell on Culbert, complacently settled into the basket chair which had been "repaired" by laying a cushion over the broken seat, there was no kindliness in my thoughts, nor, I suspect, in my expression. *He* looked the same to me as he always had—self-centered, two-faced, sensuous, lazy.

He was sitting where he had last night. I shivered to think how narrowly I had escaped killing him with the *jardinière*.

And so uselessly—so uselessly—as it had turned out.

I gazed down with hatred upon the round, bald top of his head and his plump shoulders. It was he who had forced me into the course that had so nearly been disastrous. He who had put me in a position from which there seemed no escape but murder.

"Culbert," I said peremptorily, "come up here."

He snapped his head around and up.

Anne and Johnny both started and looked upward uneasily. Neither of them spoke. I could feel myself flushing, up there by myself. After my performance in the kitchen an hour ago I was going to have some job convincing those two that I wasn't on the verge of dangerous lunacy.

Culbert sat still for a moment and then reluctantly he started for the steps. I could tell that he felt undignified, having to respond to a command issued in so short and ill-natured a manner. It made him appear like a henpecked husband. It did me good to note his disgruntlement.

I withdrew from the railing and sat on the cushioned bamboo chair. I intended to say everything that had not been said before, and I might as well take the load off my feet while I did it, for it might take some time once I got going.

"Sit down," I instructed, and pointed to the chair facing me.

"What's the matter with you?" he demanded suspiciously, but he sat down gingerly.

"Our engagement," I stated clearly, "is off."

He just sat there peering at me in the dusk, with his mouth open.

"It is no longer necessary," I explained, "for me to marry you."

"Necessar— What in the devil do you mean?"

I leaned back in my chair. I could see I was going to enjoy this.

"Let's quit playing games, Culbert. Let's put the cards right down on the table and take a good look at them. I'll give you credit. You've handled this whole affair very cleverly. Never once have you had to come right out and *say* anything. I'll even credit you with a motive for trying to spare my feelings—on the principle that anything one refuses to recognize in words just isn't *there*. But leave us not kid ourselves anymore. You knew, and I knew, and each of us knew the other knew, exactly what the score was."

"I don't know what you're talking about," he asserted stiffly.

"Don't you? Well, then, I'll just go back over it step by step. Give me a cigarette first, will you?" I interrupted myself nonchalantly. "I think Aunt Maud's tucked in for the night."

He pulled out both the cigarettes and matches and threw them into my lap.

"Thank you. Always the gentleman," I observed dryly.

I drew in the smoke luxuriously. This was turning out to be even more of a pleasure than I had expected. The fat little fool.

"You know, when I first met you," I said leisurely, "I was rather pleasantly impressed. You seemed good-natured, kindly, a good sport. What a wrong impression I got. It took me some time to learn that you're really greedy, cruel, and grasping. Well—let that go. It's water under the bridge now. And, you know, I didn't tumble to what you were up to, even when you told me—oh, so confidentially—that *you* knew the secret of my birth. How, when your father died, you found a letter among his papers from Evelyn Twilliger. She had been one of his flock in the church there in Sioux City, and I guess we Protestants have some of the same impulses the Catholics do. We like to confess to a man of God. So Evelyn had told Reverend McCauley about her predicament when she was home when Henry died. Your father, you know, must have been a pretty good Joe. Too bad you aren't more like him. Quite unprofessionally, it was he who advised her to stay out of town while her 'sin' showed and to produce the fruits of it in the city, where no one knew her. And, of course, later, Evelyn had to write him and tell him how it all came out, how her sister and brother-in-law were taking the child as their own. You know, it was careless of your father, not destroying that letter, even though he kept his mouth shut afterward."

Culbert moved restlessly. "Why are you dragging all this up?"

"Sort of a review. It's interesting, looking back on how skillful you were about the whole thing. The next time you saw me, still in a reminiscent mood, you reminded me of how Aunt Maud hated Evelyn, how she never spoke to her again after Henry Sanford's death. And then—oh, so jocularly!—you commented on what Aunt Maud would say if she knew I was Evelyn's daughter. You laughed about how I wouldn't be an heiress anymore if Aunt Maud knew *that*. And, like a dope, I laughed, too, and said she'd never know. And you said—all in the spirit of good clean fun, of course—'Well, you'd better be nice to me, then, because *I* could tell her.' And I said laughingly—silly me!— 'Well, you'd have to prove it.' And you— it was getting to be really a scream by then—you said, 'Oh, I can prove it all right. I still have Dad's letters.'"

I paused and smashed out my cigarette.

"And the next time we had a date you asked me to marry you."

"Well? And so what? Is it a crime to propose to a woman?"

"Not at all. In fact, I'll be frank with you, I was flattered. A woman is never wholly unaffected by a proposal of marriage, no matter from whom. And if you remember, I declined very tactfully. But you kept asking. And, in between times, just far enough between proposals so I wouldn't forget, you kept bringing up the 'joke' about telling Aunt Maud who I really was. At last I caught on. You wanted a wife who could support you. You figured, I suppose, that once we were married, somehow it would work out all right. Force of habit would keep me with you, even after Aunt Maud died and your hold over me was gone. In your conceit, you may even have thought you could make me care for you, in time; so that I'd *want* to keep you with me. And if I did rebel—well, there are the California community-property laws, and you would give me no grounds for divorce, and I'd have a hard time getting rid of you, and would have to make a generous settlement if I did."

I shrugged cynically. "Maybe—I don't know—maybe you intended to kill me off in some nice quiet way and enjoy the whole inheritance yourself."

"You're crazy," he shouted. "It's all a lie, every word of it. I never intended anything of the kind. It's just your nasty suspicious mind."

"A man," I said coldly, "who would blackmail a woman into marrying him is capable of anything."

"All right," he said in a congested voice, getting to his feet with a violent heave of his whole body, "all right, if that's the way you're going to treat me, I *will* tell your aunt who you are. Nobody's going to make a fool out of me."

"Nobody needs to. And you may as well save yourself a further unpleasant scene, because Aunt Maud knows already." On a sudden inspiration, I lied a little. "She's known for a long time."

He stood goggling at me, and I was sorry it had darkened so much that I couldn't see the thwarted expression on his face more distinctly. It would have been a fair treat, as the English say.

He took a threatening step toward me, and I reached out and grasped the handle of Anne's hiking stick which still leaned against the chair I had taken.

"Another thing," I said in clipped, menacing tones, "you don't know how far you had driven me into desperation. I didn't know until today that Aunt Maud knew—about me. And I'll confess it freely. You had me in a cleft stick. The thought of being in your power because of the knowledge you held and the thought of losing my inheritance were equally unbearable to me."

I stood up and faced him, the stick still clenched in my hand.

"Four times in the last twenty-four hours I've been on the verge of killing you."

For a moment he stared at me in the dusk, then his head jerked around toward the railing and back to me.

"The *jardinière*," he gasped.

"Yes, the *jardinière*."

He took a step backward and knocked against the chair. "You—you fiend," he whispered hoarsely.

"No, I'm not a fiend. I'm just a woman who was pressed beyond her particular endurance. And you might remember this in the future. It's hard to tell exactly where another person's breaking point is. So it pays to be careful when you start shoving people around. As a matter of fact, it's safer not to shove them at all."

I drew in my breath and expelled it forcefully, as one will at the end of a nerve-racking task.

"And now," I said calmly, "you'd better get yourself out of here. I won't insist on your leaving tonight, but in the morning I'm sure Aunt Maud will let Alphonse drive you to town. You can catch a bus, or a train, or anything you please. You can even hitchhike if you want to. I don't care, just so you stay out of my sight from now on."

"Children!" I heard a remonstrative voice down the wall and, glancing to my left, again I recognized the roundish white object sticking out of the bedroom window—Aunt Maud's head encased in her white mesh hair net.

"What are you talking so loud about? And what are you doing up here by yourselves? You know what I told you this morning, Vivian," she concluded admonishingly.

"It's all right, Aunt Maud," I replied sweetly. "I'll tell you all about it in the morning. We're just now going down to join Anne and Johnny."

"Well, don't stay up too late, now. Remember, we all have to get up and get ready for church in the morning. Good night, children."

"Good night, Aunt Maud," I caroled, thinking with amused relish that I would *not* tell her exactly what had passed between Culbert and me when I informed her that our engagement was broken. But my girlishly confiding reasons, like being afraid I didn't really love him, would give the old lady a further chance to exercise herself in the motherly role she had adopted toward me and which she was apparently getting such an innocent kick out of.

Culbert had turned his head toward the window and then back to me. He stood glaring at me in frustration and rage for a moment; then, with a growl, he turned and stamped down the stairs. I went to the head of them and watched him. Either Johnny or Anne had turned on the metal-shaded light over the kitchen door, and there was light again from the end bedroom window, so the terrace lay in subdued illumination.

Anne and Johnny were ostentatiously carrying on a quiet conversation, and they only glanced with pleasant vacuity at Culbert as he turned abruptly from the foot of the stairs and strode into the house. They kept on talking, as if unaware of any strain, as I descended to join them.

Johnny, however, apparently decided to retain his aplomb, no matter how strangely other people were determined to behave.

"Lovers' quarrel?" he queried brightly.

"Oh," I grunted dryly. "I suppose you could hear us yelling at each other."

"No, not exactly," Anne put in hurriedly, placatingly. I could tell she still didn't quite know how to take me. "That is, we didn't hear what you said. It was just—well, the tones, sometimes ..." Her voice trailed off lamely.

"It's nothing to be upset about," I reassured her. "I was just breaking our engagement, which, incidentally, ought never to have been made."

"Oh."

There was a moment of awkward silence, and then Johnny said, "Somebody refresh my memory. What's etiquette at this point? Congratulations, or commiseration?"

"Celebration," I said dryly, "would be more to the point in this case. You don't have any champagne handy, do you, Anne?"

"Well—ye-es," she murmured uncertainly. "I've been saving it for a special occasion."

"Break it out, then," I commanded rashly. "This is it. A very special occasion. I'll pay you back, buy you another bottle."

"Are the innocent bystanders allowed to ask why it's so special?" Johnny inquired.

They were both still appraising me dubiously, as if I were a firecracker that was likely to explode at any moment, and I began to laugh. I hadn't laughed so deliciously for a long time. I had a piece of cleansing tissue tucked into my blouse front, and I took it out and ran it under my glasses, wiping my eyes.

"I promise," I said then, in a voice that was still slightly throaty with mirth, "that this is the last exhibition I shall make of myself this week end. And I'll tell you, Johnny, why the occasion is so special. I have just escaped, by a very narrow squeak, making an awful fool of myself." My tone sobered reflectively. "I might say I have just escaped destroying myself. Naturally I feel like a new woman, a free woman. So bring on the champagne, Anne."

She pulled herself out of the long chair reluctantly, as if still unconvinced of my normalcy.

"Well, if you want it—"

"It's all right, Anne," I said quietly, "I'm going to be all right now."

I lay back, looking up at the stars. Anne was at the kitchen door when I called after her lazily, "If it's all right with you, Anne, I think I'll invite Eric and the kids down next week end. The children would love it here."

She paused with her hand on the casing. "That would be swell." Her tone sounded relieved. "Do that."

"An excellent idea," Johnny chimed in, adding slyly, "There's a new moon now, but it should be up in the evenings next week. And you know the effect moonlight is reputed to have."

"Silly!" I rebuked him indulgently.

But then— Who knew? Maybe—

THE END

Malice Domestic

Classic Women's Suspense from the 1940s & 50s

ELISABETH SANXAY HOLDING
Widow's Mite / Who's Afraid
978-1-944520-34-2 $19.95
Two suspense classics from the author of
The Blank Wall. "The author has succeeded
admirably in depicting the mounting horror
and suspense." —*NY Times.*
Introduction by Gregory Shepard.
February 2018.

JEAN POTTS
Go, Lovely Rose / The Evil Wish
978-1-944520-65-6 $19.95
A 1954 Edgar Award winner and a 1963
Edgar runner-up paired together for the first
time. "If Hitchcock had written a novel, it
would have been similar to *The Evil Wish*...
two masterpieces."—Don Crinklaw, *Booklist.*
New introduction by J. F. Norris.
February 2019.

HELEN NIELSEN
Borrow the Night / The Fifth Caller
978-1-944520-72-4 $19.95
Two vintage Southern California mysteries
from the author of *The Woman on the
Roof.* "A skillfully devised and movingly
presented drama of sin, retribution, and
supreme sacrifice."—*Chicago Tribune.*
New introduction by Nicholas Litchfield.
May 2019.

BERNICE CAREY
**The Man Who Got Away With It /
The Three Widows**
978-1-944520-80-9 $19.95
"Carey... was an adept plotter but was
more interested in characterization and
social comment... very much a forerunner
of modern *literary* crime fiction."
— Xavier Lechard, *At the Villa Rose.*
"A powerful psychological drama written
with great literary flair."—Nicholas Litchfield.
New introduction by Curtis Evans.
May 2019.

DOLORES HITCHENS
**Stairway to an Empty Room /
Terror Lurks in Darkness**
978-1-944520-79-3 $19.95
Two terrific crime novels from the author of
Sleep With Strangers. "High-grade
suspense."—*San Francisco Chronicle.*
"Expertly tautened action and style."
—*Saturday Review.* New introduction by
Nicholas Litchfield. October 2019.

COMING IN 2020:
Home is the Prisoner/The Little Lie
—Jean Potts
Footsteps in the Dark/Beat Back the Tide
—Dolores Hitchens
Too Many Bones/Blood from a Stone
—Ruth Sawtell Wallis

Stark House Press

1315 H Street, Eureka, CA 95501
707-498-3135 • griffinskye3@sbcglobal.net
www.starkhousepress.com
Available from the publisher, Ingram Books or Baker & Taylor Books.